Romance ... ***h Hess,***
**winner of the Reviewers' Choice Award
for Frontier Romance!**

TANNER

"Ms. Hess certainly knows how to write a romance . . . the characters are wonderful and find a way to sneak into your heart."

WILLOW

"Again Norah Hess gives readers a story of a woman who learns to take care of herself, fills her tale with interesting, well-developed characters and a plot full of twists and turns, passion and humor. This is another page-turner."

JADE

"Ms. Hess continues to write page-turners with wonderful characters described in depth. This is a wonderful romance complete with surprising plot twists . . . plenty of action and sensuality. Another great read from a great writer."

DEVIL IN SPURS

"Norah Hess is a superb Western romance writer. . . . *Devil in Spurs* is an entertaining read!"

KENTUCKY BRIDE

"Marvelous . . . a treasure for those who savor frontier love stories!"

MOUNTAIN ROSE

"Another delightful, tender and heartwarming read from a special storyteller!"

"Norah Hess's down-to-earth writing boldly portrays the heartrending struggle of pioneer men and women."

—*Rendezvous*

ONLY YOU WILL DO

"Although I bitterly resent it, Miss Southern Belle, I'm afraid that only you will suffice for my needs."

"You're crazy!" Serena's shocked eyes stared at him. "If you think for one minute that I'd . . . that you'd . . . " Her voice trailed off, for Josh, his eyes stormy and reckless, was moving in on her.

"No, no," she whispered. "I don't want you."

"Yes, you do," he murmured thickly, his unsteady fingers now at the opening of the robe. A cool breeze brushed Serena's breasts as her only garment was pulled apart and pushed down over her shoulders . . . and she knew that she wanted nothing more in life than to have this big rough man make passionate love to her.

Other *Leisure* and *Love Spell* books by Norah Hess:

LARK
SAGE
DEVIL IN SPURS
TANNER
KENTUCKY BRIDE
WILLOW
MOUNTAIN ROSE
JADE
BLAZE
KENTUCKY WOMAN
HAWKE'S PRIDE
TENNESSEE MOON
LACEY
WINTER LOVE
FANCY
FOREVER THE FLAME
STORM

Wild Fire

NORAH HESS

LOVE SPELL BOOKS NEW YORK CITY

To Jack and Bob

LOVE SPELL®

August 1999

Published by

Dorchester Publishing Co., Inc.
276 Fifth Avenue
New York, NY 10001

If you purchased this book without a cover you should be aware that this book is stolen property. It was reported as "unsold and destroyed" to the publisher and neither the author nor the publisher has received any payment for this "stripped book."

Copyright© 1994 by Norah Hess

All rights reserved. No part of this book may be reproduced or transmitted in any form or by any electronic or mechanical means, including photocopying, recording or by any information storage and retrieval system, without the written permission of the Publisher, except where permitted by law.

ISBN 0-505-52331-0

The name "Love Spell" and its logo are trademarks of Dorchester Publishing Co., Inc.

Printed in the United States of America.

CHAPTER
∾ 1 ∾

Two HEART SHATTERING EVENTS happened to Serena Bain on July 4, 1863. Vicksburg surrendered to the North, and her sweetheart, Jeremy Landrie, was killed.

For two days the eighteen-year-old girl had lain in bed. And though the air was stifling hot and damp with humidity, the bedroom drapes remained tightly drawn across the French window. The grieving girl could not yet bear to face the light of day, because in its bright clarity she would be forced to accept, and to live with, the fact that Jeremy was dead.

Serena turned her head listlessly and listened to the familiar sound of her old nurse, Hessie, speaking in hushed tones.

Hessie and her grandson were the only ones who had remained on the Bain plantation after Lincoln's Emancipation Proclamation had freed the slaves.

Serena wondered with a long sigh if those "freed" slaves had eaten today. And where had they slept last night? In a doorway in town, a deserted barn, or a cave back in the woods? She shook her head sadly. How could the little ones possibly survive this supposed freedom?

She sighed again, this time regretfully. Although there had never been a mistreated slave on the Bain plantation, she could not say the same for slaves on other plantations. Whereas their own slaves were healthy and unmarked, she had seen others who were terribly thin, their backs scarred with whip lashes, some old, some recent. And Mammy had told her stories about the poor women and the indignities visited upon them by their masters.

Like cousin Ira, for instance. A dark, narrow face swam before her. The conniving cousin who had been so determined to make her his wife. She shivered delicately at the thought of him. According to Mammy Hessie, the man had come from his mother's womb mean and evil as a dark stormy night. And the years had proved the brown woman right.

Serena's thoughts moved to images of Ira's tumultuous birthday celebration. On that day, as a special gift commemorating his initiation into manhood, his father presented him with his own personal slave, a pretty child a year younger than her new master. Serena squeezed her green eyes tightly as she remembered that day. Ira had rushed the visibly frightened girl straight to his room, making his parents blush with embarrassment. In a matter of minutes, his young guests playing on the lawn grew quiet and uneasy as agonized cries floated down to them. In the following weeks, Ira had beaten the girl so often and used her so harshly that his father finally had taken her away from him.

But by then Ira had discovered, and delighted in, how best to use his lust and power on the helpless slaves. No black female, regardless of age, was safe from his brutal attacks. In a short time there were more light-skinned babies being born than dark-skinned ones. Unbelievable as it seemed, when the female children from his couplings grew old enough, he would often use those. Uncle Newcomb, deeply ashamed of his son's actions, had sold those light-skinned slaves as soon as possible.

Thank God, Serena thought, that the pact made by her parents with the Newcombs when she was a baby was no longer valid. After Mama and Papa's deaths brother Dorn had decided that. After witnessing for himself Ira's maliciousness, he informed Uncle Newcomb as gently as possible that there would be no marriage between the two families. And poor Uncle, knowing the reason, had merely nodded in acceptance. But Ira had been furious and had stubbornly insisted that they would wed when he returned from the war.

But Ira hadn't returned from the war. Serena recalled with a slight curl of her lips that the last time she'd seen her cousin had been about a year ago.

She remembered it clearly, for on that same day she had received a letter from Jeremy, the words scrawled across a scrap of paper as though the writer were in a hurry. After reading the letter a couple of times she had hurried to the three-room shack where Jeremy had grown up. He and his father had lived at the edge of the swamp since his mother died when he was only three years old.

Eli Landrie, whom she now called Paw, pored eagerly over the words his son had written while his spotted hound sniffed the letter, wagging his tail as he picked up his young master's scent.

The grizzly-haired man handed back the soiled piece of paper, and then, in their usual fashion, they talked of Jeremy, recalling happy times together. Before Serena knew it, dusk was settling in, and Eli proposed that he and the hound walk her home, but she had shook her head with resolve. "There is nothing in the swamp to harm me," she said bravely.

She hadn't been so brave, however, when she left the still lighted clearing and struck out on the narrow path leading through a neck of the swamp in the gloom. Its appearance took on different shapes in the gloom, and nervously she regretted dismissing Paw's offer so lightly. Any one of those big cypresses she passed could easily conceal a waiting stranger.

It seemed half a lifetime before the big white house came in sight. Serena released a long sigh of relief when she suddenly caught a glimpse of a horse and its rider sitting among a grove of pine trees. Instinct warned her to run, to run as she had never run before.

Grabbing her dress above her knees, she sprinted up the driveway of crushed oyster shells then dashed onto the veranda as the pounding of hooves behind her came closer and closer. She grasped the big brass doorknob and turned it.

"Locked!" Her blood was a drumbeat in her ears. There was no time to knock—the man would be upon her before Mammy's slow-gaited grandson could answer it. Whimpering with terror as she rushed down the long veranda, she prayed aloud that the French windows hadn't been barred for the night.

They gave easily to Serena's frantic shove.

She slammed the double doors behind her, raced to the parlor, and knocked over a chair in her rush to reach the window. Breath coming in short gasps, she fixed her eyes on the slightly parted drapes and choked back a cry of alarm when she saw a horse pulled to a rearing stop only feet from the brick steps.

As Serena watched with bated breath, the rider swung unsteadily to the ground, then fumbled a minute in a saddlebag that had been flung across the weary mount. When he tilted his head to drink from a flask, the early moon struck his face. Cousin Ira!

Her brain raced with questions. What is he doing here? Is he dangerous? Will he harm me? With a jolt she remembered how his lustful eyes were always raking over her body. There could be no doubt what he wanted. Serena shuddered.

When Ira tossed the empty bottle into the rose garden and lurched up the steps, Serena was released from the paralysis that had gripped her earlier. She called Mammy's name piercingly as Ira's hand fumbled on the doorknob. Her eyes widened in anticipation of his entrance, but then she recalled: the door was locked. But the French windows—had she remembered to lock them?

She ran back into the hall, screaming for Mammy as she darted across the wide plank floor. And though her feet flew, she felt they had barely moved, as if they were caught in quicksand.

In seeming slow motion her fingers groped with the lock bolt just as Ira grabbed the latch from the outside. She gazed in horrified fascination at the maniacal anger on the man's face as the windows held fast. But even as her breath was expelled in relief, she saw Ira pick up a wicker chair and lift it over his head.

Dear God, he was going to break the glass. Damn, where was Mammy? She opened her mouth to shout for the old woman again, then slowly closed it. Her cousin had lowered the chair and turned his head and paused.

Faintly at first, from the river road, came the ghostlike noise of galloping hooves and yowling dogs. It grew louder in the now-arrived night as the shadowy figures of several riders took shape. When they turned up the tree-lined driveway, Ira, with a muttered curse, left the veranda in a bounding crouch. While Serena wondered at his stealthy manner, he quickly mounted the drooping stallion. A sharp jab of his heel to the sweating flank and the animal tore off toward the swamp.

Ira disappeared into the eerie mist just as a bunched group of riders came to a plunging halt a foot short of the steps, while a pack of lean yelping hounds milled around trampling hooves. They sniffed the ground and air eagerly.

Serena jumped, startled, when Mammy asked breathlessly behind her, "Is they Union or 'Federates?"

"Confederate, thank God." Serena recognized the uniform of a southern general. She pushed open the glass doors and stepped outside. The general, a man of middle age, she guessed, considering the gray in his beard, removed his hat and spoke brusquely.

"Good evening, Miss. I'm sorry to bother you, but we've been chasing an escaped officer by the name of Newcomb. The hounds have trailed him here. Have you seen him?"

"What that white trash done?" Hessie's big bulk pushed forward before Serena could answer.

The tired-looking officer frowned at the dark woman, then spoke bluntly. "Murdered his company commander."

"Oh, mercy!" Serena gasped, her face draining of all color. She pointed a finger toward the swamp. "If you hurry, you can catch him. He just rode away."

The soldiers' mounts, rearing and pivoting, streaked back down the drive after the yowling hounds. Moments later raw nerves made Serena and Mammy jump and cry out when rapid gunfire sounded along the river. The dogs barked furiously for several seconds, then grew quiet.

Some time passed before the soldiers emerged from the river area. They rode single file now, almost at a walk. In front, alongside the general, a man sat slumped in the saddle, his head bowed.

"Thank God," Serena said, silently adding that the world was well rid of Ira Newcomb.

"Amen to that," Hessie agreed. "He'll hang for killin' a officer."

* * *

A rattling of china outside Serena's door broke her reverie. Sunlight streamed in behind Mammy Hessie as she entered the room and placed a bed tray on her young mistress's legs. "Come on, child, sit up." She fluffed up the pillows. "Mammy done brought you some corn muffins and honey."

Serena pushed herself upright. Glancing at the tray, she realized how hungry she was. She reached for the warm muffin and smiled teasingly at her old nurse. "Where have you been hiding the honey?"

With a reproving frown on her face, Hessie scolded, "I oughtta smack your bottom, accusing Mammy of such a thing. Mister Eli brought that sweetness over here this mornin'."

Guilt and affection flickered across Serena's face. "Poor Paw," she sighed. "How's he faring? Does he look all right?"

Hessie wagged her white-turbaned head. "He don't look good atall. He's hurtin' somethin' terrible." She added as an afterthought, "Even the old hound looks sad."

Remorse swept over Serena. She had been selfish in her grief, thinking only of herself. She had always relied on Paw Landrie for comfort. For he constantly assured her that both Jeremy and her brother, Dorn, would come home safely, and just because she hadn't heard from her sole relative since his enlistment didn't necessarily mean that he was dead. She blinked away a tear. The one time that Paw needed her she had locked herself away from him.

Images of her dead parents appeared to Serena. How they would disapprove of her giving in to grief, giving in to anything for that matter. The Bains never gave in, no matter what the circumstances.

She reluctantly summoned the last of her strength, determined to at least make an effort.

"Take away the tray, Mammy," she said decisively. "I think I'll get dressed and go sit on the veranda for a while. I could use some fresh air."

Hessie heaved her big body off the end of the bed. "You do that, honey." Her teeth flashed in a wide, pleased smile. "Put some pink back in your cheeks."

Serena pulled a clean frock over her golden-red hair, and for the first time didn't bemoan the fact that her dress was three years behind the fashion, at least one size too small, or patched and faded. As she approached the door, she picked up an ivory-handled brush, then descended the stairs and walked out onto the veranda.

In her gray world of despondency Serena was oblivious to the dust-covered stranger who a short time later reined in at the bottom of the steps. She was startled when he awkwardly cleared his throat, then said politely, "Pardon me, but I'm looking for Miss Serena Bain?"

She stared at the soldier a moment, then nodded. "I'm she." The young man slid from his mount at that and handed her an envelope. She looked down at the soiled and wrinkled square of paper, and the bold handwriting penetrated the gloom of her mind.

"At last! A letter from Dorn!"

She motioned the hungry-looking soldier toward the kitchen house in the rear of the main house, then tore open the envelope. With trembling fingers she withdrew three sheets of paper. Her eyes flew over the words.

January 2, 1863
Oregon Territory

Dear Sister Serena,

I'm sorry I haven't written sooner, but much has happened to me since entering the war.

I was only fighting two months when I was taken prisoner. It was impossible for me to write you under those circumstances.

Then one day, after I had been in that hellhole for six months, a Yankee general came to the prison, recruiting men to fight the Indians on the western frontier. He promised if we would take an oath of allegiance and fight the Indians for two years, we would be released immediately after completing the assignment. As you might expect, I quickly took advantage of the offer.

I have finished my two years now, and have decided to remain in the West. I have settled in Oregon Territory. It's a wild and wondrous land, Serena, with vast acres of grassland over which several million long-horned cattle roam freely. They are descendants of stock brought here by the Spaniards many years ago. I have made friends with some fellows who will teach me about cattle ranching. I realize, with all that has happened, the South no longer holds a future for us.

And so, Serena dear, gather what money you can, and start west as soon as possible. You can always find a wagon train headed west. I am sending you a map drawn by an old trailfinder. He has made this trip many times and knows all the fine details of it, especially the waterholes and best places to cross rivers.

I must caution you strongly, however, not to travel once winter has set in. You must spend the cold, snowy months in some fort along the way.

Next spring I shall set up camp at the last mountain you'll have to cross, to check all the trains that descend. I have no idea when this letter will reach you, but have no fear, I will wait patiently for the day when I'll see your dear and lovely face.

Your loving brother, Dorn

The last page was a hand-drawn map. Rivers were traced, as were mountains and plains. Sparsely scattered across the map were small crosses, marking waterholes and river fordings.

Serena looked out over the fallow acres stretching away as far as her eyes could see, and for the first time in two days, life sparked in them. Had her brother lost his mind, wanting to leave all this behind, she asked herself, remembering when those fields had been white with blooming cotton.

"I will not leave it!" Her fists clenched in her lap. "I will not give up my heritage."

But by the time Mammy called supper, Serena knew that she would make the effort to join her brother in this wilderness he described with such feeling. With Jeremy gone, she didn't really care about anything.

As she sighed, wondering where the money would come from, she sat down to a meal of collard greens, potatoes, and okra.

Evidently Dorn had no idea how very poor the South had become.

When the meager meal was over, Serena lit a candle and made her way to Dorn's small office. She would go through his papers and ledgers and try to determine if there was any possible way of laying hold of enough money.

An hour later, although she had checked and rechecked, she could find nothing of importance in all the papers piled on the desk. Dorn's last entry in the large ledger, in '61, showed that their warehouse was chock full of cotton. The blockade, of course, had prevented its sale to other countries. The impact of the ban had left them destitute.

Her lips curled wryly. If, however, peace ever came again, there was a small fortune waiting for them.

Serena was about to pick up the candle and retire to her room when a soft tap sounded at the door. Leaving the candle behind, she hurried across the hall and peeked through the French windows. The days of flinging open a door to a rapping request were gone. The byways were too full of questionable characters to chance it.

Eli Landrie stood purposefully in the moonlight so that she could recognize him. He looks so forlorn, she thought, sliding back the latch bar.

"Come in, Paw," she invited and led the way back to Dorn's office. When Landrie had settled his long frame into a chair next to the desk, she asked, "May I get you some horehound tea?"

Eli smiled faintly. "I'm already floatin' in that stuff. What I need is a good cup of coffee."

"Maybe that will be possible before long." Serena smiled encouragingly at the man she had hoped would be her father-in-law. "The blockade will probably be lifted, now that Vicksburg has fallen, and trade from Europe will start up again."

Then she gave a short, dry laugh. "A lot of good it will do us now. We couldn't buy any if it were a penny a pound."

Eli echoed her sentiments, adding, "I've never stolen anything in my life, but a cup of that steamin' brew would be mighty temptin'."

A musing silence developed, then Serena said softly, "Paw, I received a letter from Dorn today."

"Ah, that's good, Serena." Landrie's face brightened a bit. "I know how worried you've been. Is he all right?"

"He's fine, now. The Yankees took him prisoner, and then he was sent west to fight the Indians. He has soldiered the two years required of him and has decided to stay in a place he calls Oregon Territory. He wants to become a rancher." She paused a moment, watching Landrie's face closely. She added quietly, "He wants me to join him."

The Southerner's shock and regret was unmistakable. He said finally, his words husky, "I'll miss you, daughter." After a short silence he asked, "When will you be leavin'?"

Serena stared down at her clasped fingers. "I don't know." Small frown lines marred her forehead. "Dorn wants me to start as soon as possible, but for the life of me I don't see how I can. I've heard of these expeditions across the wilderness and much is needed to undertake it. I'd need a team of horses and a wagon, naturally, with sufficient supplies for the long trip." She shook her head. "An impossible task, I'm afraid, Paw."

Landrie laid a deeply tanned hand over Serena's locked fingers. "I know you, honey. You'll manage somehow." He stared at a moth fluttering around the candle. "Your strength and determination would have been the makin' of my son if he'd of lived."

Serena gazed into the suffering, damp eyes. Suddenly she had an idea. "Paw, if I can somehow arrange it, I want you to make the trip with me."

Under the surprise that showed in Eli's eyes was a glimmer of animation. It faded so quickly, though, Serena wasn't sure it had ever been there. Maybe she had only wanted to see it.

The poor farmer smiled fondly at the girl he loved as a daughter. "It's kind of you to think of an old man, honey, but without Jeremy along, I'd only be in the way."

"You're not an old man," Serena scolded indignantly. "And I'm not being kind. I need you, Paw. You and Dorn are all I have in the world." Her lips curved teasingly. "Besides, who would drive the wagon for me?"

Eli Landrie gazed at Serena's earnest face for a long time before he was convinced that the girl was sincere. A shy grin lifted the corners of his mouth. "I'd be awfully lonesome without you." He squeezed her hands. "I'd be right pleased to go with you, daughter."

With a wide smile that showed her white, even teeth, Serena rose and hugged the broad and thin shoulders. "Thank you, Paw. Thank you very much."

Embarrassed, though plainly pleased at the show of affection, Eli said gruffly, "Do you have any idea how to get to this Oregon Territory . . . in case we ever get started?"

"Dorn sent me this," Serena answered, picking up the map and spreading it out on the desk. She moved the candle to cast its light over it.

Eli rose and leaned over the map. His brow furrowed as he traced a finger over the twisting, turning route. Serena sat quietly, waiting for him to speak.

It was several minutes before Landrie sat back down and brought a blackened pipe from his shirt pocket. As he crumbled a dry, brown leaf of tobacco into its bowl, he began to speak slowly, thoughtfully. "Accordin' to the map, our best approach is to board a ship and go down the Mississippi to Independence, Missouri. I heard a couple of men sayin' the other day that Independence was a favorite meetin' place for those headed west."

He scratched a sulphur match across the bottom of his boot, then held the flame to the pipe. When it drew to his satisfaction, Eli continued, "Only a fool would attempt that trip alone. The more wagons and people the better. I hear that the farther west you go, the meaner the Indians."

A long breath blew softly through Serena's lips. It was a relief to have Paw take over, make the decisions. She made a wry face. Now all she had to do was come up with the money.

A silence grew, and the moth continued its circle. Then, as though he knew what Serena was thinking, Eli scooted his chair closer to Serena. "If it would be any help, I know where there are a couple horses. I don't know if they've ever pulled a wagon, but they could damn well learn how."

Serena widened her eyes at him. "You know where there are horses? I thought my little mare, Beauty, was the only piece of horseflesh in the county that hadn't been commandeered by some officer or other. Where are these two?"

"It's a long story," Eli said, his brown eyes twinkling slyly.

"I've got nothing else to do but listen to it." Serena smiled and settled back. "Let me hear it."

A grin creasing his leathery face, Eli began. "One mornin' I went out to try my hand at catchin' a couple fish in the small stream that runs to the swamp. I'd been there about an hour when suddenly I was caught right in the middle of a fierce battle. I hurried up and crawled into an old rotted-out base of a cypress and sat there, petrified. The fightin' come right up to my tree at one point, and I could see them boys, blue and gray, runnin' and shootin' and fallin'."

Eli closed his eyes, as though to shut out the picture he had conjured. "It was like livin' in a nightmare. Anyway, the battle was being carried away from me when I see these two cavalry men shoot each other out of their saddles. When it grew quiet I slipped out of the tree, grabbed them two horses that was just standin' there, and skedaddled as fast as I could." His grin widened. "I keep them hid in that old shed of mine. Every day I cut them an armful of grass, and they're fat, sassy, and rearin' to go."

Serena's laugh rang out. "You old dickens, Paw. You certainly put one over on the war." Then gloom suddenly descended on her anew. "But that still doesn't solve the little matter of the money." She rubbed the frown on her forehead. "Or help me tell Mammy Hessie about Dorn's letter. I dread telling her what Dorn has asked me to do."

Eli simply patted her hand in sympathetic response. He knew she would find a way.

Eli had barely closed the door behind him when Mammy's voice demanded at Serena's elbow, "Tell me about Mister Dorn's letter, and what he wants you to do."

"Oh, Mammy." Serena sighed softly. "I didn't want you to hear about it this way."

"What difference how I hear it. Tell me."

Serena reluctantly picked up her brother's letter and read it aloud. Before her last word died away Mammy's tears of joy that her young master was safe had turned into a wailing outcry.

"What's wrong with that boy?" the old woman sobbed. "Wantin' to stay out there in the wilderness, and wantin' you to join him.'' She lay a heavy hand on Serena's shoulder. "You write back and say to him that Mammy says get right back here where he belong. That Mammy is gonna take care of him and his sister jus' like she always do.''

Her tear-streaked face crumbled. "I don't know I could stand it, both of you gone.''

Serena stood up and wrapped her arms around the big woman in loving understanding. "Please don't cry, Mammy Hessie,'' she coaxed gently. "Dorn's mind is made up, and nothing will change it.'' Her arms tightened around the weeping woman. "The South we knew is a thing of the past, Mammy. I expect our home to be taken away from us any day. I haven't been able to pay the taxes since the war started.

"So there's not much I can do except try and reach Dorn . . . make a new life for myself.''

When Hessie's tears continued to run unchecked, in desperation Serena offered, "Why don't you and Jebba come with me and Paw Landrie? You know that you're welcome.''

The black woman's sobbing subsided so quickly that Serena wondered if that was what the old nurse had been waiting to hear. After wiping her eyes and blowing her nose on a large white handkerchief, Hessie said, "Maybe if I was younger, child, but I'm too old now to go traipsin' off to someplace I know nothin' about.''

Serena smiled weakly. Hessie took her hands and, pressing them, said earnestly, "I don't want you worryin' about me, either. I'll find a place of work.''

"I could leave with an easier mind if you had a place of your own. It doesn't seem right just to go off and leave you.''

Serena's fingers were given a last squeeze and released. "You be Mammy's brave girl now and do what you have to do.''

The next morning Serena sat on the veranda, bitter thoughts gnawing at her. It was a while before Serena took note of the cloud of dust rolling up the drive. She squinted her eyes at the matched pair of grays pulling a light carriage and the smartly dressed man handling the reins. When he brought the team to a smooth halt and jumped to the ground, her gaze swept over him. Somewhere in his forties, she thought, and the cut of his white linen suit and the curl of that wide brimmed hat means he's got money.

The stranger removed his hat, bowed slightly, and in the short, clipped speech of the north, asked pleasantly, "Is this the Bain plantation? And might I have the pleasure of speaking to Miss Serena Bain?"

He's come to post a "for sale" sign, an inner voice warned Serena. She swallowed hard, and over the thumping of her heart, she answered coolly, "I am Serena Bain."

A slight smile tugged at the stranger's lips when he heard the unfriendliness in her voice. "I understand how you must feel toward the North at this time, Miss Bain," he said, stepping onto the veranda. "But I would like a few minutes of your time if I may. I would like to discuss something that would be beneficial to us both."

He doesn't sound like a tax man. Serena frowned slightly. One from that office wouldn't be so polite. He'd already be demanding to go through the house to count the valuables. She felt the man's eyes on her, waiting, and though she longed to send him on his way with a few scathing words, her breeding and good manners made her invite him inside.

But I won't offer him any refreshments, she thought, as with head held high she motioned for him to take a seat.

His admiring gaze ran over the dark mahogany furniture, the thick carpet on the floor. "This is a most beautiful—" he began, only to have Serena interrupt him sharply.

"I believe you wanted to discuss something with me, Mister . . ."

"John Trenton is the name, Miss." Trenton sat forward, his hands clasped on the thin, flat case balanced on his knees. "Miss Bain, the Federal authorities are interested in your cotton, now that the blockade is lifted. I have been instructed to buy your complete stock at the going rate, which is considerable."

Serena stared open-mouthed for a long moment, then sank back weakly. She hadn't expected this, but the importance of his words were not lost on her. Her money worries were over. Their warehouses were packed to the rafters with cotton.

As though to help his cause, Trenton offered eagerly, "We pay in Yankee dollars, Miss Bain. Greenbacks."

In almost a stupor of relief Serena made arrangements to meet in the Yankee's office the next morning.

His carriage was hardly out of sight before she was racing toward the swamp to tell Paw the good news.

CHAPTER
∽2∽

THE WEARY STALLION slowed to a walk when he felt the bit loosen in his mouth. He had been riding in circles for the past hour.

Josh Quade, Union soldier, reined in and swung stiffly to the ground. In the swirling mistlike fog, he'd become hopelessly lost. There was nothing to do but wait for it to lift. He concealed his mount behind a thicket of sumac, then eased himself down beneath a large cypress.

"Pray God neither army is in the vicinity," he muttered, swatting impatiently at a mosquito and slowly stretching out his long legs.

He leaned his head back against the rough bole of the cypress, his nose twitching at the rank decaying rot of the swamp. What in the hell was he doing in this god-awful place anyhow? he asked the gray silence. He should have stayed in his north woods, where the wind blew fresh and clean, making the pure blood dance in a man's vein. Let the high-nosed Southerners keep their slaves the best way they could.

It had been patriotism—he guessed that was as good a name as any—that had sent him into Tennessee two years ago to join up with crusty old General Grant. The best leader, in his opinion, the northern army had.

An entire uneventful winter had been spent in Tennessee. Hunger and cold rains had been the hardest difficulty to overcome. Not once had his appetite been completely appeased, nor had he in that time ever been completely dry.

Spring had eventually arrived, however, and in April the company had marched to a place called Shiloh where they fought the bloodiest battle of the war. After taking that stronghold, Lincoln had sent Grant to west Tennessee to take charge of the military there. It had been fairly easy in that camp; time to drink a little, brawl a lot, and once in a while, if you had the money, give a whore a fast tumble.

Then, when another spring was approaching, Grant was given the assignment of taking Vicksburg, a strong Confederate fortress. In early May they began firing cannons into the city. During the two months the rebel boys had fought bravely, but now they were tired and hungry. Vicksburg would soon fall, and two days ago Josh decided that he'd had enough of the killing, and he was tired of starving. When that brave city died, he'd be long gone.

It hadn't been difficult, slipping away from his company unit in the cover of darkness. Everyone was always so dead beat they paid no attention to each other's coming and going. It was doubtful they would have cried in alarm had they known what he was up to. Soldiers taking off in the middle of the night was an old story.

But luck had stayed with him only a couple of hours. Josh Quade crossed his legs at the ankles. After that the infernal fog had moved in. He ran impatient fingers through the longish black hair that was gray at the temples. Yawning widely, he let his lids drop over tired dark-blue eyes.

An hour later the restless stamping of his stallion roused Josh. Opening his eyes, he smiled. The fog had disintegrated, with only an occasional milky spot hovering in places.

He had just pulled his feet together to rise when the dull thud of iron-clad hooves on hard-packed clay froze him into a crouch. His hand moved to the wicked-looking knife sheathed at his waist, realizing instinctively that a rifle shot could bring either army thundering down on him.

His narrowed eyes scanned the area, but he saw nothing. He stood up slowly, then quickly stepped behind a tree. A horse and rider had just rounded a bend in the well-beaten path, coming right toward him.

Both man and animal drooped wearily as though they had traveled a long distance. Still, there was a keen wariness about the man who kept a close watch on his back trail. Puzzled lines knitted Quade's forehead. What was a rebel officer doing traveling alone?

When the horse drew opposite Quade he eased the knife from his belt. He would do this one last favor for the Union. He waited until the mount was several feet past him, then stepped out onto the path. The knife poised, its blade pointed at the narrow back of the Southerner, he ordered ringingly, "Hold, reb."

The officer's back stiffened, and Quade thought for a minute he was going to ignore the command. But as he lifted his hand, ready to send the knife flying to its mark, the enemy's shoulders drooped in a gesture of resignation. He gave a cruel jerk of the reins and the stallion whistled in pain as the bit cut into its tender mouth.

I'll have no regrets putting my knife in this mean bastard, Josh told himself darkly, eyeing a stained spur and furrows of beaded blood on a quivering shank.

The wiry body twisted in the saddle and long, slitted eyes stared insolently at Quade. "Well, blue belly, it seems you've got the drop on me."

Quade studied the narrow, thin-lipped face, then shifted his gaze to the sleeve of the wrinkled uniform. Where once there had been an insignia, only a brighter patch of color remained. He lifted a questioning eyebrow, staring significantly at the glaring evidence of stripped power. The reb stared back at him coolly, then jerked his shoulders angrily.

"Yeah," he rasped out. "At present I'm in bad order with the Confederate army."

Josh drew the knife's blade across a thumb, purposefully exaggerating the movement. Sweat appeared on the rebel's forehead, and dread looked out of his eyes. With a snort of disgust Josh slid the knife back into its sheath. He couldn't kill the cowardly bastard in cold blood, after all.

Still, as he whistled for the stallion, he couldn't help feeling he had made a mistake turning soft. But when Jake trotted up the soldier only glanced briefly at the white-faced man and said shortly, "Go on, get the hell out of here."

The sharp features relaxed. "Thanks, Yank."

Quade swung into the saddle. "I'm sick of the war too."

A knowing smile twitched the Southerner's lips, but he held his tongue when a dark, warning look was sent his way. He watched the tall, wide-shouldered body move almost out of sight before spurring after it, and calling out, "We might as well travel together, Yank. We'd have a better chance getting across country without being caught."

Quade unhesitatingly shook his head, refusing the suggestion. He was not one who liked company on the trail. Especially that of a man he'd disliked on sight and did not trust.

He had traveled twenty yards or so when common sense nudged him. The reb would know his own territory, how best to elude either army. Besides, once he was out of this god-awful country, he could say good-bye to the little weasel real quick.

Josh pulled his horse in and waited for the ex-officer to catch up. When the man joined him, he bent a hard look at the blood-stained spurs attached to the heels of the expensive boots. "Get rid of those damn things and you can ride along."

Hostility flickered briefly in the slitted eyes, then a narrow hand reached down, unhooked the spurs, and tossed them into a patch of weeds. "They are of no use anyway." The words came sourly. "I couldn't get any speed out of this bag of bones if I set a fire under him.

"The name is Ira Newcomb." A hand was stuck out stiffly to Josh.

Josh gave the soft hand a brief shake. "Josh Quade." He glanced over his shoulder at the eastern sky. "I expect it's time to look for cover. The war will be coming alive any minute now."

"That won't be necessary," Newcomb said loftily. "I know this country like I know my way to a wench's cabin. Ain't no Yank or Johnny Reb gonna see us."

Josh shot him a look of unconcealed contempt. It appeared the little man chose to forget that only minutes ago he had been very easily captured. He said nothing, however, and pulled Jake over so that the other horse could pass him. And with Newcomb leading the way, they slid the mounts down a steep embankment of a river and followed its shallow course several miles before striking across the country.

It was a land of burned-out fields and forests, towering chimneys standing amid the rubble of stones and ashes. When Newcomb swore bitterly at the wanton destruction, condemning all blue bellies to hell, Josh made no response. He'd feel the same way if it were his north woods that had been raped and ruined.

At first the two men made halfhearted attempts at conversation, remarking on the heat as the sun rose higher and hotter, and mentioning briefly what part of the country each came from. But as the sweat gathered on their brows and collected in their armpits, there was only the growling of their empty stomachs to break the silence.

It was near sunset when the hungry pair spotted the deserted shack at the foot of a small knoll and wordlessly encouraged their mounts into a long lope. They came to a halt beside a fenced-in garden patch and, without pretense, swung from their saddles and raced each other into it.

At first hurried glance there seemed to be nothing but patches of grass and matted dandelions. In hungry frustration Josh kicked out at a clod of red clay, wondering how long a man could go without nourishment. Then, as he turned to the sagging gate, resigned to another night of gnawing hunger, the glistening red of strawberries caught his eye. He tore through the ragged growth and fell to his knees among the vines. When Ira threw himself down beside him an animallike impulse made him want to growl, "They're mine! Go find your own food!"

His threatening glare gradually changed as he watched Newcomb cramming the berries into his mouth, ignoring stems and leaves. He threw back his head and laughed uproariously. What an equalizer was hunger.

When the berry plot was stripped, the men's hunger dulled a bit, the pair wandered over to the dangerously dilapidated building. "I wonder if it's safe to spend the night in there," Josh mused out loud, eyeing the canting roof of the porch, and the loose and warped boards underfoot.

Newcomb, without hesitation, hopped upon the sagging floor

and pushed open the door that hung on one rusty hinge. "These old houses are sturdier than they look. The majority started out as log cabins. Over the years the crockers have covered them with planks."

The puncheon floors of the three rooms creaked loudly as they walked. All were empty but one, which was strewn with a jumble of broken baskets and shriveled gourds.

"We'll hide the horses in here," Josh said, lightly kicking at the rubbish to discover if any mice or snakes would scurry from beneath the rubble. When only dust flew, he went outside, returning in a few minutes with an armful of long, tender grass. Another trip outside brought the stallion in, where it was unsaddled and wiped down with a rag Josh kept for that purpose.

Newcomb lounged in the doorway, a sneer curving his thin lips. "You sure do pamper that animal of yours."

Josh sent him a cutting look. "You might try coddling that poor beast of yours a little. If we should ever have to make a dash for it, you'd be run down in seconds." He ran a tanned hand over the stallion's glistening back. "Jake here is in tip-top condition. He can outrun anything in this miserable state."

Newcomb's lips retained their sneer, but after a minute he, too, brought in his tired mount and then returned with an armload of grass.

Darkness was settling in when Josh chose a room and curled up on the floor. He closed his eyes, coaxing sleep to slip in on him.

His weariness was beginning to overcome him when Newcomb began to speak. "This balmy air reminds me of nights on the plantation. I'd take a couple of wenches into my bed, and I tell you, the night wasn't long enough."

When Josh didn't respond, he asked loudly, "You ever had a wench, Quade?"

There was a long silence before Josh answered shortly, "No, I never have. Takin' a woman who is afraid to say no doesn't appeal to me."

"You're crazy, Yank. They like to be mastered, feel a little sting of the whip. They're the best there is in bed, you know."

A look of pure devilment slid over Josh's face. He raised his voice and said in pretended innocence, "Lucky for you the slaves have been freed. You'll be able to marry one of them when you get home.''

There was stunned silence in the next room. Then Newcomb bristled angrily, "I resent that, mister. I've horsewhipped men for less.''

Yeah, you little bastard: helpless slaves, Josh thought before saying in spurious surprise, "I don't know why you take offense, reb. You just said that you prefer black women over white. What was I supposed to think?''

Ira sniffed contemptuously. "Only a crazy Northerner wouldn't know that a white man would never marry a slave.''

"I wonder," Josh drawled lazily, "what you're gonna do when you have to go to a fancy pleasure house and pay for the company of a black woman. I hear they've got some real beauties there. It's gonna cost you a fortune.''

"I'll still get it free," Newcomb said complacently. "Free or not those wenches are gonna be afraid to refuse a white man.''

"You might get a knife in your gut along with your pleasure," Josh warned.

"Bah!" Newcomb snorted. "Anyway," he said smugly, "my future bride is already chosen. Besides being the most beautiful girl in the entire state, she's also pure virgin.''

Josh made no effort to smother a bored yawn. "You're a lucky man. Where do you keep this virgin hidden?''

"A southern lady doesn't have to be kept hidden. She knows her place and keeps it. Any day a person visits the Bain plantation, Miss Serena Bain will be there to graciously greet them.''

Josh shook his head, feeling sympathy for the unknown girl. Did she know what kind of man she was marrying—a user and abuser of black women, a miserable little coward?

He had an urgent need to hear no more about this Serena Bain, and he turned his back to the boasting voice.

Shafts of sunlight slicing through a dirty window awakened Josh the next morning. The years of war had taught him instant recall, and he was immediately alert to his whereabouts and what events had brought him to this crude little shack. With an agile movement he was on his feet.

In the adjoining room Newcomb still snored loudly. After checking on his stallion, out of curiosity, Josh began to rummage through the broken baskets. Most were empty, while the others contained rags, bits and pieces of harness, a rusted tin plate, and a few broken toys. Someone had been very thorough in their packing, he thought dryly, digging the last basket from the bottom of the pile.

Interest stirred in Josh's eyes. This woven container was more sound than the others, and by its weight might contain something of value. With a sweep of his hand he brushed away a covering of old newspapers to discover articles of clothing. They were mostly men's, and he hunkered down and quickly sorted through them.

Five minutes later he sat back on his heels, satisfaction on his lean face. He had unearthed two pair of homespuns and two butternut-dyed shirts. This was just what they needed. Dressed as civilians he and Newcomb wouldn't stand out as they traversed the countryside.

But later, when he tossed Ira a set of the clothing, ordering him to put them on, the Southerner balked at donning the rustic shirt and pants, declaring that his slaves wore better. Josh retorted that his slaves weren't fleeing the army, and with a sulky pout on his thin face, Newcomb stripped and put on his new outfit.

"You look right good as a crocker." Josh couldn't help tormenting the other as he ran an amused glance over wrinkled, musty-smelling apparel. "I think that garb becomes you more than Confederate gray."

Newcomb's eyes blazed at the intended insult, but the daring eyes boring into him made him swallow his anger and wordlessly stalk outside.

Josh grinned crookedly at his own appearance. There was a long expanse of wrist showing beyond the ragged cuffs and a good two inches of exposed skin above his shoe tops. Lord, he mused, I look worse than the reb.

He shrugged and, draping his dirty uniform over an arm, picked up Ira's discarded one and followed him outside.

"We've got to bury these," he said, tossing the gray at Newcomb's feet. "If either army should happen onto them, they'll be hot on our tails."

Embarrassment flushed the ex-officer's face. As a leader of

men, he should have thought of that first. After he finished adjusting his saddle, he looked up and growled, ''I intended to take care of that just as soon as I finished here.''

''Sure you did, reb.'' Josh threw him a disgusted look.

When the men had dropped the blue and gray clothes into a gully, kicking dirt and stones over them, they mounted and headed out.

Three more days passed, each more or less in the same fashion. They robbed gardens at night, shot small game when it was safe enough to fire Josh's weapon, and slept in barns when they could find one; otherwise they curled up on the ground.

As they traveled there was one happening that Newcomb wasn't aware of. Each day Josh veered more and more northward. He hadn't asked the Southerner his own destination, and he didn't care where the man went. He was only interested in the day he could leave him. And he felt that time wasn't far off. For the terrain was beginning to change. The hills were more gentle, the air drier, and the nights cooler. Any day he expected to spot familiar country.

The dislike between the two men had grown to near hate. Sometimes they rode all day without breaking the silence between them. It took but a few words from either man before the other was finding real or imagined insult in the words. By silent agreement they spoke only when necessary.

There came a day when the road they traveled suddenly forked. One way turned sharply east, the other veering north. Josh drew rein, and Newcomb shot him a questioning look as he pulled his mount alongside Jake.

''Which way, Yank?''

''Take whichever road suits you.'' Josh shrugged and turned Jake's head due north. ''I'm leavin' you, reb.''

Newcomb's eyes showed his surprise and dismay. He threw a bewildered glance around him. For the first time he seemed to realize that he was in strange territory. His pale eyes flashed with anger; the blue belly had tricked him.

He sat his restless horse, only vaguely aware of this new land as he pondered a sudden idea. Then, with a false geniality in his voice, he said, ''Maybe I'll take your way. I always fancied seeing the northern regions. Do you think those hill people will welcome me?''

"Are you out of your mind, little man?" Josh's lips curled contemptuously. "They'd eat you for breakfast.''

His face an angry red, his hands so tight on the reins the mount pranced in discomfort, Newcomb said in his most arrogant voice, "I was only joking, of course. I have no desire to look upon any more blue bellies. And it will be good to see the last of you.''

"Yeah, reb," Josh sneered. "I could see that when I told you I was driftin'.''

Pure hate glittered in the pale narrowed eyes. "We'll meet again someday, Quade, and you and I will have a reckoning. I'll not forget your insults, and you'll pay for every one of them.''

Newcomb jabbed his mount with a heel, but before the animal could move, Josh had grabbed the reins. A taunting look danced in his blue eyes as he leaned toward Ira and spoke in confidential tones. "You know your betrothed, Serena Bain? I hate to tell you this, but she's not a virgin anymore." When Ira only stared at him in stunned disbelief, Josh nodded as though in regret. "I'm afraid it's true, little man. I bedded her a while back. Broke her in real good for you. You know all those things your slave women used to do to you? Well, your little gal did them all to me. You won't have to teach her anything.''

While Newcomb stared at him dumbly, Josh touched heels to Jake. As they loped off he called over his shoulder, "If there should be a youngun from the mating, you be good to him, you heah.''

As the stallion stretched his long legs, eating up the road, Josh's face grew sober. He hoped Newcomb's stiff pride would keep him from marrying that Serena. He had, after all, uttered the lies with that intention.

The stallion's enthusiasm for speed lasting, another day and a half saw him lunging up the hill that hid Shady Valley from view. Josh drew rein at the top and stared down at the small community.

Nothing had changed. The same rude cabins dotted the hillsides, the same bleached stumps directed winding paths to places of business. He breathed a sigh of thankfulness. Right now he needed something that was lasting, enduring, a permanency he could depend on.

A soft look passed over his face. He loved this wild country and had never regretted coming here. As he quietly sat the mount, refreshing his eyes with familiar sights, his mind went back seventeen years.

His mother, a kind and gentle woman, had died when he was twelve years old. Left mostly on his own then, and without her care and instructions, he had grown into a self-willed and troublesome youngster. When Josh was fourteen, his father, a poor man who worked hard to make ends meet, decided he could not tolerate Josh's wild ways, so one spring morning he marched his son to a neighboring farmer and bound him over to the man.

Josh stayed with the farmer, who wasn't averse to taking a belt to him when he needed it, until his sixteenth year. Then one night while everyone was sleeping he gathered his clothes and slipped away, saying good-bye to New York State.

Two weeks later, tired and hungry, having existed mainly on fall apples and pears, he stood on a ridge looking down into the Ohio Valley. In the distance his gaze encountered a scattering of buildings. An hour later he was walking down a winding dirt street, bewildered, not knowing what to do. He was afraid to ask questions of the few people he passed for fear they would know he was a runaway and notify the law.

As he continued to walk on, he saw a tall figure coming down the street toward him. From the man's appearance—fringed buckskins flapping against each other as the moccasined feet stepped along—he judged him to be a trapper or a hunter. He decided hunter when he saw the long flintlock slung over a broad shoulder.

His hunger and despondency must have shown in his eyes, for when the stranger was about to pass him, he stopped suddenly and peered into the youthful face. The heavy beard stirred and a deep voice said, "Say, young fellow, how about sharin' supper with a lonely man?"

Josh and Sam Dodge had taken to each other right off. Sam was a trapper, not a hunter, and the year they stayed together, before Sam was killed in a knife fight, Josh learned all there was to know about trapping, the ways of the wilderness, and the Indians.

He also learned about whoring.

That first night, when he and Sam had met, right after supper his new friend had introduced him to a tavern wench. His eyes had almost popped out of his head when the trapper said to the woman, "Take him upstairs and make a man out of him."

He had followed the woman up the steps, nervous, a little afraid. He was big for his age, and when the woman had pulled his homespuns down around his ankles, she had given a pleased laugh. She grasped him, murmuring, "My, ain't you a big one. Most of the men downstairs ain't hung as big as you are." She gave him a sly wink. "You been pullin' it a lot, ain't you?"

He blushed red at her correct assumption.

In the hours spent with the whore she taught him the many ways to vent the raw hunger that nagged constantly at his young body. What she could not teach him, however, was the tenderness, the gentle caressing that so enriched the intimate act of love. At thirty-four, Josh Quade still knew nothing of this important fact. He continued to use women impersonally; they were vital to his needs, and nothing more.

The stallion gave a sudden shrill, glad whistle, startling Josh into action. He patted Jake on the neck and urged him down the hill. "I'm not the only one glad to be home, huh, fellow?"

Humor sparked in Josh's eyes as he approached a long building that housed a tavern and a store, which catered to most needs of the small community. Each establishment had its own entrance, with a door between them. As usual, since the first time he had entered the village all those years ago, several old men sat on the long porch, chewing tobacco and swapping time-worn tales. The ring of the horse's shoes caught their attention and they broke off the long-winded chattering to peer at him from faded, rheumy eyes.

Recognition brought toothless smiles to their lips, and high piping voices chorused, "Hey, Josh Quade!"

Josh swung to the ground and shook each gnarled hand, surprised at how glad he was to see them. They were full of questions about the war, and he took the time to patiently answer them all. When one old man suggested that Josh might be dry and would he like to step into the tavern, Josh knew that they wanted to spend some time discussing the information he had given them about the war.

Josh was not discovered immediately, standing just inside the tavern door, and he took this time to let his gaze wander around the large room where he had spent so many hours.

Ben, the bartender and owner of the place, leaned his tall angular body against the bar, talking idly with four mountain men. In a corner near an open window, five of his girls passed the time in a desultory game of cards.

His senses filled with the familiar odor of spirits and sawdust, and the presence of old and trusted friends. The darkness of the war slowly began to slip from Josh's mind. He grinned, resisting the urge to let loose a jarring, blood-tingling yell, for he knew that he would startle the lethargic group.

Then Ben straightened up to reach for a bottle and spotted him. With a smile that was genuinely glad, he yelled sonorously, "Josh, bygod. When did you get in, you old wolf?"

Josh pumped the bony hand stuck out at him, his own smile equally wide. "I just rode in, Ben."

He was surrounded then, the men slapping him on the back, shouting gruff greetings, and the whores surging forward in giggling welcome. He fell back against the bar as the women pushed and shoved, each determined to cling to an arm. Josh Quade was a favorite.

"Don't smother him, girls," Ben ordered, half joking, half in earnest. "Give me room to pour him a drink."

Josh snaked an arm between the feminine bodies and picked up the glass of whiskey. He tossed the amber liquid down his throat, then smacked his lips appreciatively. "Our grain liquor has got it beat all over the South's mash any day," he declared, drawing a pleased laugh from Ben and the customers. He nudged the empty glass. "I'd take another if it were offered."

Ben joined his laughter to the others' and tilted the bottle again. "You home on leave, Josh?" he asked, recorking the bottle.

"Nope, I'm home to stay," Josh answered after a short pause.

Concern jumped into the eyes of Jessie, the redheaded madam. "You're not hurt, are you, Josh? Wounded?"

Josh draped an affectionate arm across the small woman's shoulders. "Only in my mind, Jess," he said quietly. "I just reached a point where I'd had enough useless killin' and maimin'."

Everyone nodded sympathetically. "We heard it was bad," Ben said soberly.

The whores, not liking the somber turn the conversation was taking, moved in on Josh again, and his face showed he welcomed the interruption. "You been gettin' your pleasurin'?" one asked, rubbing into him suggestively. "I'll bet them southern belles weren't overly eager to spread their legs for a blue belly," another teased.

Josh went along with the bantering. "I found a few who lifted their fancy petticoats."

Jessie slid a slow-moving hand down the fly of his trousers, moulding her fingers around the soft manhood. "Let's go into the back room," she whispered, "and I'll show you another difference between the North and the South."

Josh was aware of the stroking fingers, the message they were sending, but he was not stirred. The old Josh Quade wouldn't have needed to be asked. By now he would have already bedded the skinny little whore and returned to the bar.

Embarrassed, he refused the redhead's offer, explaining that he was trail tired. When he noticed how the rays of the sun had shifted their pattern on the tavern floor he was relieved. Now he could say that he wanted to get home before dark, look the old place over.

The porch was deserted when Josh left the tavern. The old men had left, some to lonely cabins, others to a son or daughter. He paused to glance curiously at four bearded, black-garbed men emerging from the fringe of the forest that hemmed in the village on the north side. The four walked purposefully toward the tavern, giving him a brief nod in passing.

"Now what kind of business can them 'churchgoers' have with Ben?" he muttered under his breath as he swung into the saddle. Silas Hansen, the leader, never missed an opportunity to preach against Ben's "sinkhole of iniquity," as he called the tavern.

Josh reined Jake around, grinning. Old Ben was probably in for a dressing down for some reason or other.

CHAPTER
∽ 3 ∽

THE COTTON MONEY has certainly hurried things along for us, Serena thought as she moved along the walkway between the house and the summer kitchen. Its purchasing power had allowed her and Paw to do some haggling. Cash in hand had made the saliva gather in the storekeepers' mouths, and most of their high prices had been cut in half.

But best of all—Serena smiled contentedly—those greenbacks had bought for Mammy Hessie ten acres of good land and a sturdy, roomy cabin. The old woman was beside herself with joy, and when Paw Landrie purchased her a pair of scrawny mules from a crocker, her delight was complete. Paw had tried to apologize for their poor condition, but Mammy had dismissed his words with a wave of her large hand.

"Don't you go bein' shamed of them animals, Mister Eli. Just give me a month and them bag of bones will be fat as butter." Big tears rolled down her cheeks then, and she enfolded Serena in her arms. "You don't have to worry 'bout Mammy no more, child. Me and Jebba will do just fine. We'll plow and seed the whole ten acres. We'll be just fine."

A mistiness clouded Serena's eyes as she stepped up on the veranda. How she would miss the faithful old slave.

She sighed and sat down in a rocker, wondering how Paw was coming along with the wagon.

The sun was warm and the air soft, causing a languor to slip

over Serena. Her head began to nod, ready for sleep. Then the
heavy crunch of wheels on the driveway brought her chin up
with a jerk. She blinked, sure that she was dreaming when she
saw the large, cumbersome conveyance pull up to the steps.
After startled seconds of staring at the long, wide wagon, her
gaze lifted to a large piece of canvas stretched over three iron
curved ribs. It stood so tall, was so wobbly, surely the least wind
would make it topple over.

When Landrie asked cheerily, "Well, what do you think?"
she could only think and wonder, Is it capable of carrying us
over 2,000 miles across an untamed wilderness? She opened her
mouth but no words came out.

"It's a prairie schooner," Eli said, almost defensively. "I
know it don't look like much, but it's sturdy and dependable.
And that funny-lookin' top that's got your eyes buggin' will protect you against the elements. It's roomy enough for our supplies, plus a spot for you to sleep."

He strode to the back of the wagon, and Serena stood up and
followed Eli, though she was still unconvinced of its depend-
ability. She didn't want to hurt his feelings further.

Landrie whipped back the canvas flap and stood aside so that
she could see inside. "See. It's all packed. After we add a few
more items we'll be all ready to go."

Serena rose on her toes to look at the interior. On each side
of the narrow aisle running the length of the wagon Paw had
neatly stacked supplies all the way to the ceiling, then secured
them with rope. Directly behind the high seat a straw mattress
lay on the floor, tidily made up with blankets and a pillow.
Fastened to the back of the seat was a small mirror.

A tender smile curved Serena's lips. What a kind and thoughtful man Paw is, she thought.

To please him, she exclaimed, "Good Lord, Paw, you have a
small store in here. Will we need it all?"

"Missy, we ain't really got enough." Landrie laughed, Serena's ruse working. "You gotta remember we'll be on the trail
for at least six months. I'm hopin' we'll find a place along the
way where we can restock."

"What all do you have in there?"

Landrie took a deep breath and began. "Besides a barrel of

flour there's three slabs of bacon, a keg each of sugar, coffee, and cornmeal. Then there's a rope, an axe, a lantern, and a butcher knife for the game I'll kill along the way. We've also got a saw, a shovel, and a hammer.''

He paused to catch his breath, then continued, "In that crate under the seat there's tin plates and cups, a Dutch oven, and bags of seeds. And fastened to the underside of the tailgate is a grindstone and a plow.''

Serena grinned when Eli came to a breathless stop. "It sounds like we've got everything we'll need.''

"Not likely. I want you to gather up a few things. A clock, candles, a basin for washing up, cooking pans and a coffee pot. Then we'll need a jar of matches and a Bible.

"That's all I can think of now,'' he finished as he pulled down the canvas flap and fastened it. Then, taking Serena's arm, he led her to the front of the wagon and, glancing around to make sure they had no audience, lifted down the tar bucket that hung just over a wheel. "I've put a secret bottom in it.'' He showed her the tiny spring that released the bottom half. "You can hide your money in there.''

"Paw!'' Serena voiced her surprise and approval. "How clever of you. I've been worrying how to hide such a large amount. It's very important that I get it to Dorn.''

Landrie nodded soberly. "We'll put it in just before we leave.''

Serena stepped back and asked the important question. "And when will that be?''

"The sooner, the better. We want to get on the trail while there's still forage for the horses. If we run out of grazin' the animals won't last long. I booked our passage on the riverboat yesterday. What about we leave tomorrow morning?''

Serena smiled at him waveringly, struck as she nodded in agreement how everything was moving so rapidly, so suddenly. Through eyes that were suspiciously damp, she watched Eli unhitch the team. "I'm gonna take them back to my place. Don't want to lose them to the Yankees at the last minute.''

* * *

Two dejected women gathered the items Landrie had requested, the final act that would part them forever, and their eyes shimmered often with tears.

When everything had been carried to the veranda, Serena turned to Hessie and forced a bright smile to her lips. "Well, Mammy, there's one last thing to do, then you and Jebba can go to your new home."

"What that be, honey?" Mammy asked softly.

"Selecting the furniture for that home."

"Ah, Serena, you don't mean—"

"That's exactly what I mean," Serena interrupted. "Take anything you like. I'd rather you had it than some Yankee trash. I know that you will love and treasure it in the same fashion Bain women have through the years."

Late that afternoon the bony mules were hitched to a wagon, and Serena and Mammy helped Jebba to load the chosen pieces into it. As they struggled with a heavy four-poster, amusement tugged at Serena's lips. Mammy had picked wisely. Her four-room cabin would be the best set up place around Vicksburg. Tongues would wag about Serena Bain's foolishness.

The final parting was at hand. Jebba sat holding the reins, waiting for the two women to make their farewells. The parting was brief; both had already cried their tears and voiced their regrets that they must part. They merely embraced with Mammy saying huskily, "If ever you should need me, child, you know where I'll be."

Serena watched the wagon creak out of sight, then climbed the gentle slope to the myrtle-clad cemetery. Three generations of relatives were buried there.

It was almost dark by the time she walked among the gravestones, then said good-bye to her parents. As she walked slowly homeward Jeremy was strong in her thoughts. In what lonely place was he buried? She sighed raggedly. A part of her would be left behind with him, the young, carefree Serena.

Serena entered the big, empty house with some trepidation. The silence was so heavy it was almost spooky. She stood in the hall for a moment, listening for the echoing laughter of the black children, the hustle and bustle which Mammy had always stirred up. Only a gloomy quiet answered her.

"I'll never get to sleep," she muttered, climbing the stairs, the wavering light of a candle guiding her footsteps.

But the excitement and emotional drain of the day dictated otherwise. Midway through her prayers Serena fell asleep. Landrie's pounding on the door at sunrise awakened her.

Surprisingly, anticipation stirred her blood as she hurried down the stairs and flung the door open. Maybe brother Dorn had the right idea, a new life.

Eli stood on the veranda, his old hound at his side. Serena gave a searching glance to his stiff features. Why was Paw looking so . . . defensive? she wondered. When he lay a hand on the dog's head and said quietly, "I couldn't leave him behind, he's my friend," she understood. He was afraid she wouldn't want the old pet to come with them.

She leaned over and added her own caress to the smooth head. "Of course you had to bring him, Paw. He's family."

Landrie's eyes lit up like the first flames of an evening's campfire. To cover his relief, however, he nudged the dog and said roughly, "Go lie down and keep out of the way, you no-account hound." He occupied himself with hitching the team, then said over his shoulder, "Fetch me the money, then get dressed. We ain't got much time."

Serena pulled a petticoat over her head, and then a pink dimity. She gave her reddish-blond hair a few strokes of a brush, then tossed her treasured possession into the open valise lying on the bed. When her gown and robe were added, she closed and fastened the straps. The bag hanging from her hand, she swung a last lingering look around the room that had known both her joyful times and her sad times. She fought back a flood of tears. The familiar furniture looked so lonely somehow, as though it knew she was leaving it forever.

She firmed her lips and stepped out into the hall. Keeping her head down so that she wouldn't see into the other rooms, she fled down the stairs and out the door.

Landrie pretended not to see her teary eyes as he helped her onto the high, stiff-springed seat. He climbed up beside her and slapped the reins over the horses' fat rumps. The team, new at their use as draft animals, whinnied in displeasure and pulled against each other. Landrie swore loudly as they narrowly

avoided tangling their legs in the traces before taking off with a
lurch. Serena's mare, Beauty, tied to the tailgate, was nearly
jerked off her feet as the lead rope tightened.

When Eli steered the team onto the river road, Serena kept
her eyes straight ahead, not daring to look back. Her friend knew
what must be going on in her mind and reached over to gently
pat her knee.

The sun was warming up as the wagon rolled through town
and came to a stop at the wharves lining the banks of the Mississippi. "Well, Missy, there she is." Landrie indicated with his
whip the boat they would board and ride to Independence, Missouri.

Serena gazed at the large vessel whose twin smokestacks
puffed great clouds of black smoke as it waited for its passengers
to board. She watched with interest as two huge black stevedores
hauled down the gangplank and Landrie began to coax the nervous team onto the creaking boards. It took quiet urging from
the driver and a black hand at each rearing head to finally gain
the storage area of the ship.

Landrie jumped to the gently swaying floor, then swung Serena down beside him. "You go on up and find your stateroom,"
he said. "I'll be with you as soon as I unhitch the team and
settle the hound."

Serena climbed the narrow wooden steps to the main deck,
and then up a grand staircase to the boiler deck. When a bell
began sounding, signaling that the ship was about to take its
departure, she hurried to lean against the railing.

The big vessel moved out into the mainstay of the Mississippi.
The muddy water, laced with creamy foam, swept back from
the bow, carrying Serena Bain away from the only life she had
ever known. She straightened her spine and forced back her
tears. She must accept the fact that that part of her life was over;
she must look to the future. God willing, she would have a happy
life out west with her brother.

Josh Quade's stallion needed no guiding when he nudged him
onto the familiar trail. His eager lunging stride took them to the
top of the hill in short time.

In the still bright twilight, Josh sat quietly, gazing at the small cabin sheltered in a glade of pine and birch. How many times he had dreamed of its peacefulness as bullets screamed around him!

When he had looked his fill, he climbed down from the saddle and stepped up on the porch. He stood a moment, savoring the anticipation, then pushed open the sturdy, solid door.

Dust and age was thick in the air that met his nostrils, evidence that no one had lived here for a long time. He stepped inside and heard a rustling of mice as they scurried to secret hiding places. He ducked his head as a bat winged over his head and flapped through the open door.

In the semidarkness of the room, he hurriedly opened shutters and raised the two windows. As he savored the fresh, crisp air that rushed in, Josh stripped off the homespuns and tossed them into the fireplace. He smiled ruefully to himself as the broken shoes followed. It was decent of his friends back at the tavern not to have twitted him about his garb; surely they had laughed to themselves.

When the welcome feel of smooth, supple buckskin hugged his body, Josh sighed with satisfaction. He pulled on a pair of double-soled moccasins, tested them with a few steps, and gloried in their comfort.

His body taken care of, he glanced around the room, then grabbed up the Indian broom. In less than an hour, and just as the sun slipped over the trees, the floor was swept clean and the bed newly made up with fresh linen.

Josh's stomach growled as he sent a skeptical look to the half dozen gourds of various sizes lined up on a shelf. One properly cured, with a tight-fitting lid, couldn't be beat for preserving staples. But, after all this time, was it possible anything left in them could still be usable?

He took them all off the shelf and placed them on the table. After examination of each gourd he came up with a small quantity of flour, coffee, and salt, all in fair condition. Old routines came back to him as he started a fire in the fireplace, which quickly consumed the clothing tossed into it, then he fetched a pail of water from the deep running spring in back of the cabin. He set a pot of coffee to brew, then went outside to tend Jake and stable him in the shed. On the way up the hill he had caught the shadowy figure of a wolf sliding through the trees. There were probably others, and Jake might look appetizing to them.

An hour later, his feet stretched toward the fire, Josh sipped his second cup of coffee. It tasted more than a little stale, he mused; he'd better lay in some new supplies tomorrow. His lips took on a wry twist. The storekeeper would have to give him credit, though. He didn't have a copper cent to his name.

Josh rested his head on the back of the chair and stared up at the wavering shadows cast by the leaping flames. By the time the fire had died down to glowing coals he was more at peace with himself than he had been for a long time. He felt almost mended when he stripped and slid into bed.

The sun rose brightly on Josh's first day home. He threw the covers from his naked body and stretched lazily, lightly scratching at the black mat of hair on his broad chest. What a good night's rest can do for a man, he thought, swinging his feet to the floor.

Still undressed, he stepped out onto the porch and let his gaze wander. In shadowed spots the dew glistened on spider webs in the dark green grass, and overhead in a tamarack tree a pair of blue jays were squawking.

His eye finally swung to the valley below and rested on the winding river that skirted the village. He thought of the Mississippi and its muddy waters and hoped he'd never have to see it again.

As Josh continued to lounge against a supporting post, the sun rose higher and the mists began to burn away. Only twisted ropes of fog remained hanging over the river. A fine day to go hunting, he decided, and turned back into the cabin, sighing with contentment.

When his breakfast consisted of two warmed-over cups of coffee he also acknowledged a pressing need to make time for a visit to the village store.

His Indian-like steps made no sound as he moved over the forest floor, and the sun was barely overhead when three furry bodies were hanging from the belt at his waist.

Josh was almost home when a stealthy noise sounded behind him. He dropped the unloaded rifle and yanked the knife from its sheath as he whirled around. Then, growling a curse, he returned the broad blade to its place on his belt. A young squaw stood a few paces away, an uncertain smile on her lips.

Josh glared at her a moment, then said in some disgust, "You've been followin' me all mornin', haven't you, Ninu?"

The girl lowered her lids and nodded.

"Why? What do you want?" He stalked over to her.

"I want to be your squaw again," the girl answered, her words barely audible.

"Dammit, Ninu, you never was my squaw. Two nights with a man doesn't automatically make you his woman."

Shortly before he had entered the army Josh had grown tired of Ben's whores. He knew every move they were going to make before they made it. He had hoped the Indian girl would bring something fresh, different, to his bed. But after two nights he had known better. She was no different from Jessie and her girls. And worse, the girl had little intelligence. The first day she had driven him to distraction with her grunts and one-word answers when he tried to converse with her.

On the second day he had given her some money and explained that he didn't need her anymore.

He gazed down at the girl now and thought that she had grown thin. Why? he wondered. Surely not from hunger. She was still young, and still attractive. Any number of men would gladly provide food in exchange for her presence in his bed.

"I'm sorry, Ninu," he said in softer tones, "but I don't like havin' a woman underfoot all the time."

The girl drew near enough to play with the material of his shirt. "Ninu won't be underfoot. She stay in shed until you want her."

Josh pushed her hand away, embarrassed by the pleading in her voice. "I couldn't make you stay in the shed like an animal."

"I stay in corner, then, be real quiet."

Josh shook his head impatiently. "Ninu, I don't need a woman."

"But you a young man. Even Silas Hansen pesters me at least two times a day, and he plenty old."

Josh's eyebrows drew together and he eyed the girl suspiciously. "How come you know Hansen? He's got no use for Indians."

"I live with Hansen people now." Ninu pulled a leaf off a tree and shredded it with her nails as she added, "Help wife with chores and take care of children."

Josh watched the brown fingers tearing nervously at the greenery, then with a faint sarcastic twist of his lips he asked, "Doesn't the old goat satisfy you, Ninu? Does he run out of steam too soon?"

Ninu's chin came up proudly. "I get plenty pleasurin'. Hansen's sons also cover me."

And that's why you've lost weight, Josh thought before saying, "I don't see your problem, then."

"It's old woman Hansen. She jealous. Work me hard all the time. Sometimes even beats me."

Josh believed the girl. Big, mannish-looking Bertha Hansen was the type of woman who would be jealous of a young and pretty girl, especially if she suspected that her husband was lusting after the little squaw. And he wouldn't put it past her to treat Ninu cruelly.

Still, he couldn't take in every squaw who was mistreated by whites. He patted the stooped shoulders awkwardly. "You're gonna have to make do with them, Ninu, or get yourself another man. I have no need of you." He pretended not to see her disappointment as Ninu turned and walked away.

But Josh thought of the Indian girl as he walked homeward, and mused on her surprising story. Hansen—it was hard to think that the psalm-singing bastard would lust after an Indian squaw. The two sons, yes. They were at an age where they could drop their pants at a moment's notice.

His cabin came in view, and then Josh put Ninu and the Hansens from his mind as he skinned and gutted the squirrels. Inside the cabin he put the pieces of dressed meat in a salt bath to take away some of the wild taste. "And while they soak," he said to himself, "I'll ride down to the village and get my supplies."

As usual, the old men were gathered on the porch. He nodded them a friendly greeting then moved through the door above which hung a crude sign that simply said STORE. He paused inside the dim room, sniffing deeply of dry goods, leather, and herbs. In the fall there would be the additional mouth-watering aroma of apples and pears. And a little later yet there would be the not-so-pleasant odor of fresh fur pelts.

Old Pete Jones hobbled from a room in the back and with sparkling eyes stretched a hand across the counter. "Good to have you back, Quade. I'm glad to see you made it in one piece."

Josh shook the lean, dry hand. "It's good to be back, Pete."

"Yeah, I expect so. War is a mean business. There don't seem to be an end to this one."

"It can't last much longer. The South is hungry. They only have what the womenfolk raise, and that ain't much." Josh shot Pete a crooked grin. "Speakin' of food, do you think you could let me have a few things on loan until trappin' season? I'm flat out of money."

"Don't fret about it, Josh," Pete said, waving a dismissive hand. "Half my trade these days is done on the sale of furs."

Josh gave his order and the old man gathered up the items, totaled them, then added the amount to the end of a long list. He raked everything into a rough fustian bag and pushed it toward Josh. "Don't hesitate to come back when this is gone."

"Thank you, Pete. I appreciate it."

Gripping the well-filled sack, Josh went through the connecting door to the tavern. His eyes were dawn immediately to four unlikely patrons. Silas Hansen and three of his followers sat at a table just inside the door. Josh's lips curled in a sneer. The group looked ready to make a hasty retreat in case the devil should pop up.

He bent a dark look to the black-garbed men and was tempted to tell the other customers lined against the bar the story Ninu had told him. Then friends were calling his name, making room for him to join them. He dropped the thought as he moved forward.

"I'll have a whiskey, Ben, if you'll trust me until this winter." He grinned at the bartender.

Amused laughter greeted Josh's request. "Join the rest of us, Quade," a tall hillman remarked. "Half the village is waitin' for the trappin' season and for the blockade to be lifted."

"By God, I'm beginnin' to think that we're as poor as the South," Josh said, watching the amber-colored liquid fill a glass.

"Money is tight," Ben agreed, mopping at the rough bar with a rag that was none too clean. "I'll be glad when things get back to normal." He drew himself a small ale and, leaning his arms on the bar, asked casually, "You come in for supplies, Josh?"

"Yeah, I'm out of everything."

"It was good to see the old place again, I take it?"

"It sure was. I hadn't realized just how much I'd been missin' it."

"Don't reckon you'd care to leave it again?"

"Nope, I don't think so."

"Not even for a short time?"

Josh gave his longtime friend a raking look of appraisal that sent a guilty flush of red to the man's face. Then, making no attempt to conceal a growing irritation, he growled, "Dammit, Ben, if you're tryin' to say somethin' I wish you'd come out with it. Has somebody been here lookin' for me? The army?"

"No, no, nothin' like that," he was hastily assured as Ben, glancing around, leaned closer. "See Hansen and his friends over there by the door?" he said in a low tone.

Josh nodded, frowning. "Yeah, I saw them when I came in. I saw them outside yesterday, too. Have they taken up drinkin' and whorin'?"

"Not likely," Ben snorted. "Hansen's been askin' questions about you."

Josh's eyes narrowed suspiciously. "Oh yeah? What kind of questions?"

"Oh,"—Ben shrugged a shoulder—"things like are you honest? Can you be trusted? Things like that."

Josh set his glass down with a ringing thud. "What in the hell business is it of theirs what kind of man I am? Especially that cur Hansen!"

"Now, Josh, don't go gettin' upset," Ben urged nervously. "They only asked because they want you to do something for them."

"Do somethin' for that hypocritical sin-preachin' bunch?" Josh still bristled. "What in the hell could I do for men like them? Maybe they think I could introduce them to Satan."

Ben swiped at the bar a couple of times then blurted out, "They want you to lead a wagon train to Oregon Territory."

Josh could only stare incredulously at the tall, lanky man. "That's right," Ben said, tossing aside the bar rag.

"What do they think I am," Josh finally managed to say, "a feeble half-wit? And why in God's name would they want to go to land that lies at the end of the earth?"

"That's your answer, earth. They want all that free land. Anyone who settles there can have all he wants." When Josh only continued to glower at the bartender, he said placatingly, "I told them I didn't think you'd be interested, but I promised to speak to you about it."

Ben was called away to wait on another customer but kept an eye on Josh. A minute later when he returned to stand opposite Josh, he said, "You know, I was just thinkin'. It might be real excitin', makin' a trip through unexplored territory."

"Hah!" Josh snorted. "It might be more than excitin'. I could damn well get my head bashed in with a tomahawk. The Indians are on the warpath out there, you know. They're boilin' hot that we're grabbin' up their land."

'Yeah, there's that," Ben agreed, then added shrewdly, "That's why it's gonna take a real experienced man to get them through."

Josh sent Ben a look that let him know he hadn't been taken in by the remark.

"Forget I said that." Ben gave an embarrassed laugh. "But I do think you should give it some thought. There ain't much you can do around here until trappin' season anyhow. And they'll pay you good if you take on the job."

That night Josh lay awake for a long time rethinking his conversation with Ben. For each time he declared to himself that he positively wouldn't think of leading a bunch of greenhorns across a wilderness, equal times he argued that he could use the money. The notion of fattening his wallet while he did what he liked most, seeing new country, grew on him.

If only he didn't dislike the Bible-quoting Hansen so much!

CHAPTER
❧4❧

JOSH QUADE leaned forward in the saddle. By straining his eyes he could make out the cluster of six wagons pulled up in front of the tavern. The figures of men and women milled about, while smaller shapes of children ran about, ridding themselves of excess energy in play.

He wondered for the hundreth time if he wasn't a damn fool for undertaking this trip. "Hell, I don't even have a map," he muttered disgustedly. "I hope there are plenty of markers along the way." For not one man in the party, including himself, had ever been west of Michigan. And though his knowledge of the north woods was equal to any man's, this western country could be very different. Would he be able to read it as he did these familiar hills?

Ben had observed humorously, trying to encourage him, "Hell, Josh, what could be so different? There'll be land and sky, sun and moon, heat and cold, rain and sunshine. Why, I even bet that the sun comes up in the east out there."

"It's easy for him to talk," Josh muttered, lifting the reins and starting the stallion down the hill. "He won't be there."

When Jake broke from a fringe of pines a shout went up and the men, bright-eyed with excitement, surged forward. They gathered around the mount, calling out enthusiastic greetings, and Josh couldn't help responding in a like manner.

His glance at the women in the party was so brief he almost

missed Ninu. She stood half obscured by Bertha Hansen's raw-boned frame, each hand holding that of a crying child. The boy, around seven years old, struggled to get away from her grip. Painful tears brimmed in the squaw's eyes as his heavily shod feet kicked at her bare shins. He frowned as he watched the mother ignore her son's viciousness, but like the other women who also frowned, kept his lips closed. He didn't want to start the trip on a sour note, and he imagined the women probably held their tongues because once crossed Bertha Hansen made a formidable enemy, and the trip ahead was a long one.

Josh brought his attention back to the men. "Is everyone here?" he asked, dismounting. "Seems like we're short some men."

"Hansen and some of the men are in the tavern arguin'," a heavily bearded man explained.

An irritated scowl spread across Josh's face. Trust Hansen to spoil things at the last minute, he thought to himself. "What's not pleasin' him now?"

A wide grin stirred the man's shaggy face. "The whores want to come with us and Hansen says he won't have them sinners in the train. He's claimin' that God would never forgive their fornicatin' with the men, and that He'd bring His wrath down on everybody." The man's grin grew wider. "He ain't havin' much luck with the men. They're arguin' back that they're willin' to take their chance on God's forgiveness."

Anger darkened Josh's face. "That sanctimonious squaw-ridin' bastard," he ground out under his breath, pushing his way through the knot of men toward the tavern. As he went through the door the males pushed in behind him and the women exchanged knowing looks. If they had heard Quade's scorching remark, so had the proud, overbearing Bertha Hansen. Consequently, no one was surprised when Mrs. Hansen swung around and slapped Ninu across the face.

One woman didn't quite smother a giggle when Bertha snarled, "You slut, can't you keep them younguns quiet? A body can't hear a word around here."

As the imprint of thick fingers rose on her cheek, Ninu dragged the squalling children away, and their mother heaved herself onto the high seat of the Hansen wagon. She stared straight ahead, her stiff bearing daring the women to voice their thoughts. Back inside the tavern raised voices lost their volume and dropped to a dark muttering as Josh stalked to the bar.

Relief flashed in the bartender's eyes. Drawing a sleeve across his agitated and sweating face, he exclaimed hotly, "Maybe you can straighten this out, Josh."

Quade turned his back to the bar and let his gaze travel over the divided group of people. Sullen, angry faces stared back at him. The majority of the men, a good many of them married ones, stood behind the whores. Hansen's followers, less than one third the total, avoided his eyes. He suspected that the fear of Hansen withdrawing his financial support had forced them into the opposing group.

"All right," he said curtly, "what's this all about?"

Everyone spoke at once, each determined to be heard. Josh let the women screech and the rival groups argue heatedly for a full minute. When it looked as though some might come to blows, he aimed his rifle at the ceiling and pulled the trigger. Everyone gaped at him, their voices stilled. He pointed to Jessie.

"We'll let the ladies go first. What's your gripe, Jess?"

Before the redhead could speak Hansen roared, "Ladies! You call them sluts ladies? They don't know the meanin' of the word." When the red-faced man would have said more, an angry growl and threatening forward movement from the whore's supporters silenced him.

With her green eyes sparking fire, the little madam threw Hansen a challenging look and began: "Me and my girls want to go to Oregon, too. Hansen says we can't. He says the train ain't for the likes of us. I say he ain't got no right to keep us out."

Josh turned his gaze on Hansen, his dislike for the man thinly concealed. "What about it, Hansen? Are you objectin' to these women comin' with us?"

Hansen ran a nervous hand over his beard as he tried to match Quade's unwavering stare. He asked himself if the trapper was purposefully forcing a showdown between them, settling who would be boss on the long trek to Oregon.

The thought of losing his leadership gave the obese man the courage to bluster, "She told the truth of it."

A profound stillness settled over the room as the men and

women waited for Josh's next move. The newly appointed wagon master also knew that the time of testing had arrived, that his authority was at stake. His future of issuing orders and having them obeyed depended on how he handled this situation.

His hard blue eyes bored into Hansen's another moment, then in a voice that sounded almost friendly he asked quietly, "Do you mind tellin' me why you don't want these women along?"

Unaware that he was being tricked into a false victory, Hansen grew brave. "I'm surprised you'd ask me that, Quade," he sneered, "you knowin' personally the debauchery of these immoral women." When Josh made no answer and only listened politely, Hansen's tone was stronger as he declared ringingly, "I won't have them with us, corruptin' our young men."

Angry boos and shouts swelled in the room. When it quieted down Josh went on with his slow, even probing. "When you speak of corruptin' our youth, Hansen, do you mean the women might coax them into their beds? Your two boys, for instance?"

"That's exactly what I mean," Hansen answered loudly, full of confidence now. "My two lads ain't gonna grow up and be whore masters like some I could name around here."

Josh nodded solemnly, lowering his lids to hide the amused twinkle in his eyes. In a voice all innocence he said, as though to himself, "I guess there isn't any truth to that rumor that the Hansen boys have already been corrupted by the pretty Indian girl who lives with them."

A wave of snickering quickly built into loud guffawing. The startled confusion that washed over Hansen's face changed to black anger as he realized he'd been led into a trap. He tried to glare back at the laugh-contorted faces but could not. Then, giving Josh a hate-filled look, he turned and rushed toward the door. His sons, amusement sparking in their eyes, moved slowly after him. The oldest one, big as a man and stronger than most, couldn't resist giving Jessie a pinch on the derriere as he went past her. She squealed and started after him.

Laughing, Josh reached out, caught the woman's thin arm, and pulled her back. "Let him go, Jess. He may turn out to be your best customer someday."

Jessie's painted lips curved crookedly. "You might be right. I also gotta feelin' old lady Hansen will be gettin' rid of that

young squaw before long, and who knows, the old man might
come scratchin' at our wagon some night.''

Everyone but Josh laughed at Jessie's quip. He leaned against
the bar regarding the little madam gravely. ''Jess,'' he said,
''nothin' has been settled yet.''

''What do you mean?'' Jessie demanded, her hands on her
hips. ''I thought Hansen lost the argument.''

''That's right!'' male and female voices yelled together.

Josh slapped a hand on the bar, calling for silence. ''If you
women aren't equipped for the journey *I* won't let you come with
us. I can't allow you to trail along without food and shelter.''

''We know all that!'' Jessie exploded. ''We ain't leeches,
Quade. We've pooled our money and bought a good tight wagon
and four fine mules.'' She paused and looked down at the floor.
''I admit we ain't got much in the line of supplies.'' She paused
again, looked up, grinning impishly. ''We figured the men could
take care of our eats, and we'd take care of them. One big happy
family, so to speak.''

As enthusiastic yells of approval rang out, Josh shook his
head. Trust the enterprising Jessie to come up with a solution
like this one. She knew that the men would only think of the
free pleasuring, that they wouldn't stop and think that in the long
run it would be cheaper to pay each time they used one of her
girls. The cost of supplies was outrageous, flour alone going for
twenty dollars a barrel.

But let the hogs pay, Josh thought derisively. It served them
right not to think beyond their groins. Nodding agreement, he
said, ''It sounds a little unusual, but if it's all right with you
single fellows, it's all right with me.''

As the bachelors jabbed each other with elbows and winked
slyly, a disgruntled muttering arose among the family men. A
gruff voice demanded petulantly, ''Why just the single fellers?
I might want to contribute to the pot on occasion.''

Other voices, in tones carefully modulated so that wives outside couldn't hear, took up the man's objection. They insisted
that since they had used the whores in the past, they saw no
reason to stop now.

''You jackasses,'' Josh said impatiently at the end of the men's
argument, ''you could get away with it here, the little wife tucked

safely away at home. But on the trail there won't be nothin' goin' on that everybody won't know about.

"Now we have a long ride ahead of us, and I'm not aimin' to have no irate wife raisin' hell in camp every night. So, I'm warnin' you, if I catch any of you married men in a bed where you don't belong, I'll kick you out of the train, and let your wife know why in the bargain."

Josh stared back at the glowering faces. After a moment, grumbling darkly, the family men turned and led the way outside. When Jessie and the girls followed, Josh left the tavern also.

For the next twenty minutes, amid total chaos, untried people prepared to start their long journey. Drivers yelled and swore at teams as they pulled, jerked, and seesawed the animals into line. Anxious mothers added their noise to the din, urging children into the wagons. Josh rode back and forth in the rising dust, calming, advising, and directing.

With the exception of two drivers, Josh told the others to fall in where they pleased for the time being, but that when they reached Independence places would be allotted. He put Jessie's wagon next to the end, thinking to himself, "Jessie, my girl, that will always be your spot," and left the last position for the man with twenty head of cattle.

This man strode up to him now, objecting loudly to bringing up the rear. "My animals will be unprotected," he shouted over the noise. "The damn wolves will have them before the week is over."

With sweat making rivulets down his dusty face, the salt stinging his eyes, Josh stared down at the yelling man. "What in the hell is wrong with you, Jones?" he shouted. "Do you want to be the lead wagon so them dust-raisin' critters can choke everybody behind you?"

Jones's belligerent look slowly turned sheepish, and he muttered, "I didn't think about that."

"I guess none of us are thinkin' quite straight at the moment. I'll have some of the teenage boys trail along with you."

Josh watched the short, squat figure walk away from him with somber eyes. He knew that the argument he had just won was simple compared to others he'd face before arriving in Oregon Territory.

Finally the wagons were arranged in a long line, the teams stamping their feet impatiently. No one spoke as they waited for the wagon master's order to roll out.

A mounting excitement gripped Josh. He stood up in the stirrups and held his arm high. He waited a moment, then called ringingly, "Move out!"

The air was instantly filled with the cracking of whips, the shouting of "giddyup," and the shrilling, almost frenetic laughter of children. Mingled in the raucous din was the charged barking of dogs, from the long yowl of a lean hound to the nerve-racking yip of the whores' little feist. As though not to be outdone, the nervous bawling of cattle brought up the rear. Through the rolling dust Josh waved good-bye to the well-wishers on the porch and smiled lazily when Ben shouted, "You're gonna get rained on before nightfall."

It was toward the end of the day that Ben's prediction came true. Lowering clouds had gathered and hung over their heads all afternoon, the air smotheringly close, and finally lightning flashed to the south of them.

The teams had just been pulled in beside a fast-running creek for the night when the rain broke. It came in on a strong wind, slashing with a wild fury, blinding the draft animals with its deluge. Drivers fought the near panicked beasts to their feet and struggled to unhitch them, while the man with the cattle had additional trouble.

Bawling their fright, his small herd had bolted in every direction. Finally he was forced to leave his stoic oxen stand where he had halted them and run after his herd.

Meanwhile canvas popped like gunshot and women and children climbed onto the swaying ribs and held down the rough material with spread-eagled bodies. They were drenched to the skin almost immediately, but they held on doggedly. Precious provisions were stored inside, food to take them across the wilderness. Most had spent their last dollar purchasing the supplies, and if the essentials of survival were ruined there would be no other course but to turn back.

Working together, the wet and tired drivers finally managed to unhitch and lead the teams and pack animals to the shelter of a small stand of maples. Once sheltered out of the rain and wind they settled down immediately. Without hesitation, willing hands were turned to help the cattleman.

The storm spent its fury after about twenty minutes, stopping abruptly, its only remnants the wet and the rumble of thunder dying away in the distance. Relieved smiles touched everyone's lips, and the women hurried to the grove to search out dry wood for a fire. When very little suitable material was found, it was decided they would share a communal fire tonight.

When the hurriedly cooked meal was ready, Josh was invited to share their supper. He declined politely, explaining that the ladies on the other end had already asked him. Some smiled knowingly while others sniffed disdainfully. But when bursts of laughter pealed out from around the cheerfully burning fire in front of the red wagon, and many husbands cast longing looks in that direction, there was a universal firming of feminine lips.

It was five days later when an old man stood up in his bouncing wagon, pointing a long finger. "There it is!" he gave a reedy, exuberant yell. "Independence! Straight down the valley!"

A sharp rap on her stateroom door startled Serena out of the apathy that long days and nights of idleness had brought on. She had tossed and turned as she remembered old pains and dwelled on her uncertain future.

Eli Landrie opened the door at her invitation, a wide smile lighting his weathered features. "Come on, honey, get dressed," he urged. "Independence is just ahead. We'll be dockin' in about twenty minutes."

Forcing a brightness to her voice as she jumped to her feet, she exclaimed, "Good! I can't wait to stand on firm ground again. I'll be on deck in ten minutes."

Serena pulled a flowered blue dimity over her head and settled it over a much-mended petticoat, then gave her red-gold curls a few strokes with a brush. With a long sigh she placed her toilet articles in a small wrist-bag and repacked the robe and gown. Straightening her shoulders she left the cabin and joined Landrie, who stood on the foredeck staring down the river where much activity was going on. "That's it, honey. The jumpin' off place."

Serena studied the rude town that lay sprawled mostly along the river, and her spirits dropped. It's so squalid-looking, she thought, so depressing.

"It doesn't look like much, does it?" she said softly, moving closer to Eli as though for comfort.

"Not in the same sense as Vicksburg." He grinned down at her solemn face and laid a comforting arm across her shoulders. "It's just a little wilderness place, honey," he explained. "But the important thing"—he pointed a finger—"is to look at all those anchored boats and the wagons rollin' off them. And the ships still steaming in. Note how low they ride in the water. That's the heavy weight of teams and wagons."

In his exuberance Eli's fingers tightened on Serena's shoulders until she gasped in protest. His fingers loosened immediately. "Sorry, honey, I'm just happy to see all them wagons. We're gonna have plenty of company on our way west. Come on, let's go get in the wagon."

Josh Quade urged the stallion toward Independence to get a closer look at this starting place to the great wilderness and the end of civilization.

He entered the single street and reined in. A crowd of men jostled and conversed—plainsmen, traders, trappers, buffalo hunters, and gamblers. He felt relieved, somehow, when he saw a sprinkling of hill men, heavy, bearded, and silent.

"I'm glad I told the others to make camp a couple miles back," he muttered as he guided Jake through the mass of humanity. "I'd never be able to keep an eye on them in all this mess."

The mob was finally behind him and Josh reined his mount in just before the riverbank turned into a mire of mud from the almost constant flow of fording wagons. He crossed his arms on the saddle pommel and watched a heavily laden prairie schooner roll from the bowels of a riverboat and onto the bank. A tall, loose-jointed figure somewhere in his late forties, his spare frame all corded muscles, popped a whip over the backs of an awkwardly pulling team.

A puzzled look came over Josh's face when the man yelled a command to the animals and he recognized the soft tone and accent of a Southerner. Appreciative of good horseflesh, he ran a scrutinizing gaze over the driver. This man was not of the gentry. His features held no arrogance. So what was a crocker doing with such pampered pets?

When the thoroughbreds had been pulled to a sweating halt and the driver had climbed stiffly to the ground, Josh lifted the reins and rode up alongside the man from the South. "Howdy," he said, his voice friendly. "Are you goin' west by any chance?"

"That's our intention," the man answered politely, mopping at his face with a piece of rag. "Do you know of any wagons goin' that way?"

"I don't know about any outfits." Josh shrugged. "But I've got six wagons with me." He jerked a thumb at the line of wagons along the river. "I'm sure those vehicles are headed either for California or Oregon. It would be the same trail for quite a distance. I intend to scout around, talk to the drivers, see if they're interested in bandin' together. The more we are, the less trouble we'll have from Indians. You want to throw in with my bunch?"

"It sounds good to me," the Southerner said, holding out a long, lean hand. "The name is Landrie. Eli Landrie, from Mississippi."

Amusement deepened the fine lines around Josh's eyes as he returned the firm grip. He liked the looks of the weathered face whose sad eyes contradicted the smile on the thin lips. "Josh Quade, from Michigan." He grinned. "Think we can get along, reb?"

"Why not, Yank? Far as I'm concerned, the war is over."

"My sentiments exactly. How many in your party?"

"Just me and the girl." Landrie turned around and gazed up at the slender figure sitting on the high seat of the large wagon. "Serena, meet Josh Quade, wagon master."

God, what a beauty, was Josh's first thought, taking in the delicately boned face framed by red-gold curls. His second thought followed swiftly as he saw the hatred flashing in the green eyes. A high-nosed bitch who hates Yankees. He returned her icy glare with calm amusement, his eyes flicking boldly over her long clean lines, the round breasts that seemed almost too big for her tiny waist.

"Miss." He nodded slightly, then, raking his glance over her body again, he shrugged indifferently and turned his back on her. He took great pleasure in the audible gasp that whistled through her white teeth. He smiled at the embarrassed Eli and then said, "Come with me to talk to the others, Landrie. There may be other southern families among the new arrivals." His lips tilted wryly as he added, "They'd be more apt to listen to another reb."

Eli readily agreed, eager to enjoy the company of and conversation with men again. "I won't be long, honey," he tossed at Serena as he hurried after the broad-shouldered figure.

"That's what you think, Paw," Serena muttered under her breath. She was well aware of what the Yankee was up to. He had deliberately drawn Paw away so that she would have to wait in the heat with the sun full on her face, unless she wanted to lose her slippers in the ankle-deep mud.

"Oh, I hate that man," she mumbled to herself, her hands clenched on her knees. "Really?" a cynical inner voice whispered. "Why did your heart beat like a crazy thing when he looked at you with those cold, blue eyes?" Serena denied the thought angrily as she wiped her perspiring face with a tiny lace handkerchief. As her mind focused on those cold, blue eyes she was convinced that hate for the damned Yankee had made her heart race. What else could it possibly be?

The sun was about to set when the group of men sitting in the shade of a large tree finally began to stand up and to drift back to their wagons. Their wives and families followed them, and once everyone had settled into the vehicles, whips popped and wheels rolled.

Serena watched them move out of town and her lips firmed to a thin line. The man in buckskins, seeming in no hurry to follow the others, kept Paw engaged in conversation. The anger that had been bubbling inside her for the past hour and a half reached a boiling point at the Northerner's deliberate attempt to keep her waiting.

She jumped to her feet, determined that she would wade through the mud and give that devil a dressing down that he wouldn't forget in a hurry. But just as she tentatively put a foot on top of the large wheel, the beautiful black stallion flashed by, its rider not sparing her a glance. She stared after the wagon master, wishing she had a gun to direct at that arrogantly tilted head.

When Eli arrived shortly, muttering sheepishly about the time, Serena transferred her anger to him and refused to even speak. When he began describing Josh Quade in glowing terms she set her lips grimly.

Her cold silence dulled Eli's elation, and he, too, grew silent. The Northerner had triggered bad memories for Serena, he knew, and it would take her a while to forget that a Yankee shell had killed Jeremy. But it wouldn't be easy for him either. He drove on, reminding himself that the wagon master had seemed sincere and friendly; maybe the rest of the train would be the same.

But Serena's thoughts were not taken up with lost love as Landrie thought. Her mind was in a dark study of the man who had made her blood race and pulse leap erratically. She assured herself that her heart's odd behavior could only be the result of her deep hatred for anybody who had been involved in destroying her southland, taking away forever her well-loved way of life. There was simply no other way the man could affect her.

She pushed away the persistent images of soft buckskin clinging to broad shoulders, defining hard, muscular legs, and of heavy-lashed blue eyes.

Landrie's sudden, "There's the camp, Serena," was a welcome interruption of these disturbing thoughts.

While Eli steered the fractious stallions under a tree Serena gazed dully at the assortment of wagons halted among the stand of maple and oak. Most, like their own, were covered, but some weren't. There were even a few two-wheeled carts. She wondered vaguely what the owners would do when it rained, then suppressed a giggle. They'd get wet, of course.

Her eyes were drawn to where several fires were burning, over which women were busily preparing the evening meals. When Landrie grasped her waist and swung her to the ground she felt stern appraising eyes on her. A quick glance showed lips curled in disapproving sneers.

"I will not like them," she muttered, noting the harsh features of the drab homespun garb.

The only sign she gave of hearing was a quick intake of breath as one woman said loudly, "It will be interestin' to see how that fancy piece fares without her niggers."

But she was seething inside as she settled herself on a large rock and watched Landrie set up camp. How dare these women wrinkle those noses at her? Why, they were no better than the crockers back home. She raised her chin, her face still and uncommunicative. Who needed their approval?

Eli touched her shoulder. "Camp is all set, Serena. I'm gonna go set with the men for a while." He smiled at her encouragingly. "Why don't you mingle around a bit, get acquainted with the women."

Serena watched Landrie walk away, muttering that she was no 'possum-eyed hypocrite. She would not pretend to like these backwoods Northerners.

CHAPTER
∽ 5 ∾

WHEN JOSH RODE into the much enlarged encampment he made a swift count of the additional wagons and whistled softly through his teeth. Now there were twenty-six wagons and four carts. Most were prairie schooners, but there were a few Pittsburghs and a couple of Durhams. All good solid vehicles if they were kept in shape. That must be his number one order. Wagons kept in tiptop shape. A broken wheel could hold the train up for a full day.

His eyes lit on the girl from the South and he gazed at her broodingly, letting his scrutiny drop from the beauty of her face and linger on the ripe breasts pushing proudly against the bodice of a dress.

Unbidden the thought came: How would they feel to his lips, taste to his mouth? He shook his head to clear his mind. They would fill the senses too damn well. A man might find himself never wanting to leave them.

Grim self-mockery glinted in Josh's eyes. As if that proud beauty would ever let him get close enough to find out.

Another thought occurred to him. Why is she sitting there idle while all the other women are so busy? Why isn't she making Eli's supper? Scorn for the girl twisted his lips. She had probably never lifted her hand to a piece of work in her pampered life. That young miss would find it hard going with her own sex. The hardy women from the North wouldn't take to her ladylike ways and they wouldn't think twice before they told her so.

Strangely, he experienced the wish to punish and protect her at the same time. He realized then, with a start, the girl was coolly returning his stare. Suddenly he only wanted to punish her as tawny green eyes slashed at him scornfully. Anger raged within his soul and simultaneously a tingling burned within his loins. When the very air around him quickened, he wheeled Jake and headed him toward the group of men sitting some distance away, probably waiting for him.

"I don't like what that little witch does to me, Jake," he muttered. "She could ruin a man's peace of mind. Make him think of things best ignored."

Josh reined the stallion in, dismissing Serena from his mind and scanning the men who sat on rocks and stumps. He quietly conversed with those nearest him. They are, he thought, in general a healthy, honest-looking group. Of course, the long trek ahead would prove their true mettle. Some, no doubt, had never been tested to this extent before.

"Well, men," he said, sitting down on a rock and resting an ankle on a knee. "I guess you've acquainted yourselves with each other and are gettin' a little hungry. I'll lay down a few rules and let you get back to your wagons and supper.

"Now there're not many rules, but each one is very necessary, and absolutely has to be followed. I'll speak about the wagons first. They have to be kept in tiptop shape all the time, 'cause I want us to travel twelve to sixteen miles a day. So, rims must be kept tight, and wheels greased every morning. I hope you all have been sensible enough to bring along tar buckets."

Everyone was listening closely, and when each man nodded, Josh moved on. "On the matter of spirits. Each man will be allowed one quart of whiskey for medicinal purposes only. Anyone caught staggerin' around in a drunken state will be kicked out."

Josh didn't miss the approval that flared in Hansen's small eyes and smiled inside. The old bastard wasn't going to like his other laws. Keeping his eyes on the obese man, he continued. "Now, about the womenfolk. Any man caught foolin' around with a woman not his own, that's discountin' the whores for the single men, is also kicked out." He paused a moment to give emphasis to his next words, then said with unmistakable intent, "There are several single white women and one pretty little squaw in this outfit. I sure hope it won't be necessary to have any shotgun weddings along the way."

Some of the men laughed uneasily, having already picked out a couple of the young ladies they'd like to walk with in the woods. But Hansen, knowing that the warning was aimed mostly at him and his two sons, sent Josh a glowering look.

Josh chuckled and continued, "We will travel every day, stoppin' only for death and birthin'."

The words were barely out of his mouth when Hansen was on his feet, thundering, "That's one rule I will not accept." He paused long enough to slide intimidating looks at his followers. When they dropped their gazes before his thinly veiled threat, he roared on confidently.

"There are some God-fearing people in this train and we demand that we rest on the Sabbath and hold services." A smug sneer stirred his thick lips. "Surely you don't object to worshipin' God."

His eyes half-closed against the setting sun, Josh studied the self-appointed saver of souls. "Are you sayin', Hansen," he asked quietly, "that it's beneath you to say a prayer from the seat of your wagon, or the saddle of your mount? I remember readin' in the Bible once that prayer should be a private thing, an act that can be carried out even in a closet."

A deep voice yelled approval, triggering a similar clamoring from the rest of the men. Hansen, who had not expected such a response, glared back at the circle of faces that mocked him. Then, his face twisted with rage, he stamped away with as much dignity as his fat body could manage. While Josh's narrowed gaze followed the man he thought, we will tangle many times before this trip is over. Then he turned back to the group.

"I want you fellows to know that I have good reasons for travelin' on Sunday," he began. "I'm sure most of you must know that we can't reach our destination before winter sets in. We're gettin' too late a start. Consequently we've got to be on the move every day if we're to reach some kind of quarters before the snow flies."

Sober faces gazed at him, and Josh was reluctant to impart the one last fact the men should know before starting out with him. His gaze touched each newcomer before he said, "And there's one more thing I have to tell you: I don't have a map."

He returned the startled looks with a steady one, then held up a reassuring hand. "Don't be alarmed. I'll get you to Oregon. But a map would save me a lot of time. I'd know straightaway where the water holes are, as well as the river crossin's. So, if any of you men have a map, I'd be grateful for the use of it."

Eli opened his mouth, but before he could speak a man from Illinois said, "I don't have a map, but my cousin who's gone part of the way twice told me that you travel along the Santa Fe Trail for about forty miles and then you come to where the road forks. He said there was a sign there that pointed out the road to Oregon." The man shrugged. "I guess from there you go northwest."

"Well, that's some help," Josh said, then turned his head to look at whoever was tugging at his shirt-sheeve.

"Serena has a map, Quade," Eli Landrie said. "It's got all the things you mentioned marked on it."

Josh had the crazy desire to laugh. Of all the people in the camp, the one whose eyes flashed with hate every time they fell on him had the only map.

A wry grimace firmed his lips. "Do you think she'd let me borrow it?"

"Sure she would. I'll give it to you later."

"I'd be mighty obliged," Josh said, doubt threading his words, knowing he'd be surprised if he ever laid eyes on the map.

After glancing at the sun that was falling behind the timber-line, he said, "Go on to your families, men, and get settled in before dark. We'll talk more after supper."

The group dispersed, and, picking up Jake's reins, Josh trailed after them. Eli Landrie fell in beside him. "It was good thinkin' on your part to bring along a pleasure wagon," Eli said, his long legs matching the stride of his companion's horse. "Them whores will keep the steam out of them single hellions and the decent women won't have to worry about bein' bothered by them. Six months is a long time for a man to go without his pleasurin'."

"Gotta keep harmony in camp, you know." Josh grinned,

wondering if Eli was thinking of his own female companion. He doubted that the Southerner had cause to worry about that one. That cold aloofness she wore like a cloak would scare off the bravest of men.

The two men approached the pleasure wagon, and as they were about to skirt it, Jessie came from behind the red vehicle and detained Josh with her small hand on his arm. Eli winked slyly at him and walked on.

Surprised at himself, Josh was half irritated at the woman's action. It showed in his voice when he asked gruffly, "What is it, Jess?"

"Well, I . . .." Jessie faltered. "I just wanted to say that supper will be ready pretty soon."

Josh shifted nervously in the saddle, then, avoiding Jessie's eyes, said, "One of the new members has already invited me to eat with his family." He smiled sheepishly and repeated what he'd said to Landrie. "Gotta keep harmony in camp, you know."

"Yes, I guess so," Jessie murmured, her features deceptively composed. But her knowing eyes watched Josh closely as she changed the subject. "Have you seen the southern belle who has joined us?"

Josh looked at Jessie now, and amusement grew in his eyes. "I don't think so."

"Come on, Josh, you must have. All the other men have. They're droolin' all over camp."

The wagon master grinned crookedly. "Well, in that case I'd better look her up. Which wagon is she in?"

Jessie whacked him on the shin with a bony fist. "As if you don't already know. She's probably the one who invited you to supper. Providin', of course, the old man travelin' with her cooks it. That little beauty looks pretty helpless to me."

"Yeah, she is delicate lookin'," Josh agreed softly. "I wonder what the relationship is between her and Landrie. I can't believe it's a blood tie. Eli is only a crocker and good breeding shows all over the girl."

"Well, whatever it is, it must be a close one. He treats her like she's made of bone china." Jessie shot Josh a teasing look. "I saw her watching you."

"You did?" Josh asked, surprised. "When?"

"She was standin' back in the shade of a tree when you lit in on Hansen. From the set of her lips I'd say she doesn't think too highly of you."

Josh laughed dryly. "Yeah, I guess you could say she hasn't taken a likin' to me."

There was a strange tone in his voice that made Jessie send him a curious look. "Does that bother you?"

"Naw. She probably hates all blue bellies."

"I think it does bother you." Jessie grinned. "You're used to women fallin' all over you."

"Well . . ." Josh dragged out the word with a grin. "You're right about the last part, but the first—her attitude don't bother me in the least. Because she's gonna love me by the time we reach our destination," he said with visibly affected complacency.

"You think so, huh?" Jessie laughingly called after him as Jake walked on. "You're worlds apart, you know."

"Not in the wilderness we're not. We'll just be a man and a woman," Josh called back.

A moment later he steered Jake around wagons and laughing children, threading his way toward a large Pittsburgh. He brushed aside the image of a little green-eyed witch looking down her snooty nose at him. Why should he care if she saw him taking supper with Jessie and her girls? For all his hearty bantering with Jessie, he agreed that he and the female reb were miles apart.

Landrie came around the wagon and frowned at seeing Serena sitting idly beside a dying fire. She gave him a wan smile, then silently watched him add wood to the glowing coals. When it blazed and crackled he sat down beside her. He looked from her gloomy, petulant features to the other women who laughed and gossiped together as they tended to supper.

"Why ain't you visitin' with the women instead of sittin' here by yourself?" he asked gently.

"They don't like me." Serena broke off her contemplation of the fire. "Besides, they give me the fidgets. All they talk about are their children and husbands, and of the homesteads they're going to put up."

Landrie chuckled and patted her hand. "That's all they know to talk about, Serena. They have no idea of the world you come from, before the war, that is. All they've ever known is work and hardship." His tone turned earnest. "They're good, decent folk, though, honey, and would make good friends if you'd try to warm up to them."

"I told you, Paw." Serena jerked her shoulders impatiently. "They don't like me. You should have seen the looks I've been getting from them, the whispering and snickering they do together." She kicked out at the fire, dislodging Landrie's carefully laid wood. "They make me sick."

Eli made no response for a while, then, squatting down and scraping the firewood back together, he said thoughtfully, "If what you say is true, I can see where you'd be upset. Of course a lot of their behavior can be laid to jealousy, especially the single women." He paused for a long moment then, looking at Serena gravely, said softly, "I think, honey, the biggest thing is, they think you're useless."

When Serena's eyes widened in hurt surprise, Eli hurried to explain. "Now don't go gettin' your feelin's hurt. I know you're not lazy, the way you worked the fields so that you could put food on the table for Mammy and her grandson. But you see, honey, these women were brought up to look down on the woman who lets her menfolk do her job. In their eyes you should have set up camp, made the fire, carried the water, did the cookin'."

"Their men don't expect much, do they?" Serena remarked sarcastically, looking back into the flames.

Landrie laughed and agreed that southern ways were some different from northern ways. "But if you'll try, daughter, you can catch on to trail life real quick. Pay attention to how I do things tonight, then take it in easy stages until you get it down pat."

Serena tossed her head and answered that she'd gladly learn about camp duties, but only to help him. That she didn't give a snap of her finger whether or not the ignorant Yankee women approved of her or not.

Landrie set a pot of coffee on the flames, then sliced sugar-cured ham into a frying pan, telling himself that Serena's harsh talk came from hurt feelings, that in time she would miss the companionship of women, the friendly though sometimes sharp gossiping that seemed so necessary to females. He was sure that eventually she would fit right in with the others.

The meal was quickly eaten, and coffee was being drunk when Eli brought up the map. "Quade wants to borrow your map, Serena. I told him I'd give it to him tonight."

Occupied with adding a chunk of wood to the fire, Landrie didn't see the stiffening of Serena's back or the icy glitter that shot into her eyes. His head jerked up in astonishment when she said, "I'm sorry, Paw, but I forgot to bring it with me."

"Serena," Landrie groaned. "How could you forget something so important?"

She shrugged. "I guess I had too many other things on my mind. Anyway, what kind of leader is the wagon master to take off on such a long trek without a map of his own?"

Landrie ignored her sensible question. He started to ask if she remembered any landmarks on the map, then snapped his mouth shut when he observed an almost exultant look in Serena's eyes. Was her hate for all Northerners so strong?

A long silence passed, then Eli said quietly, "The war may already be over, Serena. We must bury our hatred and start to forgive. Keep in mind that a lot of Yankee men were killed by rebel bullets. Both sides must begin to forget."

Serena sprang to her feet, her eyes blazing. "Have you forgotten, Paw?" she challenged. "Have you forgiven the blue bellies for killing your son? Don't you have any hatred for those who have driven you from the sweet, soft land of the South?"

Eli stood and took a step toward the sobbing girl as though to comfort her, then paused. It was too early to try to reason with her. Her hurt was still too raw. In time, maybe. "I'll get supper started," he said instead.

Eli approached the brightly burning council fire, running his gaze across the faces of the men gathered around it. He spotted Quade and moved toward him, dreading what he must tell the wagon master. His relief was almost audible when Josh only nodded, then turned the talk to Eli's thoroughbreds.

"Landrie," he began, "them pets of yours will never make the long trip ahead of us. Mainly because they're stallions and will fight each other every step of the way." He propped a foot on a tree stump and stared out into the darkness. "Can you afford to buy some mules or oxen?"

Eli had suspected from the beginning that the subject of his unruly team would come up. It was decent of the Northerner to approach him about them privately.

His short laugh was mirthless. "I couldn't afford to buy a pair of shoelaces. Serena has the money. And she'll do it, once the sense of it is pointed out to her. What would you advise, mules or oxen?"

"Well,"—Josh pushed his fingers through his hair thoughtfully—"mules would be good, but I've heard that the Indians like the stubborn animals, and would probably steal them the first chance they got. Now, oxen are slower than mules, and have less sense, but they're the strongest and most reliable of all for a long haul. And they're less likely to stampede than horses or mules."

He directed a crooked grin at Eli. "And if it should come down to it, they can be eaten, same as beef." Landrie laughed, a little nervously, hoping that he and Serena would never have to get that hungry.

"Only joking, Eli." Josh's eyes crinkled at the corners, then he issued a warning. "You have to watch oxen. They're just like cows and will wander off with a passing herd of buffalo."

"How many do you reckon I'll need?"

"That wagon of yours is pretty big. I'd say four yokes should do nicely."

"The question now"—Eli put a foot up on the same stump—"is where will I get them?"

"We'll keep our ears and eyes open. Some of the other drivers may be interested in sellin' off one or two."

"Well," Eli said, bringing his foot back to the ground and straightening up, "I think I'll turn in." His lips twisted wryly. "And I imagine Serena is gettin' tired of sittin' by herself."

Josh wanted to ask Eli if the girl was related to him, but he hesitated. Those proud Southerners, you never knew how they'd take things.

I'll know eventually. He shrugged inwardly and said, "Everyone should be turnin' in. Four o'clock comes mighty early."

Josh's long stride slowed after a yard or so when he heard two voices raised in anger. He stopped altogether when he heard Eli Landrie say in positive tones, "No, by God, Newcomb. Serena never did want to marry you, and before her brother went off to war he told her she didn't have to."

A clear vision of Ira Newcomb came to Josh. How had that little weasel found his way here, the end of settled civilization?

The relationship between the girl and the crocker was made clear when Eli taunted recklessly, "I'll tell you somethin' else, Newcomb. Serena has loved my boy Jeremy since she was a little girl. And what's more, before Dorn went away he gave her permission to marry Jeremy."

Josh moved just in time to throw out an arm to catch the roaring Newcomb across the throat as he with a mad roar lunged for the older man. He then waited until Ira regained his choked-off breath and spoke for the first time.

"Take off, Newcomb, your business with Landrie is finished."

Surprise changed Ira's angry expression when he recognized the tall man towering over him. "Where in the hell did you come from, Yank? I thought you'd be back in your hills by now." Suspicion grew in his eyes. "Are you travelin' with Serena and this old swamp rat?"

"I'm the wagon master of this outfit so I guess you could say I'm travelin' with them. Are you plannin' on joinin' us?"

"I am. My intended is in this train, and I mean to keep an eye on what's mine."

Landrie's face flushed with red. "You stay away from Serena. Bother her just once and I'll put my knife in your heart."

Newcomb took a step toward the irate Southerner and Josh stepped between them. "You heard him, Newcomb. The girl doesn't want anything to do with you. Stay away from her."

After giving Josh a venomous look Ira wheeled as though to walk away, then turned back. Penning Josh with his narrow eyes, he grated out, "You ain't foolin' me Quade. I remember your words the day we parted. I'll be keepin' an eye on you."

The two men watched the reb disappear behind a wagon. "You know him from before, huh?" Eli asked.

"Yeah," Josh answered, then told him briefly of their meeting and how the pair of them had traveled together for a while.

"Serena told me that the last time she saw the man he was in chains. That he was to be tried for killing his company commander. Shouldn't we report him to the law before we leave?"

Josh would have liked nothing better. Newcomb would be nothing but trouble and aggravation, especially if he still smarted from the taunt he had made about making love to the southern girl. That was a big mistake, me doin' that, he thought. And as for turning the little bastard in, he couldn't. For he, too, had walked away from the war and Newcomb knew it.

And strangely, aggravatingly so, his mind shrank from the knowledge that the golden-haired girl loved Landrie's son. Why? The helpless piece of beautiful fluff was definitely not his type of woman. Hell—his lips curved ruefully—he'd be afraid to make love to her even if he ever got the chance. He'd be afraid of hurting her, crushing her delicate bones. Still, there was a strange yearning inside him to know this refined woman from the South on more intimate terms.

Eli shook his head and sighed. "I didn't tell Newcomb, but Jeremy was killed shortly before Vicksburg was taken."

Josh tried to deny to himself that his heart had taken a great leap at Landrie's words. He truly wanted to believe that it had only been surprise that quickened his pulses.

He murmured condolences, and then, as if it was someone else speaking, he said, "Maybe I ought to bed down near your wagon, nights."

Landrie's face lightened. 'I'd sure appreciate that. I was just thinkin' about that two-legged varmint sneakin' round at night."

"Between me and the hound, the girl will be safe. And, Eli, about turnin' him in, let's wait and see how he behaves. We may need all the gun hands we can get before this trip is over. But if he causes any kind of trouble, rest assured, I'll kick him out of the train."

CHAPTER
∽6∽

THE EASTERN SKY glowed just a shade lighter in the darkness when Josh came slowly awake. The underside of the Landrie wagon was barely discernible as he sat up on the blanket he had unrolled there after everyone had settled down for the night.

It was still outside; the night animals had returned to burrows and hiding places, and the daytime creatures hadn't ventured out yet. Josh lifted his eyes to the floorboards that separated him from the sleeping girl above. She, too, was finally quiet after tossing and turning half the night. He'd heard her quietly sobbing several times. Had she been aware of it, or had they been dream tears?

Dream tears, he decided. Serena Bain was too proud to grieve in public. Only in privacy would she allow herself to grieve her lost love.

Had any woman ever grieved for him, he wondered, loved him that strongly? He directed a snort of ridicule at himself. Whores and squaws didn't love. They just spread their legs. Enough of this mawkish musing, he thought as he reached for his moccasins. He had more important things to put his mind to, such as how to get his people out of warm blankets and onto the trail.

"This first mornin' is gonna be one hell of a mess," Josh muttered, rolling up the bed gear and carrying it over to Jake.

It was while he was smoothing the wrinkles out of his buckskins that the idea came to Josh. With amusement shimmering in his dark blue eyes he picked up his rifle and aimed it at the sky. His trigger finger squeezed, and before the echoing boom died away, a mingled chorus of angry and frightened cries, barking dogs, and the loud whinnies of highstrung horses broke the morning quiet.

He ducked, his teeth gleaming brightly in the semi-dark, when a flock of startled pigeons left the treetops with a roaring whir of wings. "Looks like I scared the livin' hell out of everybody and everything."

The shot brought Serena bolting up from her pallet, terror-stricken that she was back in the war. It took the angry mutterings of mothers trying to soothe frightened children to make her realize where she was. She leaned up on an elbow when Eli's familiar laugh sounded outside the wagon.

"Are you awake, honey?"

"Wide awake," she grumbled. "What idiot fired that rifle?"

"I expect it was Quade. Probably his way of lettin' us know it's four o'clock."

"It figures that wild barbarian would do something like that," Serena grumbled contemptuously.

"Quade knows what he's doin'," Eli defended the wagon master. "The men ain't gonna like havin' to calm down their animals every mornin', and the women ain't gonna like havin' their younguns scared half to death. You can bet that from here on someone is gonna be up at four o'clock and rousin' everybody else."

When Serena climbed out of the wagon the sky had lightened enough to throw into relief the ghosty outlines of the wagons and stirring animals. Small scattered fires were beginning to appear around the camp and grew larger as the sleepy travelers fed more wood to them. Hugging her arms against the early morning chill Serena moved to stand over Eli and watched closely how he crisscrossed large pieces of wood over a pile of dry twigs before striking a sulphur stick to it. When night camp was made at the end of the day, this chore would be added to the new one she would assume today, cooking the meals.

She wondered nervously if she could do it all as tiny flames caught hold and Eli stood up and smiled at her. "You can either wash up at the creek over there, or warm yourself a pan of water, honey. Either way, you're gonna have to fetch water for the coffee.''

Serena stared after Eli as he strode away to tend the team and hitch them to the wagon, with confusion sweeping over her. She was on her own, expected to cook a meal over an open flame. She looked about helplessly. Where to start? Get the water first, she supposed, put the coffee pot on.

Serena had hoped to arrive ahead of the others, but as she drew near the stream she found that women and children had already lined its banks. Some knelt, washing their faces, while others dipped pails and kettles into the water. She hung back, reluctant to go among the unfriendly females. Then Eli's deep, genial voice carried from camp and her eyes hardened obstinately. Paw would expect his breakfast soon, and no group of ignorant hillwomen were going to keep him from having it.

The women looked up in surprise at Serena approaching, but after staring at her a moment they made room for her to squeeze in between a heavyset woman and a young child. She leaned over the stream and wordlessly, avoiding the hostile eyes, dipped her pail and brought it up, full to the brim. She was ready to stand up when she caught sight of the sneering curl of several lips, and a quick flush of anger raced through her. She set the pail down beside her, muttering darkly to herself that she would show these rude women that she was just as hardy as they.

Her senses rebeled as the tall, dew-wet grass soaked through her dress, but she kept the fact hidden as she recklessly cupped the icy water to her face. She barely smothered a gasp, but aware of the stares directed at her she gritted her teeth and brought more water to flow over her cheeks. Then, clamping her teeth together to keep them from chattering, she dried her face on her petticoat, ignoring the more kindly look that had appeared on the stern features of her companions. If it required washing one's face in ice water to be accepted, that she could do without.

She shivered uncomfortably as she set the coffee to brewing, then began to hum softly to herself as she busied her hands with unfamiliar tasks. By the time Eli returned she had a breakfast of sorts waiting for him.

''You done real good, honey,'' Eli praised Serena, his jaws

working at the ragged slice of ham, not quite cooked in the center and burned on the edges. The coffee was good, however, and he drank three cups before the camp around them began to break up.

The sun broke over the crest of a hill, shining down on the complete chaos of drivers who yelled and swore, tugged and pulled, getting their teams into position. Amid the rolling clouds of dust kicked up by nervous hooves, mothers ran about, dodging wagons and dogs, frantically calling to missing children.

Others, not yet adept at managing a life out-of-doors, still darted about gathering up camp equipment and dousing fires. Serena and Eli, working together, soon had everything stored in its place and now sat quietly, waiting for their number to be called as the wagon master rode up and down the slowly forming line of wagons, barking an order to a man, calling a calming word to a woman.

Serena could not keep her eyes from straying to the sensuous ease of his broad-shouldered body as it moved with the motion of his mount. Her face flamed red when unexpectedly she felt a stirring just below her stomach. A confused anger brightened her eyes when suddenly the man wheeled his stallion up alongside their wagon.

"You're next, Landrie," he said curtly, ignoring Serena. "Move fast, will you? Jessie's mules are actin' up, and I want to get them movin'."

At the crisp crackle in Josh's command, Serena gave in to the tension that had been building inside her since the first time she'd seen the disturbing Northerner. Turning to Eli she sneered in icy tones, "A little authority certainly goes to some people's heads."

The big body stiffened as though she had struck him. His face a mask of dark rage, he kneed the stallion in so close Serena could see the icy glints in his eyes. His lean powerful body seemed to jab her with danger, and she drew closer to Eli. As she tried to stare him down, he shot out a hand, his lean fingers fastening around her wrist. She bit her lip to stifle an outcry of fear, wondering what the blue-eyed devil was going to do to her.

Relief whistled through her teeth when Jessie's mules sent up a discordant noise of brays and plunged and pawed at the ground.

When the little madam's high-pitched squeals rang out over the other noises, Serena was released as roughly as she had been seized. She rubbed the white imprints left from the punishing grip of strong fingers and stared after the wagon master as he loped off to Jessie's aid.

Serena's tensely held body didn't begin to relax until Eli had guided the team into the allotted position. She met his eyes guiltily when he turned to her and warned, "Serena, don't needle Josh Quade. He's not a man to fool with. I thought for a minute there he was gonna haul you off this seat and tan your little behind. And there wouldn't have been a thing I could have done about it."

"I can't seem to help it, Paw," she answered petulantly, hitching her shoulders. "The man jars my nerves . . . ordering people around."

"Good Lord, Serena, he's the wagon master, it's his job to order us around. I can imagine the fix we'd be in if everybody was doin' as he pleased. There'd be such a rush for first place in line we'd never move out."

Serena accepted Eli's reasoning reluctantly, although the excuse she had given sounded inane even to her own ears. She sat quietly until loud laughter from Jessie's wagon made her twist around and peer over her shoulder. Eli looked at the wagon behind them at the same time and chuckled when Josh gave Jessie a playful whack on her shapely rear end.

"I don't see our lordly wagon master ordering those whores around." Serena was bristling again.

Eli sent her a shrewd look. "Them girls don't need no orders from Josh," he said openly. "They know what he wants . . . and when."

"You mean that he—" Serena burst out, then stopped short, realizing that she didn't like what had been hinted, and that the very discerning Paw might read her mind.

"That's what I mean, honey," Eli answered. "Especially the redhead, Jessie."

For nearly a minute Serena couldn't speak as self-disgust washed over her. Why should she care if the blasted man slept with a dozen whores? He was nothing to her. Her delicate chin lifted proudly. "I'm not surprised that he fraternizes with that type of woman," she intoned contemptuously. "I'm sure the decent women in our company wouldn't have anything to do with him."

Eli shot her a sidelong look. "Are you blind, Serena? Every single girl in camp, not to mention half the married ones, eye him plenty. Hell, he could pick and choose among the lot of them." He pointed his long whip at the wagon in front of them. "Look how that Indian girl of the Hansens' keeps lookin' at him. It's easy to see *she* would like to have him in her blankets."

Serena reluctantly directed her gaze at the girl called Ninu. She had already, on several occasions, seen the girl's hungry eyes on the wagon master. She studied the dark, attractive face gazing from the back of the Hansen wagon, the coal-black eyes watching Josh's every move.

"What position does the young squaw hold in the Hansen household? Is she one of the sons' intended?" She diverted the conversation.

Eli gave a hoot of derisive laughter. "Not likely. Can you see that preachin' man lettin' one of his boys marry an Indian? Accordin' to Hansen the girl helps out his wife. But the whispered word is that both the father and the sons use the girl when Mrs. Hansen isn't lookin'." He paused to flick the long whip at a fly settling on one of the horses' rumps. "It's said that the old gal is suspicious, though, and she treats the girl shamefully."

As though to confirm his statement, Bertha Hansen appeared behind Ninu's slender form and fastened thick fingers in the long, swinging black hair. She jerked the girl's head back cruelly, ordering in her masculine voice, "Get up front and help me with the younguns, you good-for-nothin' slut."

Serena blinked in amazement. Why, even her slaves had never been treated that way. She turned to Eli, outrage gripping her entire being. "Why does the girl put up with such treatment? She's neither a slave nor a servant. Why doesn't she just leave that terrible family?"

"Well, from what I gather her people are just about starvin' to death. At least with the Hansens she'll get somethin' to eat every day. Maybe, too, she likes beddin' the Hansen men."

"If that's the case," Serena mused out loud, "the girl would be better off to join the women behind us. She'd escape that awful woman, and get all the men she could handle, I'd think."

She's learning quickly, Eli mused then laughed amusedly. "That's no lie. Them gals of Jessie's were plenty busy last night. I'll have to put a bug in Josh's ear about the squaw."

"Him!" Serena snorted. "He'd most likely take her into his own blankets."

"I don't think so. I've noticed that he avoids the girl. Besides, I think he prefers the pleasure wagon."

A muscle tightened at the corner of Serena's mouth. Damn, how had they gotten back to the whores again? She gave a great sigh of relief when the wagon master himself swept past them in an easy lope, his resonant voice calling loudly, "Roll out!"

Up and down the uneven line came the strident call "Giddyup!" and amid loud cries and snapping whips, twenty-four wagons of different shapes and sizes began to roll, their iron-rimmed wheels cutting deeply into the green sod.

Eli threw an arm around Serena's slim shoulders and said buoyantly, "We're off, Serena, off to a new land."

She smiled widely, her eyes sparkling in response to her friend's jubilation. Maybe a new and better future did await her in this Oregon Territory.

She turned to Eli to voice the thought, then let the words fade away. She had caught sight of a mounted figure that was all too familiar to her. Apprehension shivering down her spine, she clutched Eli's knee. "Paw," she whispered hoarsely, "I just saw Ira Newcomb ride by. How is that possible? I thought him dead by now!"

Landrie anxiously searched Serena's alarmed face. He should have warned her that the little bastard had joined the emigrants. In an attempt to soothe her, Eli covered her trembling hands with one of his own. "He must have escaped his captors, honey. I was gonna tell you that he was here but I wanted to wait until we were on the trail . . . let you get a good night's rest." His words trailed off and he sighed. "Me and him had a run-in last night."

When Serena looked at Eli expectantly, he launched into a brief but concise narration of what had passed between himself, Newcomb, and the wagon master.

Serena listened, aghast. Paw could have been killed. And he still wasn't safe, contrary to his staunch belief that Josh Quade could handle cousin Ira. Ira, like most weak men, had a stubborn streak that would make him go to any length to attain what he wanted.

As the wagon rolled and bumped along, she wondered why Ira's desire for her was so strong. Certainly not because of love. If it were lust, any female could feed that appetite. That left only one reason. Somehow her cousin had learned of her huge cotton sale and had figured out that she must be carrying a large sum of money.

She closed her eyes against an impending sense of doom she couldn't shake off. Ira would be a dark shadow on her mind the entire trip.

A wheel hit a deep rut, jarring Serena back to the present. Independence was some miles behind them now and the road had become rocky and uneven. The light morning breeze had settled down, and the sun rose steadily in a cloudless sky. The still air turned hot and humid, and the dust rolled in clouds, smarting the eyes and throat. And the rolling hills were becoming more numerous, forcing everyone to brace their feet and to grip the hard seats in order to retain their precarious positions.

Serena was holding a tiny handkerchief to her mouth and nose when Josh, his face begrimed and sweat-streaked, came riding down the line, impatiently advising the drivers to lengthen the distance between themselves.

''You're gonna choke to death, ridin' on the heels of each other.''

At the sight and sound of Josh, Serena glanced down at her slender wrist, her eyes narrowing at the bluish marks there, the shape of the lean, strong fingers. He is a brute, and I hate him, she thought. But a moment later she looked up, straight into a pair of probing blue eyes. She became deaf and blind to everything around her.

It took Jessie's cheery call to the wagon master to release her from the gaze that held her prisoner. Flustered, afraid of what the hateful man might have read in her eyes, she turned to Eli and began to chatter to him so inanely that he stared at her peculiarly. When Josh lifted the reins and loped off toward the

pleasure wagon she stopped talking as abruptly as she had
started, adding to Eli's bewilderment.

It was around noon when the shimmering water of a narrow
stream was sighted several yards to the right of the wagon train.
Mothers smiled with relief when the road turned and led directly
to what turned out to be a wide, winding creek. While squealing, laughing children splashed in and out of the shallows, cold
lunches were set out and teams were led down for a refreshing
drink.

Serena, her head aching and her back constantly throbbing,
spread a blanket on the ground and put out the leftover breakfast
of ham and fried bread. Eli wolfed down his share, but she only
picked at the food, more interested in resting her back in the
brief respite from the jolting wagon.

Eli had returned to the team and Serena was feeding the hound
scraps from her plate when with a soft rustle of buckskins the
wagon master hunkered down beside her. She felt the hot rake
of his eyes on her face and told herself to rise and walk away
from his disturbing presence. Distressingly, she seemed incapable of moving. A pleasurable warmth shivered through her
when he gently grasped her wrist and ran a thumb caressingly
over the bruise on her delicate flesh. "I didn't mean to mark
you," he said in soft, contrite tones. After a slow, audible breath
he added, "I lost control when you slashed at me with that sharp
little tongue."

When Serena failed to respond, incapable of uttering a sound,
he raised her hand and brushed his lips across the flat of her
wrist. "Am I forgiven?" His eyes gazed into hers.

Serena caught her breath as a shiver swept through her. She
gazed tentatively into the blue eyes that looked at her so tenderly.
Then she closed her own in a kind of desperate protest. She had
never felt the presence of a man so overwhelmingly in her life.

She jerked her hand away as though his touch repelled, the
color rising in her cheeks. Struggling with her unwanted attraction to him, she opened her mouth to scathingly tear into him,
but she was stopped when Eli spoke behind her.

"Ready to roll again, Josh?"

The curve of the wagon master's mouth mocked Serena for

only a moment before, with one swing, he was in the saddle. Her cheeks burning, Serena stared after him, her hands clenched in fists. The arrogant devil! He'd only been amusing himself with her.

Eli looked curiously at her flushed face. "I think the heat has got to you, daughter. You'd probably be more comfortable if you stretched out on your pallet for the rest of the day."

Serena shook her head. "It's too close in there, Paw." She didn't know exactly why, but suddenly she felt she had to have her way. She smiled at the anxious, weathered face. "I feel like I can't get my breath, and I'm afraid that the provisions will fall in on me." After a short pause she added, "Actually, I've been thinking that I'll sleep outside with you from now on. At least until this heat breaks."

Landrie mused on her words a minute, then nodded. "Keep your bonnet on, then," he said and boosted her onto the high wagon seat.

Thoughts of that darn Yankee quickly vanished.

Under the scorching rays of the sun, the country was growing rougher and wilder. There were irregular ridges to be swung around, and narrow gullies that weren't seen until a person was almost upon them.

Everyone sighed with relief when after an hour or so the land became softer, lending itself to long stretches of smooth, level pastureland. Occasionally signs of civilization, rude log cabins set many miles apart, were sighted. Dull-faced women watched them from narrow doorways as thin, ragged children hung onto their skirts. In fields cleared out of the forest, sometimes a man turned from his labor to stare impassively a minute, then go back to his work.

At one homestead Landrie silently pointed out to Serena the raw earth of a new grave. The mound was short: the burial of a child. She shivered. The loneliness and sense of futility in such an existence would smother her spirit. Please, Lord, she prayed silently, don't let Dorn's place be like one of these. I couldn't bear it.

The sun swung westward, and just as Serena was sure she couldn't ride another mile, the wagons rolled into a cool valley and stopped alongside a river. The Kaw, she heard someone say.

When Landrie swung her over the high wheel and sat her firmly on the ground, she laughed weakly. "I feel like my head has floated off my body."

"I hope you ain't got sunstroke," Eli said anxiously, peering down at her wan face. She gave him a wide smile of reassurance.

"It's that rocking-chair wagon, Paw."

"Yeah, I kinda feel the same way I did when we was on the boat. You know, honey, you'd probably be more comfortable ridin' the mare. At least part of the time."

"I thought of that, too." Serena lifted her heavy mane of hair off the damp nape of her neck, then glanced down at the dusty, outgrown dress, the tightness almost flattening her breasts. "But I'm afraid my gowns would rip apart if I tried to ride in them."

Landrie studied the straining seams of the garment and grinned. "You do fill your clothes to overflowing. Let me think on it a bit."

Serena patted his hand. "Don't worry about it, Paw. I'll get used to the wagon. You go on about your business while I get camp started."

Serena struck out down the valley in search of wood. The pealing laughter of the children faded behind her, and she felt the peacefulness that hung over the long, grassy meadow. Putting all but the search of fuel from her mind, she was shortly back to the cluster of wagons, her arms full of sun-bleached tree limbs.

She was adept now at fire-starting, and while the flames danced and bit into the wood she made a hurried trip to the river with a pail swung from her suntanned hand. On her return, a pot of coffee was soon brewing, and observing the women within her view busily engaged in bread making, a determined glint came into Serena's eyes. Grabbing up a wooden bowl she marched purposefully to the rear of the wagon. Paw was going to have real bread tonight too.

It didn't take long to scoop the flour from its barrel container; it was the other items to go with it that made Serena pause often to chew a nail thoughtfully. Finally she had gathered what she thought was necessary and was back, kneeling in front of the fire, surreptitiously watching the woman nearest her. She would play copycat.

But the woman's hands moved so swiftly as she tossed different ingredients into her pile of flour that Serena couldn't follow her movements. "At least I know what she used," she mumbled as she took a guess at the amount of baking powder and leavening. Soon enough a pan of lumpy dough was slid into the Dutch oven.

The sun had disappeared when Serena closed the cast-iron door on her culinary effort and straightened up. The dozens of crackling fires started previously now took on additional brilliance in the darkness. Mouth-watering aromas were floating in the air when she turned to preparing the rest of the evening meal.

She eyed the remaining chunk of ham with distaste, wondering if Paw was also getting a little tired of it. But who could afford the luxury of tossing it to the dog? Sighing, she poised the knife over the pink meat, then paused. The very air hummed with the presence of the man who, against her will, excited and disturbed her.

Tall and lean, with silent, predatory steps, the wagon master moved into the light of the campfire. The blue flame of his eyes flicked over her, and to Serena's blushing shame, her body responded to their heat. He stared at her a moment, like a curious cat, then with a thrusting motion of his hand said, "Here, Landrie will be glad of some fresh meat for a change."

Serena wrenched her eyes away from the hard, rugged face, then widened them as she saw two cleanly dressed squirrels, skewered through with a green-bark stick. She stared a moment then, scowling darkly, deliberately put her hands behind her back. Impatience grew in the dark blue eyes, and the offering was held forward to her again, this time none too gently.

Serena's eyes narrowed, warning him to take the stick away. Icy determination shimmered in his look, telling her that he would not. It seemed that minutes had ticked by, then, as she had known it would, her will weakened first. She snatched the wild game from him, snapping spitefully, "I hope he doesn't choke on them."

The breath ripped furiously through Josh's clenched teeth, making Serena take a hurried step backward. "It's a wonder, Miss Bain, *you* don't choke on that acid tongue of yours," he grated out. "Landrie needs to give you a good hiding, teach you some manners."

Serena's hands clenched in anger such as she had never known before. A hiding? Indeed! That would be exactly what this half-wild hillman would do to any woman of his if she dared to cross him. It was all she could do not to stamp her foot, but before she could blister him with another insult, the wagon master turned and retreated into the darkness. Her vexation a bitter taste in her mouth, she hissed, "Yankee bastard," then gazed hopelessly down at Eli's supper.

How did one go about cooking something strung on a stick? she wondered. It had to hang over the fire, she reasoned, and with much jabbing around, finally succeeded in shoving the spit into the gravelly ground, the squirrels hanging precariously over the fire. She stepped back, dusting off her hands, telling herself that it hadn't been so hard after all, when all at once the pleased expression fled her face and aggravated tears sprang to her eyes. The small carcass on the end of the stick had slid off and plopped into the ashy coals.

"Oh, no!" she cried, dropping to her knees and gingerly retrieving the smoking flesh. Would the remaining one be enough for Paw's supper? she wondered. Then she gave a despairing gasp as that one, too, began to slide slowly downward.

"Damn him!" Frustrated tears trickled down her cheeks. "He did it on purpose. He knew I wouldn't know what to do with these miserable things."

Serena gave a half-startled, half-angry jerk when a quiet voice asked politely, "Can I help you, Miss Bain?"

She gazed up helplessly at a thin, gangly youth, somewhere in his teens. She could only gulp and nod. The young man gave her a friendly smile and jumped to grab the spit that was losing its slight hold in the ground.

Serena gazed at the patch of grass where the blackened raw meat had been tossed and tears threatened again. "I've ruined Paw's supper," she wailed, dabbing at her eyes with the hem of her dress.

"No, you haven't," her eager rescuer assured her as he drove two forked sticks firmly into the hard clay, one on either side of the fire. "I'll just clean these little devils off a bit," he went on, dipping water over the squirrels, flushing away the ashes. He held them up. "See, good as new."

Serena smiled gratefully and Eli's supper was again threaded onto the spit, then hung between the two crotched limbs. "I could have done that." She shook her head. The smile still on her lips, she asked, "Whom do I thank?"

"Well," the boy blushed bashfully, "my name is Todd, but it was my maw, Nell Simpson, who sent me over here. She figured you might not know how to suspend the meat over the fire." He grinned. "That it might not enter Josh's head that a southern girl wouldn't have that knowledge."

"Hah!" Serena snorted. "I sometimes wonder if anything ever enters that one's head. He's too occupied with strutting around, giving people orders. He reminds me of a rooster in a full henhouse."

Todd shrugged, then answered amiably, "You're the only woman in the train I've heard mean-mouth Josh." He stared down at the ground in thought. "Actually, come to think of it,"—he raised his head, his brown eyes twinkling—"all the others are so in awe of his handsome face and manly body, they can't even speak to him. They just look and simper."

Serena grunted sourly. "They're to be pitied for their poor taste in men. Let's hope it improves as we get closer to Oregon."

Todd slid Serena a baffled look, then said that he'd better get going, that he had camp chores to do. Serena held out a slender hand. "Thank you again, Todd, and thank your mother for her thoughtfulness."

Her face was still flushed with hostility when some half hour later Landrie returned from tending the team. He sat down on the edge of the blanket that held a platter of crusty brown squirrel, roasted potatoes in the skin, and a pan of curiously shaped . . . something. He picked one up and looked at Serena questioningly.

"They're biscuits, Paw," she said eagerly. "Try one."

Landrie lifted a pale yellow lump to his mouth, bit down hard, moved it to the side of his mouth, gnawed, then with a rueful sidelong look at Serena, gave up.

Embarrassment and disappointment washed over her face. "Oh, Paw, are they so awful?" She picked out the smallest mound and tried to bite into it. "I've got some cold pone left over from yesterday." She sighed, tossing the teeth-defying morsel onto the grass. When the hound rushed over and merely gave it a couple of pushes with his nose, she burst out crying.

"Now, now, honey." Eli patted her back consolingly. "You tried, and that's what counts. I'm a right good hand at stirrin' up bread. Soon as I find time, I'll learn you how.

"In the meantime, I'm gonna enjoy this fresh meat." His strong teeth bit into the tender juicy flesh, his jaws working hungrily. Between bites he asked, "Where did these little rascals come from? Is some young feller in camp makin' up to you already?"

He laughed knowingly when Serena retorted that it came from no "feller" of hers. Washing a mouthful of food down with a long draught of coffee, he said, "I take it Josh dropped them off."

"I only took them because he said they were for you," Serena snapped defensively.

Landrie nodded. "I'm right glad you did, honey. As you know I'm right partial to squirrel." He glanced over at her plate holding a lone potato. "How come you didn't eat any? I know you relished it back home. That's about all we lived on one winter."

Serena shook her head. "I couldn't swallow it."

"Of course you could." Eli nudged the platter closer to her. "Come on, take a piece. Josh won't know."

But Josh did know. Hunkered down beside the pleasure wagon several yards away, he had watched the little play and knew exactly what the motions of heads and hands meant. When Serena began to greedily consume a hind leg, he grinned and muttered inwardly, "Stubborn little witch."

He continued to watch the southern girl, his eyes drifting down the white throat, where a couple of buttons were undone for coolness, to catch on the ripe thrust of her breasts. When a hungry ache knotted his loins an inner voice sneered, "Better stick to your own kind. That one is not for the likes of you."

And though Josh agreed wholeheartedly, when Jessie touched his shoulder in silent invitation later in the evening, he mumbled that he was taking a walk. As he moved away he grinned wryly, feeling the little whore's puzzled look following him.

CHAPTER

∽ 7 ∾

A BLUE HAZE of smoke hung over the camp as the emigrants made their second evening stop. The Kaw River had been crossed that morning, an easy fording, and the wagons now rolled toward the Big Blue River. Serena's anxious eyes nervously tried to pierce the darkness beyond her fire. A band of Kaw Indians had followed the train, at a distance, during the last few hours of daylight. Were they out there in the darkness now, watching? Would they wait until the camp slept, then to slip in and kill them all?

She tried to draw courage from Paw's, "Don't fret about them, honey. They're just curious." But the hushed tones of the mothers putting their children to bed added to her anxiety as she hurried to pile more wood onto the flames. But when the flames danced higher she belatedly realized that she was only making a brighter light for the savages. For fear of being snatched away in the night, Serena grabbed a stick and quickly scattered the fire.

Serena paced the small area around the wagon, wondering when Eli would return from the council meeting that was held every night. She paused at the water pail to soothe her fear-parched throat and found it empty. She was almost relieved. A trip to the spring-fed stream, which was safely sheltered by wagons, would kill some time.

The Hansen wagon blocked Serena's direct path to the water.

She frowned impatiently. Trust that pair to get as close as possible to the water supply. Not only was it convenient, they could also overhear what was said between the other women visiting the stream.

Serena was pleased to find only one figure kneeling on the trodden-down grass at the water's edge, the young squaw, Ninu. The leaping flames from the Hansen fire shone fully on the Indian girl, and Serena thought the girl was striking. It wasn't surprising that the Hansen men were attracted to her.

She noted as she knelt near the girl that several garments of homespun were soaking among the water-covered stones. Busily scrubbing some clothing with a handful of sand, Ninu looked up and smiled shyly. Serena smiled back, then gasped as she plunged the pail into the water. Goodness! she thought, it's absolutely icy—surely it comes from a spring. Ninu's hands must be numb.

"You're late doing your laundry, aren't you?" Serena commented. "Couldn't you have washed it in the daylight hours? Surely the water would have been a little warmer."

Ninu darted an uneasy glance at the Hansen men who never took their eyes off her. "The clothes aren't really dirty," she answered softly. "Only worn one time." The corners of her eyes crinkled impishly. "The big she-buffalo says that idle hands get me into trouble."

Ninu's apt description of Mrs. Hansen brought soft laughter from both girls. And though they tried to smother their giggles, when the sharp-eared woman heard them, she sat forward suspiciously, her cold stare cutting their merriment short. Hurrying to finish her chilling chore, Serena whispered, "That woman is a real devil."

Ninu nodded somberly. "All the Hansens are mean, but she is the worst. Her tongue is the sharpest and her hand the heaviest."

"She hits you?" Serena asked indignantly. "Why?"

Ninu lowered her voice until it was barely audible. "I think that Mr. Hansen does not pleasure her anymore and she thinks that he comes to me for release."

Serena recalled that Paw had hinted at that possibility, and disgust for the obese man and pity for the girl made her ask, "Does he, Ninu . . . come to you?"

A rush of blood tinged the young squaw's dusky cheek. She wrung the water from a large shirt, and then as she scrubbed at another confessed weakly, "Mr. Hansen and his sons lay and wait for me all the time."

Serena sat back on her heels, remembering other things Paw had said that morning; maybe the girl liked the attention she received from the Hansen men. She studied the slender form bent over its task for a minute, then asked bluntly, "Why do you stay with them, Ninu and take all that abuse?"

Ninu gave a short bitter laugh. "Where else would Ninu go? Nobody wants a squaw."

"You could always go to the woman, Jessie. She would treat you well, and would never strike you. Paw Landrie says she's a very warm hearted person, despite her fiery ways and tongue." Serena paused, wondering how to phrase what the move to Jessie's wagon would entail. She almost laughed aloud at her foolishness; this girl certainly knew what went on in the pleasure wagon. She added only, "At least there you could choose your men . . . get paid for it."

Interest shimmered in Ninu's eyes, then died away. "Mr. Hansen would never let me go."

"What do you mean, he wouldn't let you go?" Serena hissed angrily. "You can go anywhere you please. If you want, I'll take you to Jessie right now."

Ninu didn't respond, she only continued to rub sand into a pair of trousers with slow, measured strokes of her palm. When several seconds passed, Serena got to her feet, saying coolly, "Evidently you don't mind your situation too badly." But as Serena bent to pick up the pail, Ninu dropped the garment and jumped to her feet. The determination on the bronze face made Serena stretch a hand to the girl. Silently the girls gathered themselves together for the short dash to the pleasure wagon.

But the pair never got started. A male figure moved out of the shadows and blocked their path.

Serena's lips formed a soundless word of dismay. Of all the times for cousin Ira to show up. He stood a moment leering down at her, then peered cautiously over his shoulder before

drawling insolently, "Good evening, cousin. I've been wondering when I'd run into you. Where have you been hiding yourself?"

"I haven't been *hiding* myself anywhere." Serena tried to step
around Newcomb, still clutching Ninu's hand. "We're in a hurry
right now. I'll be going now."

"No, little cuz, I think not." The slightly built man grasped
her arm with surprising strength. "I think we'll settle things
right now."

When he threw another careful look over his shoulder, Serena
taunted, "Aren't you afraid Josh Quade will see you talking to
me? I understand he warned you to stay away from me."

"The wagon master's warning doesn't bother me none," Ira
growled, his eyes clinging to the fast, angry rise and fall of
Serena's breasts. "Just because he crawls between your legs
every night doesn't mean he owns you."

Serena gasped. Did Ira believe that, or was he only being
obnoxious, spitting out words that were meant to hurt? Well,
whatever his reasons were, the remark certainly didn't deserve
a rebuttal. Returning his leering gaze, she said coolly, "If I had
a gun, I'd shoot you for that."

"Big words mean little doings, sweet cousin," Ira drawled,
then shifted his gaze to Ninu. "What have we here?" His eyes
narrowed on Ninu's shapely body beneath its snug shift. The
devious black eyes glowed and shimmered as he shoved a hand
inside his trousers and blatantly fondled himself, his eyes never
leaving the young squaw's face.

Serena snorted her disgust, but the girl watched, engrossed,
as Ira's maleness grew and pushed against the buttons of his fly.
When Ninu swayed toward him, Serena jerked free of the fingers
pressing into her arm and tugged at Ninu's hand.

"Come on, Ninu, we've got somewhere to go, remember?"

Serena stared in blank surprise when the Indian girl pulled
free of her, muttering thickly, "Maybe Ninu go later."

"Oh, Ninu, you little fool," Serena began, then let the rest
of the argument die in her throat. The time for arguing had
passed. The three Hansen men were stalking toward them. She
threw Ninu a disgusted look then, swooping up the pail of water,
moved away. From the corners of her eyes she saw Ira making

a hasty retreat. "Coward!" she sniffed. "And that little simpleton . . ." she mumbled.

Eli was sitting beside the dying fire when Serena returned to the wagon. "I was just gettin' ready to go lookin' for you," he grumbled, then he yawned as he pulled off his boots and stretched out on his blanket. She mumbled an apology before removing her own shoes and lying down on her own bedding that was unrolled beside his. The hound padded over and curled at her feet, and when Eli's snoring came softly, she smiled and reached out a hand to rest on his blanket. Almost immediately she fell asleep.

It was just before dawn when a wild scream of terror brought Serena wide awake. Landrie jerked up beside her, exclaiming, "What the hell!"

All over camp men and women sat up and frantically reached for shoes as the squeals and angry cries of an irate woman continued. Landrie cocked his head attentively. "It's comin' from the Hansen wagon," he declared and rushed after the others running in that direction.

Serena stumbled into her slippers and arrived at the Hansen wagon just as Josh came running up. Their breaths caught in unison at the sight of the young squaw cowering against the wagon wheel, her shift ripped off one shoulder, her hair in wild disarray. Mrs. Hansen stood over the girl with a short riding whip dangling from her hand, her broad face a mask of rage. She struggled against her husband's grip on her arm, ignoring his guarded muttering. The two sons stood nearby, darting uneasy glances at the curious onlookers who had gathered so quickly.

Josh's gaze flickered over the scene, then returned to Hansen. "What goes on here?" His words stung the suspenseful air like a whip.

Hansen pretended not to hear Josh, seeking time as he waited for the rage to fade from his wife's eyes. Josh's long step shortened the distance between them. "Answer me, Hansen. What's goin' on here?"

Hansen's body stiffened, and when he looked up all his burning hatred for the wagon master shone in his defiant stare.

"Nothin' for you to stick your nose in, Quade," he ground out. "It's family business and I can handle it."

Josh hunkered down beside Ninu and gingerly touched the red welts crisscrossing her dusky shoulder. She flinched and whimpered, her eyes glassy with fear. He looked up and fixed unblinking eyes on the glowering visage towering over him. "The squaw is not of your family, so it looks like it is my business. Why was your wife beating the girl?"

The self-appointed savior of souls glared back at Josh, nervousness twitching his loose, weak mouth. After shooting his family a warning look, he blustered, "The wife had to get after her to do the camp chores."

Josh glanced up at the sky; it was only a dark gray. "You start her chores uncommonly early, don't you? Daylight is still a good hour away."

"The Injun didn't finish the washin' last night, and the missus told her to finish it this mornin' before startin' breakfast."

An angry, low muttering rose from the crowd, and a woman's voice, sounding to Serena suspiciously like Jessie's, warned loudly, "Don't let him take you in, Josh. The louse is lyin' through his teeth."

When others joined in, a few baritones included, Josh stood up. It grew so quiet the hoot of an owl was heard distinctly before he said coldly, "All right, Hansen, the truth now. The girl was beaten for another reason, wasn't she?"

Hansen licked his dry lips, opened his mouth, then snapped it shut at the low sound of mischief coming from the wagon. When all eyes turned to the young boy sitting on the tailgate, he took a threatening step toward his son. He was seconds too late.

"Maw beat her cause she caught her layin' with Paw under the wagon," the boy explained for all to hear.

Her son's blatant words penetrated Bertha Hansen's jealous rage. In the thick, shocked silence her heavy hand swept across the full, petulant mouth. The boy toppled over backwards, landing on the ground with a loud wail. Satisfied grins jumped to the lips of the onlookers. Josh's expression didn't change, but those who watched him caught an unmistakable twitching of the corners of his mouth.

He spoke over the outraged yells of the young boy. "Hansen,

I said in the beginning that I wouldn't tolerate women trouble in this train." He nodded over his shoulder, out across the valley in the direction they had come. "Gather up your things and prepare to leave."

Disbelief glared in the Hansen tribe's eyes. Stepping away from his wife and sons, Hansen shouted, "You can't kick us out of this train! It was me who hired you to lead us."

Forbidding glowed in Josh's eyes, and it echoed in his voice when he said, "Your hiring me doesn't give you special privileges." With finality in the words he repeated, "Pack up and get out."

He turned to tell the anxious audience to return to their wagons, then slowly spun back around, as in unison everyone cried loudly, "Behind you, Quade!"

Silas Hansen, his face almost grotesque in its twisted rage, had rushed the wagon master's back. But Josh had been warned in time and took a quick sidestep then received the ramming shoulder with his own. However, the surprise and momentum of the man's great weight brought both men crashing to the ground.

The younger bounded immediately to his feet and went into a crouch as the slower-moving Silas pulled himself up with the aid of a small sapling. Then, snarling with hate and without caution, Silas rushed his enemy. Josh's knotted fist landed flush on the bearded chin. The large shaggy head snapped back, the big body sagged, then slowly folded to the ground. Josh stood over the inert form, his breath coming in short pants. He whipped around at another shouted warning.

The sons were moving in on him. Sighing, he squared away, his lean, tough body held in readiness.

The Hansen brothers came in opposite directions, their intention to box him in. No time was wasted in feinting. The air was filled with harsh breathing, shuffling feet, and the muffled thud of blows against flesh.

In a short time a well-placed fist, driving straight from Josh's shoulder, put the younger brother out of the fight. The elder one fought on like a wounded bear. Blood streaming from his nose, he groped for Josh, trying to catch him in his powerful arms. Bloodied and battered, his shirt hanging in shreds, Josh continued to fight, the corded muscles in his arms working like pistons.

And Serena, her breath almost stilled, felt a strange sensation at each blow Josh received. Forgetting that she must hate the loathsome Yankee, she gripped Landrie's arm with biting fingers.

"Why doesn't someone help him? He's ready to drop. It's not right that he should fight all three."

Eli looked down at her, and his surprise turned to humor. It would seem that Miss Bain doesn't dislike the Northerner as much as she claims. "He's our leader, Serena," he explained, keeping his face blank. "His authority is at stake and he must show every man here that, if necessary, he can lick any one of them."

It was a relief, for the women at least, to see the fight nearing the end as the young Hansen put all his remaining strength into an uppercut that led from his knees. However, Josh's rock-hard fist caught young Hansen on the temple, and as the big body went limp and sprawled on its back, muttered approval was sounded from the emigrants. Then the father began to stir and all attention turned to him.

Grins and snickers were not suppressed as Bertha helped her husband sit up, then roughly jerked him to his feet. Almost simultaneously the younger son staggered to his feet, stood a moment gathering his wits, then moved to squat beside his brother. Swiping an arm across his sweating face, Josh stalked over to the parents.

"Load your boy into the wagon, and get!"

Sullenly hostile, the pair glared at him. Mrs. Hansen opened her mouth as if to speak, then, aware of the unfriendly faces staring coldly at her, she closed her lips in a tight line and slowly began gathering up equipment while her husband and son loaded their unconscious relative onto the awaiting tailgate. Her chin in the air, and her eyes avoiding the smug looks of the women whom she had always bossed about, she sat waiting, the reins in her capable hands.

Elbows jabbed ribs and eyes swung to Josh as Hansen, his bearing sheepish yet stubborn, edged his way to Ninu who had regained her footing and now leaned weakly against a tree. "Come on, girl," he growled. "We're leavin' now."

"Hansen, damn your hide!" Josh exploded, his eyes blazing, his patience exhausted. "Get your ass in that wagon and get the hell out of here!"

Hansen swung his great bulk around, a ready protest on his lips. But before he could voice it, Bertha had left the wagon and clapped a beefy hand on his shoulder. Her strong fingers biting into his fat flesh, she said grimly, "You and your whore have brought enough shame down on me and the children. You choose between us, right now."

Daylight was approaching as the creaking axles of the Hansen vehicle pulled out with Silas handling the reins. With satisfied grunts the people began straggling back to their wagons, carrying with them the source of many days' gossip. About to follow them, Serena held back when her glance fell on Josh and Ninu talking to Jessie. She watched interestedly when Jessie smiled at the girl and motioned her head toward the pleasure wagon. The single men congregating near that particular vehicle grinned appreciatively when Ninu readily joined the young whores standing nearby.

Well, that's that, Serena thought, turning in the direction of her own wagon. After a few short steps, she paused, her attention shifted this time to her cousin Ira. He leaned against a tree, his eyes thoughtfully on the ground.

He's plotting how to get the girl away from Jessie. Serena sighed, knowing that he'd get no resistance from the young squaw; the foolish girl was fascinated by her cousin.

As she resumed walking, unpleasant thoughts of Ira and the squaw were dislodged from her mind when she bumped into a hard, muscular body. When strong fingers closed around her arms and steadied her, she looked up into the dark blue eyes of the wagon master.

Her feelings turbulent and mixed at his touch, she tried to pull away but was held firmly by the lean, strong fingers. "Don't fret about the squaw, Miss Bain," Josh said softly. "She'll be fine with Jessie. After the Hansens, it will seem like heaven to her."

Serena's green eyes suddenly flashed fire. "I'm sure it will also for the men who will seek out the new flesh like a pack of dogs. Will *you* be the leader?"

"Damn you and that slashing tongue." The words were growled in her ear as she was molded against a long lean frame. Her chin was grasped roughly and jerked up, forcing her to stare into sparkling blue eyes. Then, just when she was sure that her neck would snap, the dangerous expression in Josh's eyes softened as his gaze fastened on her trembling mouth and the little pulse beat at the base of her throat.

And while she was telling herself, Get away from him, he's a threat to your very being, his lips parted on a hungry sigh and swept down to cover hers. All thoughts sank into nothingness. The urgency in his lips turned her blood molten, for never had she felt so needed, so wanted. Her arms came up around his shoulders, and her hand stroked the back of his head as his kiss deepened, demanding that she respond to its heat with that of her own. She quivered in answer.

Eli's familiar hearty laugh resounded from the grazing post and suddenly brought Serena out of the deep dream that had swept her up. She pulled her mouth away from the sweet lips that seemed to devour, then whispered raggedly, "Let me go!"

If she was heard, there was no indication, for the hard chest continued to flatten her breasts, and the legs remained pressed to hers. When she began to struggle she was grasped by the hips and lifted until she was pressed against a hard manhood that throbbed in unison with the tongue that once again probed her mouth.

Serena commanded herself not to feel the heat of his passion, but when she was abruptly released she would have fallen had warm fingers not taken hold of her elbow. Scalding tears of shame burned the backs of her eyes. "I hate you," she hissed, "hate you, hate you!"

"No, Miss Southern Belle," he returned smoothly. "It's yourself you hate, because you fell so low as to want a hateful Yankee in your arms, and perhaps in . . ." His words trailed off as his eyes gleamed with desire.

He was walking away from her then, his beautiful body seemingly mocking her. Humiliation rushed over her in a dark tide.

The dreadful man had only been toying with her emotions again, deliberately making her respond. He'll never do it again, she vowed as she ran back to the wagon. But as she built a fire, a small, perplexed frown creased her forehead. Where Josh Quade was concerned, was her mind stronger than her body? Her body had let her down dreadfully this morning.

Serena had just put on a pot of coffee when Eli walked into camp and tossed a bundle to her. "Buckskins." He smiled widely. "You can start ridin' your mare today."

Serena unfolded the pants and long shirt and ran her palms over the velvet smoothness of the garments. "They're beautiful, Paw," she exclaimed. "Where did you get them?"

"Mrs. Nell Simpson sold them to me. Her son, Todd, had an extra pair."

"Oh, yes, I met him." Serena smiled. "He helped me to set up a spit for the squirrels that smart-aleck wagon master brought over. Seemed like a nice youngster."

"Yes, he is, and so are the other Simpson younguns. There's two girls, younger than Todd, who's seventeen, then another boy around five."

"Their parents must be awfully proud of them."

"I expect the father was. Nell's a widow now, only a short while. The Simpsons are from Kentucky. They had only been on the trail three days when Mr. Simpson was struck by a copperhead. Its fangs punctured a big vein in his leg and the poison just raced through his body. He was dead within hours."

"Oh, how dreadful," Serena cried compassionately. "Poor Mrs. Simpson and the children." She stared into the heart of the fire, shuddering, realizing anew the hidden dangers they could encounter on the long trek to Oregon. "I'm surprised the woman didn't return to Kentucky to be with family and friends."

"Nell is a strong woman, in both mind and body. Everything they owned was invested in their wagon and team, and she was more or less forced to go onward."

"I hope the men traveling with us have her courage and determination to make a fresh start in a new land."

"Amen to that," Eli agreed, then jerked his head in the direction of the wagon. "Go put on your new duds. Let's see what kind of squaw you'll make."

Inside the cramped quarters of the schooner Serena tugged the tight, worn dress over her head and slid her legs into the doeskin trousers. The jerkin-type top came next, its softness caressing her naked breasts. Enjoying the feel of her new outfit, she smoothed her palms down over her hips and decided the fit wasn't too tight, not as revealing as she had feared the men's clothing would be.

But if she'd had a full-length mirror to look into, Serena would have seen that despite the comparatively loose fit of the buckskins, all of her enticing curves were well defined. When Landrie called to her to come out and check the burning meat, she jumped to the ground, a pleased smile on her face.

Eli's eyes widened as Serena walked toward him, an image of Ella Bain coming to his mind. The girl had her mother's slight frame, a figure that startled a man when he lifted his eyes and beheld her ripe breasts. And, he sighed, just like her mother before her, men would lust after the daughter too. He knew that even the way she walked would be a sorry temptation to any young man.

He hid a tickled grin behind his hand. The Yank was going to have his hands full. There could be many a fight over this proud beauty. He might have to turn out half the train before the journey was over.

Eli was quiet for so long that Serena frowned and demanded suspiciously, "They're too tight, aren't they?"

"Naw, honey," he hurriedly assured her. "They're supposed to fit just like they do. They have to be a little snug so they won't catch on brush and tangle you up."

"I don't know." Serena looked doubtful. "Mammy Hessie would skin me alive if she caught me wearing britches."

"You're livin' in a different world now, Serena," Eli remarked, pulling aside the boiling coffee. "On the trail them britches will do you just fine."

But as Serena moved about, making breakfast, she was conscious of the sidelong looks slid her way. She knew that whenever two women drew together and whispered, they were discussing her new attire. She hoped that Paw knew what he was talking about.

Josh was astride his stallion, waiting for everyone to mount up and take their places in the wagons, when he noted the open-mouthed stares of some men. He turned around in the saddle and followed their gaze, and for the first time saw Serena in her new clothes. She was walking toward her mare, her full breasts moving under the sensuous fabric with each stride of her long legs. A molten liquid shot through his veins and, much against his will, a surge of gnawing jealousy pulsed within.

Hell, he fumed, she might as well be naked. Parading around for all the men to gawk at her. He shot those men a dangerously dark look and, in a voice noticeably irritated, shouted, "Roll out!"

CHAPTER
❦ 8 ❧

A MONTH HAD PASSED; the Vermilion and Big Blue had been forded. The wagons now traveled along the Little Blue, where the dust rolled so thick that each morning drivers traded places, back ones moving to the front and leaders taking their places. Only the pleasure wagon remained in its usual position, despite Jessie's frequent complaints.

I wonder how Ninu is making out these days, Serena mused as the mare plodded along, way in front to avoid the clouds of dust. At least the girl was still under Jessie's protection. Ira hadn't gotten to her yet. She hadn't spoken to her cousin since that night Bertha Hansen had taken the whip to the young squaw. But he was still around. She'd seen him at a distance.

Come to think of it, she hadn't spoken with the wagon master either since that fateful night. However, much to her self-disgust, she was always aware of him with every fiber of her being.

Her searching gaze picked Josh out of the group of riders several yards ahead. She watched him, telling herself sternly that this burning infatuation she felt—she refused to call it anything stronger—must be smothered, put out. Besides, the intensity of her attraction to him was frightening. It would be so easy to lose control.

Serena determinedly pulled down a mental barrier between herself and Josh Quade and stared out over the vast, empty land she and Beauty traveled. Someone had warned that there were no trees between the Little Blue and the Platte, and so far who-ever had said it had been right.

She looked up at the sky, and there wasn't a cloud in sight, only a red ball of fire that sent its scorching rays indiscriminately over human and animal alike. If only it would rain, she sighed. It hadn't rained since the trek began, and the grass, what there was of it, was seared yellow. The animals were beginning to take on a gaunt look.

Serena glanced down at the hound plodding alongside Beauty. "But you're fat and sassy, huh, boy?" She received a slow wag of a thin tail. "Why aren't you walking in the shade of our wagon, you foolish hound?" The tail moved once again, this time half-heartedly.

Just then she glanced over her shoulder at the sound of trotting hooves approaching behind her. A young, freckled-faced girl, around fourteen, Serena thought, slowed her mount and matched its pace to Beauty's.

Serena returned the friendly though shy smile. "You're Mrs. Simpson's daughter, aren't you?"

"Yes, I'm Susan. Sure is hot, isn't it? Hard to believe there was frost this mornin'."

"Yes, it is." Serena remembered the patches of white shim-mering in the cool air. "September is only a few days away and frost is to be expected, I guess."

"You're so beautiful, Miss Bain," the little girl said suddenly.

"Why, thank you, Susan." Serena blushed at the guileless compliment. "So are you."

"No, I'm not. I'm too scrawny. Todd says so all the time."

"Oh, honey, brothers are like that. They love to tease. Believe me, you're going to grow into a beautiful young woman."

Pleasure suffused Susan's face in a soft pink blush as she ducked her head shyly.

Serena was surprised at the enjoyment she derived from the young girl's company as they rode along, speaking of inconse-quential subjects. For the most part she was still ignored by her female traveling companions. A few of the older married ones did nod to her occasionally, but the younger, and especially the single, ones hadn't changed their attitudes in the least.

Susan suddenly broke the short silence with a statement that

snapped Serena back to the present. "Mama says it's good that
the wagon master has marked you for his own."

"What?" She gaped at the girl.

"She says it will keep the other men away, keep them from
fighting over you." Before Serena could open her mouth, the
girl had turned her mount around and explained hurriedly, "I'd
better get back to our wagon, see if Mama needs help with my
little brother Davy."

Serena stared after the slim back as it retreated. Where had
Nell Simpson got such an idea? Certainly not from Josh Quade's
actions. Why, he didn't even speak to her anymore.

Serena was so immersed in Susan Simpson's baffling pro-
nouncement she had been oblivious to the sun's sudden disap-
pearance behind a dark, hovering cloud. Were they to have rain
at last?

The wagons had just pulled in for the night when the rain
came, cool, fine, and misty at first, then a heavy patter that
dampened the dust. Then it poured, visions were blurred, and
pack animals struggled and floundered in ankle-deep mud. Over
the wild whinnying of horses, deep braying of mules, and loud
screeching of children, Josh's baritone shouted out orders.

"Fall out, and unhitch teams."

Serena repressed a giggle at some of the outlandish threats
made to teams as drivers fought to control them. Her mirth turned
to anxiety when she became aware of her own highly nervous
team, which was squealing and rearing in fright, almost lifting
Eli off his feet as he hung onto them.

She flung Beauty's saddle under the wagon, tied her to one of
the locked wheels, then hurried to assist her hotly swearing companion. She leaped and grabbed at a tossing head, then two
strong hands clasped her waist and lifted her aside.

"Get in the wagon before you drown."

She peered up through wet lashes and met the dark blue eyes
that coolly commanded as well. She was too wet, too cold, and
too tired to argue.

Shivering in her soaked clothes, her teeth chattering, Serena
clambered into the wagon and dug deep into the trunk that held
her scanty supply of clothing. By the time Landrie joined her
she was in a soft, high-necked flannel gown and her buckskins

were draped over the back of the wagon seat. She turned her back while Eli changed into dry clothing, then, lighting the lantern, she laid out a meal of cold pone and wild honey.

"It's not much, Paw, but it's nourishing." She gave him a wide grin.

Eli grinned back. "We've had less, daughter."

The rain was still coming down in sheets as Eli smoked his evening pipe. Nor had it abated when later he donned a slicker, picked up a tarpaulin and his bedroll, and prepared to leave the wagon. Serena's green eyes widened at him. "Paw, you can't sleep out there in the mud and rain. Stay in here with me. There's plenty of room."

"Honey, I won't be sleepin' in the rain and mud. I'll spread this canvas on the ground under the wagon to keep me dry and snug. I want to be near the horses in case they act up again."

A few minutes later Serena turned the lantern down and stretched out on the pallet. Her lips tilted in amusement as Eli's loud snores reached the wagon. In his tired, dreamless sleep Paw wouldn't hear the horses if they were whinnying into his ears.

Serena was on the verge of falling asleep herself when a persistent scratching on the canvas startled her. Who could it be? She crawled to the rear of the wagon, parted the long slit, and gasped in surprise. Josh Quade gazed up at her, looking much like a spoiled, mischievous youngster as he said with a drooping lower lip, "I've got nowhere to spread my blankets."

Serena's mouth twisted mockingly. "What about the pleasure wagon? You seem to always be welcomed there."

"Not always," Josh answered, an amused glint in his eyes. "Jessie is filled to the rafters tonight even underneath the wagon."

His words were followed by a sneeze and Serena relented enough to say, "I suppose you could squeeze in beside Paw."

"And listen to that racket all night?" Josh's expression hinted that she was unfeeling as the coarse rasping below grew even louder in short, unrhythmic snorts. "I'd get no sleep at all."

"Well,"—Serena began to close the opening—"I can't think of anything else."

Josh reached up and stayed her hand, asking, "Are you sure?" as he peered over her shoulder at the straw mattress.

"Are you suggesting that you sleep with me?" Serena asked incredulously, jerking her hand free.

The wagon master tilted his head and narrowed his eyes as though considering her question, then: "Naturally I'd love to sleep with you, but I'll settle with sharing your wagon."

Serena felt the angry blood rush to her face. "Don't twist my words. You know very well what I meant."

"I'm sorry." The blue eyes grew soft and beseeching. "May I please come in? Look, I've got my own blankets." A tanned hand held up a bedroll. "I didn't mean to share yours . . . unless you invited me to." The blue eyes glimmered teasingly.

"What will the others think?" Serena felt herself weakened by the soft tone.

"They'll never know. I'll be gone before anyone is awake."

"What about Paw?"

Josh smiled wryly. "Eli is in a sleep so deep it's near death. Nothin' is gonna wake him up."

Undecided, Serena watched the rain pouring down on the black head, flattening the hair. Josh nudged her hand and coaxed, "I'll catch pneumonia out here, and then what? If I die who'll look after you?"

"Oh, you're impossible." Serena sat back on her heels with a resigned sigh. "You make darn sure you stay in your own blankets."

"Yes, miss," Josh said meekly, scrambling into the wagon, flinging off the dripping slicker. "I wouldn't dream of getting into your . . . blankets."

Hah! Serena thought, sliding between the warm covers and turning her back. You wouldn't dream of it, you'd just do it if the notion took you.

She closed her eyes, wondering what she was allowing to happen. Had she became witless, letting this . . . this *rake* share her sleeping quarters? And what was he doing? Why wasn't he settling down? She raised her head and looked over her shoulder, then quickly lowered it back to the pillow. He was stripping off his clothes. She had glimpsed one long muscular thigh and calf as the wet buckskins were pulled down over a narrow foot.

"Is that necessary?" she asked coldly.

A throaty chuckle sounded very close to her ear. "Not even for you, Miss Southern Belle, will I sleep in wet bucks."

Serena said no more as she watched the masculine shadow finish its work. I'll never sleep tonight, she thought, very conscious of the warm, naked body which had finally stretched out beside her.

But bone tiredness and the deep, even breathing only inches away lulled her into dreamland, a land where Josh Quade's lips moved tenderly, coaxingly over hers. A delightful warmth simmered in her lower body, then spread upward to meet the tingling of the breasts being stroked by lean, supple fingers. She sighed softly, arched her back, and was clasped tightly against a hard male frame while a husky voice moaned her name raggedly.

The sound of her name brought Serena reeling back to consciousness. She jerked her mouth away from the demanding lips and pushed at the broad, hairy chest hovering over her. "What are you doing?"

Josh gazed down at her in the gray dawn, his eyes glazed with passion. "I'm thanking you for sharing your dry quarters," he answered huskily, "although they were reluctantly given."

While her sleep-misted mind tried to summon up a sharp retort, the warm mouth was moving on hers again in a kiss that burned its way to the very soles of her feet. And the hands that had been prepared to fight now unconsciously moved to clasp broad, smooth shoulders.

Then Josh set his whole being to intensifying the fire he had kindled within Serena, and she was hardly aware when her gown was pulled over her head and tossed aside. When a warm mouth closed over a breast and sucked urgently on the hardened nipple and a rein-callused palm ventured over her body, all rational thought became impossible. Josh pulled away from her once, and she moaned a protest. Slowly, he took her hand and guided it to his throbbing maleness.

"Look at me, Serena," he coaxed soothingly. "Explore me with your eyes and hand. Feel it grow with the desire to enter your warmth, the desperate need it has of you."

The seductive whispered words gave impetus to the sensations coursing through Serena's blood. Her fingers curled around the hard, smooth length, and with a deep-throated moan, Josh drew her back into his arms. His mouth came down and covered hers, and she stroked him in the rhythm of his tongue sliding in and out between her lips.

Josh groaned softly as he became sensitive to her touch. He then turned Serena over onto her back, gently parted her thighs, eased between them, and hung over her a moment. She heard him catch his breath sharply, then he was expertly guiding himself into her waiting moistness. Filled with the need of him, she was unprepared for the hot tearing of his turgid manhood.

Excruciating pain washed over her. "Stop it!" she cried, writhing desperately beneath him. "Please don't!"

He cupped her face, and his features strained in the gray light.

He whispered, "Serena, you're a virgin. There's no way I can make it easy for you."

"You can stop! I demand that you stop!"

Josh sighed frustratedly. "Yes, I can stop." Slowly and gently he withdrew from her and as she buried her head shamefully in the pillow, he dragged on his damp buckskins. He then knelt beside the pallet and stroked the red-blond curls that were spread on the smooth, white shoulders. "I can make it good for you if you'll give me another chance. The next time won't hurt."

"There'll be no next time! Never! Never!" The words were muffled, but the intent was clear.

"I'm very sorry for hurting you, Serena," Josh murmured, then quietly left the wagon.

He stood outside a moment, willing his blood to cool and his desire to dissipate. Serena was his first virgin. Even though their love hadn't reached fruition, he was inordinately pleased that he was the first to have her, no matter for how short a time, and that no other man had ever been there before him.

When he sighed and walked away there was a dispirited droop to his wide shoulders. The southern beauty would undoubtedly hate him now.

CHAPTER
∽ 9 ∽

IT WAS MID-OCTOBER and the wagons followed the course of the Platte, a wide and sandy river. Wood was scarce now and campfires were fed with buffalo chips.

Sentries were stationed about when the wagons were in their nightly circle, for they were now in Indian country. The emigrants faced danger from the Pawnees, Cheyennes, Arapahoes, and Sioux. So far only small bands had been sighted at a distance, watching the travelers as though gauging what power they'd have in a battle.

A day came when the fork of the Platte was reached. It was crossed with relative ease, and the wagons rolled on toward Nebraska and the immense mountains that would have to be crossed.

At present, they were some fifty miles from Laramie and the hills were becoming high and rough. The first such one faced the wagon master.

Josh Quade sat the restless stallion, his blue gaze scanning the brush-covered rise, knowing that farther on there would be mountains that would make this one seem like an anthill in comparison.

But this one looked imposing enough to make untried men a little nervous. He looked back over his shoulder when he heard the rattle of trace chains and the creak of wheels. The long, winding wagon train was almost upon him, and watching it approach he decided that it would be best not to let the drivers have time to think and become anxious.

With a wave of his hand he motioned them onward and sent Jake lunging up the steep slope. Whips popped and encouraging words were called to teams as the animals leaned into traces and labored upward. Thankfully, halfway up the climb the steepness softened to a more gentle slope, allowing the drivers to relax a bit.

Still, it took a good hour to reach the top, which was fairly level with enough room to halt the wagons. The women lost no time in setting out cold lunches and the men began to wipe down sweaty teams. The older children took turns keeping an eye on the livestock, seeing to it that they stayed together.

Serena took her plate and sat down at the base of a large rock and leaned back, more interested in relaxing than eating. Her nerves had been so taut lately, she sometimes thought they were near the breaking point. This is because of him, she thought bitterly, her eyes falling on Josh hunkered down with Jessie, hurriedly eating whatever she had given him for lunch. He stood up suddenly and stretched, and her eyes, like a magnet, were drawn to that spot several inches below his waistband. His buckskins were so tight they clearly emphasized his maleness.

Her face blushed rosily as she remembered how one rainy night she had been coaxed into caressing that manhood, and how it had grown into an astounding size. She recalled how stroking hands and hot lips had made her yearn to feel that vibrating strength inside her, the sure knowledge that only then would there be an end to the agony of her need.

Serena shivered involuntarily. She had gotten her wish, and much more, as that long, hard length had plunged inside her, making the warm blood trickle down her inner thighs and stain the blanket.

She realized suddenly with a start that her intent gaze was being returned. She looked away.

What causes those faint, dark smudges under her eyes, Josh wondered, his gaze wandering over Serena's face. She's a delicate little thing. Is this long trek proving too much for her?

He had asked himself that question before, concerned when

he saw the fatigue on her lovely face. He had tried to talk to her once since that traumatic time in her wagon, but the icy, contemptuous look she'd turned on him had frozen the words in his throat.

What had made him stop that night? he wondered. Never had he wanted, needed to possess a woman so strongly. He'd have never stopped for any other female who had built his desire to such a point of no return.

But then Serena had been a virgin. Josh's eyes softened when he remembered hearing that the breaking of the membrane that protected the core of femininity where no entrance had been made before was very painful for some women.

His lips curled self-deprecatingly. She was so delicately constructed and he was so damned big. "I hurt her all right." His slim hands clenched into fists.

He would try once more to straighten out things between them. He decided to apologize, to explain how sorry he was for hurting her. He meant it.

Serena knew immediately whose mount had stopped beside her, but she refused to open her eyes. She always lost control when that smoky blue gaze reached out to her. She continued to keep her face tilted to the sun, her long lashes touching on her cheeks. When she felt Josh's anger wrapping around her she knew a deep satisfaction and inwardly hugged the sensation gleefully.

The saddle creaked, the horse moved, then his voice said sneeringly: "Still playin' Miss Southern Belle, I see."

Serena opened her eyes, looked at the big wagon master, then turned her head from him, arrogant and withdrawn.

A nerve twitching angrily at the corner of his mouth, Josh struggled with the mad desire to yank her behind some bushes and make such love to her that those red lips would never again sneer at him.

But since that was out of the question he relied on words to crack the haughtiness imposed on the fine features.

"So, fancy lady, you're still hating yourself, huh?"

He had captured Serena's attention then, the green eyes full of astonishment. "Hate myself? Why should I do that?"

Josh's glinting eyes raked her slender curves with easy familiarity. "Because," he shot at her, "you desired a Yankee one rainy night, and wasn't woman enough to finish what you started." His steady gaze bore into her. "And because at this very moment you desire me."

The truth of the words brought the red rushing to Serena's face. She clenched her fists and opened her mouth to hotly denounce his claim, but had no chance.

"Don't deny it. I know, because the same need is eatin' at me." His gaze dropped to her breasts, where for a moment it lingered in hunger. "Oh, yes," he murmured hoarsely, "we'll get together again, and then I'll show you how good it can be."

As though hypnotized by the smooth, seductive voice, Serena could only stare up at the determined face and shake her head.

He returned her denying gaze a moment, then with a mocking smile he wheeled the stallion and called out an order to the wagons to roll.

Horses, mules, and oxen braced themselves, holding back as words of encouragement urged them downward. No whips sang out, for the way down had a sharp pitch. Dust rose, settling thick coating on everyone and everything.

Several yards ahead of the wagons Serena, along with the others who were mounted, gave Beauty the reins, letting her choose where she would place her dainty hooves. Small avalanches of earth and stone dotted the hillside while in some spots, mounts were forced to sit on their haunches and slide. Serena worried about how Paw and the team were doing.

Every morning the two beautiful animals, unaccustomed to work collars, sidestepped and reared nervously to fight the harness. They get worse instead of better, she thought with disappointment, glancing over her shoulder, trying to spot their wagon. It was useless. She couldn't distinguish one vehicle from the other through the rolling, choking dust.

She had seen, however, with much aggravation, that Josh Quade's big stallion was close behind her. Had she the room and strength to spare, she thought irritably, she'd maneuver the mare away from him. But she dared not alter Beauty's course. Drawing an arm across her sweating forehead, she turned her attention back to the mare, softly praising and encouraging her forward.

Those on horseback were finally nearing the foothills, but it was an area thickly overgrown with brush. As her mount slid and scrambled toward it, Serena eyed the ground with some concern. There could be holes hidden in that scrubby growth, easily bringing a mount to its knees with a broken leg.

But thankfully Beauty was doing splendidly, carefully picking her way. With the mount's safety in mind, Serena leaned over the mare's glossy neck to lighten her load, and to scan the ground for holes. Consequently, she was unprepared when the large stallion to the left of her gave a terrified snort and sidled, its heavy rump ramming solidly into the smaller mount. The startled animal automatically braced her forelegs, and as Serena sailed over her head she caught a blurring glance of a coiled rattlesnake.

Cries of alarm smothered Josh's anguished cry as the slender body hurtled downward, landing inert against a large rock. As his stallion danced past the crumpled form he flung himself from the saddle. His face dread-filled, he ran to kneel beside Serena and was struck by her pallid skin.

"Dear God," he whispered hoarsely, "is she dead?" He began chafing her limp wrists, anxiously calling her name. When her lids fluttered, then slowly opened, he was washed with relief. But when she looked at him without recognition he grew frantic and wildly called for help. Riders went by, unable to stop the stumbling horses. When Serena's heavy lids closed again he swept her into his arms, running and slipping on gravel as they reached the foot of the hill. Dismounting riders gathered around, firing anxious questions as he laid the injured girl in the shade of a cottonwood. He stared up at the worried faces, his eyes wild.

"Don't crowd so close, dammit! Give her air! Get me some water!"

Half a dozen canteens were shoved at him. Cradling Serena's head against his chest he grabbed the nearest one and pressed it to her lips. And though most of it spilled down her chin, some trickled down her throat. She swallowed eagerly, and he tilted the canteen again.

Landrie's wagon was the third to reach the bottom. Dark apprehension grabbed Eli when he noted the people clustered in one spot and the mare standing nearby, favoring a hind leg. He jumped from the wagon and the people fell away, giving him a clear view of Serena's limp form held in the wagon master's arms. Dropping to his knees beside them he threw Josh an anxious, questioning look.

"She's alive, Landrie," Josh quickly assured the white-faced man. "But she may be badly hurt. Let's get her into the wagon."

Eli ran to pull back the canvas flap and watched Serena being lifted up with caring gentleness. Inside the wagon Josh's eyes flickered with remembrance as he laid her down on the same spot where once they had almost made love. She moaned softly and Eli lay a hand on her forehead.

"She's burnin' hot," he muttered, then looked at his still-faced companion. "Turn around, Josh. I've got to get her clothes off and see where she's hurt."

"Check her head first, Eli. She fell hard against a rock," Josh advised, then turned to find a score of women looking up at him inquiringly. His voice rough with distress, he ordered curtly, "Go on about your business. Landrie is takin' care of her."

Indignant looks were shot at him and one woman sniffled angrily, "You'd think we ain't good enough to lay hands on Her Majesty."

Quade stared after the miffed women, hating them for the cold, harsh treatment they had shown the southern girl. "They call her a high-toned bitch for no other reason than jealousy," he muttered under his breath. "Well, it'll be a damn rare day when I ever let any of them help my Serena."

"My Serena?" Josh raked a hand through his hair, staring bewilderedly, seeing nothing. When had he started thinking along those lines? Probably from the very beginning, unaware, but in that frozen minute of agony, when he didn't know if she were dead or alive, he'd realized that he loved the obstinate, self-willed little rebel. Lusted after her, yes, but also loved her desperately.

His face became sardonic. He had about as much chance of making the lovely Serena his as he did leading the wagon train to its destination blindfolded. He was startled when Eli spoke behind him.

"Josh, go fetch Jessie." The order came hoarsely. "Serena's

got an awful bump on the back of her head. I'm afraid she's fractured her skull.''

Josh stared a moment at the ashen face then, swearing bitterly, jumped from the wagon and took off running.

In minutes Jessie was climbing into the wagon, a small carpetbag in her hand. When she ordered Eli out, he left feeling ashamed of the relief that washed over him. It had been almost more than he could bear, listening to the girl moan in pain and unable to help her.

Eli was still pale when he joined Josh hunched over a fire. The fall air chilled considerably when the sun went down and he stretched his hands to the warmth of the flames. He glanced at the strangely quiet wagon master.

"We're gettin' a lot of curious looks from the women. I expect they'll come nosin' round pretty soon, the hypocrites, makin' off as if they care how badly hurt Serena is."

"Yeah, I know," Josh answered, almost savagely. "Don't look at them; maybe they'll leave us alone."

Josh's idea seemed to work, for the women kept their distance and contented themselves with speculations. Eli filled his pipe, but before he could light it, Jessie hopped from the wagon.

"The girl has one hell of a bump on her head, and she's in a lot of pain. I'm pretty sure, though, there's nothing broke. I gave her some laudanum. That should put her out the rest of the night. I'll check on her later, though."

A warm look on his seamed face, Landrie offered his hand to the small woman. "I can never thank you enough for helpin' Serena, Jessie. If ever I can help *you*, just ask."

The sharp-tongued Jessie was left without words for a moment. Voiced appreciation to a whore was almost unheard of. She smiled and shook Eli's hand. Pulling a tough grin to her face she said, "It's time I got back to my own wagon. The girls would never think of starting supper on their own."

Josh took hold of her skinny arm. "I'll walk you to the wagon. You can never be too careful in the wilds." Jessie burst out laughing at the devilment in his eyes. His expression, however, was serious when on arriving at the pleasure wagon he gave her thin shoulder a quick squeeze and said, "Thanks, Jess. I owe you."

There was a brooding sadness in the little whore's eyes as she watched Josh turn and walk out of sight. "You've finally fallen, huh, big man?" she whispered over the tightness in her throat. The high laughter of one of her girls broke upon her, and, sighing, she turned to respond to the familiar sound. The men would start coming soon. But as she climbed into the wagon she knew that Josh would never again visit her at night.

When Quade rejoined Eli at the campfire, the man looked up, shaking his head in bemusement. "Who would have ever thought that Serena's first new lady friend would be a whore?"

"She couldn't find any better." Josh sat down beside Eli when the older man nodded in agreement. "How is she?" He motioned toward the wagon.

"Quiet. Sound asleep."

Josh and Eli sat in silence, each occupied with his own thoughts. True darkness gathered, and because neither man felt like cooking, Eli put on a pot of coffee, then dug into the hamper, pulling out the cold remains of his lunch. Ready to dig into the cold pone and brown beans, spoons were returned to tin plates at the sound of light crunching footsteps.

Nell Simpson walked toward them, a steaming kettle hanging from her hand. Eli's eyes kindled when he saw the sway of her rounded hips and the bounce of her heavy breasts, an almost forgotten tingle stirring his loins.

"Howdy, Miz Simpson." He smiled broadly, jumping to his feet. "You bringin' us bachelors somethin' to eat?"

The widow hadn't missed the glint that jumped in Eli's eyes, and though her voice was formal when she answered him, her eyes twinkled invitingly. "I know that your girl is laid up from her accident, and since I made more than enough stew for my family I thought you and Josh might like some."

"We sure would," Eli declared, taking the kettle from Nell and setting it on the ground.

"How is she doin'?"

"She's hurtin' some. Has a god-awful bump on her head."

"She's a very lucky young girl," Nell said. "She could have broken her neck in that nasty fall. At the least she might have scratched up her face in all that rock and brush."

There was no tone of humor in Eli's short laugh. "I gotta feelin' there were some who probably wished that she had."

A guilty pink flushed the widow's face, highlighting her brown eyes and brown hair. "I won't lie to you, Mr. Landrie, that some of the young ones probably felt that way, but not me and some of the older women." She paused then added with a coaxing smile, "In all fairness, though, the other young women don't have a chance with the fellows when your girl is around, Mr. Landrie."

Eli nodded. "I know what you're sayin'. Serena is right good to look at. But them girls ain't got nothin' to worry about. Serena is still gettin' over losin' her sweetheart to the war—my son, actually—and she's got no interest in any other man at the present.

"But you wanna know what really riles me?" Eli's eyes were suddenly shooting fire. "It's the way them women, from the very beginning, snubbed her and whispered behind her back because she was green to their ways, because she acts in a genteel manner. But let me tell you, just because she acts the way she was brought up doesn't mean that the girl is lazy, by God. I've seen her work harder than any slave, in the boiling sun, so that the black younguns left behind by their mothers would have some food to put in their little bellies.

"If you northern women think you had it hard durin' this damnable war"—Eli was finally winding down—"you ain't been in a southern woman's shoes."

There was a long, thick silence in which Josh and Nell Simpson indulged bitter reflections. Nell's contrite voice sounded first. "You're right, Mr. Landrie. The women shouldn't have acted like they did. But most of them feel differently now. They've seen how she's taken hold, and they'd like to be friends with her."

When Eli made no response, only grunted, the widow finished lamely, "Well, we've got a long way to go yet. I'm sure that after a while Miss Bain will forgive the ladies and accept their friendship. And now"—she smiled timidly at Eli—"I'd better get back to my younguns before they start thinkin' the Indians have grabbed me."

The two men watched with interest as the shapely form retreated. Josh grinned. "The widow Simpson wouldn't be bad in bed, I'm thinkin'." He waited a moment, then added, "That's where she wants you, you know."

Eli chuckled. "I've been givin' it some thought. But I don't know. It's been a long time since I've had me a regular woman. She's a lot younger than me and would probably want lovin' every night."

Josh lifted the lid off the steaming pot, sniffed appreciatively, then drawled, "Hell, what have you got to lose? Give it a whirl. You might find that you've got more vinegar in you than you suspect."

Eli grinned and scraped the cold beans from his plate before ladling it full of spicy-smelling stew. Sitting back down he spooned a generous amount of meat and vegetables into his mouth, chewed, swallowed, and smacked his lips.

"By God." He winked at Josh. "I'm gonna chance embarrassment. Her cookin' alone is worth hangin' round her camp. Serena can't cook worth spit, and she don't show much promise of improvin'."

A softness entered Josh's eyes. He didn't care if Serena Bain couldn't boil water. If she were his wife he wouldn't know what he was eating anyway.

CHAPTER
∽10∽

IT WAS AROUND EIGHT O'CLOCK that evening when Jessie stepped into the light of the campfire and smiled at Josh and Eli. "How's the patient?"

"She seems to be all right, Jessie." Eli stood up. "She does cry out once in a while, though."

The tiny woman nodded. "That's to be expected. She's got quite a bump on her head, not to mention a couple of bruised ribs."

She shifted her attention to Josh. "One of your scouts has a piece of news for you. He came across a fur post of sorts about three miles from here. He hasn't talked to you about it because you've been busy with Miss Bain." She hopped up on the tailgate of the wagon. "Why don't you two go look the place over? I'll stay with the girl."

Curiosity sparked Josh's ice-blue eyes. Maybe someone there could give him some information about the trail to Oregon. A couple of times the road had eluded him, the ruts filled in with sand and soil. He had gone on by instinct alone, luckily stumbling back onto the route after a few miles.

He looked at Eli questioningly and, receiving an eager nod, went in search of the scout to get directions.

The moon was full and the sky clear as Josh and Eli slowly cantered along, having no trouble spotting the two rudely constructed buildings sitting among a grove of cottonwoods at the

113

bend of a river. The high laughter of women erupted from the smaller building as the two men swung from the saddles. A knowing grin passed between them.

"There's Newcomb's nag," Eli muttered as he looped the reins around a well-used hitching rail. "You look out for that snake, Josh," he warned. "I've seen him watching you, and there's pure hate in his yaller eyes."

"I'm wise to his feelin's for me," Josh answered and led the way into the flow of traffic between the post and whorehouse.

The two brushed elbows with frontiersmen dressed much like Josh, buffalo hunters, their stench arriving long before they did, gamblers, their well-cut black suits showing up the paleness of their skin, and the big mountain men who stepped aside for no one. And mingling in this world of rough and violent men were the satin-clad whores.

A group of men from the wagon train ambled by, and Eli muttered, "I hope they don't try to brawl with this bunch of characters. Them men make my back crawl somethin' awful."

Josh grinned in sympathy. "Let's step in the post and get a slug of whiskey to stop that back crawlin' of yours."

The long, low-ceilinged room was dimly lit by suspended kerosene lamps, their flickering flames shining on the dirt floor that was thickly covered with sawdust. Ever-widening dark spots in the coarse material told tales of spilled spirits and spilled blood.

Josh and Eli made their way to a corner table. A tavern woman spotted them immediately and, picking up a tray, hurried over. The once attractive woman leaned boldly against Josh's shoulder, her thin, dirt-spotted dress gaping at the neckline.

Her heavily painted face creased in a smile as she asked coyly, "What can I do for you, big man?"

Josh, used to whores and their open, friendly ways, ran a hand up her short skirt and bantered back, "There's a lot you could do for me, lady, but right now, how about a bottle and a couple glasses?"

As the woman moved away Eli's sharp elbow nudged Josh. "Look," he said, his eyes narrowed on the figure shoving its way through the throng of men lining the bar. "There's Newcomb, and he's ugly drunk."

Josh lifted indifferent eyes to Ira's liquor-flushed face. "He is that. Maybe one of the men he's pushin' will put a bullet through his rotten heart."

Their bottle arrived then, and Newcomb was forgotten as Josh filled their glasses with the clear liquid.

The whiskey was raw, burning down their throats, bringing tears to their eyes. "God, that's awful stuff," Landrie gasped, used to the South's aged bourbon.

Josh sighed resignedly. "I expect we might as well get used to it. It's probably all we're gonna find from here on."

The second drink slid down a little smoother, and Josh was about to pour himself a third when a scuffling at the far end of the bar drew his attention. He stiffened and swore angrily. "Look over there to the right of the bar, Eli," he said softly. "That's Ninu wrestling with them two buffalo hunters. Newcomb's got her away from Jess."

Eli nodded. "Serena said that he would. Do you think he's gonna let them two manhandle her that way?"

"Hell yes. They've probably paid him to let them use her."

Landrie stared at him in disbelief. "Naw."

"You'll see," Josh answered grimly. "He's talkin' to the bartender right now, tryin' to get a room in the back."

It became apparent from the stubborn shakes of the barman's head that Ira's request was being refused.

His mood dark and dangerous, Newcomb stamped back to his table where several more men had gathered. He glanced down at Ninu, forcibly held on a man's lap while he openly fondled her. When her eyes pleaded dumbly with him, Ira slapped her across the face.

Josh swore soundlessly, helplessly. He dared not go to the girl's defense. There would be a dozen guns to face from the lust-filled men, and there were men, women, and children depending on him to get them to Oregon.

A bright glint shot into his eyes as an angry muttering began among the men. "There's trouble brewin', Eli." He leaned forward in the chair. "From those scowlin' faces, I'd say that Newcomb has told them the deal with Ninu is off."

As the two men watched intently, Ira tried to back away and

came up against a solid barrier of flesh. The wild look of a trapped animal glittered in his eyes.

"He's gonna get a knife slipped between his ribs and the squaw carried off," Eli said quietly and uneasily.

"It sure looks like it," Josh agreed. He half rose to his feet, then sat back down. From the corners of his eyes he saw the bartender reach down behind the bar and bring up an old army muzzle-loader, and for all his heavy weight, he walked around the end of the bar swiftly. The gun cocked and ready, he moved in on the group, swinging the loader slowly, its barrel covering every man.

"I got this thing loaded with lead and ten-penny nails," he snapped out. "If the whole bunch of you don't break this up I'll nail your hides to the wall."

The offenders scattered, blending with those who had gathered to watch. Ira glared at the tavern owner a moment, then his infuriated eyes reached across the room and straight into a pair of blue ones that glistened with satisfaction. Too angry to hide his hate, Ira started across the floor.

Josh jerked to his feet, his chair toppling over backwards. He stood firmly on his feet, his thumb stuck in his waistband, only a scant inch from the broad knife stuck in its sheath. A hush fell over the room, and pleased grins spread over harsh features. The big trapper would squash the little bug.

Ira came to a faltering halt when he took in the lean fingers hovering over the deadly implement. The threat left his eyes completely when Josh asked contemptuously, "Did you want to say something to me, reb?"

Newcomb was painfully aware that all eyes were upon him and that everyone knew he didn't have the courage to face the wagon master out. It seemed for a moment the Southerner would direct his violent impulses to the young squaw when she touched him on the arm and asked quiveringly, "We go now?"

Newcomb glared down at her, then to everyone's disgust he pretended to honor her request. "Another time, Yank," he blustered. "We'll have it out, have no doubt of that."

Josh smiled thinly and called after him, "In the meantime I'll keep a watch on my back."

Newcomb swaggered out into the night, the stiffening of his back the only indication he'd heard the insult hurled behind him.

Voicing their contempt for the "little coward" the patrons turned back to forgotten drinks and conversations.

"Blast the little snake!" Eli snorted with disgust. "I hoped he'd carry through his bluff so you could do him in and be through with it. He's gonna be a constant piece of trouble."

He is that, Josh thought grimly, but I want to be closer to our destination before I throw him out of the train. He smiled calmly at his companion. "Don't fret about it, Eli. I'll keep a close eye on him." Josh picked up the bottle. "Let's have one more then head back to camp."

Eli nodded and let his gaze drift over the room. His casual glance paused on a man sitting alone across from them.

Nudging Josh's arm, he whispered, "There's a gent over there eyein' you."

Josh followed his friend's jerk of the thumb. He took an instant dislike to the man who smiled and nodded his head at him. Barely concealing his annoyance, Josh made a brief scrutiny of the stranger.

He saw a tall man, almost as tall as himself, a little huskier and a few years older, with blond hair worn rather long and topped by a large-brimmed hat, and a square clean-shaven jaw.

"From his clothes and that gun strapped to his waist, I'd think he's a rancher," Eli said as Josh finished sizing up the stranger. Landrie quickly picked up his glass, swilled its contents, then sat it back down. "He's comin' over to our table."

When the rancher stopped in front of him and held out a hand, Josh stood up and, hiding his unreasonable aversion to the man, took the offered hand.

"The name is Jovan, Foster Jovan," the handsome man said as he pulled out a chair and sat down. When Josh reseated himself, he continued, "I'm told your handle is Quade, and that you're the wagon master of a train headin' Oregon way."

Josh nodded, and Foster Jovan leaned his elbows on the table and stated his business briskly. "I own a cattle ranch out that way, and I'd like to ride along with you. With the Indians warring, my chances of making it through alone aren't very good."

"They're still after the white man, then?" Josh frowned.

"Yeah, worse than ever. From here on you're gonna come up against all the western nations. The chiefs are wise to the fact that most of our soldiers have been called back east to fight in the war so the danger of being attacked by them is always present."

"Have you made the trip before?" Josh asked, lowering his eyes, concealing the hope that lay there.

"Yes, up to the Nevada–Oregon borderline. My ranch is in Nevada."

Josh waited for the man to go on, to say something enlightening about the route ahead, averse to admit to this man that he had no map, that twice already he had floundered. His sigh of relief issued slowly through his lips when Jovan spoke again.

"We'll go through Nebraska, then up the Sweetwater to the Southern Pass." Then, as an afterthought, he added, "The first fort we'll come to is Fort Kearney."

Eli slid Josh a sympathetic look. Poor fellow, he wouldn't be able to make much out of that scrap of information. Darn Serena for leaving the map behind.

Jovan pushed back his chair, ready to rise. "Well, what about it? Do I join you?"

There was no logical reason for refusing the rancher, yet it was with reluctance that Josh said, "We leave at first light, day after tomorrow."

When the rancher nodded and walked away, Josh mused out loud, "I wonder why I don't like the man?"

Eli shrugged. "It's just a natural feelin' a man gets sometimes. I didn't cotton to him much, either."

Josh tossed the glass of whiskey down his throat and stood up. "Let's go."

When Serena awakened, she knew immediately that the hour was late. It was too loud for the general early hubbub of camp when everyone was still half asleep. It sounded more like night camp, when women chatted together and the children darted about, laughing and yelling. Then yesterday's events rolled over her and she realized with a pang of guilt that she was the reason the train was still camped.

Her fingers gingerly felt the aching lump on the back of her head, then moved down to tentatively stroke the strips of cloth wound tightly around her midriff. Two bruised ribs, Jessie had said.

Jessie, Serena thought as she curved her lips ruefully, a feisty little redheaded whore, and the nicest woman she'd ever met. That Jessie was a whore made no difference to her. She had learned early in her young life that all too often women were forced into situations that were beyond their control. Hadn't she herself ended up working like a field hand so that she could eat?

Serena stared up at the ribbed, arched ceiling of the wagon. Jessie didn't act ashamed of the way she earned her living. Just last night she had talked freely about it, spouting jokes about her customers and laughing at their personal peculiarities.

There were a tense few minutes, Serena remembered, when the growing friendship between them had been threatened. Jessie had mentioned Josh, spoke of his prowess as a lover and his preferences during lovemaking. She brusquely cut Jessie off in feigned surprise.

"That one a good lover, with his rough, crude ways?"

She hadn't looked at Jessie when she tossed the scathing words into the air, but she could feel Jessie's green eyes gazing at her speculatively, and wasn't surprised when she was quietly reprimanded.

"I imagine, Serena, that you've only known southern men who were well bred and sought proper southern ladies. But you musn't compare Josh Quade to them. He's a backwoodsman, a trapper, rougher than most men. The women in his life, mostly whores and squaws, haven't known, or cared, to teach him the niceties a girl like you would expect. He may not know any flowery speeches, but he sure as hell knows how a woman's body works, I suspect much more than your southern gentlemen."

With an inward sigh, Serena reluctantly admitted to herself that Jessie was right. Josh Quade certainly knew how to make the female body sing. And regardless of what the little woman thought, she knew he could also be gentle.

She thought of Jeremy and their time together and knew there was no comparison to the fervor Josh put into his kisses and caresses. He made Jeremy look like a schoolboy. She knew now

that her love for the childhood sweetheart had been a deep
friendship that she had unfortunately mistaken for love.

But, Serena thought, just the strong physical attraction between us doesn't necessarily mean that we share anything that
has to do with love. No, I must stay as far away from him as
possible. I must be cool and aloof. I will not be known as one
of Josh Quade's women.

Foster Jovan arrived at the campsite shortly after noon, his sturdy,
well-equipped wagon pulled by a pair of black mules. With a
heavy thread of insolence in his voice, he demanded of a stoop-
shouldered farmer, "Where's the wagon master?"

The angular man finished greasing an axle then squinted up
at the stranger. He shifted a cud of tobacco in his mouth, then
aimed a stream of brown juice at a bee buzzing around his mule's
rump. He grunted, "I dunno."

When Jovan came across Landrie chatting with a full-bodied
woman, his patience was all but gone. "Where in the hell is
Quade?" His thunderous question startled the pair.

Eli's back stiffened, and when he turned around and looked
at the rancher, anger shimmered in his eyes. "He's off scoutin'.
He left me in charge. What can I do for you?"

"You can tell me where to pull in for the night, for one thing."
He spit the words impatiently. "I assume I'll be the lead wagon
when we pull out tomorrow morning."

"Well, mister, you're assumin' too much. Josh is placin' you
midway in the train to begin with. We reverse places every day
except for the pleasure wagon and anybody who's travelin' with
livestock."

"But I've been over the trail before," Jovan, red-faced, argued hotly. "I can take the train straight through."

Remembering Josh's aversion to the stranger, and more heartily disliking the man himself, Eli answered staunchly, "So can
Josh. You're just gonna have to eat dust with the rest of us."

Nell Simpson giggled and Eli chuckled as Jovan laid the whip
to his mules and sped away.

As the sun rose higher, the air in the wagon grew warmer, and
Serena was beginning to feel cramped in the narrow confines.

Jessie had broken the monotony by bringing her bowls of venison broth. And though the tasty concoctions helped her to grow stronger, the energy it produced made her restless and yearn to be outside in the fresh air.

She was debating about leaving the wagon when the other women suddenly began stopping by. All were friendly and inquired about her health and brought her gifts of homemade jellies or jams. One woman went as far as to proudly hand Serena a small sachet of dried flowers.

Serena was courteous to the women's friendly overtures, but she still held herself slightly aloof. She remembered their previous behavior toward her, so she would wait and watch.

When it appeared there would be no more visitors, Serena stretched her cramped muscles and sighed. She was bored, and now the wagon was positively stifling.

She eased herself up, sat a moment, then impulsively reached for her pale blue poplin robe. Careful of her bandaged ribs, she eased her arms into the sleeves, wrapped the garment around her tiny waist, and tied it securely. With the aid of the spring-seat she pulled herself up, calling Eli's name.

Landrie's eyes lit up when he saw Serena standing, but there was concern in his voice when he asked, "Do you think you should be on your feet so early, honey?"

"Paw, my head doesn't hurt much anymore, and if I don't get some fresh air pretty soon, I think I'll faint."

"Well now, we don't want that, do we?" Eli grinned. "Let me help you down." He took her arm and helped her climb carefully down the tall wheel spokes. "I've got us a fine supper," he told her. "Beans that have been cookin' over a low fire all day, and crispy fried prairie hen."

"It sounds delicious." Serena smiled up at Eli as he eased her down on a blanket spread in front of a saddle for her to lean on.

The meal was consumed rapidly and with relish. When Serena finally leaned back with a comfortable, satisfied sigh, Eli handed her a cup of coffee. While sipping the strong, hot brew she suddenly became aware she was being watched. Her face clouded indignantly. It was Josh Quade, of course. His blue gaze was always piercing her.

Eli laid a chunk of pine on the fire and flames licked hungrily at the rings of pitch. Serena stared into the blaze, determined not to look over her shoulder. But the warm spot on the back of her neck grew warmer, and despite her intention, she turned her head and surprisingly gazed into the handsome face of Foster Jovan.

When the rancher first spotted Serena sitting before the fire, he mused that he had never seen a more beautiful woman. As he watched her, there grew inside him the determination to make her his wife. What a gem she would be, placed in the setting of his ranch.

When she glanced at him, he rose and walked toward her fire. Eli watched Jovan's approach through narrowed eyes and drew in his lips. He still rankled from his earlier confrontation with this high-handed rancher. When Jovan's booted feet stopped outside the circle of the campfire, Eli mumbled a short greeting. When Eli continued to puff on the pipe clamped between his teeth, Jovan ignored the action that said plainly to move on, and asked jovially: "Aren't you going to introduce me to your daughter, Landrie?"

Eli puffed silently. Then Serena stirred uneasily, and, taking the pipe from his mouth, Eli spat into the fire then muttered grudgingly, "Serena, this is Foster Jovan. He joined us today."

His white teeth flashing in a wide smile, Jovan bent over Serena and took her offered hand politely and formally. His eyes gleamed softly as if to tell her that she was beautiful, desirable. Then he said smoothly, "I am very happy to meet you, Miss Landrie."

"Miss Bain," Serena corrected, returning the smile. When he raised an eyebrow she explained her relationship to Eli briefly. Then, attracted to Jovan's good looks and hungry to converse with a gentleman again, she ignored Eli's scowl and invited the new man to join them.

When Jovan had taken a seat beside her, Serena poured and passed him a cup of coffee, hiding a smile of amusement when he managed to brush her hand with his. "Why are you going west, Mr. Jovan?"

Jovan's teeth gleamed again. "I'm not *going* west, Miss Bain. I'm *returning* west. I left New Orleans about four years ago to fulfill a dream, a dream to become a cattle rancher. Business took me back to my home state about a month ago.''

Serena sat forward eagerly. "And did you establish your dream, Mr. Jovan?''

The rancher's handsome face glowed. "I certainly did. I don't want to brag, but I believe I have the biggest spread in all the West.''

Raising a fine arched eyebrow, her eyes bright with merriment, Serena teased, "Oh? My brother has a ranch in Oregon Territory.''

Jovan's eyes widened in surprise. "Whereabouts in Oregon?''

"Somewhere around Baker.''

"Baker, that's where the Oregon trail ends, I believe. My place is in Nevada, near the territory border.''

"Are we neighbors, then?''

"Distant ones. About fifty miles apart. But you won't find any much closer," he added.

Eli removed the pipe from his lips, knocked the bowl out, and quickly joined the conversation. "Serena's brother thinks that ranchin' is the thing to get into. What's your opinion?''

"A man couldn't get into anything better," Jovan answered promptly. "When the war is over there's gonna be a loud cry for beef. The cattle roaming free on the range have multiplied like rabbits for several years. There are hundreds of thousands in the West right now. They're wild as hell, but the man strong enough to round them up will have his fortune made in a short time.''

"The people livin' there, what are they like?''

Jovan thought a moment before saying, "Well, with minor variations, they're a tough bunch. There's a good number of convicts, a lot of army deserters, hunters and trappers. The majority are ambitious, willing to go any length to get what they want." He paused to drain his cup. "There's no law in the West, only the gun in a man's holster.''

"What about women?" Serena wanted to know. "Are there many?''

Jovan's expression held a note of contempt as he said, "Not unless you count the squaws. You trip over them every time you turn around." His lips curled. "A lot of the men have given them the name *wife*. But of course that will change when decent white women begin arriving.''

He ignored Eli's sour grunt and continued: ''There are a few white wives on the ranches, but they live so far out a person doesn't see them very often. The decent women stay home mostly.''

Serena ducked her head to hide her amusement. This man had strong opinions about women. What would he make of her friendship with Jessie? she wondered.

The rancher continued to charm Serena by spinning his entertaining descriptions of the West. When she finally looked around the campsite and discovered that most of the fires were reduced to glowing embers, she couldn't believe that the time passed so quickly. She suppressed a giggle when Eli yawned loudly and pointedly. Mr. Jovan had better take the hint, otherwise Paw would tell him straight out to leave. She hadn't missed the fact that her friend didn't particularly like the new man.

The twinkle suddenly disappeared from Serena's eyes. The wagon master was making his nightly check of camp and Jessie walked alongside him. The pair conversed in hushed tones as they moved from wagon to wagon, occasionally laughing softly.

Had the two of them just left the pleasure wagon? she wondered. As she pictured Jessie's arms clasped around Josh's broad, bare shoulders an empty feeling filled the pit of her stomach.

She jerked sharply when Jovan spoke with unmistakable animosity in his voice. ''I wouldn't have figured Quade for a whoremonger. I've seen his type before. Usually they can get any woman they want.''

Serena's back stiffened, and she surprised herself by saying curtly, ''He hasn't necessarily been in bed with the woman. The whores are a part of the train. He has to look after them also.''

Eli gave Serena a startled glance. Was she defending the wagon master? A glint of devilish amusement crept into his eyes. He would test her a little further.

''I don't know about that, Serena,'' he said. ''There's a dozen men who look after Jessie and her girls' welfare.''

He was pleased with the heated look she threw at him. Foster Jovan was not similarly pleased at her defense of Quade. Was she involved with the wagon master? He frowned darkly. The thought that his eventual ownership of the beautiful woman might be threatened caused an active hostility to root inside him. When the strolling pair halted in front of the Landrie fire, he purposefully scooted closer to Serena.

The firelight reflected the amused twinkle in Josh's eyes as he drawled, "Well, Jovan, I see you're gettin' acquainted with some of your neighbors."

"That's right." Jovan squinted up at him.

Josh's gaze focused on the rancher's scowling face a moment longer then moved to Serena. Her hands closed over a stout stick as she was gripped by a sudden desire to strike out at the handsome face as the blue eyes slid over her body with a lazy, knowing look. Just when she thought she could restrain herself no longer, Josh took Jessie's arm and walked on, disappearing into the darkness.

"He and I are gonna tangle before this trip is over," Jovan growled to himself.

After a hard stare at Eli, who was unrolling his blankets near the dead fire, Jovan picked up Serena's hand and brought it to his lips. "I hope we'll be able to spend much time together, Miss Bain," he said softly. "I'd like to get to know you better."

She smiled up at him. "I'm sure we will, Mr. Jovan." She watched him walk away, then moved toward the wagon.

"He and Quade certainly didn't take to each other, did they?" She removed her mocassins and slid between her blankets.

"That often happens between two big men," Eli answered sleepily. "They're like two fightin' roosters, each determined to be top cock."

It would be interesting to see who won, Serena acknowledged, then closed her eyes to allow sleep to steal over her, softly, like a caress.

CHAPTER
∞11∞

JOSH URGED THE STALLION into a long lope, heading toward his group of outriders. These were mature young men, carefully chosen for their trustworthiness to keep an eagle eye out for Indians. He gave his orders to the serious-faced riders, then watched them ride away. Josh hoped that when they returned they'd have nothing to report other than a shortage of grass or a high river crossing.

Later, while riding at the head of the long train, Josh congratulated himself on how well everything had gone so far, discounting the ousting of the Hansen family and Serena's tumble down the mountain. He looked out across the prairie. There was tall grass for the stock, streams providing water, and plenty of small game.

His eyes grew sober. Only one ripple marred his smooth waters, Foster Jovan. The man had set his sights on Serena Bain, and it appeared she was responding to him. Josh's lean fingers tightened on the reins. Women were so thick-headed sometimes. A handsome face, polished manners, and smooth compliments left them blinded.

And dammit, although he had told himself countless times to forget the little beauty, she still invaded his mind and disturbed his sleep. Even a distant sight of her would send his blood pounding. He could only hope that once the trip was over and he had returned north, each mile put between them would reduce the frequency of his thoughts of her.

A sudden movement on the skyline drove Serena from Josh's mind. His face became grim and tight-lipped as he spotted his first band of warring Indians. The sun, glancing off their naked bronze bodies, showed in relief the feathers stuck in their hair, the sign they were out for blood. He had no doubt that had he been close enough to see, he would have viewed faces smeared with red paint.

He swiftly counted twenty riders. What tribe? he wondered, then gave a self-deriding snort. "What difference, fool?" he muttered. "They're all after the paleface these days."

He reined the stallion off the dusty track and pulled him in. As each driver or rider moved past him they were informed that Indians were in the area. "But don't be afraid," he added when he saw the startled faces of the women and children. "There are too few of them to attack us. If you happen to see them, ignore them and don't let them see that you're afraid."

The remainder of the day was nerve-racking. Josh wondered if his assumption had been correct. What if the Indians he had seen were only scouts waiting to signal a camp of thousands? His eyes drifted to the distant line of bronze bodies keeping pace with the wagon, casting a feeling of doom on the emigrants.

Josh insisted that routines not be broken, for to do so might alert those who followed them. When lunch break was called, however, it was hurriedly eaten as the sun-bronzed men stoically watched them from a quarter of a mile away.

It wasn't until dusk, when the wagons were being maneuvered into the usual circle, that the Indians whirled their mounts and raced toward the setting sun, and out of sight. While everyone heaved sighs of relief, Josh wasn't so sure that his people had seen the last of them. Tonight he would double the night sentries and have draft animals and mounts tethered closer in, ready to be brought inside the circle if necessary.

The interior of the large circle resembled a small settlement, Serena thought, complete with individual fires crackling and the aroma of cooking filling the air. And the children, confined to wagons all day, now ripped, roared, and stumbled into everyone's way. But no one minded, she noticed. The youngsters' spontaneous cries of laughter lent a sense of the commonplace and stability to the travelers' lives.

Kneeling in front of her own fire, heating a pan of beans and turning long strips of salt pork in a blackened skillet, Serena glanced up at the musical sound of jangling spurs. Foster Jovan was coming toward her, a small covered pot swinging from his hand. His face cheerful, he asked, "Any chance of sharing your fire? I've brought my own grub."

Serena returned the rancher's smile then joked, "Pull up a piece of sod and sit down. We're about ready to eat."

Back at the end of the wagon, an irritated scowl on his face, Eli slapped the lid on the tar bucket. If Jovan thinks he's going to make a habit of taking his evening meal with me and Serena, he thought angrily, I'll tell the man straight out that he isn't welcome. He disliked Jovan becoming too familiar with Serena. When she called him to supper, he barely acknowledged Jovan's genial greeting.

Nor did Eli talk during the meal, but sat stiffly as conversation flowed smoothly between the couple sitting across from him. As soon as the meal was eaten, and one cup of coffee each was drunk, he stood up and muttered darkly, "Let's get over to the council fire, Jovan."

Jovan squinted at the older man, a frown gathering between his eyes. "You go on," he said gruffly. "I'll be along shortly."

Serena watched Eli's lips set in a stubborn line. She knew, even if Jovan didn't, that Paw had no intention of leaving without his unwelcome guest. After a few tense minutes Jovan realized that he would not be left alone with the little lady tonight. With a smile that belied the anger boiling within him, he rose and bid Serena a reluctant good-night. As he stalked along behind Landrie, he muttered inwardly, "You old swamp rat, you won't stand between me and Serena."

Serena was left to stare into the fire, watching it snap and spark. Night sounds surrounded her, the twittering and rustling of grouse settling in for the night, while away in the distance an owl hooted dismally. She jumped when a pack of coyotes commenced a string of staccato cries, and she sat closer to the fire. Her gaze lifted to nervously probe the shadows that were lurking closer and closer to the wagon.

Were those really coyote cries, she worried, or was it Indians signaling to each other? Foster had mentioned once that the Indians were masters at imitating birds and animals. Was the enemy out there in the dark somewhere, waiting until the camp slept so they could creep in and kill them all?

She raked her gaze over the women sitting closest to her and noted that they also hugged their fires, tense and watchful, talking to each other in hushed voices. Even the children were less rowdy in their play, making sure that mothers were always in sight.

The tense lines in Serena's face eased a bit when Jessie walked into the light of her campfire. "It's kinda spooky around here, huh?" the little woman remarked, helping herself to a cup of coffee before sitting down beside the younger girl.

"I'm a bundle of nerves," Serena admitted. "Do you think we'll be attacked?"

"I don't know." Jessie shook her head. "I've never had much experience with Indians. The ones in Michigan were more or less friendly."

Jessie sipped the hot coffee appreciatively, remarking on its good flavor. "None of my girls can make a pot worth drinkin'," she complained. "I'm amazed sometimes that the men keep showin' up."

Serena's eyes twinkled. "I expect they're better at something else."

"Hah!" Jessie snorted. "They are if they want to be. It's irking the ungrateful wretches that they're not making any money for their favors. I'd be out of business if there was another pleasure wagon around." She reached down and, scratching the hound's ears, said, "I was sorry to lose Ninu. She's one of those rare women who enjoys the work. She handled twice the men the other girls did.

"That bastard, Newcomb, knew that too. That's the main reason he was so hot to take her away from me. It's too bad." She sighed. "The girl won't last long under the conditions he'll set up. She won't get proper rest or decent food."

Serena rose, then blinked when Jessie asked abruptly, "What about your love life, honey? I see the handsome rancher makin' eyes at you. Has he made any moves toward gettin' you in his blankets? He certainly hasn't been around the pleasure wagon.''

Serena's first instinct was to tell her friend that her love life was her own personal business. But she remembered that bluntness was Jessie's way, and her lips curved humorously. "Foster is a slow mover, Jessie. We haven't got past the hand-holding stage yet. It's even made me wonder if Foster isn't one of those gentlemen who thinks that a wife doesn't enjoy lovemaking, that she only tolerates it.''

Jessie's small body bristled. "I wouldn't give you that," she snapped her finger and thumb, "for a hundred gentlemen. They are so ignorant about women. Give me a passionate man like Josh Quade any time.'' She swiftly finished the last of her coffee and stood up. With gentle teasing yet dead seriousness on her elfin face, she said, "Look, honey, if Jovan should change his mind about blanket sharin', I've got this concoction you drink every time you . . .'' She shrugged. "You know what I mean.''

Serena felt a warmth rush to her face, while her mind fumbled for an answer to this unpredictable woman's remark. Jessie, embarrassed for the blushing southern lady, simply smiled goodnight and walked away.

Foster Jovan, having purposely left his grub pail at the Landrie campfire in order to see Serena again, arrived there in time to see Jessie's flashy green dress disappear around the corner of the wagon. Dark disapproval settled over his features, and his distaste was heavy in his voice when he spoke.

"Serena, I don't like you in the company of that woman.''

Serena's welcoming smile faded and was replaced with a grimace of irked impatience. "That *woman*, Foster," she said coolly, "is a friend of mine. I like her and I'm going to continue our friendship.''

"But she's a whore, Serena. A lady doesn't associate with her sort.''

Serena arched a fine eyebrow at Jovan and, scooting away from him when he sat down beside her, snapped, "Who says I'm a lady?''

"Don't talk foolish, Serena. A man has only to look at you and know that you're gently bred.''

"You can't tell a lady by looking." Serena's eyes flashed dangerously. "You have to know the woman. Jessie is more lady than ninety percent of the women in this train. She is kind, generous, and considerate. And, she's honest. She doesn't try to hide the fact that the men she sleeps with pay her for that privilege. Would you care to lay odds on how many of your so-called ladies sneak and lay with men other than their husbands?"

Jovan glanced around nervously. Seeing the curious eyes turned toward Serena's raised voice, he scooted up next to her. Picking up her hand and stroking it, he soothed softly, "I'm sure you're right, Serena, I just never thought of it in that light before."

Serena shrugged to calm herself. "I didn't mean to preach, Foster," she said finally.

Jovan's lips twisted into a smile that didn't quite reach his eyes. There was much he'd have to teach this willful young woman, he told himself, and once she was his, breaking off her friendship with the whore was number-one priority. No wife of Foster Jovan's was going to hobnob with that kind of trash.

No hint of his thoughts showed on the rancher's face as he brought Serena's hand to his lips. "I'll have to treat Jessie better from now on. Whoever is a friend to my girl is a friend of mine, also."

His *girl*? Serena drew her hand away. Wasn't Foster being a little presumptuous? He was arrogant enough to assume she would welcome his romantic advances.

She studied the attractive features of the man beside her and mused that Foster had made the past month pass more pleasantly. Flirting with the man had somewhat taken her mind off that other, insufferable man.

"I'll appreciate it, Foster, if you become a friend to Jessie," she said softly and raised her face, inviting his first kiss.

A crunching of footsteps startled the pair apart just as their lips were about to touch. Serena, her face flushing guiltily, managed a strained smile at the two men glaring down at her. Jovan, however, was completely at ease as he looked mockingly at the wagon master. "You men shouldn't sneak up on a man when he's courting his girl."

Eli grunted, and Josh's eyes questioned Serena for confirmation of Jovan's claim. But she was unable to meet his gaze and dropped her eyes, making no response. He studied her bent head a moment, a muscle in his cheek twitching angrily. Then, his blue eyes dimming flatly, he wordlessly turned and walked away.

Eli gave Serena a mean, hard look, then, muttering darkly, he too spun on his heel and hurried after his friend.

Jovan sensed from Serena's stiffly held body that she was suddenly unhappy. He tried to strike up a conversation, but when she only answered him in curt monosyllables, he wished her good-night and left for his wagon. He would claim his kiss when she was more disposed to give it.

He was no sooner out of sight when thoughts of the threat that lurked just outside their camp came rushing back to Serena. They were out there, she knew, watching and waiting. And God, it was awful, not being able to see them.

She pulled her knees up and clasped her arms around them. She couldn't keep her eyes from straying to Nell Simpson's wagon. Was Paw there? He had become quite chummy with the widow lady lately.

When it appeared that she was the only one in camp other than the sentries still awake, Serena rose and extinguished the fire by kicking dirt over it. Then, bidding the hound to jump into the wagon, she scrambled in behind him. She pulled the blanket up around her ears, and the old coon dog scratched and turned, making himself comfortable. Good old fellow. She smiled wanly. He hadn't deserted her. And no Indian would get past him.

Serena knew that she hadn't been asleep for long when the first volley of shots rang out. Her heart hammering, she lay stiff and still, gripped in a paralysis of fear. The hound leapt from the wagon and stood outside, barking furiously, while all around sounded the frightened cries of children, whinnying horses, and bawling cattle and oxen.

"Oh, Paw, where are you?" she whimpered. "Do be careful out there." And Josh, she worried, he'd be in the middle of the fighting. . . . No, he'd be leading it, his beautiful body exposed for the first bullet fired.

She was seeing him in her mind's eye, lying on the ground, a bullet lodged in his heart, when suddenly, above the ear-splitting sound of shots and yells, his rich, strong voice rang out.

"Women and children! Get inside your wagons and lie on the floor."

A semblance of calm came to Serena at the comforting sound of his voice, giving her the courage to lift a corner of the canvas and peer outside. Her heart fluttered wildly as she saw dim forms darting about, and guns and rifles flashing fire. In the soft light she glimpsed several figures sprawled on the ground but could not distinguish whether they were red or white.

When the booming of guns increased and several yells of pain sliced through the din, Serena dropped the heavy cloth and lay back down. Her body wet with cold sweat, she prayed, "Please, God, let our men keep the savages away, and please look after Paw and Josh."

Long tense minutes followed, filled with the constant crackling of firearms. Serena was ready to join her cries with those of the children when silence abruptly claimed the air. She waited a full minute before easing up on her knees and lifting the canvas again. A wild scream of terror rose in her throat when she looked into a face that was level with her own. Then a roughly handsome face smiled reassuringly at her while she fought the wild desire to throw her arms around Josh's neck.

"Oh, Josh, I was so frightened," she sobbed, silently willing him to climb into the wagon and take her in his arms. She wasn't surprised when he didn't. Then she remembered that she couldn't expect such an action from him after what he and Paw had interrupted earlier in the evening, especially after the remark Foster had made.

Still, she was sure she caught a momentary flash of tender concern in his eyes as he said quietly, "You'll be all right now. They've all gone."

"Was anyone hurt? Killed?" she asked fearfully. "Paw? Is he all right?"

Josh looked down, hiding his pleased surprise. Strange, she hadn't asked about Jovan. His voice was warmer as he assured Serena that Eli was fine. "One of our men from Michigan caught an arrow in the shoulder, and a couple of men were

winged by bullets. I guess half the cattle are gone, spooked or
driven off.''

''What about the Indians?''

''Six dead, a lot wounded. I don't think we'll be bothered by
that tribe again.'' While Serena listened closely, he went on,
''We were being tested tonight. The chief knows now that we're
too strong for his braves.''

Silence lingered while Serena sought for a topic that would
hold Josh there, keep him talking to her. She could think of
nothing. It was as though her mind had gone blank. Finally, she
could only whisper ''Good-night,'' and she sank back on her
pallet. She listened to Josh's footsteps fade away, thinking how
humiliating it was to dislike a man and still ache for his lovemaking.

She was still puzzling over her rebelling body when Jovan
peeked into her wagon. When the hound growled warningly, and
she pretended to be asleep, he went away. Not only did she not
wish to talk to him, Paw would be upset if he should find the
rancher at her wagon at such a late hour.

Sleep finally nudged Serena, but she pushed it back. Paw
Landrie hadn't returned to their wagon yet. The camp grew quiet
once more and still Eli didn't return. Damn Foster Jovan and his
big mouth, she thought dejectedly as she curled into a ball and,
wet-eyed, fell asleep.

Seated beside the council fire, Josh and Eli discussed in low
voices whether or not the Indians would make another raid on
the train.

''Are you up to splitting the rest of the night with me?''
Josh tossed some buffalo chips on the fire. ''You could have
the first watch, be able to get a couple hours sleep before we
head out.''

''Sure.'' Eli puffed on his pipe.

Josh was the first to break the silence. ''About what we saw
tonight, Paw—the kiss between Serena and Jovan, and him saying she's his girl, do you think it's true?''

''I sure as hell hope not.'' Eli tapped out his pipe and stuck
it in a shirt pocket. Sliding Josh a pensive look, he said, ''She's
a stubborn little cuss with a vengeful streak inside. If she got it

in her head that makin' up to Jovan might jab it to another man, she's capable of a good pretense."

Josh smiled in the darkness. "If that's the case, it would be funny if her actin' backfired on her, wouldn't it?"

"Sure would." Eli smiled also. "Providin', of course, that was the case."

Josh's elation ebbed away as he sought his blankets. He stared up at the star-filled sky. Was that a cloud, he wondered, or just the darkness of gloom?

CHAPTER
∽12∽

A WEEK AFTER the wagon train entered Nebraska, Fort Laramie was sighted, the first real fort along the rutted way. It stood on a high slope, looking down on the tepee village of a Sioux tribe. It was constructed of adobe, its roof topped with spiked posts.

Josh lifted his gaze beyond the large building to the Black Hills, dark with cedar and pine, then farther on to the rise of Laramie Peak. After a few minutes of gazing in awe, he dropped his eyes back to the village, wondering about the Indians.

His chest lifted as he quietly sighed. Since leaving Independence the train had covered nearly six hundred miles, and probably another twelve hundred or so lay ahead.

His eyes then followed the Platte as far as he could see it. When he and his travelers left the fort they would travel close to the stream. According to Jovan, farther on the river would turn and run through Colorado, leaving them to follow the Sweetwater then.

The wagons rolled to a jangling, creaking halt about a quarter of a mile from the fort. Relieved smiles lit everyone's faces, especially the women's. The constant bouncing on a hard wagon seat under a boiling sun was beginning to take its toll.

Eli jumped to the ground and darted Serena a tentative smile as she swung from the saddle. "Josh tells me that we're gonna be restin' here a couple of days," he said. "I don't expect you'll mind that."

Serena returned the hesitant curve of his lips and assured him that she didn't mind in the least. "I think I'm becoming bowlegged, sitting in a saddle so much."

As she reached under Beauty's belly to uncinch the saddle, Eli said hurriedly, "Serena, I'd like to borrow the mare for a while. Me and Josh are gonna ride into the fort to inquire where we can camp. I don't want to bother saddlin' one of the horses."

Serena quickly nodded her assent, and a few minutes later she smiled happily as she watched Eli and Josh ride off at a canter. Paw hadn't been so pleasant to her in quite some time. His manner had been cool and reserved ever since the night he saw Foster trying to kiss her.

They had quarreled over Josh, Paw claiming that Josh was his friend and that she never made him welcome at their fire. The dread of losing the affection of a dear friend had made her eventually relent. "Invite him, Paw, I'll treat the man as civil as I can," she offered.

Josh had stopped by their fire a few times after that, but had stayed only a short time. The air around the campfire had been tense with the hostility flowing between him and Jovan. And from Josh's cool, aloof attitude toward her, it was plain to Serena that he only came there to please Paw.

The time had lengthened between each visit; finally they ceased altogether. Paw had blamed her and had begun visiting either Josh or the widow during the evening. And she, too proud to tell him of the fears and loneliness that claimed her after dark, had only the hound to keep her company and calm her jittery nerves. For, unknown to Paw, she had pointed out to Foster that it wouldn't seem fitting for him to visit her when Paw was away. It had been a weak excuse she knew, but if Foster was offended, he didn't show it. And amusingly, she had felt piqued at his acceptance of her dictate.

At any rate, night after night she had sat alone in the small circle of light cast by her fire and let her imagination fly. Her overactive mind suggested that Indians slinked through the tall grass and lurked behind each boulder, just waiting to grab her.

A hand fell on Serena's arm and she started. "You sure was woolgatherin', Miss Bain." An emigrant laughed. "I just wanted to ask if you know about startin' camp. My younguns are gettin' hungry.''

"Paw and Quade should be returning any—" Serena began, then broke off as the two men came loping up the slight incline toward them. She and the woman joined the group that gathered around when the pair reined in.

"We can't camp on the military grounds," Josh said promptly. "But there's a small settlement within sight of the fort, specially erected for the benefit of wagon trains and their people." A cheer went up, and Josh lifted a hand for quiet. "I must tell you that it's a rowdy place, consisting mostly of saloons and gamblin' dens. One of the officers warned me that the owners of these establishments take advantage of people passin' through, so be on the alert.

"We'll be here a couple days, so do all the things you've been puttin' off. There's a blacksmith shop where you can get necessary repairs made on your wagons, and there's a post office of sorts if you want to send out some letters. You'll also find some newspapers—I don't know how old they are—if you're interested in how the war is goin'.''

Pleasant smiles lit the faces of most of the women. A post office, a piece of civilization. Messages to loved ones left behind could be sent out. As for war news, most were happy to forgo all knowledge of it.

When some twenty minutes later the wagons rolled into the rough settlement, Serena's high spirits began to sag. Never had she seen such squalor as in this place of sparsely scattered buildings, structures rudely constructed, warped and weatherbeaten, the majority with no windows. The single street, inches deep in dust, wound around with no semblance of order. As the train rolled through mushrooming dust a miscellaneous group of men and women assembled outside the taverns and dens to watch the emigrants pass.

"They're a frowsy, disreputable-looking bunch," Serena said softly to Eli, her gaze lingering on the women, blunt-spoken and hard-edged creatures. Most were not thirty yet, she judged, but already old and gaunt-looking.

Beauty became nervous as the crowd edged further into the street and sidled along, drawing attention to Serena. Muttered insults from the street whores reached her, but it was the wolfish grins of the men that made her flesh crawl. She was relieved when suddenly Josh was riding beside her.

Finally the settlement was left behind and a stand of trees was reached. As drivers pulled out of line and halted where they pleased, broad smiles lit their faces. For the next two days there would be no seesawing back and forth, forming the usual circle.

Eli unhitched the team and Serena unsaddled the mare, then together they walked the animals to a clear-running stream where teams and mounts were already slaking their thirst. On their way back, Josh passed them, his great stallion snorting fire at any other that came too close. Eli spoke a pleasantry to him, but Serena only nodded coolly. Eli shot her an irritated look but held his tongue.

His voice was curt, however, when he said, "I'll go hunt up some wood for the fire."

Serena watched him walk away and sighed. She had upset Paw again. She sat down in the grass and stretched out her legs and thought about how she regretted the widening discord between her and the man who was her closest friend.

While she worried her mind with what to do about her perplexing problem, the familiar noise of camp settled around her. As she shifted into a comfortable position against the protective shade of a tree, her tense body finally relaxed and she dozed.

Once again, Josh Quade entered her dreams. His fingers caressed her throat, moved up her cheek, then tickled her nose. She caught his hand, to bring it to her tingling breasts, and a soft chuckle brought her eyes flying open.

She gazed into the smiling face of Foster Jovan.

Disappointment surged through Serena. Then some impish devil made her lie quietly, to let Jovan see the desire she knew still lingered in her eyes. If he could see that she was a woman of flesh and blood, passionate, and eager for his caress, maybe he'd respond in like manner, hopefully putting an end to the unwanted thoughts of Josh Quade.

Seconds ticked by and Serena grew uncomfortable. She knew that Foster was aware of the intense urgency beaming through her eyes, but not even a flick of an eyebrow betrayed his innermost thoughts.

Jovan broke the awkward silence at last by sitting back on his heels and reaching behind him. "Look what I bagged for your supper." He held up a brace of sage hens.

Serena first felt humiliation at Jovan's rejection, then hot anger. What kind of man was he? What flowed through his veins— ice water instead of red blood? Josh Quade would have devoured her, had her eyes given him such an invitation.

That's the difference in the two men, she told herself sternly, rising gracefully to her feet. Foster is a gentleman and would never take advantage of a vulnerable moment, while that other one . . . he would watch like an eagle and, like that predatory bird, waste not a second in claiming his prey.

"Thank you, Foster," she said, forcing a smile to her lips.

Jovan smiled back and rose beside her. "I'll go clean them for you."

Eli returned in time to see the frustration and annoyance on Serena's face, and hid a tickled grin. Daughter might have convinced herself that Jovan was all a woman could desire, but wait until the day she discovered that a real man would not feel fulfilled himself if his woman had not delighted in full satisfaction as well. She would realize then that she needed a man who would leave all that high-handed, gentlemanly behavior outside the bedroom door.

Dumping the armful of wood onto the ground, he hoped fervently that this lovely, passionate girl would learn in time that Foster Jovan was incapable of truly sharing himself—before she heard the rumors that he fancied more the young Indian lads that lived on his ranch.

The sun had dipped over the horizon and it was dark when fires were built and burned bright. Merry laughter and jovial voices were a comforting and calming sound as suppers were cooked and the day's events discussed. For later there would be a store for the women to wander through, and a tavern where the men could clear the trail dust from their throats. Even a stroll through that outlandish place called a settlement would be a welcome respite from the monotony of rolling through endless miles of wilderness.

The festive atmosphere had touched Serena also. She sat relaxed, lazily contemplating the contented look on Eli's face as he tended the spitted chickens slowly roasting over the fire. He has become a changed man, she thought, and he looks at least ten years younger. How much did Nell Simpson have to do with it? she mused. Could there be a marriage between the pair? And if so, how would she feel about it? She had looked upon Paw as her own for a long time.

If I ever do resent Nell, I'll never let it show, she promised herself silently. Paw has been without a wife since Jeremy was a little boy, and it would be good for him to have a woman in his life again. But he will have his hands full, taking on a ready-made family, making them a home, providing for them. Still, these same children could help lighten the grief of losing Jeremy.

An hour later, when supper had been eaten and Eli was having a pipe, he glanced at Serena staring into the fire and asked, "Wanna take a walk over to that hellhole after a while?"

Serena looked at him and grinned. "I was afraid you weren't going to ask me."

"Well, I couldn't let you go alone, now could I?" His eyes twinkled mischievously. "Nor with Jovan, for that matter. A young woman has to be careful of her reputation."

Serena shot him a surprised look. "My being alone with Foster hasn't bothered you before. What about all the times you went off and left us together while you visited the widow? He could have taken advantage of me a dozen times."

Amusement was mirrored in Eli's eyes. "Jovan hasn't been sittin' with you, miss. But even if he had I wouldn't have worried. Jovan is slick; he's made up his mind he's gonna marry you, and he wouldn't risk steppin' out of line and makin' you angry."

"Land's sake, Paw," Serena said impatiently, "correct me if I'm wrong, but I somehow get the impression that you'd like to see me married to that Yankee wagon master."

The creases alongside Eli's lips deepened in a teasing grin. "I could rest more peaceful if the pair of you were hitched up. I wouldn't have to worry every time the two of you were out of my sight."

Serena pounced on Eli's remark. "Ah-ha! So it's your fine friend that you don't trust."

"Well . . ." Eli looked away sheepishly. "I've seen him

watching you with a hungry look in his eyes. I don't think he'd have the control your fancy rancher friend has. Josh is pretty predictable, practices no guile. If he wants you, he'll go after you. That's why I keep an eye on him.''

"So,'' Serena half laughed, "to give you peace of mind, you're hinting that I should marry the man?''

"I don't know if Josh has marryin' on his mind, but you could do a lot worse.'' Eli cocked an eye at her. "Better than takin' on that one swaggerin' over here.'' He nodded his head at Jovan, who was stepping briskly toward them. "You ever tie up with him, honey, you'll regret it within a week.''

Serena could not reply for the man in question was upon them, his teeth flashing in a wide smile. "I thought you might like to take a walk into the settlement, Serena,'' he said.

Eli stood up. "We was just startin' over there.'' He ignored the frown that momentarily darkened the handsome features opposite him.

Jovan was silent a moment then, crooking an elbow for Serena, said with a false brightness, "Let's get going, then.''

Josh rode down the narrow twisting street of the settlement, the stallion picking its way through a milling, mostly drunk and disorderly crowd of men and women. He nodded to several of his men who had arrived ahead of him.

The saloons and gambling places were packed with pleasure seekers, their raucous laughter almost drowning out the tinny pounding of piano keys. He scanned the faces of those passing through the swinging doors, and a frown etched lines between his dark eyebrows. Maybe he'd better shorten the layover. His honest and simple people wouldn't have a prayer against this unscrupulous-looking bunch.

Josh reached the end of the street and turned Jake around. The large horse had retraced its steps midway when Josh spotted Serena and her male companions. He frowned in displeasure at Jovan's possessive hold on Serena's arm and held the stallion back, fighting to control his racing pulses before confronting the pair.

The trio was almost upon him when a burst of excited voices erupted from the tavern in front of them. Eli and Jovan conferred a moment, then, keeping Serena between them, the three entered the building. Josh waited a minute before swinging from the saddle and tethering the mount. He followed them inside.

The long, narrow room was crowded, the majority of the patrons pushed into a tight group at the far end of the bar. Josh swung a searching look over the area and spotted Serena and Jovan sitting at a table close to the door. He turned his head to look for Landrie, and the Southerner spoke at his elbow.

"Looks like we've got a piece of the South here tonight." Landrie jerked his head toward the knot of men at the end of the bar.

Josh cocked a raised eyebrow at his friend. "I don't get your meanin'."

"They're havin' what you might call a slave market over there," Eli explained with heavy disapproval in his voice.

"There's blacks this far west?"

"Naw. Not blacks . . . squaws and youngsters."

"I didn't know that kind of thing went on out here. Who sells them, do you think?"

"Sometimes their own people, I hear tell, but mostly the poor devils have been captured by enemy tribes during a battle. The red man has learned that the settlers coming west are finding few men willing to do the hard labor farming involves. So, for a few dollars, a healthy squaw can be picked up. She's used to hard work and probably makes a better hand than the louts who hang around the taverns."

"Not to mention—" Josh broke off as a squealing commotion erupted, rising over the heads of the spectators gathered to watch, and bid for, those offered for sale. He and Landrie edged through the press of people, then the older man exclaimed in angry surprise: "That's Ninu, and I'm damned if that bastard, Newcomb, isn't tryin' to sell her."

The young squaw, one sleeve and half her bodice torn away, struggled in the Southerner's grip as he tried to boost her onto the cleared spot on the bar. Newcomb ignored her tearful entreaties, aware of the lustful gaze of the men who eyed hotly the red, dark-tipped breast bared for all to see.

But each time he tried to hoist her up, Ninu would relax her body and slide back down. The audience began to laugh at his ineffective efforts. Frustrated and angry, Newcomb finally balled a fist and clipped the girl on the chin.

As the unconscious figure slumped into the man's arms, Josh plowed through the bodies, roaring, "Newcomb! You miserable whelp!"

The Southerner's body went ramrod stiff and Ninu slipped from his suddenly nerveless arms. His eyes bulging with the dread of what would surely come, he started backing away. Then a foot was purposefully stuck out by a big mountain man. He tripped and sat down hard. The tavern whores, always alert to a brewing fight, ceased their maudlin laughter and gravitated to a far corner. The regulars picked up on their movement and hurriedly took themselves off to safer distances.

The air grew hushed as Josh dragged Newcomb to his feet and slammed him up against the bar. "How would you like a fist in the face?" he grated through clenched teeth.

Newcomb shook his head dumbly, but the action didn't stop the punishing fist that caught him in the mouth and nose. He staggered back into the tensely staring crowd, his blood spraying those who hadn't moved fast enough to avoid it.

Josh stalked after him. "Ride out of here, you cowardly bastard. If I catch you around the train, I'll put my knife through your heart."

Newcomb swiped at his bleeding nose, then growled, "You haven't seen the last of me, Yankee. Everything will be settled to my satisfaction farther along the trail." He spun around and pushed his way toward the door.

Josh knelt beside Ninu's limp form, muttering, "You crazy wench," as he pulled the torn shift over her nakedness. He hefted her into his arms, stood up, and paused, unsure of what to do with the unconscious squaw. As his eyes skimmed the room they were caught and held by Serena Bain's scornfully flashing ones. Confusion swept over him and he looked for Landrie. His friend had disappeared. When one of his men walked past him, he shoved the girl into the surprised man's arms.

"Take her back to Jessie," he instructed brusquely.

Smarting from Serena's contemptuous look and raging inside, Josh shoved his way to the bar and ordered a bottle and a glass. Those standing near him sensed the big man's black mood and were careful to keep a wide space around him. They had seen the destruction his rock-hard fist could do and had no doubt that the broad blade at his waist could be handled equally effectively.

Josh picked up the bottle and filled the waiting glass with the raw, white whiskey. The sale of flesh at the end of the bar picked up where it had left off and he watched the transactions through narrowed eyes as the liquid contents of the bottle slowly inched down.

An old squaw was sold for ten dollars; two girls around fourteen went for fifty dollars each. Then an old hag was pushing a teenaged boy onto the bar. Clad only in a breechclout, his skin the color of rubbed copper, the young Indian stood with stone-like immobility as the aged street whore ran a dirt-grimed hand up his naked thigh, her whiskey-roughened voice pointing out such features that might whet the interest of a low percentage of the males in the room.

Josh lost interest as the woman droned on about the youngster and let his gaze drift to the table beside the door. He lifted an eyebrow at the dark disapproval on Serena's lovely face. Surely she was used to this sort of thing, having once owned slaves herself. He looked at her companion and received another shock. There was a feverish excitement burning in Jovan's eyes as they traveled over the Indian youth.

While he watched the man, unable to believe what his eyes had clearly seen, the rancher bent his head to Serena and spoke earnestly to her. When she smiled and nodded, he jumped to his feet, knocking against a nearby table, spilling a glass of ale. He slapped some money down between the two men who had surged to their feet in loud complaint and rushed to the bar.

Josh knew that what he suspected was true when the boy directed a faint, suggestive smile at Jovan as the rancher hurriedly struck a deal with the old whore. He jumped to the floor and with a barely hidden smile of complacency followed his new master back to his table. Josh swore under his breath as Serena naively greeted the boy with a friendly smile when Jovan introduced them.

A grim voice spoke at Josh's elbow. "I can't let things go on between her and that buggerin' bastard, Josh."

"Don't worry about it, friend," Josh growled back. "I'll put my knife in him if I see things goin' too far."

Eli clasped Josh's shoulder in silent thanks. "I'm goin' back to camp now to see Nell. You keep an eye out for Newcomb. There was killin' hate in his eyes when he left here."

"I'm wise to him, Eli." Josh smiled thinly, then turned his attention back to the auction. His eyes widened in interest. Waiting quietly beside the bar was a white woman, still youngish and quite comely with dark brown hair curling around her oval-shaped face. When she caught his eyes perusing her soft features, her brown eyes welcomed him, so he let his gaze continue to drift over her shapely body. This one, he thought, could take the sneer off Serena Bain's face.

He motioned the bartender over. "Who's sellin' her?" he asked with a jerk of his head in the woman's direction.

"That one is not for sale," the man informed him. "She used to work for the old gent standin' beside her, but his wife died last week and he's goin' back to Ohio. The woman wants to go on to Oregon, and she'll work for anyone who'll provide her a place in a wagon train." He winked slyly. "I can think of a way she could pay me for her passage. What about you?"

Josh ignored the comment and made his way to the pretty woman in the midst of the interested men gathered around her. He nudged the old gentleman's arm. "Mister, I'm the wagon master of a train goin' to Oregon. The woman can work for me." The farmer turned and looked at Josh, and a smile of relief brightened his weathered face. He looked at the woman, she nodded, and he held a hand out to Josh.

"Her name is Jane Scott," he said, and after Josh gave his name, the old man continued, "She's a good lass and a hard worker. I hope you'll treat her well." After a quick peck on Miss Scott's cheek, the Ohio farmer turned and was gone.

Josh looked down at the woman smiling up at him, and for the first time was struck with the weight of responsibility for his actions. What in God's name had he done? What in the world was he going to do with her? Hell! He didn't even have a wagon. Then his gaze encountered Serena's, and his spirits soared. The furious blazing eyes that drilled into him definitely said that she didn't like what he had done.

A triumphant smile tugged at his lips. To hand back, even in small measure, what that little witch had given him the past months, he would find a place for Jane Scott *somewhere*. And under the sparking eyes, he pulled his new responsibility up tight against his body and, lowering his head, kissed her soundly. But when he raised his head to mock the southern girl, she was gone. He tasted ashes now, and his arms dropped abruptly from the soft body that pressed against him. "Come on, let's get out of here," he said shortly.

CHAPTER
❧ 13 ❧

JOSH SENT THE STALLION loping toward camp. Jane Scott wrapped her arms around his waist, and though she wondered at the wagon master's change in attitude, she possessed a self-esteem that brought a smug smile to her lips. She nestled her head against the broad back in front of her, confident that she would change his mood later . . . in his blankets.

The heightened twist of the new woman's lips fell, however, when upon reaching the emigrant camp Josh led her to a wagon where a man and woman sat before a fire. Her new employer reached behind him and helped her to the ground.

"Eli, Nell," he said from the saddle, "this is Jane Scott. Put her up for me, will you?" The three stared after him, their mouths open as the grim-faced man galloped away.

When Serena and Jovan, along with the boy, Sato, arrived back at camp, Serena told the pair good-night and went straight to her wagon. As she stripped off the buckskins it occurred to her vaguely that Foster seemed in as much a hurry as she to end the evening.

As Serena luxuriated in the freedom of nakedness a moment, trailing light fingers across her breasts, a thought of the wagon master eased into her mind. So, she mused contemptuously, the very virile Josh Quade needed the regular comfort of a woman's body. Evidently he had tired of Jessie's girls, and realizing that

Serena Bain had no intentions of providing him that service, tonight he had found one who would.

Good, I'm glad, she told herself, shrugging into the blue robe. But as she jumped from the wagon to reheat the remains of supper's coffee, the picture of the dark-haired woman lifting her head to receive Josh's kiss flashed in front of her. At that moment, she knew a wretchedness of mind that was almost unendurable.

Bending over, poking at the fire, she told herself fiercely that she didn't care how many women the bastard Yankee kissed. Serena straightened up and listened at the sharp clang of hooves on stone. She peered through the darkness, then drew in her breath sharply as the very man pulled in his mount and swung to the ground. His eyes raked hotly over her thinly clad body as he came toward her.

She felt breathless excitement flow through her, then quickly struggled against the sensation when she remembered that less than an hour ago this same man had obtained a woman with whom to share the long trip. She could not control the erratic beating of her heart, but her voice was cool when she sneered, "Where is your new woman? Don't tell me that you are tired of her already."

Josh smiled at her lazily and stroked her cheek with slim fingers. "Where's your Indian lover?" he mocked, dropping his hand. "Don't tell me that he's abandoned you for his new toy."

His sarcastic innuendo held no meaning for Serena and she jumped in quick defense of Jovan. "How dare you call Foster that. He did a fine and decent thing tonight, taking that boy off the block, giving him a good home."

Josh searched her face for a long moment then, shaking his head, said softly, "Serena, you little fool."

"You're the fool!" she flashed back, her breasts rising and falling rapidly. "Taking on the responsibility of a strange woman. You don't even have a place to take her. Of what use will she be to you—outside of bedding her, of course? I thought Jessie's girls took care of that need sufficiently."

"No, no, Jessie's girls don't." Josh shook his head. "Nor will Jane Scott." He locked her eyes with his blue ones. "Al-

though I bitterly resent it, Miss Southern Belle, I'm afraid that
only you will suffice for my needs."

"You're crazy!" Serena's shocked eyes stared at him. "If you
think for one minute that I'd . . . that you'd . . ." Her voice
trailed off, for Josh, his eyes stormy and reckless, was moving
in on her. She read his intention in his gaze and quickly stepped
backwards until she bumped against the wagon.

"No, no," she whispered, her hands held out to ward him
off.

"Yes, yes," he whispered back, reaching for her.

Their eyes locked as his lean, tanned fingers gripped her arms,
hers wide and denying, his glittering with desperate need. "I
don't want you," Serena gasped as the heat of Josh's hands
burned through the material of her robe as they traveled up to
her shoulders.

"Yes, you do," he murmured thickly, his unsteady fingers
now at the opening of the robe.

A cool breeze brushed Serena's breasts as the garment was
pulled apart and pushed down over her shoulders. "You're
wrong," she whispered weakly as his eyes fastened on the twin
mounds like a man thirsting for water.

"I was never so right," he answered on a groan and lowered
his mouth, warm and seeking, to cover a breast and to flick his
tongue over the rosy tip, teasing it until it grew hard, then drawing it between his teeth and nursing it slowly. Oh, God, how
can I want this? Serena's hands clenched as his hand smoothed
its way down her waist, across her stomach, down to the downy
center between her legs. But when his finger entered her and
gently stroked, she knew that she wanted nothing more in life
than to have this big rough man make passionate love to her.

As hot liquid rushed through her veins Serena forgot the fact
that anyone, at any time, could come upon them and see her
nakedness as Josh was seeing it. But she was helpless now, could
only draw long, ragged breaths and yield to the need that had
called out for relief for so long.

She trembled uncontrollably when Josh's lips finished their
sweet tormenting and traveled a moist path up her throat and
settled possessively on her parted lips. As his tongue plunged in
and out of her mouth, her arms wound themselves around his

waist, meeting the drive of his slowly bucking hips. She moaned softly as his hard arousal, in rhythm with his tongue, nudged against her stomach.

And in answer to her wordless assent, Josh's hands tore at the lacing of his shirt, murmuring thickly, "Touch me, Serena."

Serena raised a hand and, laying it on his broad chest, tentatively moved her fingers through the short, curling hair. She felt his heartbeat quicken and she became brave. Running her palm lightly over the rippling muscles, she discovered a small, hard pap. "Oh, God, yes," Josh rasped hoarsely when she lay her lips against it and slowly circled it with her tongue.

His breath coming in quick, shallow gulps, Josh released her throbbing lips and swung her into his arms. As in a dream she felt him set her in the saddle then climb on behind her. She leaned back in his arms and his free hand cupped a breast, the pad of his thumb moving gently across the pink, puckered nipple.

Serena was hardly aware when a few moments later Josh reined the stallion in and slid to the ground. When he lifted his arms to her she fell into them eagerly, and he carried her to where the grass grew tall and thick. Then, dropping to his knees, he laid her down in the green softness. With slow deliberation he pulled the robe apart and slid it off her arms.

Her slender, perfectly shaped body shone luminously in the moonlight, and the breath caught in his throat as he gazed at it. His hand reached out, and with trembling fingers he caressed the ivory-tinged mounds a moment, then reverently lowered his head to let his lips draw a swollen, taut nipple into his mouth. As his lips worked urgently, Serena moaned and caressed the corners of his working mouth.

Minutes passed while Josh teased and tantalized both breasts until they were rigid with desire, making Serena purr with pleasure. And when his lips moved downward, trailing sweetly across her silken stomach, she writhed and moaned his name, her fingers flying to his waistband. He helped her unlace the buckskins, and she gasped with delight when his large manhood seemed to jump into her palm. She stroked and squeezed him gently, and their fast, harsh breathing mingled in the soft evening air.

Then Josh rose to his knees, whipped the shirt over his head, and slid out of the buckskins. He stretched out beside her and gathered her in his arms. For a long moment he only held her, savoring the feel of her body.

But Serena's body had cried out for his too long. Feeling the long, firm length of his arousal throb against her thigh was almost more than she could bear. She wanted him inside her, to make them one. She slid her hand between their bodies and curled her fingers around his hardness. Josh caught his breath at her touch and he wanted to ravish her then and there. But he forced himself to lie quietly, to let her take the lead. This moment must not be spoiled as it had the other time.

As though she read his mind, Serena's lips, hot and sweet, moved over his throat, across his shoulders. She lingered twice to flick her tongue across desire-ridden nipples, then traveled down his firm, lean midriff, drinking in his clean, healthy male scent. When she scattered tiny searing kisses across the hard bones of his hips and seductively stroked his inner thigh, Josh was no longer able to control himself.

"God, Serena," he gasped, "I can't take much more."

She lifted her head to gaze at him out of passion-filled eyes, then slid up his body, making him hold his breath, before turning over on her back and lifting her arms to receive him.

Josh climbed between her slender long legs with loving care and hung suspended over her, waiting. Serena, heavy-eyed, gazed up at him, filled with the knowledge of what he wanted. She lifted a hand and stroked his cheek. "Make love to me, Josh," she murmured, "I've waited so long."

His heard pounding at her urgent plea, Josh hesitated. "It might hurt again, at first." His eyes searched her face. "And I can't promise you that I can stop this time."

"I know," she whispered, running her hands up his arms and clasping her fingers at his nape.

She felt his hands slide beneath her hips and lift them off the ground. Curving his body over hers, he entered her slowly, but still she gave a gasp of pain as his largeness began to fill her.

"Should I stop?" The question came raggedly, its tone begging her to say no.

And though Serena felt the warm blood trickle down her thighs, she withheld her cries and caressed his cheek in silent acquiescence. Josh's soft eyes beamed with admiration in response, as carefully, bit by bit, he drove deeper into the warm core of her.

She sensed that he was exercising a gentleness that was probably new to him, but the pain was sharp, growing. Finally she could bear it no more, and her lips parted to beg him to stop. But suddenly the words trailed off in a murmuring sigh. The burning had ceased and was replaced by a warm, flowing sensation. In a weakening rush that left her heart racing and her body trembling, she shuddered uncontrollably. As she clung to his shoulders, his mouth clasped onto hers, muffling her cries of delight. She was aware of his own sudden spasm, and then their bodies relaxed breathlessly.

Later, lying on their sides, legs tangled, still united, Serena smiled lazily and arched her body into Josh's like a cat rousing from sleep. She gazed into his blue eyes and they reflected her own sense of well-being. His lips curved into a soft smile and she felt him growing inside her.

"Again?" she teased.

"Yes! Again and again." His hand left her hip to brush the damp hair off her forehead. "Don't you want it, too?" She let her actions answer by running her palm down his stomach, stopping where he disappeared inside her. She felt him begin to move swiftly, and her eyes glinted in the moonlight when once again he was on top of her, grasping her hips, holding them steady to take his powerful strokes. She braced her heels on the ground and met each long, increasingly desperate thrust.

As Serena was enveloped in a cyclone of sensation, a hoarse sob escaped Josh, and together they cried out in pleasure.

Several moments passed while their breaths returned to normal and heartbeats slowed. Lying in the cradle of Josh's arms, completely exhausted, Serena's drowsy gaze focused on the moon; she was surprised at the distance it had traveled since she had last noticed it. Then the low croaking of frogs, night insects and the scent of crushed grass invaded her senses. She was brought to earth when Josh began to speak as he brushed a damp curl off her forehead.

"Serena," he said softly, "I'll not forget this night if I live to be a hundred."

Oh, God, what have I done? Serena wailed inwardly, thinking of her total surrender to this man. Not only was he an enemy to the South, he was a noted womanizer. And in his arms she had allowed herself to become like all the others before her.

It struck her with cold clarity that Josh had deliberately set out to do just that, to show her that she was no different from Jessie and her girls, or his new woman. The dewy softness left her face, and before Josh's unbelieving eyes the old familiar coldness quickly settled over her features. Looking away from him she clipped coolly, "I'll forget it. Just as fast as I can." She sat up and reached for her robe, and felt lean fingers grasp her shoulder, biting into the flesh.

And the old hardness raced back in his eyes as he demanded icily, "Are you tellin' me that our lovemakin' meant nothin' to you, that you didn't find fulfillment and enjoyment?"

"Enjoyment?" Serena jerked away from him. "You . . . you wild barbarian, how can a woman enjoy rape?"

Furious, and cut to the core by her lie, Josh rose to his knees, and, gripping her arms, he shook her until her hair fell over her face. "You lie, you lie!" he ground out. "You asked me to make love to you, and damn your shallow heart you wallowed in the pleasure I gave you. You were worse than a whore who spreads her legs for any man."

Her eyes wide and staring at the stinging insult, Serena jerked free of the punishing fingers and, dashing the hair out of her eyes, slapped Josh across the face as hard as she could. His head rocked from the blow's force, and for a moment he could only stare at her blankly. Then anger surged, and quite deliberately he slapped her back.

Astonishment overriding the stinging of her cheek, Serena's eyes glared brightly at him. Josh stared back, panting heavily. "Whether you like it or not, Serena Bain, I'm in your blood. Before this night is over you'll hunger for me again. And God help me, I'll ache for you. But I can appease my need with my new woman, while you won't have *anyone* to cool your hot passion."

"Oh?" Serena shot back. "You seem to forget Foster. I too have an outlet."

"Hah!" Josh snorted. "You'll get no help from that quarter.

He'll only hold your hand and make pretty speeches. But when it comes to putting out the fire that smolders inside you, only *I* can do that.'' He grabbed her and jerked her to her knees. His eyes bored into hers as he ground out, "And I swear to you, lady, the next time you'll make it *very clear* what you want from me."

With a hard shove of his hand, Serena sprawled back into the grass. She lay there, hating him. With firm resolution in her voice she hissed at him, "Never, you Yankee bastard!"

"You will," Josh answered calmly, climbing into his buckskins. "And I may just make you beg a bit." He laced his fly and ran a suggestive palm down its length, sending Serena a mocking look. When he swung into the saddle and turned the stallion's head toward camp, Serena looked wildly about for something to fling at his back, but there was only the bent grass where they had lain. She dropped her head to her drawn up knees and cried in anger and despair.

And Josh, already bitterly ashamed of the demeaning words he had flung in Serena's face and the hard slap he had returned her, stared unseeing before him as the stallion carried him back to camp.

CHAPTER
~14~

Josh had allowed his people two days to make necessary repairs on wagons and to replace shoes on teams and mounts. The women used the time for washing and mending clothing. Serena and Eli spent most of their time at the small post, haggling over the price of food and other goods to replenish their depleted supplies.

And now Fort Laramie lay three hundred miles behind them, along with the Platte and Sweetwater. A week back ten wagons had taken a fork that would lead them to California, and the rest of the train followed the Snake River.

So far the new country had been the easiest land to cover, discounting that it was buffalo range and everyone had to be always on the alert for stampeding herds. The big animals, according to Jovan, could wipe out an entire train.

Another week passed, leading into Indian summer. The weather changed and became as hot as mid-summer. The sun beat down, creating heat waves, and a hot, dry wind blew endlessly.

Swaying along in the wagon, her dust-grimed clothes sticking to every limb, Serena felt that her entire life had been spent on the trail; that there had never been a plantation, a war, or a gentle, laughing boy who had gone off to fight and never returned. She glanced down at the trail-worn buckskins. Had all the fancy dresses, outgrown and left behind, also been a dream?

She flicked the long whip at a fly on one of the oxen's rump, relieving some of her unrest with its sharp snap. Danger of Indian attacks was still a cloud that hovered over them all. But happily, since that one incident, the train had been left alone, the natives seemingly content to watch them from a distance.

Still, their constant presence kept everyone nervous, and the strain was beginning to show on the weary emigrants, especially the mothers.

Other things were also taking their toll. There had been no rain for weeks, and everything was bone dry. Where in the beginning the grass had been green and lush, it was now shriveled and brittle, rustling in the wind. Often there were long stretches where the grass had died completely and the slightest breeze sent the topsoil spiraling away. The livestock were becoming lean and gaunt, and even the plodding oxen bawled occasional complaints.

Serena reached for her canteen, but as she uncapped it Paw's dire warning came to mind. "Use your water sparingly, Serena. With this drought on, there's no tellin' when we'll come onto another water hole."

The lead ox called its need for water and Serena felt a flash of guilt. The poor thing, it was probably thirstier than she was. Paw had purchased the patient animals shortly after leaving Fort Laramie. The previous owner had forgotten to set the brakes on his wagon one night, and the next morning it lay at the bottom of a deep ravine, smashed to bits. The man had sold the six beasts to them, bought a horse from another member, and joined the others who traveled the miles in the saddle.

Paw was pleased with his new acquisitions, remarking that the animals could be hitched to a plow once he had established a homestead. A shyness had come into his warm brown eyes as he had informed her that he and Nell would be getting married when they reached Oregon country.

Serena's eyes clouded. The sharp pang that had stabbed her at his news hadn't lessened when he went on to say that he wouldn't be surprised if Josh and Jane Scott weren't thinking along the same lines. "Jane is a fine woman," he'd added. "She's a hard worker, and she's crazy about Josh. She'll make him a lovin' and willin' helpmate."

For a moment, when she shot him a startled look, she imag-

ined she saw a slyness in Paw's eyes, mixed with something like
. . . triumph? She had dismissed the thought when he said, "You
were right, not cottonin' to Josh. His ways are much too rough
for a delicate little thing like yourself." Paw had left her then
before she could overcome her surprise and make some comment.

Serena lifted the heavy, damp hair off the nape of her neck,
a petulant scowl settling over her features. Paw continued to sing
that woman's praise, however, and she was sick to death listening to it. And it didn't help matters, her sharing Nell Simpson's
wagon. This made it awkward for her to visit the widow and
become better acquainted with Paw's future wife. She truly
wanted to be friends with the good-natured woman. But that
would be next to impossible with that simpering female always
about.

She stared gloomily ahead, recalling the first time she accepted Nell's invitation to have supper at her wagon. It was the
only time Josh had put in an appearance.

While Nell and Miss Scott had fussed over a couple of steaming pots, she had been talking with the three young Simpson
children when suddenly she sensed Josh's presence. She glanced
up and her heart fluttered wildly. She hadn't been this close to
him since that long night of lovemaking. And though his buckskins were worn and dirty, and his brown face looked weathered
and tired, he had never looked better to her. She longed, almost
desperately, to be alone with him, to feel his strong arms around
her. But as she nodded to him coolly, she made sure none of
her thoughts were etched on her face.

Serena gave a long, ragged sigh. It had hurt painfully when
he, equally cool, acknowledged politely, "Miss Bain," and hunkered down beside the fire. She tore her eyes away from the
muscular thighs molded by the soft buckskins as he asked mockingly, "How are things with you these days . . . and nights . . .
the coyotes howlin', and all."

She caught the double meaning of his words, telling that he
was aware of her restless nights, that she ached for the release
only he could give her, and that he would withhold that healing
until she asked him for it.

Her amber eyes, wide and falsely innocent, lifted to him.

"I'm just fine, Mr. Quade. Day and *night*. The yowling of wild coyotes doesn't bother me in the least. I hear it's the supposedly tame ones that you should watch out for."

"Is that a fact?" His brief smile mocked her as he poured two cups of coffee and handed her one. He sipped at the steaming brew then said, "There's one coyote you let get awfully close to you."

A light of combat in her eyes, Serena retorted, "I did until a certain time at a certain fort, then I learned to stay clear of him."

Admiration twinkled in Josh's eyes as he bowed slightly, saluting her. Her heart racing excitedly at his flirtatious response, she waited for his next sally. It did not come. Instead, after swallowing his coffee in one long draught, he turned to Jane Scott, who watched them with narrowed eyes, and said, "Let's take a walk before supper." The suggestive tone of his voice left no doubt about the purpose of the walk. Nell, however, looked after the pair, a mixture of surprise and speculation in her eyes.

Now Serena sighed again, bringing her attention back to the oxen. Josh was still keeping his promise to her. Not once had he hinted that he wanted her again. She had, however, the comfort of knowing that he hadn't forgotten her completely. She was aware that his smoldering gaze raked over her when he thought she wasn't looking.

"Enough of Josh Quade," she muttered bitterly, dragging an arm across her perspiring face. She had been so deep in recalling the past that she had almost forgotten the present. For the first time she was aware of the eerie approach of dusk.

As she gazed perplexedly at the sky, a rider raced along the line of wagons, shouting at the top of his lungs, "Storm! Dust storm comin'!!"

Serena glanced over her shoulder and gasped. Great yellow clouds were sweeping along, bearing straight down on the train. Mesmerized, she watched them grow larger and larger, rolling across the earth like a threatening giant. When the frightening phenomenon of nature blotted out the sun completely she jerked out of her hypnotic state. Standing up in the wagon, she called encouragingly to the oxen, which were rapidly becoming uneasy.

The animals tried to heed her voice and her grip on the reins, but as long streamers of grass, roots intact, lashed and caught at their legs and hoofs, the creatures became half crazed.

Serena hung on, feeling as though her arms were being pulled from their sockets as the oxen tried to bolt and run. She was crying aloud when, over the roaring din of the wind and sand, she heard Josh's shouting voice: "Give them the reins, Serena, and get inside the wagon and cover yourself up."

It was the first time Serena did not balk or argue at an order given by the wagon master. She dropped the reins and dove over the seat of the careening wagon, landing on the pallet with a hard jolt. Then, fighting the gale that peppered the canvas with small stones, her trembling fingers struggled with the blanket, finally drawing it over her head. Clutching it tightly, she braced herself against the violent rocking that sometimes lifted the back wheels off the ground.

Then the wagon gave a shivering shake and a lean body stretched out beside her. Strong arms gathered her closely and excitement surged through her veins. She did not have to look to know who held her. It could be only one man.

The storm raged on, but the wagon finally came to a halt as the oxen's strength waned. Lying quietly, Serena felt Josh's body heat and was overwhelmingly aware of his clean, intoxicating scent. The desire to turn in his arms and lock her lips to his expressed itself as a pulsating knot in her stomach.

She had almost acted on the thought when she remembered that Josh was probably waiting for such a move on her part. She recalled him threatening to make her beg, and drawing on all of her willpower, she pushed back her intense craving and lay still. She would not humiliate herself once again.

Twice Josh took away the arm covering her to push up the blanket, clearing it of the sand that rapidly weighed it down. The wind gradually lessened, then ceased altogether. In the deadly quiet left behind, Josh removed his arms from Serena's waist and, as he carefully lifted the blanket, spoke for the first time since entering the wagon.

"Thank you for sharing your quarters with me."

Serena blinked back tears as he jumped from the wagon and walked briskly away. She raised up on her knees and watched him disappear into the hazy light. Then she had a comforting thought. *It was her safety Josh had thought of. Not Jane Scott's.*

Eli rode up as Serena was climbing back onto the hard seat. She burst out laughing at his dust-covered face, and he looked at her quizzically, wondering at the near-hysteria in her voice. He reined the horse closer, then saw the moccasin tracks in the sand.

Suspicion jumped into his eyes. "Are you all right, honey?" he asked tightly.

Alerted to the sharp concern in Eli's voice Serena choked off her laughter and assured him that she was fine. Eli eyed her a moment then growled, "I thought maybe that long-legged Quade might have gotten some ideas in his head."

"If he did, he kept them to himself," Serena answered sourly.

Eli hid his grin with a grime-covered hand. His hopes were high as he wheeled his mount and rode away. Those two mule heads might still get together.

On Friday morning of the second week since the dust storm, Serena sat in front of her fire, contentedly sipping her second cup of coffee. These early hours were her favorite time of day. It was a busy time, with the swearing voices of men as they gathered their livestock, the rattle of pots and tin plates, and fussing children objecting to the early rising.

But it would settle down as hearty breakfasts were eaten, fueling the travelers for another grueling day. And later Josh would mount his stallion and call the order to roll out.

Serena frowned into the fire. Much too often lately she had caught herself waiting for that deep, rich voice. Had she, she wondered, arrived at the point where even the sound of his voice was important to her? She jumped impatiently to her feet and began gathering up plates and cookware. Thoughts of Josh Quade must stop. His actions stated plainly that he had lost all interest in her. Evidently Jane Scott had driven Serena Bain from his mind.

At the last minute Serena decided she would ride in the wagon with Eli. She seldom got to visit with him anymore. Most evenings he didn't even take supper with her, and he never returned from Nell's wagon until long after she had retired.

She sighed, feeling sorry for herself. She'd had a lonely time of it lately. Foster hadn't had an evening meal with her for ages. It was probably her fault, she admitted. She had objected to Sato sharing their food. It had sickened her to see him dip his fingers into her carefully prepared meal. And that terrible habit he had of wiping his greasy fingers under his armpits when he had finished eating. But just as disgusting to her was the stench of the boy. She didn't know how Foster could bear sharing his wagon with him. Foster claimed that it was the bear grease Sato used on his hair that made him smell, but in her opinion it was a lack of soap and water.

Serena and Eli didn't converse as much as she had planned. They spent most of the time admiring the beauty of the land, a place of buttes and mesas, sprinkled with the tangy odor of sage, smooth gnarled mesquite, and the dark green of juniper and pine.

Once Eli indicated with his whip a huge sprawling cliff and remarked, "There's another one."

Serena nodded. They had passed so many along the way, wind-carved shapes that had been given names like "Courthouse Rock" and "Chimney Rock." She mused for a minute on the men who had created this trail and given names to the bluffs and cliffs. What a hardy lot they must have been.

A nervous muttering from Eli brought Serena from the past and back to the present. "What's wrong?" She squinted at him.

"I don't care much for this stretch of trail," Eli grumbled, "and I'll be glad when we're off it."

Serena noted for the first time their perilous position. The way had become winding, running along the face of a towering cliff. The wagon was just rolling onto a spot where only a foot or so of solid rock lay to the outside of the wheels. She threw a quick look over the drop that led out of sight and shivered. What if something should spook the oxen? She gripped Landrie's arm, urging tensely, "Go slow, Paw. Don't let them run."

"Don't worry about them runnin'. They wouldn't run if I took the whip to them. Them beasts know as well as we do that they're on dangerous ground."

Landrie drove tight-lipped; guiding the team that along with the others were inching their way along in the quietness that had settled over the train. The only sound was a creaking of wheels and the jangling of traces.

The road widened finally, and in one voice Serena and Eli muttered, "Thank God." Several yards later the oxen made the last curve and came out on a stretch of level ground about a mile wide. Josh had called a halt to those preceding them and already women were busy with grub sacks. As the rest of the wagons moved cautiously around the bend Eli pointed out to Serena that between each team of horses and mules, a brace of oxen plodding along.

"That Josh, he's sure smart. He knew those wise old beasts would calm and lead the others safely around the cliff." Serena only sniffed and busied herself with setting out lunch.

Three more days passed and the grass grew more abundant on gentle, rolling hills. On the fourth day, shortly after the noon break, the travelers spotted their first herd of buffalo. Wagons were brought to a halt as men, women, and children stared, spellbound. The animals were a black mass against the skyline, not unlike a long, rolling cloud of black dust.

"They're on the move," Eli whispered in awe. "Huntin' new grazin' land."

Serena stood up beside Eli, her lips slightly parted, unable to believe the sight before her. Then suddenly she gripped Landrie's arm and exclaimed excitedly, "Paw, there's cattle mixed in with them."

Landrie shaded his eyes with a hand and peered against the sun. "Danged if you're not right," he cried, spotting several head grazing with the buffalo. "I bet Indians have stampeded them from settlers goin' through. Some might even be from our own train. You remember how them varmints chased off a lot of cattle that night?"

Serena and Eli were still discussing that possibility when the herd's leader lifted his shaggy head abruptly and stared at the gaping people, thus releasing the men into action. With jubilant cries of "Buffalo!" they reached for guns and ran toward the herd. To the sound of booming and cracking, the slaughter began.

Serena's eyes widened in horror and disbelief. The poor stupid, defenseless beasts, her mind agonized, why did they just stand there? Why don't they run? Can't they see their companions dropping all around them?

She was about to faint at the sight before her when with pounding hooves Josh's big stallion thundered among the herd, his authoritative voice ringing out. "That's enough! There will be no needless killin'."

A few more shots were fired, then under the cloud of gunpowder hanging in the air it grew quiet. Serena dropped back onto the wagon seat, her legs trembling. "That man never ceases to amaze me," she muttered, shaking her head in bemusement.

Eli shot her an impatient look. "You don't give Josh credit for anything, do you, Serena?" he said gruffly. "If you'd care to dig beneath that roughness of his you'd find a man full of carin' and compassion. He wasn't only thinkin' of them dumb critters, he was also thinkin' of the food that was wantonly being taken away from the Indians. Some of them buffalo, which will only lay there in the sun and rot, might mean the difference between life and death to a tribe this winter."

Serena slid the irate man an amused look. She had never heard Paw string so many sentences together at one time. She did agree with most of his heated tirade, though. This unnecessary slaughtering of buffalo probably had helped to turn every western tribe against the white man.

As Landrie had predicted, only about half the kill was brought back to the wagons. And of that half only the choicest cuts were taken. Under Josh's disapproving stare the men looked shamefaced as they handed the meat over to the women.

In the time taken to kill and butcher the sun had swung far westward, and Josh directed that the wagons be pulled into the circle for the evening. As the sun sank and dusk settled, steaks sizzled over fires, permeating the air with a delicious aroma. Spirits were high and when supper was finished a banjo and fiddle were brought out. Inside the circle of wagons husbands grabbed wives and much hopping and stamping began. Jessie arrived with her girls, and they were seized immediately and whirled into the dancing throng. Those men lacking female partners grabbed each other around the waist and spun around together. Howls of laughter rose as the men taking the women's roles minced and pranced daintily.

Inside her wagon, her eyes aglow with excitement, Serena gave her hair a final pat. Maybe Josh would ask her to dance. God, she hoped so. Sometimes the desire to be held in his arms again coursed throughout her body so strongly it was frightening. She worried that in a moment of this deep need she might go to him, ask—maybe even beg—him to make love to her.

"You'll only be teasing yourself if you dance with him," an inner voice pointed out.

"I know," Serena muttered. "But who's to say what might follow." She had complete faith in the fire she and Josh sparked in each other. If she could only get his arms around her for a minute the rest would be easy. Josh would take matters into his own hands. She shivered in anticipation of Josh leading her away in the darkness, laying her down in the tall grass, and . . .

Humming lightly to the music, Serena descended the spokes of the wagon, stepped onto the ground, and froze. Josh and Jane Scott had just joined the dancers. She stood statue still, watching the pair, pain in her eyes. Miss Scott was all bubbly smiles, her dark eyes snapping as the sprigged muslin twirled around her dancing feet, her hands curved around Josh's neck. And he, damn him, gazed into his partner's uplifted face, his firm, sensual lips curled as if on the edge of laughter.

Suddenly wanting to cry with despair, Serena began to climb back up the large wheel. She would not expose herself to that little witch's sly, smug looks, or the possessive glint in her eyes when she looked at Josh.

She was about to swing a leg into the wagon when a pair of hands gripped her waist. "Were you waiting for me?" a laughing voice asked as she was swung back to the ground.

"Foster, you startled me." Serena laughed and would have pulled away from him but his hands tightened, holding her fast. She looked up in surprise when he pulled her up against his body and lowered his face to hers. For the first time in their courtship, his kiss was long and urgent.

When she was finally released, she gazed up at him, breathless. "Well," she said softly, "what was *that* all about?"

Foster didn't answer that it had occurred to him that he had neglected her recently, that he might lose her through his absorption with Sato. That he was afraid he'd acted foolishly, risking so much for one heathen Indian. After all, the boy could easily be replaced, whereas a woman like Serena Bain came into a man's life but once.

"I couldn't resist you, Serena," he answered softly. "That's what it's all about." He stroked her hair. "I haven't trusted myself to be around you lately, but I'd like to try again if you'll let me."

Serena looked away from Jovan's gravely questioning eyes. She wasn't sure she wanted things to return to how they'd been. She and Paw were getting along better now, and due to Foster's absences, Jessie dropped by more often. Then Jane Scott's gay laughter rang out and she could only think of one thing.

Revenge. She would be so loving and attentive to Foster that the soft-voiced, double-dealing Yankee couldn't help seeing that it didn't mean a snit to her that he danced with his fancy Miss Scott.

Giving Jovan her most brilliant smile, she murmured, "Shall we dance?"

Foster pulled her into the circle of his arms and swung her among the dancers, forcing Josh and Jane to come to an awkward halt or be knocked to the ground. Serena darted a surprised glance at the rancher and knew that his wide-eyed innocence was a lie. He had deliberately put them in Josh's path.

And Josh was furious. Serena peeked at him through her thick lashes then caught her breath. His rage was directed at her. Why? Was it the sight of her in Foster's arms that made his blue eyes look like silver lightning?

Jovan apologized, and Josh, after giving their tightly pressed bodies a raking look, nodded, a stolid look of withdrawal coming over his lean face. Then he turned his attention back to Jane.

Serena loved to dance and had missed doing so. She and Jovan moved well together, keeping perfect step. As she and her partner dipped and swayed, she was unaware that men's mouths watered as they watched her graceful figure in the snug buckskins, or that the wagon master seldom took his stormy eyes off her.

But Jane Scott knew. She knew by the tenseness of Josh's

body and by the way his head was always turned in the direction of the southern girl. Nell Simpson's words came unbidden to her: "Don't fall in love with Josh, Jane," she had warned. "Everyone knows he's marked Serena Bain for his wife. That's why the single men only look at her. It amuses them to watch Jovan court her. They're all bettin' that the wagon master will walk away with the prize."

Jane's lips firmed stubbornly. What did Nell know of love, planning to marry that tough old Southerner, Landrie? She listened to him pleasuring Nell every night, and it was sickening, the noise the pair of them made.

Passing over the fact that Josh had never made any romantic moves toward her, Miss Scott clung to the notion that the haughty girl from the South didn't know this. Serena Bain pictured them together in a much different light, and because of this her pride would never let her have anything to do with the wagon master. And in the end, the big man would turn to her, Jane Scott.

As the music played on, Serena waited for Josh to ask her to dance. But after deliberately sitting out a couple of rounds, giving him the opportunity to seek her out, it became apparent he had no intention of approaching her. He danced only with Jane, and the intimate way he held the woman narrowed Serena's eyes with rage and hurt.

Josh kept Serena in the corner of his eye as she remained stoically out of his way. A muscle along his firm jaw knotted and jerked. He had thought that by now Serena would have weakened and given some indication that she wanted him. He had thought each evening would be the one to bring her to him. For regardless of what he had said to her that night after the two of them had exhausted each other making love, all he needed was a look from her that said she was ready.

"Well, I've waited long enough," he muttered decisively, his big hands clenched into fists. He looked over to where Jane Scott was talking to some of the other women, then he brought his gaze to bear on Jovan walking Serena to her wagon. His eyes narrowed dangerously. If he kissed her, he'd kill him.

He relaxed when the rancher only lifted Serena's hand and rested his lips against its back. When he left, heading toward his own wagon, Josh signaled the banjo picker and the fiddler to

put away their instruments. Neither man seemed reluctant to do
so. Some of the younger travelers grumbled, but the older ones
were happy to seek their blankets. It had been a long and ex-
hausting day.

Josh faded back into the darkness and waited for the camp to
sleep.

The long flannel gown Serena had dug out of the small trunk a
couple of weeks ago helped ward off the cool air seeping through
the bottom of the wagon. She added another blanket to the pallet, then slid beneath the covers and pulled them up around her
shoulders. She snuggled her head on the pillow and waited for
sleep to come. But stealthily, like some predator, the sweet,
sharp ache she was coming to know so well came over her.
Never again would Josh hold her in his arms, never again would
his body relieve the agony inside hers. Only Jane Scott would
know that rapture now.

She lay staring into the darkness, wanting to howl with hurt
and discontent like Paw's old hound did when the moon was full
and bright.

She was finally drifting off when the wagon bounced. Someone was climbing into it. Her eyes flew open and a hand was
laid across her lips, stifling her outcry. Even in the darkness she
knew who the invader was.

"What do you want?" she whispered breathlessly when Josh
removed his hand.

"You ask me that?" The question came hoarsely.

"Yes, I ask you that," Serena hissed, a picture of him dancing
with Jane Scott coming to her. "Why aren't you with Miss Scott,
your intended? Doesn't she take care of your lust?"

A soft chuckle accompanied the soft rustling sound of buckskins being removed. "Only you can do that, Serena." Josh's
long length slid down beside her.

"What are you doing?" she whispered fiercely, her small fists
beating at his chest when he pulled her into his arms. "Get out
of my wagon. I'll call for Paw."

"You don't mean that," he murmured back, and before she
knew it, he had deftly pulled her gown up and over her head.

And while she lay there, stunned, his lips parted against her throat, gasping her name on a long, tortured breath.

She opened her mouth to protest, then she felt the pressure of his arousal against her stomach and couldn't say a word. It took all her willpower to ignore the heated desire that scorched through her and to finally whisper, "No, no, no."

"You can say no all you want to, Serena,"—Josh threw a long leg over hers, holding her captive—"but it won't make a blind bit of difference. You hunger for me almost as strongly as I do for you. Why don't you admit it?" His lips slid down to her full breasts and fastened on a hardened nipple.

"I don't hunger for you," Serena denied raggedly. "I don't want you."

"You do, you obstinate little vixen," Josh argued savagely before his mouth sought the other breast.

And as his lips tugged urgently on the swollen nipple, Serena groaned. In love and in hate, her arms came up around his shoulders as she arched her body into his in total surrender.

Josh's sigh of relief fluttered against Serena's breast as he lifted his head to fasten his mouth on hers. While his tongue flickered in and out, he slid his hands beneath her hips and lifted them off the pallet. He bent his head to kiss the soft triangle of hair, then gently parted her legs as he carefully climbed between them to hover over her.

"Take me, honey," he whispered. "Sheathe me deep inside you. It's been so long, and I'm in such pain."

Serena's smooth palm curved around his long, hard length, caressed it a moment, then guided its pulsing strength inside her moist warmth.

Keeping a firm hold on the desire that surged through his veins, Josh slowly, steadily filled her. She sighed contentedly as, holding her narrow hips steady to take his powerful drives, he stroked in an agonizing rhythm. Tonight he intended to bring her to heights no other man ever could. Whether or not she'd ever love him, he would make sure that she never forgot him.

In seconds Serena's pent-up passion for the tall lean man who was loving her so thoroughly was climbing toward its crest. She moaned his name, and he responded to her need, rocking more quickly in the well of her hips.

When her body finally ceased shuddering and grew limp, Josh lowered Serena's hips to the pallet, but he kept his unrelieved maleness firmly inside her. As she floated in sweet ecstasy he bent his head to her breasts and sucked the nipples into flaming desire again. When she sighed softly and bucked her hips toward him, he smiled in satisfaction. Pulling her hips up again to meet his, he resumed his slow, smooth stroking.

This time Serena was determined that the wondrous working of Josh's body would last longer, to make last as long as possible the incredible sensations he caused to roil inside her. She leaned up on her elbows to watch his long strength move in and out of her body. And almost immediately she was overwhelmed by waves of passion that threatened to draw the life out of her.

This second time Josh dulled his own need, crushing Serena's lips with his as wave after wave of weakening passion rolled over him. When his body finally stopped shuddering he moved over on his side, still clasping Serena tightly. He would let her slender body rest a while and gather the strength it would need for the long night of loving he had planned.

The moon had disappeared when the exhausted lovers collapsed in each others' arms for the last time. Josh gave a tired, contented smile and laid a possessive hand on Serena's smooth stomach. He had led the way in this wild night of lovemaking, and she had followed him eagerly and willingly.

Serena also smiled, fulfilled but tired. She listened to Josh's heart throb in her ears and waited for his talk of love. For although he had murmured loving words of encouragement and gasping praise when she had proven to be a good pupil, not once had he said the three most important words.

Seconds stretched into minutes and the man lying beside her remained silent. Her heart gave a hopeful leap when finally Josh stirred to prop himself on an elbow. Now he would tell her; speak the words that would find an echo in her heart. His lids heavy with spent passion Josh gently smoothed the damp curls off her forehead.

"You are wonderful, honey," he whispered.

Serena's body stiffened. Those weren't the words she had been holding her breath to hear. They were only what a man would say to a woman, *any woman*, who had pleased him in bed.

A Special Offer For Love Spell Romance Readers Only!

Get Two Free Romance Novels

An $11.48 Value!

Travel to exotic worlds
filled with passion and adventure—
without leaving your home!

Plus, you'll save $5.00
every time you buy!

Thrill to the most sensual, adventure-filled Romances on the market today...

FROM  LOVE SPELL BOOKS

As a home subscriber to the Love Spell Romance Book Club, you'll enjoy the best in today's BRAND-NEW Time Travel, Futuristic, Legendary Lovers, Perfect Heroes and other genre romance fiction. For five years, Love Spell has brought you the award-winning, high-quality authors you know and love to read. Each Love Spell romance will sweep you away to a world of high adventure...and intimate romance. Discover for yourself all the passion and excitement millions of readers thrill to each and every month.

Save $5.00 Each Time You Buy!

Every other month, the Love Spell Romance Book Club brings you four brand-new titles from Love Spell Books. EACH PACKAGE WILL SAVE YOU AT LEAST $5.00 FROM THE BOOK-STORE PRICE! And you'll never miss a new title with our convenient home delivery service.

Here's how we do it: Each package will carry a FREE 10-DAY EXAMINATION privilege. At the end of that time, if you decide to keep your books, simply pay the low invoice price of $17.96, no shipping or handling charges added. HOME DELIVERY IS ALWAYS FREE. With today's top romance novels selling for $5.99 and higher, our price SAVES YOU AT LEAST $5.00 with each shipment.

AND YOUR FIRST TWO-BOOK SHIP-MENT IS TOTALLY FREE!

IT'S A BARGAIN YOU CAN'T BEAT! A SUPER $11.48 Value!

Love Spell ◆ A Division of Dorchester Publishing Co., Inc.

GET YOUR 2 FREE BOOKS NOW–AN $11.48 VALUE!

Mail the Free Book Certificate Today!

TWO FREE BOOKS

Free Books Certificate

YES! I want to subscribe to the Love Spell Romance Book Club. Please send me my 2 FREE BOOKS. Then every other month I'll receive the four newest Love Spell selections to Preview FREE for 10 days. If I decide to keep them, I will pay the Special Member's Only discounted price of just $4.49 each, a total of $17.96. This is a SAVINGS of at least $5.00 off the bookstore price. There are no shipping, handling, or other charges. There is no minimum number of books I must buy and I may cancel the program at any time. In any case, the 2 FREE BOOKS are mine to keep—A BIG $11.48 Value!

Offer valid only in the U.S.A.

*Name*_____

*Address*_____

*City*_____

*State*_____ *Zip*_____

*Telephone*_____

*Signature*_____

If under 18, Parent or Guardian must sign. Terms, prices and conditions subject to change. Subscription subject to acceptance. Leisure Books reserves the right to reject any order or cancel any subscription.

A $11.48 VALUE

Get Two Books Totally
FREE —
An $11.48 Value!

▼ Tear Here and Mail Your FREE Book Card Today! ▼

**PLEASE RUSH
MY TWO FREE
BOOKS TO ME
RIGHT AWAY!**

Love Spell Romance Book Club
P.O. Box 6613
Edison, NJ 08818-6613

AFFIX
STAMP
HERE

The shock stabbed sharply and spread throughout her stomach while she felt herself turn crimson with humiliation. Naturally he hadn't spoken words of love to her. He didn't love her. He loved Jane Scott.

And while Josh thought, Damn, what made me say that? Serena jerked away from him and sat up. Her voice matching the cold knot in her stomach, she said, "Really, Quade? I didn't think it was all that good. I've had better."

For a fraction of a second Serena's remark hit Josh like a slap across the face. Then amusement flickered in his eyes. She'd had no other man to compare him with. He stroked a hand down her slender back.

"Are you sayin' that you and Jovan are lovers?"

Serena shrugged away his hand. "What do you think?" She jerked her gown over her head. "You and Jane Scott aren't the only couple who are courting."

"That may be," Josh agreed, watching her yank the soft material down over her rounded hips. "But you're not gettin' any lovin' from the rancher."

"Oh? How do you know? Have you been sneaking around my wagon at nights?"

"No, I haven't been sneakin' round your wagon. Maybe I've been checkin' out Jovan's."

In her hurt and anger, Serena missed the dryness in Josh's comment. "I don't know what that proves. The nights are long. You have to sleep sometime, and if a man is determined, well . . ."

"Let's not argue." Josh tried to coax Serena back into his arms. "These past hours have been so perfect. Let's make the rest of the trip that way."

Rage burst inside Serena. "Oh! You'd like that, you randy tomcat!" She almost spit the words at him. "You've got it all worked out, haven't you? Since the proper Miss Scott won't act the whore for you, I can play that role. Well, you can go to hell, Josh Quade!"

Her voice grew louder with each word, bringing Josh to his feet in alarm. If Eli heard her, found him naked in her wagon, God only knew what the short-tempered Southerner might do.

Maybe he wouldn't shoot him, but he'd lose all respect for him. The older man had great love for Serena Bain.

Josh was scrambling into his buckskins as Serena almost shouted, "Get the hell out of my wagon and don't you dare come near it again."

As Josh jumped to the ground and made a hurried exit, he swore impatiently under his breath. He still hadn't told the little spitfire how deeply he loved her.

CHAPTER
∽15∽

JOSH RODE FAR AHEAD of the train this early afternoon, a worried frown creasing his forehead. How had he strayed away from the river? For the hundredth time since embarking on the wilderness trek, he muttered, "Damn, I wish I had a map."

Another half hour passed in which the big man debated the possibilities open to him. Stop the train right now and send scouts out in all directions before continuing on, or listen to his gut feeling that he was still on the right track, or, the least attractive one, swallow his pride and ask the rancher, Jovan.

His lips drew into a firm line. The latter would take a large chunk of willpower. He could barely be civil to the man, much less admit to him that he needed his help.

Sometime later Josh was still straining his eyes ahead, about to reluctantly give in and approach Jovan, when he realized that the stallion had quickened its pace and was straining impatiently against the bit.

With a relieved sigh the wagon master's uneasiness faded away. The big animal smelled water. He gave his mount the reins and it immediately veered to the right, loping in a direction entirely opposite to where he had steered it. In another ten minutes the velvet-soft nose was whiffling the water of the mighty Snake.

Josh hooked a leg over the saddle horn and studied the swiftly flowing stream. "You're a mean-lookin' bastard," he growled, "and accordin' to Jovan, noted for your quicksand."

When he feared the stallion was in danger of foundering, he pulled the sleek head up and turned it toward the wagon train. In a half mile he spotted the long, snaking line and wondered glumly if he would lose any of those wagons—and more important, any lives—while fording the river. This would be their hardest crossing to date; the men would be tested severely by the Snake's treacherous waters.

Standing up in the stirrups, Josh raised his rifle and snapped off a shot, a prearranged signal to the wagon train. His action was answered by loud distant cheers. The orderly line of vehicles was broken, and in minutes the river bank was lined with thirsty livestock.

Upstream, safe from trampling hooves, women and children eagerly dashed into the shallow depths, a blissful look on their faces as chafed skin drank in the wet coolness. Serena was about to join them when she paused at the sound of hard-galloping hooves coming up behind her.

"You women! Get out of there!" two male voices yelled. "There is quicksand in this river bottom," Josh's deep voice warned, echoed by Foster Jovan's.

Their eyes mirroring terror, mothers grabbed children and hustled them back onto the sandy river bank. One white-faced woman voiced the question that had occurred to everyone. "How are we gonna cross it if there's quicksand in there?"

Josh let his gaze rest briefly on each anxious face, lingering a little longer on Serena's. She noted the lurking disquiet in his eyes, even as they twinkled at the women's fears. There was a reassuring calmness in his tone when he answered them.

"There's nothin' to it, ladies. We hit the water at a run and keep the critters movin' as fast as we can."

He turned his lean body in the saddle and looked down into the uneasy faces of the men who had come up silently behind him. His quiet, matter-of-fact words were like a soothing balm to them.

"Men, for the first time this drought we've been in is gonna benefit us. The river is low because of it, and you should be able to keep your teams at a full gallop until you're across."

When relieved smiles replaced dread on the weathered faces, Josh raised a cautioning hand. "Bear in mind now that it's very important the teams don't slow down to a walk. You'll be takin' a chance on losin' your wagon and team if that happens."

Everyone nodded agreement, with only one man venturing a suggestion. The owner of a small herd of purebred cattle wondered if perhaps they should lay over for the rest of the day, suggesting that animals, as well as drivers, would be more refreshed after a night's rest, and would have a safer crossing.

Josh glanced over his shoulder to the north. "Ordinarily I'd agree with you," he said. "But by the looks of them clouds buildin' back there it could rain tonight. If it does, this river will double its size and we could be stuck here for a week waitin' for it to go down."

Everyone, including the cattleman, acknowledged that Josh made sense. And squatting down in a semicircle, they began discussions as how best to carry out his plans to get them to the other side of the river.

It was decided finally that half the men on horseback would cross first then wait on the other side with ropes ready. If a wagon should get bogged down the chances were good that these men could pull it out. And the other half of the riders would swim alongside the wagons, helping in any way they could, even rescuing passengers if necessary.

A somber group of people then gazed across the wide expanse of the Snake, asking themselves if everyone would set foot on the other shore. In one accord the women knelt down to pray to the Lord for a safe passage. The bared heads of the men bowed solemnly over them, and Jessie and her girls clasped hands and silently mouthed long-forgotten prayers.

Amens were murmured, and those chosen to cross first swung into saddles and charged their mounts into the river at a dead run. The animals plunged and splashed, snorting in displeasure, but beneath the slash of riding quirts and shouted encouragement, the opposite shore was reached. The men waited there with anxious eyes and coiled ropes in hand.

The first wagon waited, its driver standing with feet planted firmly and reins gripped tightly. His family knelt huddled together in the back, their eyes wide with dread. Josh sat his restless stallion, waiting for the man to nod that he was ready. When the sign was given he pointed his rifle skyward and pulled the trigger.

The driver's sonorous yell echoed the ringing shot, and accompanied by the crack of the long whip over their backs, the startled team lunged ahead, hitting the water before they were fully aware of it. Yelling and cracking their whips, several riders swam their horses alongside the galloping team while their owner, his arm moving frenziedly, lashed at their backs.

Serena sat Beauty, straining her eyes to watch the wagon's progress. It was next to impossible to see anything through the misty clouds of water being churned up. She imagined that it had crossed safely when another wagon hit the water.

Four more wagons crossed without incident, including Jessie's. The terrified high screams of her girls frightened the mules so, little additional help was needed to spur them on.

Then the Landrie wagon was next. Serena studied the cumbersome vehicle apprehensively. Could its great weight and size be pulled swiftly across the river by the plodding oxen?

It did not ease her concern when Josh rode up and cautioned, "Use the whip with a heavy hand, Paw. Don't give them beasts time to think." And while she sat, ready to hit the water with Eli, he turned somber eyes on her.

He wanted to tell her to be careful, that if anything should happen to her he didn't know what he'd do. But the words never came. After a hesitant moment he caused the rifle to crack again.

Eli let loose a bellowing roar, and the startled oxen lunged into the yokes and shot into the water. At Serena's command Beauty splashed in behind them, her uneasiness showing in her rippling muscles. Serena felt the cool water moving up her legs and sighed with relief when she felt the mare swimming.

Everything went well until the wagon was halfway across the stream. Then those watching on both sides of the river gasped in unison when the big prairie schooner gave a shuddering lurch, then stopped. A wheel had caught on something. Eli yelled and snapped the long whip, and the oxen tried to respond, bawling and straining into the yokes. But their efforts only managed to drag the wagon a few feet before coming to another halt.

Her heart in her throat, Serena joined the flurry of motion

around the wagon and, with the other riders, yelled and flayed the water with her whip. Their eyes rolling, terrorized now by the noise and their inability to move, the oxen bunched their solid shoulders and gave one last mighty lunge. With a loud sucking sound the quicksand released its hold. Shortly thereafter water was pouring from the wagon as the weary oxen pulled it up on shore.

Eli and Serena had just hugged each other in thanksgiving when a shout went up. "Horse in trouble!"

Squinting her eyes, Serena stared across the water, then felt like a giant hand had closed around her heart. Josh's big stallion was caught in a strong current and was being swept swiftly downstream, only its fine head showing above the water. Josh was submerged well past his waist as he struggled to keep the mount's head up and steered out of the current.

Serena stood frozen a moment, her thoughts a mixture of fear and dread. Then without thinking she ran to Beauty and swung into the saddle. But as she lifted the reins, ready to dash back into the stream, Landrie grabbed hold of the bridle.

"Stay here, Serena," he ordered firmly. "You'll only be in the way. The men will handle it."

"But, Paw—" Serena struggled to free the mare.

"Mind me, missy." Eli's tone said he would brook no disobedience. "Just get down off the mare and be quiet."

There were no more outcries as with bated breath everyone tensely watched the two riders swim their mounts to the floundering stallion. There was a thankful murmuring as with unerring skill two ropes snaked out, one settling over the terror-filled horse's neck, the other coming down around Josh's shoulders. The horse might be lost, but the man would survive.

The trained quarter horse obeyed the pressure of knees and strained toward shore. The rope tightened on the stallion and, bit by bit, it was slowly turned, then steadily and carefully towed free of the sucking current. A great shout went up when the tired animal's hooves hit solid bottom and galloped toward shore.

Josh was quickly surrounded as he stepped from the saddle, and Serena, forgetting their last encounter, obeyed the dictates of her heart and moved to join the group of well-wishers.

She froze in mid-stride as she saw Jane Scott run up and push her way to Josh's side. His gaze caught Serena's just as the woman threw her arms around his waist and rested her head on his chest.

For an instant Josh stiffened as Jane clung to him, a distinct aversion clouding his eyes. Then, so swiftly Serena knew she must have imagined the expression, Josh put a hand under Jane's chin and tipped her face to his. Just before his lips touched the woman's, his eyes slid to Serena, the light in them saying that he was enjoying her fight to regain her composure.

Serena bit her lip and looked away, sensing that many eyes were upon her, assessing, some showing pity, others spiteful pleasure. Suddenly Eli was beside her, his hand gripping her elbow. "Put your chin up, missy," he ordered softly, turning her away from the watching faces. "Don't let your hurt show. It would give some of them jealous witches too much pleasure."

Eli's words stabbed through Serena's misery. She straightened her spine and smiled brightly at the stern-faced man walking beside her. His face softened, and he returned an approving smile.

But as Serena unsaddled Beauty, then began setting up camp, her mind was still at variance with the front she bravely put up. Inside she felt empty. She couldn't deny what she had witnessed. She must accept the fact that Josh really did love Jane Scott.

Josh, however, on seeing Eli leading Serena away, had put Miss Scott away from him so roughly that she almost fell. *God, you dumb bastard, what have you done?* He directed the angry question to himself as he pushed through the crowd. What had induced him to humiliate Serena so . . . and, almost as bad, encourage Jane Scott? Hell, she'd be hanging around him worse than ever now.

By the time the last wagon made it across the river the sun was almost down, and a tired and weary group made camp.

Serena had just put a pot of coffee to brew on a bed of red coals when to her surprise Josh walked into their camp. She pretended to ignore him, but she didn't miss a move of his as he silently began helping Eli unyoke the oxen, then drag the wet items out of the wagon.

He's got a lot of gall, she thought as she banged pots and frying pans. *He flaunts his woman under my nose, then shows* his scraggly face at my fire. Her brows drawn together with an affronted frown, she raised her head to order him away, then faltered when she found his gaze on her. She stared. Was that entreaty in his eyes, asking for forgiveness?

She dismissed the thought with an inward snort. It had to have been a shadow shamelessly playing on his face.

"Your mattress is ruined, honey." Eli broke the tense silence. He smiled at Serena apologetically and tossed it aside. "Even if we dried it out, you wouldn't want it. It will never lose that musty smell wet straw always gets."

Serena shrugged indifferently as she stirred a pot of beans bubbling over the fire. Eli turned to Josh and suggested they now go to Nell's wagon and straighten it out. Serena doggedly kept her eyes on the pot of beans.

It was midafternoon, and Josh reckoned the wagons had covered around forty miles since the river crossing when he spotted Fort Hall in the distance. He signaled to the lead wagon to pull up and loped toward the large, open cantonment.

His eyes took on a wary look as six soldiers, led by a captain, trotted out of the fort and came toward him. Was his train to be turned away? His eyes narrowed, as he prepared himself for an argument. The teams were beat and his people bone tired. Both animals and men needed a couple days of rest.

He had worried needlessly. As the small group of riders pulled up before him there was a genial smile on the young officer's face. He leaned from the saddle and offered his hand.

"Welcome to Fort Hall. Captain George Rush in command."

Josh liked the man's firm handshake and returned his smile. "Josh Quade, wagon master of a train originating out of Michigan. Can we make camp here?"

"I'll be glad to have you," Rush said, then motioned with a thumb over his right shoulder. "You can put your livestock and wagons over there on the parade grounds and set up camp inside the fort." After a polite pause he asked, "How long will you be with us?"

"Only a couple days. Just long enough to give my people and animals a rest and to make a few repairs on some of the wagons."

"Where are you bound for?"

"Oregon country, somewhere around Baker."

A small frown furrowed the young man's forehead. "You don't plan on going straight through, do you?"

"Naw." Josh grinned. "I've got too many greenhorns in the company. I'm gonna have to stop somewhere before winter sets in."

"And that's not too far off, according to the Indians," Rush said. "They claim we're in for an early winter this year; something about the bark on the trees and the extra fur the animals are growing.

"But I think you can make it to Fort Bridger before the first snowfall. Old Jim Bridger has a fine setup there. He built the place especially for emigrants. There's a store, tavern, and several cabins."

"That's good to know." Josh smiled with relief, some of the weariness lifting from his shoulders. "I've been worryin' about winter quarters." He lifted a hand to the captain and turned the stallion back in the direction of the waiting wagons. There he ordered that the women and children be let off at the fort to set up camp and the animals be taken to the parade ground.

The women and children moved stiffly between the two huge cottonwoods that made a natural gateway to the inside of the fort, grateful to be stretching their legs again. The wagon master had pushed them hard all day, and Serena was convinced that the team had deliberately drawn the wagon over every rut in the road. She longed to rub her aching buttocks, but was too aware of the male eyes fixed upon her.

The cantonment scattered itself over a large area. Long barracks and officers' quarters stretched neatly across one end, while a trading post, a blacksmith's, and other small buildings gave the rambling appearance of two additional walls boxing in the fort.

Surprise and alarm showed on feminine faces, for among the soldiers who quickly gathered there were many Indians. The children, wide-eyed and apprehensive, gathered close to mothers, hanging on to their skirts and stepping on their heels. Jessie nudged Serena and whispered, "If the Indians are warring against the whites, what are they doin' among all these soldiers?''

"A good question," Serena answered, feeling a shiver run down her spine.

Their question was answered by the proprietor of the store where the women gathered to wait for the men.

"There's an Indian village and cemetery a mile or so away," he explained. "And though they trade with the pale-face today, tomorrow they might try to kill him. The Indians are a strange people."

The women agreed, peering across to the parade ground, anxious for the men to join them.

A good half hour had passed when, with spirits high, the men headed for the fort. And though each man respected Josh's strict rule of no drinking on the trail, a man's throat got awfully dry after a while. After their families were settled in, the men quickly headed for the tavern. Everyone, that is, but Foster Jovan. He went in search of Serena.

His faced darkened disapprovingly when he found her sitting beneath a tree with Jessie and her girls. His eyes narrowed when gay laughter erupted from the group, drawing the attention of several soldiers standing nearby. "Why does she insist on being in that woman's company all the time?" he growled through his teeth. "Those men will think she's a whore too."

Whether Jovan did not see, or simply chose to ignore, the heated looks shot his way when he interrupted the light chatter of Serena and her friends was hard to say from his expressionless face. However, everyone caught the suppressed anger in his voice when he said to Serena, "We've got at least an hour before sundown, so come take a walk with me."

Serena's lips compressed. *He will never accept Jessie as my friend,* she realized, and wondered if she'd been wise in encouraging his attention. Nonetheless, she forced a smile to her face, and with a resigned sigh she rose and took Jovan's proffered arm.

They had walked just a short distance from the group when Jovan stopped and turned to face her. She blinked in surprise when he asked soberly, "Will you marry me, Serena? Let me announce our engagement tonight."

Surely he isn't serious, Serena thought wildly. Doesn't he realize that there's no spark between us?

Jovan saw the bafflement on her face and hurried to add what he thought would be an enticing inducement to his proposal of marriage. "You'll never be sorry, Serena. I'll treat you like a queen. I promise to use you gently, and not too often. I want a son, badly."

Serena could hardly keep from crying out, "Foster, I don't want to be used gently. I want you to make love to me as though I mean everything in the world to you, like you can't get enough of me. The way Josh—" For never have the words *love* or *marriage* passed his lips.

At least Foster honored her with an offer of marriage before asking to share her bed, she reminded herself. That was love, wasn't it, respect? And maybe that love would take heat, approach the same kind of intensity Josh had fired in her, if she and Foster should marry.

Serena shook her head at this last thought. She could never marry Foster. The pair of them were like oil and water together, never quite mixing.

She chewed the side of her lower lip, methodically choosing the words that wouldn't let him down too harshly. Finally she looked up at the rancher, who waited hopefully.

"I really can't give you an answer now, Foster," she explained. "There's my brother Dorn to consider. Before I would marry any man I'd want Dorn to meet him first, to give me his blessing."

Jovan stiffened, and when she saw his mouth tighten with irritation, she was glad of the lie she'd told him. Had he shown hurt or disappointment, she'd have added some softening word. But now it was no longer necessary.

She looked at Jovan blankly. "I'm sorry, Foster, that's the only answer I can give you."

Foster steeled his face not to show the rage boiling inside him. The coy little girl, did she think she was too good for him? Well, she'd find out differently.

His eyes hooded, hiding the anger that still burned in his blood, his teeth flashed in a quick smile. "I can understand that,

Serena. However, I hope you won't mind if in the meantime it pleases me to think that we have an understanding of sorts.''

"Well"—Serena shifted uneasily—"if you want to think that. But I want it understood clearly that I've made you no promise.''

"But you didn't say a definite no," Jovan reminded her, tightening his arm around her waist.

Before Serena could make a suitable response, he brushed a chaste kiss across her lips and pulled her to her feet. As he hurried her back toward the fort, he kept up a constant chatter on his ranch, his cattle, making it impossible for her to return to the original conversation.

Nor could she broach the subject when they reached the encampment, for after giving her hands a gentle squeeze, Jovan hurried away. She stared after him, wondering why she felt this sense of uneasiness. She shook her head and, with a little sigh, set about lighting a fire and starting supper.

Thankfully her hands worked with a will of their own at the familiar task, for Serena's mind was far from what she was doing. She couldn't shake the disquieting sensation that some vital fact was escaping her.

Half an hour later, as she was testing a potato with a long-handled fork, there began to unfold a justification for the anxiety that had plagued Serena for the past hour. It started with Jovan swaggering into camp with an expression of relish on his handsome face. "What's he up to?" she muttered under her breath as the man hopped up on a large rock, drawing everyone's attention.

"Ladies and gentlemen," he called, his voice ringing complacent, "I want you all to share in my great happiness." He paused as though to impart the importance of his announcement. When he was satisfied that he had everyone's attention, he sent Serena a warm look and continued.

"It has been agreed between me and Miss Bain that after I have met her brother, we will become engaged.''

Silence gripped those who had gathered around, and a stolen look was sent from Josh's cold, still face to Serena's red flushed one before the frying pan in her nerveless fingers dropped into the fire, sending sparks and ashes flying.

She took a step toward the obviously satisfied rancher, ready

to hotly denounce his words. But then her sparking eyes took in
the fact that Jane Scott had an arm tucked possessively in Josh's,
a mocking light in her eyes as she smiled smugly at her.

"Bitch," Serena hissed between her teeth, refusing to look
again at Josh, sure that she would read sardonic amusement in
his eyes. She turned coolly back to the fire and retrieved the
frying pan from the ashes, telling herself, without too much
conviction, that she was glad Foster had told his lie. Josh would
stay away from her now and in time she would get over her
foolish idea that they were necessary to one another.

Her head bent over the frying meat, Serena missed seeing the
perplexed expressions that flashed over the faces of the men.
The wagon master was a fine man, and in their opinion the little
beauty had chosen the wrong man. But in order to hide the
sympathy they knew Josh would not want, the men reluctantly
offered Jovan congratulations.

Jane Scott, who had immediately searched Josh's face at Jovan's announcement, had seen the agony that flickered in his eyes.
She firmed the satisfied curl of her lips, and, smiling up at him,
she asked gaily, "Shall we go congratulate the happy couple?"

She flinched at the cold glower that preceded his brusque,
"I've got to attend to some business." And pulling away from
her grasp he walked quickly away, disappearing into the gathering darkness.

Eli, his face a cold study, did not offer any good wishes either.
Shooting Serena a glaring, disgusted look, and grabbing Nell by
the arm, he growled, loud enough for the uncomfortable girl to
hear, "Let's get out of here. Serena just threw her life away."

Serena stared glumly into the flames. Damn Foster to hell.
Because of his lie, this time Paw was really upset with her,
probably finished with her forever.

But why? Her chin jutted out defiantly. Why was he so set
against Foster? Even though she was raging angry with the man,
and had no intention of ever marrying him, she still liked and
respected Foster. He was a successful rancher and was always
courteous to Paw, and still the older man had this unreasonable
dislike for him.

She tossed a piece of wood onto the fire. Of course I know
the reason for Paw's attitude toward Foster, she thought. He

wants to see me married to Josh, the man he *thinks* is so perfect. Well, I could tell him a few things about his perfect man that would make him change the tune of his song in praise of that long-legged wolf.

Serena's eyes were still snapping when a masculine voice rose behind her. "Are you awfully angry with me, Serena?"

"Yes I am, Foster." She swung around on him. "You told those people an out-and-out lie."

"I know, and I'm sorry." Jovan hunkered down beside her. "I saw Quade looking at you, his eyes all hungry, and before I knew it, I was blurting it out." He touched her shoulder gently. "Am I forgiven?"

Jovan's apology was so unexpected it took Serena a while to answer him. She could understand him being jealous of Josh, wanting to strike out at him, for hadn't she felt that way about Jane Scott many times?

"Do you want me to tell them the truth?" Jovan asked after some time passed and Serena still hadn't answered him.

Serena shrugged her shoulders wearily. "It really doesn't matter." She fixed Jovan with stern eyes. "As long as you remember our conversation about an engagement between us. Remember that nothing has been settled."

"I won't forget, Serena, I promise." He motioned toward the coffee pot. "May I have a cup of your brew?"

Serena filled two cups, then handed one to Jovan. As they sipped the steaming liquid silently tired parents and children around them began to yawn and nod. Soon only Serena's fire continued to burn as she and Foster sat before it, while the Indian boy, Sato, remained lurking in the shadows.

CHAPTER
∽16∽

ANOTHER SIX WEEKS had passed since the wagon train rolled out of Fort Hall, and bleak November was upon the travelers. Fort Bridger couldn't be too far ahead, the wagon master hoped.

Hunched in the saddle, his collar pulled up around his ears, Josh rode several yards ahead of the other riders, gazing across the endless miles of rock and granite. This new land, he frowned, was a desolate place, draining the nerves of an already depleted people. Tensions were high and quarrels were becoming common among the men and women. And yesterday, to add to everyone's discomfort, a cold wet rain that threatened to turn to snow had descended upon them.

He sighed heavily. The trust placed in him put a heavy burden on his weary shoulders. Could he come through for them?

Serena, some distance behind Josh, also hunched against the chilly wet and shivered when a blast of cold rain blew against her face. Lately she had felt frozen most of the time. She glanced at a passing rider and envy sparked in her eyes. She could easily resume her dislike of the hardy people from the northwoods, she thought with a rueful smile. While she added more shawls to her shoulders the women from the North let their jackets flap open, stepping along as though new blood pumped in their veins.

And Josh Quade glowed with so much health his big body was like the presence of some feral animal as he moved about camp.

Like now, she grimaced, eyeing the loosely held body moving in unison with his mount. He hadn't even donned a coat. His only concession to the growing cold was to lace the buckskin shirt up to his muscular throat.

What does this silent, reserved man think about, she wondered, as he rides along, never seeking human companions? With the exception of Paw he had formed no real friendships along the way.

She was deeply saddened as she realized that she and Josh had never had a real conversation, had not gotten to know one another. Between them it had either been hard, insulting words or the ragged breathing of mutual pleasure.

Did the pair of them have anything in common, she mused, other than the deep attraction they shared for each other? Did Josh have a good sense of humor? Did he like children, old people, animals? Did his hard features hide a kind heart? There was tenderness in him, she knew.

A sigh feathered through Serena's lips. Josh hadn't been near her since that night Foster announced the false engagement. And Paw, she thought, her eyes dulled, she saw very little of him, usually only in the mornings when he hitched up the wagon. And the constrained feeling between them hadn't lessened either.

Serena suddenly tightened her grip on the reins, making the mare snort in displeasure. Jane Scott had just spurred her mount up alongside Josh's.

She patted the mare's sleek brown neck in apology for having caused the bit to bite into her tender mouth. "Sorry, Beauty," she murmured, "my brain must be waterlogged, wasting my thoughts on that long-legged wolf." She looked away when Jane leaned seductively toward Josh, an inviting smile touching her lips.

The woman dropped her eyes before the frosty look she received from Josh and stammered, "I . . . I thought I'd ride along with you for a while."

Turning his profile to her and looking straight ahead, Josh said gruffly, "You'd better get back to Nell. I'm sure she'll need your help when we make camp."

His weak excuse for sending the hired woman away was like

a slap in her face. It would be at least two hours before night camp was made. She stared bleakly at his stiff back. She should have known from Nell's dubious expression when she asked the widow for the loan of her mount that Quade wouldn't want her company. Resentment leapt in her eyes when she spotted the dainty mare stepping along just a short distance behind Josh.

Wheeling the borrowed horse she raced back toward the Simpson wagon, throwing Serena a vengeful look as she splashed past her.

Josh listened to Jane's wet retreat, thinking that the woman was becoming a bother and a bore. He knew what she wanted—marriage. He smiled sourly. The man she would finally hook would be in for a disappointing discovery. The warmth and promise in that lady's eyes was only a façade. Underneath she was cold and calculating. Twice he had caught her unaware, each time reading greed and ruthlessness in her unguarded face.

He rode on, his thoughts unconsciously turning to Serena in comparison to the other woman. Nothing was withheld with her. The hot, eager response of her lovely, soft body melted a man, drove him on, even when he was ready to drop.

Josh's shoulders suddenly sagged in his wet shirt. Serena was marrying another man, and he would never possess her again. But he had one small consolation. Jovan would never replace him when it came to lovemaking, of that he was sure. For the kind of passion he and Serena had shared came but once in a lifetime between a man and a woman.

He shook himself and straightened his shoulders. He mustn't hammer at that thought anymore, he thought, and forced his attention back on the surrounding area. The sky had gone from a dull gray to almost black. Any minute now the fine drizzle was going to turn into a full-fledged blizzard.

"We're in for it," he muttered, anxiously scanning the tall granite walls that hemmed the train in. There was no protection here for his people. There was nothing to do but pull up and ride out the weather the best they could.

The word to halt had barely traveled the long line when the storm broke with a fury. Gales of wind swept down the canyon, driving frozen pellets of snow before it. It lashed at people and animals, striving, it seemed, to push them backwards.

Blinded and maddened by the icy onslaught, teams and horses fought the straining hands that kept them from succumbing to the raging storm.

Josh's stallion was behaving remarkably well until a piece of brush came whipping along and lodged against his forelegs with a crackling thud. Terrorized instantly, the animal neighed and reared, pawing at the sky. Josh slid from the saddle, fought the horse to a stand, and, whipping the scarf from around his throat, tied it across the wild rolling eyes.

He sighed with relief when the great beast relaxed and stood still. Then, ready to swing back into the saddle he caught a flurried motion from the corner of his eyes and whirled around.

"Serena!"

A few yards behind him the delicate girl struggled to hold back the mare that strained to bolt and run. As Josh rushed to her aid, dodging rearing horses and plunging teams, he could see by the paleness of her face that she was about to collapse.

After what seemed forever he was finally at the small mare's head, grabbing hold of the bridle. It took several seconds of soothing words before the frantic animal heeded the calm voice and settled down. Serena turned to Josh then, exhausted, she leaned weakly toward him.

All noise and confusion was shut out; nothing outside of themselves existed as their eyes met and locked. Josh's slightly trembling hands grasped Serena's small waist and lifted her out of the saddle. Their eyes still tight on one another, he held her level with his face a moment before he slowly slid her down along his hard body. She felt his cold, wet frame begin to simmer, and when their hips met he groaned throatily and held her there.

Serena gave her own little gasp of pleasure and need when she felt his blatantly rigid manhood pulsating madly against her thigh. Her arms flew around his neck as her act of desire caused Josh to place his hands on her rounded buttocks and pull her tightly into the well of his hips.

I'll surely faint, Serena thought as she squeezed her eyes shut. Eagerly Josh sought her lips and bucked urgently and suggestively against her. But the threat of swooning did not deter her from opening her lips to receive his thrusting tongue, or cease the straining of her body against his need.

"Oh, God, Serena, I need you," he whispered huskily in the hollow of her throat. "I lay awake nights thinking of you, wanting you in my arms."

He moved slim fingers beneath the damp, heavy shawls she wore and took a firm, round breast in each hand. When his stroking thumb tantalized each nipple until it tingled he fumbled at the laces at her throat. "I've got to feel their velvety smoothness again, know their sweetness in my mouth."

"Oh, yes, yes!" Serena moaned helplessly, her fingers flying to aid his desire.

And keeping Serena captive in the tight circle of his arms, Josh stepped behind a tall, narrow boulder and there his hot mouth claimed first one breast and then the other. And while his tongue flicked and teased, Serena hurriedly groped at his buckskins and gently stroked his throbbing maleness.

It took Landrie's outraged cry to bring the pair back to earth. Even so the return was not rushed. Serena's hand slid out of Josh's buckskins with reluctance, and he took time for one last stripping of the nipple held between his teeth. He lowered her until her feet touched the ground, then stood in front of her, hiding her until she had retied the laces and adjusted the shawls. And if Eli expected to see embarrassment or regret on the lean face when it turned to him, he was disappointed for he saw only unabashed desire.

The Southerner shook his head in utter disbelief, and after darting glances around to see if anyone else had viewed what he had, he sighed with relief. Everyone was busy battling the storm. He brought his stern gaze back to the heavy-lidded pair and snapped, "Get inside here, Serena, before you freeze to death."

Silently Josh swept Serena up and set her down beside Eli. Then, tying the mare to the tailgate, he returned to the stallion, swung into the saddle, and loped away to the head of the train. For the first time, concern for those in his charge did not take precedence as he stared ahead blankly.

All his thoughts were taken up with the girl who had melted so lovingly in his arms. Dammit, she couldn't love Jovan. Why, she had responded to him just now the way she always did in his arms.

His lips firmed in determination. This foolish pride each was guilty of must come to an end, otherwise there would be no happiness for either one of them.

Far back in the line, sitting beside Eli, Serena was also in deep thought. Surely Josh didn't love Jane Scott after the hungry way he had just sought to make love to her.

The memory of his bruising kisses and the fire of his mouth on her breasts sent a recurrence of desire shooting through her veins. She had stifled a little moan, then started when Eli spoke softly to her.

"Are you all right, daughter?"

Serena's first instinct was to tell Eli everything, to lay her head on his shoulder and howl like his old hound as she told him of her doubts and uncertainties about Josh. She didn't love the rancher—it was Josh she loved and wanted to marry.

She shook her head; she couldn't do that. She couldn't trust Paw not to go to Josh and angrily demand that he state his intentions toward her. She'd be so embarrassed that she'd never be able to look Josh in the face again.

She managed a weak smile in Eli's direction and murmured that she was fine, only a little tired and cold. "I'm looking forward to a fire and some hot food."

Eli respected her unspoken request not to pry, and he put an arm around her narrow shoulders. Pulling her up close to his side, he teased, "I think this old body can still generate enough heat to warm you up a little."

His levity brought a giggle from Serena, and Eli smiled, happy that he had brought a little pink back to her cheeks. Nevertheless, he told himself, one of these days he was going to have a serious talk with Josh, whether Serena wanted him to or not. Whatever they shared between themselves couldn't continue as it was now. In the end they would destroy each other.

Total darkness was not too far off when the train inched from between the towering walls of granite and entered a shallow valley. Shouts of elation ripped through hoarse throats as the emigrants peered through the blowing snow and feasted their tear-blurred eyes upon Fort Bridger. The wagon master's teeth flashed in a white, relieved smile as mothers hugged children and then smiled happily at their husbands. Finally, Josh thought, a respite from bouncing wagons and bone-chilling cold, for three months at least.

The fortress, with its palisade walls and buildings erected from cottonwood trees, was not overly large. The main building, the post, wasn't much larger than the several cabins scattered about the courtyard, and much smaller than the two buildings jutting out from either side of it. One side was clearly a smithy, considering the clanging and hammering going on inside. And on the other side, it was learned later, was a tavern.

Regardless of its size, however, seeing the Stars and Stripes fluttering from a flagpole stirred everyone's blood and raised their spirits as the wagons rolled into the compound.

The noise of the emigrants' arrival brought several men spilling from inside the tavern. For the most part it appeared trappers made up the majority of the males who gathered for a look at the women in the train. And Josh, recognizing his own kind immediately, mused to himself that the lean, somber men had probably come down from the hills for a bit of company and some relaxation.

Josh's glance was caught by the group of women and children standing off to one side, and he couldn't suppress the sympathetic smile that touched his lips as uneasy looks were cast at five blanket-wrapped Indians who stared back stoically at them. He could almost see what the group was thinking. Would they find Indians at every fort?

"My own thoughts," he muttered, reining in the stallion and swinging to the ground. As he stretched his stiff back, a tall, thin man with a bobbing adam's apple separated himself from the men idling before the tavern and walked in his direction.

Well past his fifties, Josh thought, as he was greeted with a wide smile and a proffered hand.

"The name is Jim Bridger." Pale blue eyes blinked against the snowflakes caught in light, skimpy eyelashes. "Welcome to Fort Bridger."

"Thank you." Josh released the bony hand, gave his name, then added, "We're right thankful to be here."

"You should be. You folks, just beat gettin' caught in a blizzard comin' down from Canada."

Josh gave Bridger a rueful look. "We got a taste of it comin' through that pass."

"A taste is right. You just watch a few hours from now."

"We'd like to watch from permanent quarters if it's all right with you." Josh grinned. "I've pushed my people hard to get here before the snows set in."

"Your people will be welcome," Bridger answered cheerfully. "It gets danged lonesome here in the winter. Don't see too many people 'cause the trails are shut off by drifted snow."

"There's quite a few of us," Josh warned, glancing over his shoulder at the emigrants who watched him and Bridger with anxious faces. "Do you think you can put all of us up?"

Bridger waved a dismissing hand. "Don't fret about it. I have a system here that works just fine. See them cabins back there?" He jerked a thumb over his shoulder. "They're for the married couples. A place where they can continue to be a family while waiting out the winter.

"Now the buildings ain't big but they're good stout places with fine drawing fireplaces." He directed Josh's attention to his right. "You see them two long barracklike structures? They're for the single people in your group. The first one is for all the men over age fifteen, and the one next to it for the women."

Josh managed to say, "It sounds fine," when behind him a muttering began to rumble. It was soon clear that some of the company wasn't happy with the old man's setup.

Irritation flickered across his face. The damn fools, didn't they know how lucky they were to have found any kind of shelter with a blizzard whistling at their rears? However, he and Bridger were soon in the middle of clamoring, buzzing arguments.

The single women declared vehemently that they would not spend a winter cooped up with six whores, while the single men shouted just as determinedly that Bridger had no right to keep them from Jessie and her girls. And Bridger, hemmed in by them, his adam's apple bobbing crazily, shouted back, "There will be no whorin' goin' on in my fort. It only leads to trouble." He swung around to face the women. "As for you wimmen," he roared, "maybe you'd rather keep rollin' up in your blankets out here in the snow. I can tell you right now it gets darn cold in this here valley.''

When he continued to get a few glowering looks he said testily, ''It's my place and I can run it any damn way I please. Take it or leave it.''

When the yammering settled down in the face of Bridger's firm stand, Josh walked over to Jessie, who was leaning against her wagon listening to the angry debate. And though her lips were tilted in a scornful smile, he knew that she was resentful of the words being shouted by both men and women.

Smiling into the gaminelike face, he ruffled the red hair. ''Don't let them bother you, Jess. They're just ignorant.''

''That's right, Jessie.'' Serena approached and spoke behind Josh. ''The seven of us will scout out a corner and the others can go to blazes.''

Jessie trilled her usual gay, careless laugh and linking her arm with Serena's, said, ''I don't pay any attention to words like those anymore.'' Her eyes twinkled mischievously. ''Actually, I'm thankful for the old goat's rule. It'll give me a chance to rest and get some meat on my bones.''

A laugh began to gather in Serena's and Josh's throats then died in confusion as their eyes met and hunger leapt between them.

''Let's go check out our quarters, Jessie,'' Serena murmured, avoiding her friend's knowing grin.

''I've got to get goin', too,'' Josh said. ''Find out from Bridger where to put the stock.''

As Serena and Jessie walked away, Serena could feel Josh's burning gaze following her. Her whole being suddenly tingled with the desire to turn around, run back to him, and throw herself in his arms.

Josh caught up with Bridger as the irritated men stamped toward the post. ''Jim, I'm sorry for the way them damn fools been carryin' on.'' He fell in step with the older man. ''But they're just a small portion of the emigrants. The others are fine men and women, and are very thankful for your hospitality.''

When Bridger didn't answer, only kept stamping along, Josh asked hesistantly, ''Where can we unhitch the teams and house the stock?''

It seemed as if the irate man would take back his previous welcome; the black look on his face undoubtedly said that he might be considering it. Finally, though, as Josh continued to walk determinedly beside him., some of the fight left the pale blue eyes. Taking Josh by an arm, he steered him past the corner of the palisade and, pointing a long finger southward, explained, "Go past that stand of spruce and you'll find shelter and feed for your animals. When you come back I'll settle you all in."

"I'm much obliged," Josh called after Bridger as he disappeared into the post.

Relief washed away the worry on the men's faces when Josh informed them that, no thanks to some, old Bridger was allowing them to put up for the winter.

Wagon wheels creaked and whips snapped, and for the first time in months the weary animals would be sheltered from the elements. And though their owners wondered what the testy Bridger would charge them for the hay being forked into feeding cribs, all were thankful that at last the poor beasts would eat regularly.

"Serena!"

Serena turned her head at the cheery call and a smile lit up her face. She took Jessie's outstretched arm and they turned their steps toward Nell Simpson's. She hadn't had a nice chat with the pleasant woman in a long time.

Her pleasure at seeing the widow was soon overridden by annoyance when Jane Scott appeared next to Nell, her arms full of clothing. How did that woman always manage to show up every time she was about to have a conversation with Paw's intended? When Miss Scott ignored Jessie as if she wasn't there, hot anger gripped Serena.

Damn her, she thought, looking down her nose at Jessie, trying to make off like she's better than her. She deliberately turned her back on the woman and said teasingly to Nell, "So, lady, you've got your own quarters, have you? Are you going to associate with us poor commoners anymore?"

Nell's brown eyes twinkled. "Eli asked me the same thing." The corners of her lips drew down pensively then. "I wish we didn't have to be separated." Her pleasant face blushed fiery red. "What I mean," she stammered, "is that . . . I wish that we could have come across a preacher before making winter camp."

"He can still visit you, Nell." Serena smiled at the unhappy face. "You can make his meals and—"

Jane Scott's smooth tones cut Serena off. "Yes, Nell, you're very lucky. As Serena pointed out, you can at least visit with Eli every day, all cozy in front of a fire." She paused and looked sad, simulating shyness, before looking slyly at Serena and adding, "Josh and I have nowhere to court now." She sighed. "Josh doesn't like these living arrangements at all." She lifted innocent eyes to Serena. "He's a very passionate man. He said he didn't know how he was going to stand it, being kept away from me for such a long time."

Blinding pain from the hurtful words kept Serena from seeing the incredulous look Nell sent Jane Scott. And while the widow glared at the woman who shared her campfire, acute outrage roared in Serena's head.

The bastard! The no-good randy bastard. All this time he had been making love to both her and his hired girl. She choked back a tear. If one woman couldn't satisfy his lust, and lust was all she could call it now, she was glad he hadn't asked her to marry him. Any woman who wed that man would soon find out that she had to share him with any skirt that caught his fancy.

Serena became aware that Nell was talking to her. "You're always welcome to come visit, Serena. You're like a daughter to Eli."

With a suspicious moistness in her eyes, and a voice far from steady, she murmured, "Thank you, Nell."

"And you, too, Jessie. Come any time," Nell called out to the two friends as they struck off for the long building Bridger had assigned to the women.

"That bitch was lyin' through her teeth," Jessie spat angrily when they reached their quarters.

Serena wanted to rail out at her companion and tell her not to give her false hope, that she had lied to herself like that for months. Instead, she answered quietly, "I think not, Jessie. And if you don't mind I'd rather not talk about either one of them."

Jessie gave her arm a sympathetic squeeze, and together they stood quietly, examining the structure that would shelter them all winter. It ran about forty feet in length and twenty feet wide. The walls were constructed of whole logs and the roof of wooden pine shakes.

After a while the pair smiled at each other, then Serena pushed the door open and stepped through onto a puncheon floor of pine. Jessie stepped on Serena's heels, almost knocking her over as the rest of the women pushed in behind them. Serena caught her balance, then froze. Wood mice, scampering about in their unceasing search for food, had paused to peer with beady eyes at the sudden square of light in the doorway. When alarmed squeals escaped a half-dozen throats, the creatures scattered for secret hiding places and everyone relaxed and laughed self-consciously.

The long room was dark and poorly ventilated, so Jessie moved to the one fairly large window and swung the shutters away from the glass panes. In the dim illumination of near dusk, the huge fireplace in the center of the room was the first thing to catch the women's attention.

The large structure and the hearth that circled it was a crudely erected affair but if, as the old man claimed, it drew well it would provide cozy warmth.

Eyes grew accustomed to the gray darkness and the women began their inspection of the furnishings. There were bunk beds built along the two long walls, a broad plank resting on two poles at the end of each bed, a step-up to the bunk above, and a long table with benches of equal length on either side of it.

While some of the older women poked about in a large pantry at the far end of the room, the younger ones gathered around a barrel full of water, and a wooden tub placed next to it. When a voice surmised that this was where they would have to bathe and wash their clothes, two young women, more affluent than the others and used to porcelain hip-tubs, immediately began to complain. The others, although they had no idea that such fancy baths existed, were not about to let on that they had washed their bodies in wooden ones all their lives. They, too, added their complaints.

Serena sent the whiners an impatient look and went to check out the bedding on the bunks. She could still feel the chill in her bones from shivering through the cold nights on the trail. If she could sleep warm and soundly in this great barn of a place, any other inconveniences could easily be borne.

She patted a mattress of sweetsmelling hay stuffed into several fustian sacks sewn together. Slipping a hand beneath the woolen army blankets, she felt the muslin sheet tucked around the rough ticking. She was disappointed that there was no slip on the pillow. However, it looked new and unused, and she was thankful for that.

Straightening up, she pushed back the memory of a canopied tester bed with soft feather mattress and fine linen. She walked to the group which was still fault finding. What had these women expected? Serena thought impatiently. Here in the middle of the wilderness! Didn't they realize how fortunate they were to have found any kind of accommodations? And from words she'd heard dropped along the way, most had left homes so poor they could not compare to Bridger's offerings.

When Jane Scott joined the voices of discomfort, Serena banged a fist down on the plank table so hard the pewter candlesticks on its top bounced in the air. The grumbling ceased as startled eyes stared at her.

"You women!" she half shouted. "If a person didn't know better he'd think you were all raised in the lap of luxury. For God's sake remember your roots and shut up."

When Jessie snapped, "Amen to that," those who squirmed at Serena's accurate assessment of their previous circumstances covered their embarrassment by darting glowering looks at the redhead.

"Miss Bain is right, you know," a young, hardy woman who had been with the wagon train since its beginning said. "Instead of yammering on about unimportant things we should get organized."

"Such as?" someone asked, willingness in the question.

"Well . . ." The northwoods woman chewed on her thumbnail thoughtfully. "Everyone must take their turn at chores, such as keeping the fire going, cooking the meals, washing up the dishes, and keeping the floor swept. Of course each woman makes up her own bed and washes her own clothes."

She swept her gaze around the long table where most had

gathered, and when she was met with nods of approval she pulled a scrap of paper and pencil stub from her rucksack. She tore the paper into smaller bits and began to laboriously print each woman's name on a piece.

The slips of paper were drawn from a hat someone produced, then the room stirred as the busy women went about appointed duties. A tall, heavyset woman from Ohio built a roaring fire from a plentiful supply of wood right outside the door, and one woman moved around the room lighting candles. As warmth began to fill the room moods brightened and, before long, bursts of laughter erupted as the women began to settle in.

Beds were chosen and clothing hung on pegs that had been driven into the walls. The four women who would be in charge of cooking for the first seven days inspected the pantry when complaints of hunger sounded throughout the room.

Ample staples were found, but there was still the lack of meat. The cooks, ready to discuss this problem, were interrupted by a loud rapping on the door. Jessie, standing nearest, opened it and found one of her former customers grinning down at her, and shoving a large chunk of venison into her hands.

"Old Bridger said give this to you ladies." When Jessie thanked him and started to close the door, it was caught and held. "We're sure gonna miss you and the girls," the man said suggestively, his eyes questioning her.

She let her lips part in a sweet smile. Encouraged, he smiled back eagerly, loosening his hold on the door. Then, before he knew what she was about, the little whore jerked the door from his hand and slammed it shut. Grinning at his muttered curses she shot home the bolt. Some of the men might not intend to abide by old Bridger's rule, but she would see they did.

Everyone was ready for bed soon after supper. The warmth that had been denied them for so long was now making itself felt by the weary bodies. For several minutes there was the sound of rustling mattresses and good-nights being called out. Gradually only the soughing of the pines and the whisper of snow against the windows was heard.

Surprisingly, sleep did not come to Serena right away. She thought that the hustle and bustle of settling into new quarters would be enough to lull her directly into a restful sleep devoid of thoughts of Josh. However, she soon found that she was sadly mistaken as she tucked her hands under her cheeks to protect her bedding from the tears. She had no illusions left regarding Josh's feelings for her. There was no doubt he desired her body, but as she was now fully aware, it was Jane Scott he loved and would take as his wife.

And she, Serena reflected with bitterness as her lids finally began to droop, had set herself up for another bout of painful memories.

CHAPTER
∽17∽

THE WIND built during the night, and the storm grew and howled down from the hills until dawn. A few hours later when Josh, using his full strength and weight, managed to push open the door of the men's quarters his eyes widened at what they beheld. The fort was now an evenly white world, broken only by roof and chimney tops, and an occasional glimpse of a window or door that had not quite been covered by the drifts.

Stepping back inside, he roused the others. The women would never be able to force their door open, and if they hadn't had the foresight to stock in a good supply of wood it would be mightly cold in their quarters by now. A tenderness softened his eyes as he thought, ". . . especially for the slender girl from the South."

Grumbling to themselves and to each other, the men picked up the shovels that were stacked in a corner and, moving outside, barely returned the greetings from husbands who were already shoveling outside of their cabins. At a sharp word from Josh all hands fell to, and began working in shifts. It was close to ten o'clock when a clear path to the women's lodgings was finally made.

The women charted the men's progress from inside, and when they had reached their door, it was immediately swung open with wide smiles and loud cries of welcome. Eager hands ushered them inside and hurried to fill tin cups with steaming coffee.

"I see we're just in time." A husky young man noted that the last of their fuel was only glowing coals in the fireplace.

"We weren't worried," a buxom woman simpered, looking coyly through her lashes at the attractive bachelor. "We knew that strong arms and backs would soon clear away the snow for us."

Annoyance dimmed the woman's bright gaiety when the target of her overtures slid his eyes to Serena. "Miss Bain wasn't worried either," she snapped, then went on with a hint of warning in her voice, "She knows that the wagon master wouldn't let her stay cold for very long."

At first Serena felt anger rise in the tight silence that followed the churlish remark. Then, turning her head, she caught Jane Scott's burning gaze on her and knew a keen pleasure at the woman's jealousy. When Serena saw Jessie's pleased grin, she slyly returned it.

And the young man who had started it all ducked his red face, then growled, "Come on, men, let's see to some more firewood."

Shortly, amid loud laughter and much horseplay, enough split logs were carried in by brawny arms to last a month.

When flames licked hungrily at the new supply of fuel, a large cast-iron skillet was placed over the fire. Once the lard inside melted and sizzled, the cooks took turns frying plate-sized flapjacks. Meanwhile, a fresh pot of coffee brewed on a bed of coals raked to one side, and mouth-watering aromas permeated the air.

Shortly, to the background of giggles and low-toned masculine voices, the jacks and coffee, along with dark, full-flavored molasses, were placed on the long table. "Come and get it," a gay voice rang out, and the rescuers didn't need a second invitation. Benches scraped across the rough board floor as the men seated themselves, and the women were momentarily forgotten as their guests took the edge off their hunger. Smiling knowingly at each other and murmuring, "Isn't that just like men," the hostesses hovered around them, keeping cups filled, urging more flapjacks on them.

In the beginning Jessie's girls had rushed forward to resume serving the men their food as they had done for the past three months. The young whores hadn't got near the men. They were met with cold looks and contemptuous remarks. "Your help isn't wanted. We decent women are taking care of the men now. Save your services for when you're back in the pleasure wagon and the men's baser side needs you."

Once again chairs scraped against wood and female lips smiled seductively. The room took on an atmosphere of celebration as bursts of laughter rang out and everyone talked at once.

Serena watched her young companions with a cynical smile on her lips. Away from their mothers' watchful eyes they had unbent and now flirted recklessly with the men they previously only dared look at. Then Serena's roving glance picked out Jane Scott, her enemy. With her head tilted provocatively and red lips smiling, she conversed animatedly with one of the older men. *I'll bet she's put out that Josh didn't come in to visit with her.*

Serena's eyes twinkled gleefully. *It aggravates her that she's missed the chance to show the others that she's captured the best man in the entire wagon train.*

Serena's enjoyment of Miss Scott's displeasure faded, however, as she admitted to her own disappointment that Josh hadn't joined his men. She nudged Jessie. "Look at Jane Scott making up to that man. You'd think she'd be afraid that Josh would walk in and catch her."

Jessie directed a disinterested glance at the couple and shrugged her thin shoulders. "I think Miss Scott is lookin' for a little romance. I'm afraid our wagon master isn't good at sentimental-like love." She sent Serena a sly look from under lowered lashes. "Does he strike *you* as being fanciful?"

Serena dipped her head, feeling the scarlet spread over her face at the memory of what Josh had whispered as she lay cradled in his arms, his passion-hard body thrusting against hers rhythmically. *Oh, yes, Jessie,* she cried silently, *he knows the language of love; he knows just what to say to spur me on, to do his every bidding as he guides me in the ways of pleasing him.*

She sensed Jessie's quizzical gaze at her long silence and,

affecting a careless shrug answered evasively, "I've never given it much thought."

Jessie stretched and changed the subject. "I notice your handsome rancher isn't around. Where do you suppose he is?"

"Probably sulking somewhere," Serena laughingly answered. "Seems ever since we settled in here he's been puffed up about something or other." She stood up and moved to the window to gaze out at the white world beyond.

About to turn back to the room, Serena was arrested by the sight of a male figure coming toward their quarters. Her lips tilted in a tickled grin. The angular body of Jim Bridger was scurrying up the freshly dug path, and from the grim look on his bony face the women would soon lose their male companions.

The older man didn't say a word when he flung the door open and stood sternly, waiting for the men to leave. When the last one walked sullenly past him, he craned his head around the room. Satisfied that no male lingered in a hidden corner, he closed the door behind him on the women's disappointed faces.

In the gray monotony of winter's icy bleakness the emigrants' routines varied little as the weeks passed. The women spent many daylight hours making "jerk," venison cut into thin slices then roasted slightly over a slow fire. It was the staple food of the Indians, and it would also suffice for the white man when he was out of fresh meat. Jim Bridger informed the women that jerk was also the basis of which pemmican was made. When asked, he spent an afternoon showing those who were interested how to make the Indian delicacy.

The thin strips were found to be quite tasty, and soon became a favorite with the men. The treats were often stuffed into their pockets to dull hunger while out hunting.

When it was too cold to go hunting the men gathered at the post, some playing cards and others talking of their futures in Oregon Territory. The bachelors were always restless, their pacing taking them often to the window to stare longingly at the long building a few yards away. If one was caught with a hand in his pocket, some married man was sure to say slyly, "I'm sure catchin' up on my pleasurin' since arrivin' here and goin' out huntin' most days. Every time I bring home fresh meat I know that come bedtime *I'm* gonna be thanked properly.''

Amused glances would be directed to those men who had once bragged that they had easy access to six willing bodies as often as they wanted. But they were now reduced to going without favors even though they had to continue providing for these same women.

The usual retort to this teasing was the boast that once on the trail again the loving would be better than ever: The girls would be rested up, and it would be well worth the waiting.

During the good-natured bantering, wondering glances were sent to Josh, but no one had the nerve to chaff him about his love life. Some felt sure that he slipped the Scott woman into the widow's cabin and laid with her, while others wondered if the southern beauty pleased him through the long night. All agreed he was getting his loving *somewhere*, for the man was too relaxed and too at ease.

Some nights, when the flames from great glowing logs sent shadows jumping on the walls, the women spoke of their past, telling where they came from and what their lives had been like. One night Jessie told her story.

"Now some of you young ladies," she began, "believe that whores are born whores. That, of course, is untrue. We all start as innocents, some lovin' mama's little darlin'. There was a time, not too far back, when I was just as respectable as any woman in this room.''

Staring into the fire, as though she read her past in the flames, the words spilled out of Jessie's mouth, sometimes toneless, sometimes vibrant with anger.

"My early years was spent in a small village in Ohio. It was a carefree time, filled with love . . . until I got to be fifteen. That winter my father was caught in a blizzard and took a deep chill. In three days he was dead from pneumonia.''

Jessie paused and curled her lips. "Our farm was a fairly large one, and my mother being a soft and helpless sort, soon married a man pretty much like that Bible-spouter Hansen.

"From the beginning my stepfather and I didn't hit it off. I guess I was mad my mother would replace my father so quickly. And my stepfather didn't cotton to me because I looked so much like the man who had known his wife first. It wasn't long before he was droppin' hints that I should be thinkin' of marriage. His next move then was to bring men home, hopin' that one would ask for my hand.''

The fire reflected the twinkle in Jessie's eyes. "I naturally discouraged them in every way I could think of, giggling, talkin' too loud, and often wearin' ugly clothes or leaving my hair unbrushed.

"Then one day my new Papa brought home a man who was handsome and had pleasin' ways. And though he was nearing forty years, I agreed to marry him when he asked me to. After knowing him for only three days we was married and we left for New Orleans. There my husband got us a room that was so fancy it nearly made my eyes pop.

"After our supper and a bottle of wine in our room, we got into the big bed in the corner." Jessie paused to give a short laugh. "I won't go into detail about what happened there—some of you are too young to hear it—but, ladies, I could talk all night and not cover half of what my husband taught me on my wedding night. He turned out to be a real bastard later, but I've only met one other man like him since.''

Serena almost cried aloud with the pain she felt at these last softly spoken words. She knew that Jessie was referring to Josh.

"For two weeks I led a life of pure bliss," Jessie went on, "rarely gettin' out of bed. Then one mornin' when I awakened I found myself alone. Pinned on the pillow next to me was a note. That's when I learned my husband already had a wife, plus three children, and that he was returning to them. He wrote that the room was paid for another week, and that he hoped I would return home to my mother.

"Well, the no-good had left a roof over my head for a few days, but hadn't left me a cent to purchase any food. The first day I cried so hard I wasn't hungry. But the next day I felt faint from the lack of food. And there I was, with nothin' of value to sell and no experience in anything that would get me a job in the city.

"It took the ogling of the desk clerk to make me aware of the one thing I could sell. In desperation I went out onto the streets seeking those who would pay for my services. Thanks to my husband's lessons, I knew just how to please the gentlemen I slipped into my room. I was paid handsomely by them, and I sure hoarded my money. At the end of the week I was able to buy a steamship ticket back to Ohio.''

A bitter laugh preceded her next words. ''Naturally my mother's husband wasn't overjoyed to see me, and had the nerve to say that I should have been more careful of whom I went off with. Then he said that I could stay a few days, find myself employment somewhere, but I'd have to leave. I waited for my mother to speak up, insist that I stay with her, but she only sat by the window and kept on mending a pair of that bastard's socks.

''I was boiling mad at that, and I told them both to go to hell. I slammed out the door and went straight to the largest whorehouse in town.'' A wry smile lifted the corners of her lips. ''I guess that was my second mistake, but at the time all I could think of was gettin' back at my mother.

''At any rate, I worked hard at my trade and got to be the favorite girl in the house. But one thing stuck in my craw. I was bringing in a lot of money, but the madam was taking most of it. Remembering my hunger, and feelin' the fear of it ever happening again, I hated every cent that went into her pocket.

''You see, a whore ages fast; once your looks is gone you're kicked out onto the streets. There you'll be reduced to sellin' yourself for a night's lodging and a cheap meal, and later it could be for a bottle of raw whiskey to make you forget, and give you the strength for the hours ahead.

''I had been working for about six months when I met a couple trappers from the north country. While eatin' ham and eggs with one, he kept remarkin' that he wished I'd come back with them to their village 'cause the whores there were gettin' old and that I could make a lot of money.

''Well, his words stuck with me.'' She smiled over at her girls, sitting in their usual corner. ''So, I went quietly about, makin' friends with five of the most attractive girls in the house. Eventually I convinced them to go north with me.

''We were heartily welcomed by the male population and were kept busy. And I must admit I was content until Josh was talked into leading our present train to Oregon country. Something told

me to take my girls and go with him, that our future lay there.''
Jessie grinned her most charming smile and added brightly, ''I
have a dream too, to own the biggest and finest fancy house in
all the West—and to find one man to love.''

When Jessie stood up and walked across the room to her bunk,
the only sounds were the sighing of the wind and the creaking
of ice-filled branches. Some of the girls dabbed at damp eyes;
all understood that the same calamity could befall any one of
them. A respect for Jessie and her girls was born that night.

CHAPTER
❧18❧

THE BONE-NUMBING WINTER days passed, the air biting even through the buffalo robes of those lucky enough to own them. The women from the north had donned their linsey-woolsey frocks. With the addition of heavy knitted shawls they were quite comfortable in the big drafty room. But the women from the southern states constantly hovered around the fire in their light-weight clothing, seldom going outside.

Serena kept warm, thanks to a set of long-legged underwear donated to her by Nell's son, Todd. She was even more appreciative of their extra warmth when it was her turn to bring in the split logs stacked just outside the door.

Then, one December morning, surprised expressions followed by excited cries greeted Jessie's announcement that Christmas was only a week away. "We must celebrate! We must have a tree," a fifteen-year-old exclaimed as everyone gathered around the fireplace.

"We'd better check with old Bridger first," someone interposed sourly. "He's just ornery enough to let us put one up, then calmly toss it out the door."

Serena picked up the fur-lined jacket that had mysteriously appeared on the foot of her bed one afternoon and caught Jessie's attention with a wave of her hand. "Come on, Jess, let's go talk to Bridger about the tree."

Surprisingly Bridger met their wishes with an excitement that matched their own. He not only agreed to personally bring down a big spruce from the hills, he would see it set up in the post's community room. "So we all can enjoy it," he explained. When he handed Serena a bag of dried corn for popping, saying gruffly, "My mother used to string it and put it on our tree," Serena planted a smacking kiss on his cheek and suppressed a giggle when his face turned red.

Caught up in the holiday spirit, trunks were thrown open and eager fingers, though occasionally reluctant, brought out treasured pieces of ribbon and bits of colored cloth. Word was sent to the wives in the cabins to do the same. Then everyone would gather in the community room that afternoon to cut out ornaments to hang on the tree.

During the first community meeting, the weather-bound women were too hungry for "women talk" to settle down with needle and thread. Mothers and daughters made small groups around the roaring fire that had been built for them while they caught up on news and gossiped. Evidently Jessie's story had been relayed, for suddenly, softer looks were sent her way.

The men in the tavern part of the post craned their necks to catch glimpses of the young women, for Bridger made sure that no one crossed the threshold separating the two rooms.

Serena and Jane Scott guiltily sent searching looks into the room beyond, but neither saw the man they looked for.

On the second meeting day the ladies settled down and allowed their nimble fingers to produce stars and other shapes from the bright material assembled. The remainder of the week would be a busy time.

The women's quarters were buzzing with laughter as willing hands turned out their specialties for the coming party. All except Serena had produced something good to eat.

She stood staring out the window now, chewing on her lower lip. She was the only one in the group who could not distinguish herself by creating some culinary treat. It did not bother her that others' triumphs were prettily displayed on the table. It was only Jane Scott's four-layered chocolate cake and remembrance of the woman's jeering remark to her the day she finished icing it that set her teeth on edge every time she looked at it.

"I haven't seen you around the oven, Miss Bain. When are you going to turn out your masterpiece?"

Damn the woman, Serena thought with her hand clenched. Jane Scott knew as well as the other women that she was no great hand in the kitchen.

I could get Nell to help me with something, she mused, then dismissed the idea. That would be cheating, and her conscience would never allow her to claim the final result as her own.

A big bearded man passed Serena's line of vision out the window, and she absentmindedly returned his smile and wave of his hand. Two weeks ago this mountain man had discovered a cache of wild honey in a hollow tree. After smoking out the bees he had shyly presented their sweetness to her. The women, with the exception of Jane Scott, good-heartedly teased her about her new admirer.

As her new friend passed out of sight, he triggered the memory of a candy Mammy Hessie used to make. Its main ingredient had been honey. She turned and walked tentatively toward the pantry, trying to remember the exact steps in the recipe, wishing she had paid more attention as she helped her old nurse turn out the confection.

Everyone watched with interest when Serena left the supply room and deposited the items she had gathered on the table. "Well, well." Jane Scott's strident voice beat against her ears as she took a heavy skillet from a cupboard and poured the last of the honey into the cast-iron vessel "It appears that our Southern belle is going to try her hand at the fire, after all."

Jessie jumped to her feet and took a menacing step toward the much larger woman. "Shut it up before I shut it for you."

A young girl threw herself between the two women, facing Jane Scott. "Why don't you stop pickin' on Serena, Jane? We're all gettin' tired of listenin' to you."

"Hear, hear," came the call from several throats.

With a loud sniff and her chin stuck in the air, Josh's hired woman walked to her bunk and sat down stiffly.

"Go ahead, honey." Jessie nodded to Serena. "Ain't nobody gonna bother you now."

Serena couldn't remember ever being so nervous as under her companion's watchful eye she gently stirred the bubbling, golden liquid. She tried to remember if Mammy had said to let it boil until it spun a thread. Or was that the icing she made for her mouth-watering cakes?

Finally, realizing that only goodwill was directed toward her, she relaxed, remembering everything clearly, as though Mammy stood at her side directing each move.

She knew just when to remove the skillet from the fire, and exactly how to add the walnuts so they wouldn't settle to the bottom. When she poured the finished product onto a large platter to cool, the women gathered around and with wide smiles clapped their hands. Jane Scott chose to sit off by herself, pouting.

Her sullenness turned to annoyance about an hour later when Serena's mixture had set, and each woman who sampled it declared the candy delicious. Her emotion became anger at last, when Jessie quipped, "You're gonna have to watch Josh, Serena. He's got a sweet tooth you wouldn't believe. He'd make short work of this."

"I think he'd eat her up, too, given the chance," the same young girl teased, sliding Jane a sly look.

Serena couldn't help darting a look at Jane and couldn't help the pleased sensation she felt at seeing the rage on the Scott woman's face.

Christmas morning finally arrived, and while everyone rushed to dress in their best finery, Serena leaned against the frame of her bunk bed. She was acutely conscious of her trail-worn buckskins, and just as aware that there was nothing in her trunk that would fit her anymore.

Against her will her eyes strayed to her enemy, and she gritted her teeth in frustration. Jane Scott wore a pretty blue dress with ruffles around the V-shaped neckline and the edge of the short sleeves.

"Her neck is too short and plump for all that shirring," she muttered to her hurting ego. "She looks like one of Mammy Hessie's banty hens."

"Your face is gonna freeze that way," Jessie teased behind her. "What dour thoughts are pickin' at you?"

Serena plopped down on her bed, running an appraising eye

over her petite friend. "You look very fetching in that green satin, Jess. Are you out to catch that special man you spoke of?"

Jessie blushed at Serena's compliment. "Any man worth havin' in this train is already took. I'll start lookin' when I'm all settled in Oregon country." She ran a sharp eye over Serena. "Don't you think you should start gettin' changed? We have to leave pretty soon."

Serena hunched her shoulders and revealed reluctantly, "I haven't anything to change into. None of my dresses fit me anymore. The last time I wore one the seams busted."

"I see." Jessie took her arm and steered her toward the young prostitutes who looked like colorful birds in their bright gowns as they chattered excitedly. "Dolly is about your size and coloring; she'll be happy to loan you a dress."

"Oh, but Jessie . . ." Serena's objections died on her lips as Jessie ignored her and pulled a golden-haired girl to one side. A few minutes later a dark blue dress was slipped over her head and Jessie was settling the satin over her hips.

As to be expected the garment was cut to show off a figure to its best advantage. The neckline plunged daringly, the waist fit snugly, and the material clung softly around the thighs. Jessie turned Serena slowly around, giving a low whistle.

"Whew-ee, are you gonna cause a ruckus among them woman-hungry men! Josh had better carry a big club."

Jane Scott's angry gasp was audible to everyone. Her furious eyes ran contemptuously over Serena, then with a meaningful look at Jessie's girls, she sneered, "Don't stand too close to your friends, Miss Bain—the men might think you're one of them."

Dead silence followed the sharp crack of Jessie's palm across the irate woman's face, and the small woman's deadly warning was clearly heard. "If you dare to insult Serena at the party I'll see that you'll regret it. Do *you* understand?"

Her hand nursing the red prints on her cheek, Jane nodded sullenly.

Wraps were donned, and the women set out for the post, their arms and hands laden with turkey and venison roasts, pots of dried maize and string beans, and a basket of potatoes to be baked in Bridger's fireplace. There were dozens of loaves of

bread, plus the sweets the women had worked on all week.
Bridger had sent word that there would be a prayer meeting
before the tree trimming, and everyone except Jessie and her
girls carried a Bible.

Serena brought up the rear of the chattering women passing
single file into the post. Her gaze met Josh's immediately. He
was leaning against the stone wall of the fireplace, and as his
eyes sent her messages of desire, everyone around her ceased to
exist. How good he looks, she thought, her eyes trailing hungrily over the broad shoulders straining at the buckskins and
the narrow hips blending into long, muscular legs. She remembered the feel of his firm, smooth flesh against hers and a weakness settled in her lower region.

Breathing his name softly, she started toward Josh, then was
knocked off balance as Jane Scott brushed roughly past, her
voice calling, "Josh! It's so good to see you!"

Serena numbly watched Jane link her arm in Josh's and hug
it to her breast. "Idiot," a taunting voice inside her jeered. "He
wasn't even looking at you. The lovelight in his eyes is for the
woman he intends to marry."

The joy of the day was gone, her heart a hardened rock inside
her. Blindly she moved toward the table where the food was
being deposited.

Jessie saw the dangerously dark look Josh turned on the hired
woman as he pulled his arm free.

"Serena, Josh doesn't care a thing about that witch," she
whispered beside the trembling girl as they put their dishes down.
"She forced herself—" She broke off with a frown when Foster
Jovan arrogantly stepped between them. When the rancher put
a possessive arm around Serena's shoulders, she turned and
walked away.

"I've been watching for you," Jovan murmured softly to Serena. "I thought you'd never get here."

Serena gave Jovan a wide smile. She needed his attentive
presence today to make Josh Quade aware that she was loved
and had no need of him.

The rancher stayed close beside Serena as she moved about
the room, and she wished he'd stop talking, even though his words
were making little inroad to her mind. Her hope that he would

be a buffer to the pain that raged inside her was fading. She wished desperately that she could slip away and nurse her hurt and disappointment.

"Would you like a cup of cider?" Jovan's voice jarred her from her thoughts.

"Yes, thank you, that would be nice." She smiled at him wanly.

He moved away, and stepping back to make room for a man carrying a basket of potatoes to the fire, Serena came up against a hard male body. She turned her head to apologize, and gazed into Josh's handsome, rugged face.

Gazing into her eyes, Josh's went soft at the tenderness he saw in Serena's green depths. His gaze moved to sweep over her face, lingering on her lips. Slowly, then, his heavy-lidded eyes moved down to her heaving breasts, and it was with conscious effort he raised his sight back to her face.

"I've got to see you, Serena," he said hoarsely. "Alone. If I don't hold you in my arms soon, I think I'll go out of my mind."

Her own need reflected in her eyes, and praying that Josh would tell her that Jane Scott meant nothing to him, Serena asked falteringly, "What . . . what about Jane?"

She died a bit when he frowned impatiently and answered, "Miss Scott has nothin' to do with the fire that burns between us . . . nor does Foster Jovan."

Serena's thick lashes swept down on her cheeks to hide the pain she knew was visible in her eyes. Josh had practically said, "I love Jane, but I lust for you."

When she continued to look at the floor Josh commanded, "Serena, look at me. Tell me that you'll meet me in the men's quarters when the dancing begins."

Scalding tears burned the back of Serena's eyes as she sought some cutting words that would hurt this callous man as he had wounded her. But nothing would squeeze through the knot in her throat.

She was never so glad to see Foster as when he came up and slipped an arm around her waist. He handed her the cup of cider then, speaking quietly, but loud enough for Josh to hear, said, "Drink up, then let's take a walk. There's so much I have to say to you."

The means to lash hurtfully back at Josh were handed to her and she rushed to take advantage. Directing a provocative look at Foster, she spoke with a husky laugh. "And I want to hear it all, Foster."

The curl of her lips was stopped at the sound of a sharply indrawn breath. She sent Josh a glance through her lashes and started at the anger in his eyes and the stiff set of his jaw. Then he deliberately opened a path between her and Jovan, sneering over his shoulder, "Keep in mind while you're walkin' that old Bridger doesn't tolerate any whorin'."

Pain and anger fought inside Serena as she stared after the sinewy back as he stalked through the door. She was blinking rapidly when Jessie spoke at her elbow. "I just passed Josh. He's got the very devil in them snappin' eyes of this. What started him off, do you reckon?"

"Who knows, with that wild man?" Serena replied nonchalantly.

Jessie wasn't fooled as she studied the stiff features and suffering eyes. After a moment she took Serena's arm and, pulling her along, said gaily, "You're needed to help trim the tree."

Both girls ignored Jovan's muttered oath.

Although Serena watched for Josh during the trimming of the tree, and later during supper, he did not return for any of the events. When the fiddler and the banjo picker tuned up, she, with a single-minded determination to put the blasted Yankee out of her mind once and for all, threw herself into the festivities. Jovan pouted as she danced and flirted with a long line of men. She wasn't even aware when the rancher left the party.

The noise of the holiday celebration had long since faded into the crunch of ice-crushed snow as Josh tramped the hills with his hands shoved in his pockets and his head bent in thought. Why had Serena become cool and aloof so abruptly? It had been clear to him after that last night of lovemaking that everything was fine between them. It was true that no plans for the future had been made, but he had taken it for granted that she felt as he did about a life together.

He paused in his tireless strides to look up at the cold, white moon. Until a few hours ago he had pushed to the back of his mind a promise given to Eli—Foster Jovan would never marry Serena Bain.

At the time he had felt sure no preacher would come along in the dead of winter. But seeing the pair together and so cozy, a warning bell had gone off in his mind. Winter was slowly drawing to an end, and before long they would be on the trail again. There was every possibility that a man of the cloth might join them along the way. And to see that delicate beauty marry that man would be more than he could bear.

Depression hovered over Josh in a murky gray cloud as he turned to retrace his steps. "I may have to kill the bastard, after all," he muttered half an hour later as he pushed open the door to the big room that had been his home for over two months.

The low flames in the fireplace gave the only illumination in the large room. The quarters were reasonably neat but carried a distinctive air of male habitation. Josh's nose wrinkled at the sour, rancid smell of unwashed clothes and bodies. "Damn boar's nest," he muttered.

A long sigh escaping him, he lowered his long length onto the hearth and, propped on an elbow, stared into the flames. One seldom found the room empty, and he was thankful for the solitude that would be his until the Christmas party broke up.

He lay quietly, visualizing the cheer and hilarity taking place at the post: Serena and Jovan dancing, holding hands, smiling into each other's eyes.

His thoughts were suddenly too devastating to bear and he stood up. He might as well go to bed and try to sleep, or at least be ready to feign it when Jovan returned. One smug look from the man and he would smash his face.

Josh was unlacing his knee-high moccasins when a rustling sound from a corner bunk stayed his hands. He peered into the soft shadows, then swore softly under his breath. In a tangle of bare bodies, Foster Jovan and the young Indian, Sato, were oblivious to everything around them. Neither heard the quietly approaching footsteps. Several seconds passed before Jovan's eyes flew open and looked squarely into the contemptuous eyes staring down at him.

Guilt and confusion washed over his face when Josh drawled sneeringly, "Enjoyin' yourself, Jovan?"

Jerking erect, tumbling the boy out of his way, Jovan stammered, "I . . . I know . . . how this must look, Quade, but the little bastard just won't leave me alone. He's pestered me ever since I bought him, and tonight I finally gave in so he'd leave me alone." He grabbed up his trousers, adding nervously as he awkwardly slid into them, "I'll make it worth your while if you don't let this out."

An impatient scowl flicked across Josh's face. He could hear the party breaking up and he had only minutes to conclude this dirty business, to achieve that which would end for all time anything between this man and Serena.

He pierced the waiting man with dark, dangerous eyes. "Like what?" he asked shortly.

The tension left Jovan's face, and with a hint of arrogance that set Josh's blood to boiling he said smoothly, "Well, like helping you get your own ranch going. I'll lend you the help of my men to gather a herd."

When no response issued from Josh's firmly held lips, the assurance left Jovan's face and his tone took on a pleading note when he added finally, "You name it. Anything you want."

For what seemed an unbearably long time to the rancher, the wagon master stared down at him. Then, his voice softly dangerous, Josh named his terms.

"What I want, and what I intend to have, is very simple, Jovan. Starting right now, put all thoughts of marryin' Serena Bain out of your mind. Start coolin' your attention to her, and when it comes time for you to leave the train you're not to even tell her good-bye."

Jovan's face turned livid. He wanted Serena Bain with a passion. Not the passion of a man for a woman, but for a desired possession. He jumped to his feet, his eyes shooting sparks in the light of the dancing flames.

"You ask too much, Quade. That would be a dastardly thing to do to a lady."

There was no relenting on Josh's face. Making no effort to hide the disgust in his voice, he retorted, "I wonder if she, and the others, would think that what you just did in that bed was a dastardly thing also.''

Jovan's entire body seemed to go limp with defeat. His sneering smile was bitter with hatred as he chanced goading his enemy one last time.

''I hope, Quade, you aren't planning to replace me in Miss Bain's affections. She's not for the likes of you.''

If Jovan's words hurt Josh, only the slight sagging of his shoulders gave any indication of it as Jovan stamped from the room, Sato at his heels. He stretched out on his bunk, sighing raggedly. ''God,'' he whispered. ''I'm weary, down to the marrow of my bones.''

CHAPTER
∽*19*∾

THE LAST DAYS of February were upon them and there came a night when big drops of rain splattered on rooftops and melted the snow. The deluge that lasted for three days and nights was viewed by the emigrants with mixed feelings. Spring could not be far behind, and though everyone was eager to reach their destination and to get settled in, no one looked forward to the hardships of the trail again.

Housebound people became restless, and as each day dragged by, tempers became short. The older, wiser heads were responsible for harsh words never coming to blows.

On one of the rain-filled days Josh leaned against the bar at his usual spot, half listening to an old man reminisce about the places he had trapped in his youth. Lost in his thoughts about Serena's behavior and what awaited the wagon train once it was on its way again, he paid little attention when the outside door was flung open and a white man and five Indians entered the room. He felt vaguely uneasy as the group made their way to the warmth of the fire. However the arrogant tone in the white's voice when he ordered whiskey claimed his awareness and brought his gaze to settle on the group hugging the fireplace.

At first he didn't recognize the whiskey-bloated, bewhiskered face. Then the man spoke again and he smiled thinly. He'd know that dictatorial voice anywhere. Ira Newcomb.

Josh studied the ex-officer sprawled out in a chair, the requested bottle of whiskey at his elbow. How had the little rat arrived here at this time of year? Surely he hadn't traveled all winter.

He nudged the old man who continued to ramble on and asked in low tones, "That white man down there with the Indians, have you ever seen him around here before?"

"That one!" the old man snorted contemptuously, sliding Ira a dark look. "He showed up here in the early fall and picked up with them renegades. They've got a shack up in the hills . . . and a couple squaws. Used to be three. Word has it one came down with pneumonia but that devil kept usin' and abusin' her until she died. He's a mean, evil bastard.

"I ain't seen 'em lately. They must have run out of supplies. Until they got snowed in they came down once a week, checkin' if any wagon trains had come in."

Josh's face turned grim. "Did he ever mention what his interest was . . . in the trains?"

"Yeah. Claimed his fiancy would be comin' through on her way to Oregon. Bragged that she was carryin' a lot of money and that after she married him he was gonna build a big ranch out there."

The old fellow talked on, but Josh didn't listen. He had but one thought. Get the hell out of here before Newcomb spotted him. If the bastard thought the members of the train weren't aware of his presence he would be less careful as he followed them on the trail. For he had no doubt about the Southerner's intent: He meant to have Serena Bain . . . at any cost.

Another two weeks went by and Newcomb didn't visit the post again. He doesn't have to, Josh thought, thin-lipped. The little weasel had learned all he needed to know in that one day. He visualized the man up on one of the hills, with a watchful eye on the fort. Once the wagons pulled out he would be right behind them.

When the wild geese began to sweep in on the rivers with a raucous clamor, weary from their flight against winds and wet weather, the emigrants prepared to leave. The women washed and ironed and packed chests and hampers, while the men spent their time in the large shedlike barn, generously greasing wagon wheels and going over traces, lines, brakes, and singletrees. Together, husbands and wives carefully went over supply lists, purchasing what they could afford and stowing the items in their wagon.

And on a blustery March morning the people stood ready to roll out of Fort Bridger, to leave Wyoming behind.

Jim Bridger and the old-timers were on hand to wish them an easy and safe journey. And when Josh shook hands with the eldest trapper the old man gave him a toothless smile and urged, "If you don't like that Oregon country, Quade, come on back here. The hills and streams are full of any kind of game you could want." His dry, bony hand gave another squeeze to the firm, young one. "I'll tell you all my secret places to set traps."

As Josh led the snaking line of wagons away from the fort, leaving the nation's flag with twenty-four stars waving over the tallest building, he mused on the old man's words. He might just take old Jenner up on his offer some day—that is if he didn't return north.

I'll have time to think about that decision later, he told himself, looking over his shoulder, wondering how far behind Ira Newcomb trailed them.

Typical spring weather accompanied the train, a time of gusting winds that sent soaking rains ahead of it, stopping abruptly, then several minutes later starting all over again. The people grew weary of the great scudding clouds that moved perpetually overhead, and the men worked in slow motion, the strength pulled out of them from coaxing and pushing teams and wagons, mired in axle-deep mud.

The women, spent and wilted, cooked the evening meals in an almost trancelike state, while tired children quarreled and whined.

The emigrants had been back on the trail a little over a month when they came to a branching of the road. A third of the train turned onto the road that would lead them to California. Some of those who continued to follow the Snake through the lava wastes of Idaho wondered often if they had chosen the wrong direction. Never had they seen such hot, breathless, and desolate country.

And Josh, his lean visage strained as the stallion plodded along in the heat, searched ahead through narrowed eyes. For the past two days he found it more and more difficult to stay on the right road. Time and again he had come to places so crisscrossed with other rutted roads he had been hard put to choose the right one. But today, he led the way by pure instinct. The heavy rains of March had completely obliterated all roads.

He took a cheroot from a breast pocket and struck a sulphur stick to it. Drawing deeply on the brown cylinder, he pondered his dilemma. He could ask Jovan the directions, but after what had transpired between them back at the fort it would be awkward, to say the least. "However," he muttered, "if it becomes necessary, for the sake of the people, I'll go to the man."

He pinched out his smoke and reined the stallion around. But first he'd talk it over with Eli to get his opinion.

Riding several yards behind Josh, Serena concentrated on the muscular gracefulness of the man up ahead. A mental image of him making love to her came to mind, their bare bodies fused together, loving each other. But, she acknowledged inwardly, there was much more than desire in loving him. Besides the total fulfillment he always gave her, there was the comfort she derived from his very presence. The darkness surrounding the campfires at night was less frightening when he was around; even the yowling of coyotes didn't seem so threatening when he was near.

She sighed softly, her shoulders sagging. What a mess . . . pretending to be engaged to Foster in the hope that it might hurt Josh. And that was a laugh. Josh Quade couldn't care less that she was engaged to another man.

And now Foster would be hurt when he realized she had no intention of marrying him. An indecisive light glimmered a moment in her eyes as she dispiritedly urged the mare on. Lately, she sometimes got the feeling that he courted her only because he felt that she expected it.

Since resuming their journey she seldom saw Foster anymore. It was almost as if he avoided her. As if he were waiting to flee.

Maybe he's accepting the fact that he's wasting his time with me, she thought, watching Josh catch up with Paw's wagon and ride alongside it.

Eli's strong white teeth flashed a welcome to Josh. "Why the long face, son? Have the whores gone out of business?"

A half smile stirred Josh's lips. "I wish it was something that simple. It's the road, Eli. It's gone, washed away by the rain." He ran slim fingers back through his hair. "I don't mind tellin' you, I'm almost at an end of my knowhow."

Landrie's concerned gaze ran over his friend's tired-looking face, the drawn lines on it more from discouragement than fatigue, he suspected. The responsibility this man took so seriously was beginning to tell on him.

"Don't fret about it, Josh," he advised kindly. "Like I've said all along, you're evidently goin' in the right direction, otherwise Jovan would be quick to tell you about it. Just keep your eyes on him and you won't get lost."

"Maybe," Josh answered glumly. "In the meantime I'll keep goin' accordin' to the sun."

It was a couple of hours to sunset when Josh, by pure chance, picked up the road again. His spirits lifted, for the ruts cut into the sod were so deep he doubted the harshest rain could wash them away. He looked up at the cloudless sky. "Damn," Josh murmured. He knew rain wouldn't fall for some time in this scorching wasteland.

Almost a week later the train wound around a mountain and came upon what seemed to be miles of grazing buffalo. And although evening camp was hours away wagons were quickly drawn into a tight circle, all livestock hustled inside the enclosure. Too many cows had already been lost to roving herds.

Serena stood with Eli and Nell, staring in awe at the horizon as a massed black line came closer and closer to camp.

"How many do you think there are, Paw?"

"Four or five thousand. Maybe more."

As the thick dust roiled up by the cloven hoofs rose toward the sky, sometimes obscuring it, Josh's rich voice questioned behind Serena, "It's quite a sight, isn't it?"

Serena's pulse leapt and raced so fast she felt dizzy. He stood so close she could feel the heat of his body enveloping hers. Drawing a trembling breath she looked over her shoulder at him. Their gazes met and she felt a shock run through her. Raw desire and deep longing blazed in his eyes.

"Yes, it is," she answered breathlessly.

"I'm thankful the breeze is blowin' against them." Nell Simpson laughed nervously. "Otherwise there'd be an unbearable stink."

"I thank God that it's a grazing herd and not a stampeding one," Eli grunted. "If them beasts was on the run, this camp would be smashed to smithereens, us along with it."

Alerted for the first time that these placid-looking animals could present danger to them, Serena instinctively moved closer to Josh. She felt his hands take hold of her arms and pull her protectively against his broad chest. She swallowed spasmodically as she felt a hard arousal against her spine.

Pink tinged her cheeks when Josh ever so slightly bucked his hips suggestively against her buttocks. She glanced around guiltily; was anyone watching them? She sighed a breath of relief. All eyes were on the moving herd.

The disquieting sensations flowing between Serena and Josh were interrupted when Eli said, concern in his voice, "Josh, I think it's becomin' a ticklish situation."

Other mumbling voices could be heard also. The ragged edge of the herd had moved much closer, some barely skirting one edge of the circled wagons. Josh nodded grimly, but before he stepped away from Serena he whispered thickly, "Lay your blankets beneath the wagon tonight, please."

With all her heart Serena wanted to refuse his urgent request, to cry out that she would not allow him to use her again, that it was wrong of him to play her against Jane Scott. In the end, however, she nodded helplessly, the plea in his eyes making a reproach impossible. Hating herself, she watched him walk toward the group of anxious men, her heart racing in anticipation of the night.

The gray wave of wagging heads continued to move in. At one point the wagons were hemmed in, the constant flow of animals passing on either side. Rifles were then quickly hauled out of wagons, and an occasional shot kept a wide space between a nervous people and the river of buffalo.

It was also an uneasy group that ate a cold supper, crowded to one end of the circle, as far away as possible from the stock herded at the other end.

No one tried to talk over the deafening din of trampling hooves.

When darkness fell Serena put her lips close to Eli's ear and informed him that she was going to retire under the wagon tonight.

"You'd better hang up some blankets," Eli advised, his voice raised so that she could hear him. "Otherwise you're gonna choke to death."

She nodded and climbed into the wagon. Minutes later she jumped to the ground, her arms full of gray army issue.

Serena had a neat little room when she finished hooking the blankets on any projection she could find. Leftover blankets were spread on the ground, then, climbing out of the buckskins, she slid her arms into the robe she remembered to bring along. She stretched out on the scratchy material, her body aching, her ears straining to hear Josh's footsteps.

She didn't hear him approach, but suddenly he was there, reaching for her, bringing his familiar scent, clean flesh with the tang of outdoors. In total darkness she raised her aching lips and he ravaged them hungrily. Eagerly she wrapped her arms around his shoulders and thrust her fragile fingers through his silky hair, stroking as their tongues parried and thrust wildly at each other. Then Josh lifted his head to say huskily, "Serena, I need to be closer to you. Let me get out of these."

Serena sensed more than heard the soft rustle of buckskins being hurriedly discarded. She moaned softly when she felt the heady sensation of his lips sliding over her breasts. Fire rushed through her feverish veins and her lingering hands groped restlessly over his bare back and powerful shoulders when he drew a swollen nipple between his lips and nursed it deeply. And as his sensuous mouth tugged and drew, her hands fluttered across his firm, rippling stomach, hesitated a moment, then lightly grasped his pulsating manhood.

"Oh, God." Josh's breath rasped against her breasts. "I've waited so long to feel your touch again. Serena, Serena," he begged, "stroke me in your loving way."

The husky request fueled the passionate flame that was already ablaze within Serena, and squeezing gently, she tentatively began to ease her hand up and down.

Josh's breath grew ragged, and his hand trailed down the length of her trembling body, coming to rest on the soft blond sheath between her thighs. She whimpered and strained toward his working fingers.

"Please, Josh," she whispered, "now, take me now."

"Oh, God, yes," he groaned.

And kneeling between her silken thighs he lifted her writhing hips up to his and slowly slid his luxurious length inside her.

For a moment he merely held her, allowing himself to glory in the eager, moist well. And when Serena cried out in ecstasy, Josh lovingly eased her back to the blanket, then cupped his strong hands under her silky rear and, stretching out on top of her, his weight on his elbows, began a slow, satisfying thrusting.

She shifted beneath him, desperately yet eagerly awaiting each plunge of his manhood. Her frenetic action quickened his urgent thrusts, and as his hips rose and fell, driving deeper into buried treasure, she thought with added excitement of all the people milling around, none of whom had any idea what was going on beneath the Landrie wagon.

She was quietly moaning; then, her fingers biting into the firm shoulders hovering over her, she sobbed a final cry of joy. Josh instantaneously caught her cry in his mouth, at the same time muting the sound of his own shuddering release.

With a contented sigh Serena took the weight of Josh's relaxed, slippery wet body and inside her she felt the occasional pulse of his spent arousal. When his breathing returned to normal, he attempted to withdraw his length from her, until she grabbed his narrow buttocks and held him fast.

"Why leave now?" she murmured in his ear. "You know that it will only be a short time before . . ." Her words trailed off as she bashfully lowered her lashes and giggled. She felt his responsive chuckle, and raising up on her elbows she began stringing kisses across his thick throat, then down his furry chest. Her tongue flicked through the crisp curled hair until it found the bullet hard paps. She closed her teeth over one and nibbled teasingly.

Serena laughed softly and triumphantly when Josh began to grow inside her. She lifted her lithe, lean legs and wrapped them around his waist. And when Josh started moving on her, Serena stopped him.

"Hold still," she whispered.

And while Josh hovered over her, his hands braced on either side of her head, Serena rhythmically bucked her delicate hips, her velvet soft core sliding smoothly up and down to meet his throbbing length. She held back her own release, thinking only of wanting to give pleasure to the man she loved with all her heart.

And when his large body began to tremble and his arms buckled, giving her all his weight, this time it was her mouth that silenced his loud, shuddering groan of relief.

"Ah, honey," he whispered finally in her throat, "you've sapped me. Please, let me rest for a minute." Then he smiled.

All through the night Serena and Josh loved, rested, then loved again. They vaguely knew that just beyond their cozy little nest men were taking turns sitting up, intermittently shooting into the darkness, keeping the wagons from being engulfed by the ever moving herd of buffalo.

Serena was unaware when she fell into a deep sleep and was somewhat dazed when she awakened to the shining sun and the dead quiet outside. As she climbed into the buckskins she wondered when Josh had left her. Would their faces tell everyone of their love-filled night together?

"It's about time you're up," Eli greeted her as she crawled from beneath the wagon. "I was about to call you." He pulled a skillet off the fire. "I've got breakfast made."

"I see our visitors have left." Serena laughed lightly, dragging her fingers through her tangled hair.

"Yeah," Eli answered gloomily. "We saw the last of them about an hour ago."

"You don't sound very happy about it." Serena looked searchingly at him. "What's wrong?"

"Somethin' we greenhorns hadn't thought about. The beasts have left very little grass for our stock. With the size of that herd, we may have to travel for miles before we run into any grazin'."

Another worry for poor Josh, Serena sighed, walking stiffly

to the fire and bending down gingerly to scoop the heated water over her face. Her eyes twinkled. Her muscles were so tired and sore; would she be able to ride the mare today?

As she ate her breakfast she kept an eye out for Josh. She couldn't wait to see him, to touch him.

She had scraped her plate clean and drained the last of her coffee when her searching gaze found him. He stood some yards away, staring out over the landscape, and dropping her cup she hurried to join him.

"Good morning," she said softly, lying slim fingers on his arm.

Josh turned his head and smiled down at her, his eyes softening at the passion-exhausted eyes, the slightly swollen lips. "Good mornin', love," he said gently. "You look a little tired."

"I wonder why." Her sparkling eyes teased. After a searching glance at his lean face, she said, "With the exception of that frown on your forehead, you look pretty much the same. What's bothering you, Josh?"

"Take a look," Josh answered, flinging his arms out. "The road is gone. Every trace of it for miles has been cut to ribbons by those damn cloven hooves."

Serena looked where Josh motioned, her face going strangely still. Then, her eyes not quite meeting his, she asked, "Is that so bad?"

"Not really. We can keep headin' west and sooner or later get to where we're goin'. The only thing, the road would have taken us past water holes and the best places to ford rivers. You'd better get packed up. We'll be leavin' soon."

"Josh, I want . . ." When Josh waited for her to go on, she shook her head as though what she had started to say was unimportant. She smiled weakly and asked, "Will I see you tonight?"

His eyes glittered. "Tonight, and every night."

CHAPTER
∽20∽

"JOVAN says he's as lost as I am and has no idea which way to go."

"He knows, Josh," Eli snorted. "The vindictive bastard is just gettin' back at you because you put a stop to his deceiving Serena."

Josh agreed and both men fell silent for a time. Then Eli asked, "What are you gonna do, son?"

Josh gazed into the red coals of the fire where he and Eli were hunkered down. "What can I do but start scoutin' again?" He stood up. "God knows how long it will take me . . . days, I expect."

"Do the rest of us stay put?" Eli rose also.

"No, keep the wagons rollin' in a westerly direction. You've got to find grazin' for the stock. I'll catch up with you as soon as possible, and pray that I have good news.

"I'll start out at first light," he added hurriedly as from the corners of his eyes he caught Serena's inviting look just before she climbed into the back of the wagon. Love her good and hard tonight, he told himself as he walked away from Eli, it's got to hold you for a while.

As Josh rode along, he kept a ceaseless vigil on the barren ground, ever hopeful of finding the double ruts of the wagon trail.

For three days now he had ridden in this land of towering walls of unscalable mesa, where only bighorn sheep and eagles lived. He patted the nearly empty saddlebag flapping against the stallion's belly and smiled thinly. When he had started out it was full of dried deer meat, parched corn, dried apples, and several chunks of corn bread. And now, if nothing else, hunger alone could force him to return, his quest unfinished.

It was early afternoon when Josh suddenly reined the stallion in and gazed onto a narrow valley, a wide smile spreading across his face. There it was, sharp and clear, running out of sight: the lost wagon road.

Josh figured he'd catch up with the wagon train before dark when he noticed for the first time a broken mass of storm clouds gathered east of the tallest mesa. "Damn!" he muttered. "Not more rain. I swear if it does and washes away the tracks again, I'll put a gun to my head."

It was an hour or so before night camp when falling sheets of rain coming toward the train were spotted by the people. The storm approached swiftly, like a moving wall, enveloping everything before it. Sodden, windblown brush flew about, keeping horses and teams constantly nervous. Everyone was thankful when Eli called a halt in the lee of overhanging granite ledges.

Eli unyoked the oxen and unsaddled the mare, then prepared a shelter for Serena—a tarpaulin fastened to the tall spring-board seat, then stretched out about five feet and secured to sticks stuck into the ground. He gave Serena a wet grin. "Build your fire under the tailgate."

She smiled and nodded, then climbed into the wagon to load her arms with a pile of dry wood that Eli had taken to carrying along with them. Back on the ground again she stacked it the way he had taught her, then taking a sulphur stick from a tightly sealed jar, struck it against the wagon wheel and held it to the small pieces of kindling. The slivers of wood curled and wasted, but the larger pieces had caught.

After starting a pot of coffee brewing, Serena hugged the fire, her shoulders hunched beneath a slicker, her eyes studying a much-handled piece of paper. Each night for the past two months she had secretly pored over the map her brother had sent her.

She knew that Josh was finding it difficult, leading them without a map, and though for a long time she was sorry and ashamed she had lied to him about it, she shrank from the thought of admitting it to him. She would be unable to face the scorn that would leap into his eyes.

Lost in the perusal of river crossings, water holes, and mountains, Serena didn't hear the approaching footsteps. When buckskin-clad legs hunkered down beside her, alarm drained the blood from her face.

The gentleness on Josh's face disappeared. Serena took one look at Josh's cold, furious features and, cringing away from him, her fingers fluttered in nervous haste as she strove to shove the map back into its oiled wrapper.

Josh's lean, brown hand shot out and grabbed her wrist in a painful grip. "I thought you left the map behind . . . isn't that what you said, little lying . . . ?"

Serena felt pain in her eyes that Josh should speak to her in such an insulting way—and also guilt for keeping the map from him—Serena gazed into his cold, accusing eyes.

"I wanted to give you the map, Josh, but I couldn't get up the courage to tell you I'd lied about it. But"—her lips began to tremble—"I had made up my mind if you didn't find the road this time I was going to give it to you."

There was no sign of relenting in Josh's eyes or grim, forbidding mouth. "Sure you were," he taunted sarcastically, "after we arrived at our destination."

"No, Josh, you're wrong. I really . . ." She couldn't bear the jeering look on Josh's face and broke off the faltering sentence. She didn't resist when he jerked the map from her nerveless fingers, only watched in mute wretchedness as he struck out blindly into the surrounding darkness.

Josh paid no attention to the increased patter of rain or its slash across his face. This last blow had left him dead to all feelings except the rage that boiled against Serena Bain. How could he have been so mistaken about her? How could she be so unfeeling as to jeopardize dozens of human lives out of pure spite?

He kicked out at a rock, loathing himself for once having

loved the southern girl beyond all reasoning. Bitterness rode his features as he rounded a wagon and walked headlong into Eli.

His friend stared at his drawn face in concern. "What's wrong, Josh? Didn't you find the road?"

"I found it, about three days from here." Snatching the map from a shirt pocket, he shoved it at the older man. "Here's what's wrong," he ground out. "She had it all the time. I just caught her lookin' at it." His hands clenched convulsively. "I could smash her lyin' mouth."

Eli's face blanched, his shock and regret unmistakable as he recognized the white piece of paper. Yet when he spoke, it was to justify the young girl's action.

"Try not to think too badly of her, Josh. I know Serena real good, and there's not a mean bone in her body. You've got to remember how she hated the Yankees the day she lied about this." He tapped the map. "They had killed her sweetheart, made a prisoner of her brother, and driven her away from her home." He handed the map back to Josh. "There was no way in the world she'd have given you the map then."

Josh's dark scowl didn't lessen at Eli's reasoning. He would only concede that it might have been that way in the beginning, but argued vehemently that later she could have forgotten her hatred, considering all the people depending on his ability to take them across the wilderness.

Having no response for the truth of the passionate words, Eli could only offer weakly, "I'm sure she's been keepin' a tight watch on our progress. If you'd gotten into serious trouble I'm sure she'd have given you the map."

"I've got my doubts about that," Josh growled. "Anyway, we'll never know now, will we?"

Eli's back stiffened in defense of Serena's integrity. His voice filled with confidence, he retorted, "Maybe you won't, but *I* don't need any proof. For all of Serena's sharp tongue and stubborn pride, I've never known a more lovin' and carin' person."

When Josh snorted, "Hah!" he spun on his heel and walked rapidly toward his wagon. He stopped in the shadows when he saw Serena huddled close to the fire, the old hound hunched close up against her. She suffered, he knew, and he would not add to it by scolding her. Everyone acted as they did for some reason, whether it was right or wrong.

Although the deluge of rain hadn't lasted long, it left the earth underfoot slippery and dangerous. Wagons slid and swerved, teams went down, and those bringing up the rear were mired hub deep. Much time was lost in untangling harnesses and dragging wagons from the sucking mire.

However, with the aid of the map, the train was now making good time.

But the wagon master rode with a new worry these days. The wagons rolled through dog soldier country now, according to Jovan the morning he and his wagon parted company with the emigrants.

"These Indian outlaws are not like the usual brave," the rancher had taken spiteful pleasure telling. "They're bold and murderous, attacking trains at the most unexpected times and places."

And the emigrants had found proof of his claim several times since leaving him. There had been looted wagons, dead teams and dead men, their scalps torn off. The only evidence of women and children were feminine apparel and scattered toys. Josh had advised husbands that if ever it looked like his family might be taken prisoner by the vicious renegades, perhaps he should shoot his loved ones to save them from untold torture.

Twice a body of dragoons passed them, and though there had only been a hundred or so soldiers in each group, it lightened the people's spirits. Josh kept to himself the grim thought that if they should be attacked, the chances were slim that the soldiers would be nearby. They had too much country to cover.

Two weeks later Josh had another worry preying on his mind. He had spotted a lone brave on a distant knoll, the telescope in his hands trained on Serena. Her hair, now bleached almost white by the sun, would work like a magnet to the Indian. The Nez Percé would go to any length to snatch her away from the train.

"But maybe it's not a Nez Percé," Josh muttered. "Maybe it's one of Newcomb's Indians." He knew that the man was out there somewhere, just waiting for a chance to grab Serena. The words of the old trapper back at Bridger's fort had made clear the motive of Newcomb's desire to marry his cousin, not undying love for the beautiful girl, but the money she carried with her.

Since he hadn't told Eli of Newcomb's presence at Fort Bridger—it was enough that one man worry—he had resumed sleeping close to the Landrie wagon.

And now just thinking about the little rat getting his hands on Serena caused a cold knot to form in his stomach.

It had taken but a couple of hours that traumatic rain-drenched evening for him to calm down and think Eli's words through. Paw had spoken logically, while he, in anger and hurt, had spewed out harsh and hateful words, words that Serena would never forgive. And Eli hadn't quite forgiven him either.

His big shoulders sagged a bit. "Thank God the journey is nearing its end," he muttered. "And there I must make a decision. Return north, or settle near Fort Bridger. There's no future for me in Oregon now."

Josh shaded his eyes with a hand, trying to gauge the distance up the mountain. He could only conclude that it was a long climb. After a nourishing feed for man and beast, they would test themselves against it.

As lunches were eaten, husbands pretended to have only the food in their plates on their minds as they shunned eye contact with their wives. The wives were not taken in, however. They didn't miss the anxious looks sneaked at the steep, dangerous route that must be followed. Their own fears were hidden by talking calmly and brightly of the future that awaited them.

Serena's gaze seldom left the mountain as she chewed and swallowed, tasting nothing. Was it possible to climb that threatening, wild wall of rock? The Blue, as it was called, loomed over the Grande Ronde, a place of tall, rich grass, timber, and streams. At last they were on the final stretch of the long, hard drive. Before too long she would be with brother Dorn, trying to build a new life.

The sadness and confusion that often came to her eyes these days clouded them now. Before, she had looked forward to settling in a new land, building a home, and rearing children . . .

Josh's children. That, of course, was out of the question now. Josh wouldn't even look at her.

Serena heaved a long sigh. It would be a lonely and barren existence, for she couldn't visualize falling in love with or marrying anyone but Josh.

She cast an uneasy eye at the mountain again, and as though he read her thoughts, Eli swallowed a mouthful of beans and comforted, "Others have done it, daughter." She smiled and nodded, but the tenseness did not leave her face.

All too soon the noon break was over, and the number-one wagon stood ready to move out. The driver was nervous, his knuckles white on the reins. What had once been an envious position was now quite the contrary. He glanced at his wife, and she smiled at him encouragingly. Still, he had a fleeting wish to be a child again, holding on to his mother's hand as the steep climb was made.

Serena reined Beauty in alongside their wagon, giving Eli a quick, warm smile. Then she, like the others, kept her eyes on the wagon master, waiting for him to order the first wagon out. Unlike the day she had resented his presence on their first mountain climb, today she wished he'd stay as close as possible to her. Sadness shadowed her eyes again. She knew he wouldn't be there this time.

The call came. The driver firmed his lips, cracked his long whip, then his team started climbing through brush and briar. Josh waited several minutes, then passed the word that the others should follow at similar intervals.

Very little dust was raised as the teams, seemingly aware of their danger, placed each foot carefully as the wheels jolted over rocks, moved around huge boulders, and skirted deep crevices. Some stumbled occasionally, but while drivers held their breath the animals regained their footing and climbed on. The women and children prayed silently.

According to the sun it was around two o'clock when the trail narrowed dangerously and began to wind around the shoulder of the mountain. For half a mile, at no point did it widen.

Eli looked over his shoulder to see how Jessie was faring behind him. He wasn't too concerned about Nell; Josh was looking after her and the children. But the little whore's mules were a stubborn, contrary pair, unpredictable at all times.

Thankfully, today the dark-colored team plodded along as though they knew this was no time to act up.

They had finally reached a straight stretch of road when from the corners of his eyes Eli glimpsed a shape that froze his blood. Only yards away a brown mountain grizzly was emerging from a thick growth of brush. Huge and red-mouthed, the bear was headed straight for Jessie and her mules.

Maybe he doesn't see them, Eli hoped. Their eyesight is very poor.

The thought was shattered when, with a rumbling roar, the great shaggy form reared straight up and pawed the air. His breast tight, Eli prayed that the animal would remain on his hind legs—they didn't charge when upright—and that the spunky Jessie, now aware of the danger, wouldn't try to use the old cap and ball rifle she always kept nearby. Even if she was lucky enough to hit the great beating heart, the voluminous blast would spook half the teams strung along the mountainside. He shuddered, seeing in his mind teams and wagons tumbling and rolling, disappearing out of sight.

The mules sighted and caught the rank animal smell at the same time. Loudly braying with terror, the pair came to a frozen halt. Jessie jumped to her feet, the freckles standing out starkly on her blanched face. She took a braced stance on firmly planted feet, and gripping the long whip tightly, she called tensely, "Move on, Paw, give me plenty of room."

The oxen responded to his urgent call and the sting of the whip across their rumps. When they had lumbered along a good hundred yards from the white-faced woman, Eli pulled them in and jumped to the ground. As he flexed his arms and shoulders, praying they were strong enough to stop a runaway team if necessary, he looked around for Serena. He did not see her and was thankful. Knowing her, she would rush in to help her friend, probably only to get in the way.

He turned back to Jessie. While he watched, his eyes never leaving the grizzly, she let out a piercing scream and swung the whip just as the brute began to lower his forelegs. With a plunging rush the startled mules galloped straight for the bear, their only desire to get away from the stinging lash that bit into their flesh. In surprised alarm at the unexpected charge, the bear wheeled and loped off into a stand of stunted spruce clinging to the mountain.

With Jessie using all of her strength on the reins, and Eli hanging on to the halter of each wild-eyed head, the mules were finally brought to a halt only a few feet away from the oxen. Jessie gave the Southerner a triumphant smile as he wiped the cold sweat off his face.

"That was a close one, girl." He grinned and climbed back into the wagon.

It was twilight in the valley below by the time all the wagons had reached the crest of the mountain, a wide, flat stretch that seemed to run for miles. Amid relieved laughter and much bantering, camp was made and darkness settled in. Families sat close to their fires, tired and not too talkative. The day had seemed a week long. And tomorrow, after their descent, their destination would be reached.

CHAPTER
∽21∽

SERENA DRANK the last of her coffee, then rose to pace about, almost ill from jealousy. At the widow Simpson's fire Jane Scott sat close to Josh, heaping his plate with food and keeping his cup filled with coffee. And across from the pair, Nell did the same for Paw. Tears blurred her eyes. The four looked so cozy, so contented.

She could have sat with them. Nell had invited her, pointing out that it was senseless to have two fires going, not to mention her eating alone. She had hated lying to the friendly woman when she explained that she had a fierce headache and would be poor company. But the thought of the hate and scorn she would see in Josh's face was too much to be borne.

Unbeknownst to Serena, Eli had been watching her for several minutes. She still suffered, he knew, still longed for things to be right between her and Josh.

He said a quiet word to Nell, then rose and crossed over to Serena's fire. He sat down on a smooth rock, silently filled and lighted his pipe, then studied her through the rising tobacco smoke as he puffed on the narrow stem clenched between his teeth.

Serena started when he said abruptly, "Are you gonna pace all night, honey? You're makin' me dizzy, walkin' 'round and 'round."

239

She sighed and threw herself down beside his lean frame. "Oh, Paw, what am I going to do?"

Eli gave her a sidelong look. "About what, daughter?"

"You know what I'm talking about." She jabbed at the fire with a stick. "What am I going to do about Josh?" She slid Eli a half-defiant look. "You know very well that I'm in love with him."

Pleasure warmed Landrie's weathered face. Finally this headstrong girl was admitting out loud that she loved the Yankee. He laid his hand on her knee, pressed it, and said softly, "I always thought you did . . . well at least hoped that you did. He's a fine man, Serena."

Serena tilted her head and stared up at the stars, blinking back hot tears. "I know he is, and a lot of good it does me, loving him."

"Why do you say that?"

"Oh, Paw . . . after that incident with the map he hates me. He avoids me, never speaks to me."

"Yes, I've noticed all that." Eli nodded soberly. "I've also noticed that you act the same way. How do you account for that, seein' how you claim to love him?"

"For heaven's sake, Paw, I've got some pride left." Serena shot Eli a pouty look. "I'm not going around him unless he gives me some sign that he's forgiven me. You weren't there that night, you don't know how awful he spoke to me, looked at me."

"Did you ever stop to think that maybe Josh is waitin' for a sign from *you*?" Eli raised an inquiring eyebrow. "Maybe he regrets his words and actions and is afraid that you won't forgive him. I see him watchin' you all the time when he thinks nobody notices. I think he'd be happy to talk to you."

Eli paused, watching the hope grow in Serena's eyes. "Why don't you go talk to him."

"I don't know, Paw." Serena pushed back a wayward strand of hair. "His dislike for me seems awfully real. I think you're mistaken about what he feels."

Eli reached over and gripped the cold fingers that twisted nervously. "There's only one way to find out. And you shouldn't put it off much longer, honey. I think Josh is plannin' on return-in' north once he gets rid of us. Once he's headed home you got no more chance."

Serena's response was drowned out by a sudden barking from the camp dogs. The hackles on the old hound rose and deep warning growls sounded in his throat. Josh hurried by, a lantern swinging from his hand. Eli rose to intercept him.

"What do you think, Josh? A coyote snoopin' round?"

"Probably. I'll take a walk around camp and check it out."

Eli reached for his rifle. "I'll go with you."

"No. You'd best stay here."

Eli hesitated a moment, then nodded, although Josh's tone suggested he suspected more than a coyote. And as his friend faded into the darkness he turned his back to Serena and stealthily checked the priming of his firearm.

Josh walked but a short distance when his weak light picked up a set of moccasin prints. He swore softly. They were made recently and right behind the Landrie wagon. He knew instinctively the tracks were made by one of Newcomb's dog-soldier friends.

"He's a crafty little bastard," Josh growled under his breath. "He's hung back all this time, knowing that he'd have his hands full tryin' to control Serena for several hundred miles."

He grimly followed the tracks to a patch of grass, the crushed dew-wet blades evidence that the Indian had sat there a while, watching the camp—and Serena. Moving the lantern slowly over the area, he spotted the toed-in prints leading down the mountain, the distance between them telling him that the Indian had been running. "Probably when the dogs started barking," Josh muttered.

He stood a moment in thought, then walked slowly back to the wagons. "I saw an old she-bear scampering off into the brush," he answered the anxious questions put to him. "Most likely the one that scared Jessie. She's probably hungry after hibernating all winter, so don't anyone stray away from your fires."

Voices raised in uneasy discussions. "Shouldn't the men take turns setting up all night, keeping the fires going?" "Would a fire really deter a hungry bear? I heard once that . . ." The words faded as Josh walked away to have a private word with the night guards he had already posted.

"I saw no sense in upsettin' the women and children," he added after telling the six men the truth. "So keep your ears tuned and your eyes peeled. If you see anything suspicious, fire off a shot."

Serena watched Josh return to Nell's fire, settle himself comfortably against a boulder, then stretch his long legs out to the warmth of the leaping flames. Her eyes grew stormy when Jane Scott rose and stretched sensuously, making sure the sight of her full shape wasn't lost on the handsome wagon master. When he smiled up at the woman, she knew a hurt that penetrated to the core of her being.

Eli, still puffing on his pipe, did not miss the pain that shot into Serena's eyes, or the cause of it. "If I was you, Serena,"— he took the pipe from his mouth—"I'd go over there right now and tell Josh plain out that you want to talk to him; ask him to walk with you and tell him that it's private."

"Paw," Serena answered impatiently, "don't you have eyes in your head? Can't you see he's too busy to consider talking to me, much less take a walk with me?"

"Serena." Eli's stern brown eyes jabbed at her. "If you love that man like you say you do, you'll chance his rejection. God knows you've turned *him* away often enough. Maybe you won't be successful tonight, but at least you'll give him something to think about. Maybe hang around for a few days so that you can talk to him again."

Serena stared pensively into the fire. Paw was right. So many times in the past she had repulsed Josh's attempts to mend some dissension between them. Her stubborn pride had stood in the way then; was she going to let it happen again?

"No! Never again!" she cried inwardly. "To hell with my dignity and my high notions. The single most important thing in life right now is to regain Josh's respect and love. And I will do, or say, anything that will bring back the tenderness in his eyes."

Landrie smiled encouragingly at Serena when she stood up and nervously smoothed her hands down her buckskin-clad thighs. "Go on, honey, you'll never regret makin' the first move."

She gave back a weak smile, then took the first step toward arguing her cause.

Although the Simpson fire was no more than thirty feet away, it seemed miles to Serena before she stood in front of Josh, a strained smile on her face. She swallowed hard when his steely gaze lifted to her, devoid of any expression. She felt despair creeping over her, closing around her throat. He had no intention of making it easier for her to speak. Her lips moved but made no sound.

Then Jane Scott snickered, and pride and courage came surging in.

"Josh," she said, her voice low but clear, "I would like to talk to you. Will you walk with me?"

Surprise flickered briefly in Josh's eyes before changing to almost savage hunger. Damn, he thought, she's so lovely, so desirable.

He pulled up his knees, hiding the evidence of his arousal. The twig his fingers tugged at snapped between his tightening grip. Tonight he must put aside his love and desire for her and risk turning her away for all time. For a renegade Indian skulked out there in the darkness and they dare not leave the protection of the firelight.

And though it was the hardest thing he had ever done in his life, he forced himself to look away from Serena and say brusquely, "I've had enough walkin' for one night."

Serena was vaguely aware that Nell gathered her children and quietly ushered them into the wagon. But Jane Scott had no intention of giving Serena any privacy with the wagon master, and she inched even closer to Josh. For a second Serena was tempted to forget it all, to turn her back on the cold, stoic face and the hateful, simpering one. Then the stubbornness and determination that had enabled a slender young girl to toil under a boiling sun came to the fore.

She blinked back her tears and set her trembling lips. "It's important, Josh," she insisted, a hint of pleading in her voice.

For a fraction of time Josh's face lost its hardness, a look of tenderness breaking through the cold blue of his eyes. Still, he answered coldly, "It will have to wait."

Serena's small gasp came on the heels of the short reply that seemed to explode in the tight silence. When she caught the other woman's pleased, hateful smirk, it was too much to bear. With a choked cry, she wheeled and raced away.

Josh fought the overwhelming desire to follow her, to explain his refusal, to wipe away the hurt in her eyes. His conscience wasn't helped any when Nell jumped from the wagon, clucking her tongue in sympathy for Serena.

"You didn't have to be so rude and hateful to the girl, Josh Quade. Eli's not gonna like it one bit. You know how he feels about her."

But before Josh could respond to the widow's charge, Jane was demanding snappishly, "Why shouldn't Josh talk that way to her? Who does she think she is, marchin' in here and demandin' that he walk with her?"

Nell shot the woman an annoyed look. Her tone sharp, she said heatedly, "It didn't sound to me like Serena was demandin'. It sounded more like beggin'."

"It would do that one good, to beg once in her life," Jane sniffed, then twitched her shoulders indifferently. "She thinks she can have any man in this camp."

Nell arched an eyebrow. "And can't she?"

The anger and jealousy that leapt into Jane Scott's face overshadowed her attractiveness. For a minute she was downright ugly as she pointed out triumphantly, "She just failed with Josh, didn't she?"

Nell glanced at the northwoodsman and was pleased to see by the dark scowl on his face that he did not like what his hired woman had said one bit. A teasing sparkle in her eyes, she asked, "Well, Josh, did Serena fail with you?"

Serena had not failed with him, Josh thought as he stared into the flames, he had failed with her. The first time she had ever come to him she had been forced to swallow her pride and speak before this vicious woman seated at his side.

God! he thought savagely, never would he want his darling to beg. He loved her proud spirit, a spirit that would have bent in most women, under the same circumstances.

When Jane tugged at his arm, demanding doggedly, "Tell her, Josh, tell her that Serena Bain don't mean a thing to you," he turned a look on her that silenced any other word she might have voiced.

"Woman," he growled, "I haven't noticed it before, but you have a fretful, ugly disposition." Leaning forward and laying a piece of wood on the fire, he added with finality, "I don't want to hear another word about Serena Bain."

The two women grew quiet, one greatly pleased, the other seething inside. And Josh continued to gaze into the fire, thinking ruefully that not talking about the little beauty didn't keep her from his mind. He saw her image in the new flames, her red-gold hair tumbling around her shoulders, her tawny green eyes gazing imploringly at him. Even as he had spoken so cruelly to her, he had wanted to crush her in his arms and bruise her red lips with his own.

After several silent minutes had passed, he glanced over at the Landrie fire and a worried frown creased his forehead. Serena hadn't returned yet. Surely she hadn't left the confines of the camp. His frown deepened. She was awfully upset when she dashed away, probably wasn't thinking straight. When a painful knot formed in his chest, he suddenly knew that he must go look for her.

"I see she's not back yet." Josh hunkered down beside Eli.

"No, she's not." Eli glanced at him, his eyes reproachful and somehow threatening. "And I'm gettin' worried. I don't know what you said to her, Josh, but damn your hide if anything has happened to that girl—I'll come lookin' for you."

"You don't know yet if anything has happened to her," Josh cut back, his voice made sharp by his own worry, "so don't drop dead before you're shot." He stood up. "I'm gonna take a walk around camp and see where she's poutin'."

Josh took the time to light a lantern then, moving from fire to fire, posed the same question. "Any of you folks seen Miss Bain?"

Each time he was answered with shakes of the head. The flickering light swinging at his side, and more and more appre-

hensively, Josh stepped outside the circle of wagons and began
to search the surrounding darkness.

With a dread he couldn't shake, he moved to the mound of
crushed grass he'd seen earlier back of the Landrie wagon. A
low distressing sound swelled his throat as he moved the light
over the spot. Serena's small footprints crossed those of the
brave, sprinting in the same direction.

His heartbeat a thunderous sound in his ears, Josh lifted the
lantern shoulder high and played its weak beam over a small
area at a time as he moved slowly among a stand of stunted
trees. A band of pain gripped his chest when the rays picked up
a short growth of soft brush. It was uprooted and tangled, mute
evidence that a struggle had taken place on the spot. He sagged
against a boulder, the pain he felt exquisite as his fear-stricken
imagination took over.

What was happening to her? Why hadn't he talked to her? he
berated himself. He could have ordered Jane to leave them and
let Serena tell him in private what was on her mind.

Josh's hands balled convulsively. And now he must face Eli's
condemning eyes.

With a sigh of resignation he pushed away from the boulder
and almost walked into the older man. Concern pinched Eli's
craggy face and, wasting no time, Josh told him bluntly what
had happened. "An Indian renegade has her, Paw. A friend of
Newcomb's."

"Newcomb? Ira Newcomb? You mean he's here? I thought
we left that bastard a thousand miles behind us."

"So did I, until I saw him at Fort Bridger one day."

"You knew all this time and you didn't tell me? I had a right
to know, Josh. Serena is like a daughter to me."

"I know that now, Paw. I should have let you in on it. But at
the time I thought if I could handle it I could save you worry."
Josh stared off into the darkness. "It's all my fault, hurtin' her
with my hateful words, makin' her careless of her safety."

His eyes sick with worry, Eli opened his mouth, but before
he could speak Josh said earnestly, "I'll find her, Paw, before
this night is over. I'm leavin' the train in your charge," he rushed
on, not giving Eli time to respond. "You shouldn't have any

trouble gettin' down the mountain. Hopefully Serena and I will catch up with you before you reach the bottom.''

He gripped Eli's sagging shoulders, then hurried away to saddle the stallion.

Serena's captor had made no effort to hide his pony's tracks, and had it been daylight, Josh could have overtaken them in a short time. But it was dark, and a light fog was creeping up the mountain. As he moved, always downward, visibility was soon cut almost completely. He finally patted the stallion's neck and gave him the rein. The intelligent animal would sense danger long before he would.

In the meantime, he must content himself with the knowledge that while Serena and the Indian were in motion, she would not suffer too badly.

CHAPTER
∽ 22 ∽

JOSH WAS MISTAKEN that Serena didn't suffer. Besides a fear such as she had never known before, her head ached dreadfully and her ribs felt crushed from the muscular red arm that held her tightly.

And the memory of that terror-stricken moment when the racing hoofbeats reached her ear and she stood rooted to the ground was still vivid in her mind. She would never forget staring wildly through her tears as the pony and its rider bore down on her and, before she could cry out, snatched her from the ground. As she was settled with a hard jolt in front of the Indian, his rough hand had clamped over her mouth.

Dazed and shaken, she could only grab hold of the mount's shaggy mane and hang on. For if she should fall as the animal rushed headlong down the mountain, those galloping hooves would surely crush her skull.

After what seemed like hours to Serena, the little pony's pace slowed to the gait of a tired mount. She felt sorry for the animal but was grateful for the lessening jolts to her body.

Had she been discovered missing yet? she wondered. If so, Paw would be sick with worry. And what about Josh? He would probably be stamping around, swearing, thinking that she was deliberately hiding somewhere so that he would have to hunt for her.

He would come after her, she knew. It was his duty to look

after the people, and Josh Quade took his responsibilities very seriously.

The little mount stumbled, jerking Serena back to the moment and the awareness that a dewy mist was rolling up the mountain. It settled over her like a cloud, reaching through her clothes. And if that wasn't enough, a wind came up, whipping her hair across her face and making her increasingly aware of the rancid odor emanating from the broad body that had captured and now held her. She wrinkled her nose: bear grease.

The pony plodded on, always downhill, and Serena could have cried from weariness and apprehension. What was going to happen to her? The question beat like a drum on her mind.

Serena was shivering and her teeth chattering when she spotted the small fire shining weakly ahead in the darkness. Her fear grew as every act of Indian savagery she had ever heard passed through her mind.

It seemed to her that she blinked her eyes and in the interim they reached the fire. The pony was brought to a sliding halt, and as her companion jumped to the ground her eyes leapt to the four unkempt, blanketed Indians hugging the sparse warmth of the flickering fire. Her gaze was returned by dark, expressionless eyes. And as she searched the outer darkness, debating whether she should make a dash for the pony and for freedom, her ankle was grasped roughly, and a guttural voice grunted, "I have brought white squaw."

Serena gave a startled jerk of her head when a familiar voice said, "Thank you, Ta'sun."

"Cousin Ira?" she asked, dumbfoundedly peering in the direction from whence the words had come.

At first she could make out nothing but shadows of brush and boulders. Then a movement focused her eyes and widened them with a look of incredulity. In view of anyone who cared to look, her cousin had a naked Indian girl penned beneath him, taking the savage thrust of his body. And while she watched, unable to tear her eyes away, the minutes ticked by and the driving hips moved faster and harder, bringing smothered cries of pain from the girl.

It seemed like forever to Serena before the slight, wiry body shuddered, then collapsed on the worn-out female form. And when the young squaw turned her face to the fire, her heart twisted at the tears in the soft black eyes.

"You monster," she yelled, trying to jerk her foot free, to spring at the despicable user of women and scratch the flesh from his face.

The grip on her ankle tightened, and her cousin laughed tauntingly. "Be careful of what you call me, little cousin," he warned dangerously, withdrawing from the limp body he had used so harshly. "If you think back, you'll remember that I take no sass from my women."

"I'm not one of your women," Serena shot back.

"Oh, you're gonna be one of my women, and you'll soon learn to keep your mouth shut."

Serena was praying for Josh to appear and take her away or, if not, for death to strike her. She heard crunching footsteps approaching, then felt her other ankle grasped. Reluctantly she turned her head and was shocked as she gazed at the bewhiskered face that bore little resemblance to the man she had known before.

She scanned the narrow face, and as she looked into the cruel eyes she knew that not a vestige of decency remained in her cousin. There had been so little to begin with, but the ruthless wilderness had destroyed it all.

"Come on down." Ira tugged at her ankle. "We've got important things to talk about."

"I've got nothing to say to you, you depraved excuse for a man," Serena cried contemptuously, trying to free her foot. "Take me back to the wagon train and I'll forget I've seen you . . . for Auntie and Uncle's sake."

"Never mind them," Ira growled. "They're both dead, killed by our own niggers." He laughed harshly. "The black bastards thought it would hurt me."

The tears that shimmered in Serena's eyes for her dead relatives died in shock as Ira jerked her off the pony and stood her before him. From the corners of her eyes she saw the young squaw drag on a doeskin shift, then slowly make her way to the fire. The despair on the thin face brought home to her that in a short while she, too, might look and feel that way. She wanted to cry, to beg the unfeeling man to let her go, to remind him that they were cousins, had grown up together.

"Get control of yourself, Serena," an inward voice ordered. "You know that you would be wasting your breath. Don't let him see your fear. Stand up to him."

And though Ira still gripped her shoulders and her knees were shaking, she asked in a controlled voice, "What do you hope to accomplish by bringing me here, Ira?"

"To fulfill a dream, little cousin." Ira's lips curled in a leer. "We're going to spend the night together, then tomorrow morning we'll go down the mountain and find a preacher."

"You're crazy!" Serena strained to free herself, her whole being revolting against his words.

"We'll see how crazy I am," Newcomb snarled confidently, then grasped the hair at her nape and twisted her face up to his. She caught the scent of whiskey on his breath as he sought to kiss her, and fear returned. She twisted and turned, trying to wrench herself free, but the hands in her hair only tightened. Finally, when a hand began to move over her breasts, painfully squeezing and probing, desperation gave her the added surge of strength to break loose from the punishing hands.

Ira laughed an ugly sound and reached for her again. She swerved away, panting, "You fool, Josh Quade will kill you for this."

"Ah yes, the wagon master." He stalked after her. "Your lover, huh, little cousin?" Surprise flickered in Serena's eyes and a mirthless smile twisted his thin lips. "Yes, sweet Serena, I know all about your Yankee lover. The first time he laid between your legs was back in Vicksburg. The Yankee dog took your virginity, didn't he? That which should have been mine."

"You're wrong, Ira, I never even knew Josh back in Vicksburg. I'd never laid eyes on him until Paw Landrie and I joined his train."

Anger at the Yankee for having lied to him flashed in Newcomb's narrow eyes. One more score to settle with the arrogant wagon master someday. But first things first. He took on a look of lecherous, confident expectation as he began walking slowly toward Serena.

"So, little cousin, I'm not to be denied your virginity after all. It's been a long time since I've had the pleasure of breaking in a virgin.''

"Never!" Serena panted, leaping nimbly from his clutching hands. "Dorn lives at the foot of this mountain, and he'll come after you, you know it.''

"Hah, not after tonight, he won't. Because for the next few hours I'm gonna ride you until you're overflowing with my seed. Tomorrow morning when he's faced with the fact that you might bear a bastard, your proper brother will insist that I marry you.''

"I'd never live with you!" Serena cried, making no effort to hide the disgust in her voice.

"That would matter little to me," Ira grunted. "I'm only interested in controlling your share of the money that old river rat is carrying for you.''

"It will never happen." Serena gritted the words through her teeth. "There are no circumstances under the sun that would make me marry you.''

Her sharp declaration was hardly uttered when she found herself backed up against a tree. Ira was upon her then, his fingers sinking into her arms. "We'll see." His eyes narrowed to thin slits. "Now, if need be, I'll have the braves hold you down," he threatened thickly. "I thought to save you that embarrassment.''

Powerless, Serena could only glare her hatred and declare again, "Quade will kill you for this. He'll track you down and put his knife through your rotten heart.''

Ira's jeering laugh cut across her scathing warning. "You're only wearing yourself out, little cousin. Even if your big mountain man tried, he'd never trace you through this fog. Besides, my Indian friends will keep a tight watch." He licked his lips, his eyes glittering. "And I can ride you at my leisure all night long.''

While Serena stared at him, helpless and wild-eyed, mutely shaking her head, Ira's fingers left her arms. Fastening them in her shirt, he ripped it apart. As she cried out, he bore her to the ground, ignoring her flaying fists on his back and shoulders. Then, when she gave him a good clip on the temple, he swore savagely. Holding her down with the weight of his body he caught her hands and stretched them over her head. And while she flinched in sickened revulsion, he lowered his head, his whiskered face scraping her tender flesh as his lips moved over her breasts, then fastened on a shrinking nipple.

She began to struggle violently when she felt him fumbling with the opening of his trousers. Bucking her torso, she tried to throw him off. When he forced one of her hands down on his turgid manhood, she forced back the bile that rose to her throat, and clenched her fists defiantly, refusing to hold the muscle that had violated so many women.

"Touch it, or else." The threat was muttered around her aching nipple. And to give substance to his words he bit down sharply.

Serena forced back a cry of pain, uncurled her fingers, and, sick to her soul, did his bidding.

Newcomb's smacking lips made a vulgar sound in the night, filling Serena with loathing and disgust. She endured as tears of shame ran down her cheeks. Oh, dear God, where was Josh?

After what seemed an eternity, Ira muttered against her ravaged breast, "Get out of them buckskins."

Her mind frozen with the terrible knowledge of what was to come, Serena's trembling fingers moved to the lacing of her buckskins. Then, as she turned her head away in shamed despair, she glimpsed a broad figure hunkered down in the shadows, only feet away from the fire.

Her heart leapt and raced with hope, then it slowly died. What if the man who crouched there didn't know she was there, didn't know what was going on? The flames from the fire could be blinding whoever was out there.

She knew that somehow she must alert the man to her predicament. So, pretending to work at the lacings of the soft leather trousers, moving her fingers in such a way that would make Ira think she was obeying him, she waited with held breath to see if the ruse was working. She knew that it was when he eased away a bit, giving her more room to work.

It didn't give her much of an edge, but she would gladly take it, for only seconds from now this animal would possess her.

She took a long breath, held it, and praying as she had never prayed before, with one quick movement brought up both knees with all her strength and drove them into Ira's groin. When he rolled off her, roaring in pain, she jumped to her feet and sprang into the firelight.

But Ira, holding himself with one hand, was right behind her, doubled over but still moving swiftly. His free hand reached out and, catching her long flying hair, jerked her back into the shadows. A long, pealing scream ripped from her throat, and before it died away a tall figure leapt inside the circle of light. A sharp, glinting knife was held in readiness in a slim, tanned hand.

"Oh, Josh," Serena cried softly as she sank to the ground.

It was Josh's nose rather than his ears that told him first of the human presence. Indians smoked a mixture of tobacco leaves and bark they called *Kinnikenick*, and he had smelled it many times along the way as ever-watching Indians had camped nearby.

He lifted his head and sniffed like an animal, and so intent was he on discovering the aroma's origin, he barely had time to muffle the stallion's soft whinny of discovery. He moved on cautiously, his head cocked for any sound. It wasn't until he rounded a thorny, close-knit locust thicket that he pulled the mount in. Only yards away, against a huge boulder, a small fire burned. He peered through the curtain of twisted and gnarled foliage and counted six hunched figures. Five braves and one squaw. Sweeping his glance over the encroaching shadows he spotted seven bone-thin ponies.

His forehead knitted. Where were Newcomb and Serena?

Josh dropped the reins over the stallion's head, confident that the animal wouldn't leave the spot, and swung stiffly to the ground. Moving swiftly and quietly, he concealed the lantern in a crevice of a huge rock. Then, dropping to the ground, every sense alert, he began to move forward on stomach and elbow. When he reached a jumble of dead brush, just to the right of the grouped Indians, he carefully raised his head. As his eyes slowly ranged the area, his hand went to the broad blade, making sure it was handy to his reach. If there were sentries about he would need its silent power.

When he saw no lookout, his gaze went back to the ragged, half-starved Indians. A hard knot of alarm formed inside him. Had he followed the wrong brave? Were these Indians only a hunting party? he asked himself, remembering that the rider he had followed hadn't exerted himself by covering his tracks.

Josh pushed shaking fingers through his hair. Now what? He had wasted precious time and would lose much more waiting for daylight, searching for other tracks.

He was about to squirm his way back to the stallion when a mirthless smile twisted his lips. The red men were suddenly showing a lewd interest in something going on behind them. He hadn't followed the wrong man after all.

Josh raised up on one knee just as a slender figure, blond hair flying, sprang out of the gray darkness.

"Serena." He groaned her name, seeing her torn shirt and bared breasts. His body tightened and his muscles tingled as he saw Ira Newcomb stumble after her in hot pursuit, his face twisted in rage and pain. The Southerner's outreached hand fastened in her hair. And when she gave a sharp cry of pain, Josh's whole frame leapt into action.

His hand jerked the knife from its sheath and startled glances jumped to him as with catlike quickness he leapt into view.

With a muttered oath Newcomb released Serena's hair and stared at Josh, a sickly-looking pallor spreading over his face. When Josh started stalking toward him, the knife in his palm poised to fly at his heart, the shivering man slid a pleading look to the group who stared back stoically.

Grim humor twisted Josh's lips. "Don't expect any help from that quarter, Newcomb. They know this is a white man's fight, a trifling matter over something as insignificant as a white woman."

His voice calm yet resolute, Josh added, "You're gonna die, scum. Go for your gun when you're ready."

The color left Ira's face, his fear and hate piercing the dead silence. Then hope flared in his eyes. His longtime enemy read it easily; a bullet was faster than even Josh's knife.

Josh's body went rock still, when with a clumsy hand Ira grabbed for the ivory handle sticking out of its holster. Josh waited until it cleared leather and was aimed with malice-filled eyes to send the broad blade winging through the air from his hand.

The mortally wounded Southerner clutched at his chest, star-

ing in wild surprise. After a moment a film came over his eyes
and his chin dropped. While everyone watched, he uttered a
gasping sigh, then folded slowly to the ground. After a convul-
sive jerk, he lay over on his back.

Josh stood looking down at the sprawled figure until a whimpering sound from Serena brought him hurrying to her. When
she lifted her arms to him like a frightened child, he knelt and
gathered her in his arms, keeping a tight watch on the Indians
at the same time. He would be one against five, should they
decide to take up Ira's fight.

But the renegades' attention wasn't on the man and woman.
The five braves and one squaw huddled together, their guttural
voices muttering in half whispers. Josh's muscles tensed when
one rose and stepped forward. He relaxed when a bronze hand
was held out, the palm up, in a gesture of peace. He too lifted
his own hand, but he didn't relax until all six sprang onto their
ponies, and without looking back took off down the mountain,
disappearing into the mist.

When the sound of the hooves faded away, Josh put Serena
gently away from him, then stripped off his jacket. Helping her
into it, he warned in a low voice, "We've got to get out of here.
I don't trust that pack. Although they didn't side with Newcomb,
they might plan to slip back and wage a war of their own." He
smoothed back her tangled hair. "Do you feel strong enough to
move on?"

Serena nodded and he drew her to her feet. "Stay here," he
said. "I'll be right back." She watched him walk over to Ira's
still body, reach down, and take hold of the knife's hilt, then
withdraw it from the narrow chest. She shivered as he held it
point down, letting the carmine rivulet trickle off its point.

While Josh busied himself wiping the blade clean on a patch
of grass, she walked over to her cousin's body. She knew a
moment's sadness as she looked into the sightless eyes. Although Ira had been vile and brutal, a menace to all he came
across, her last link to the South had gone with his passing.

Serena stepped aside as Josh joined her and scooped up Ira's
heavy body, explaining as he hoisted it to a tall fork in a pine,
"I'll send a couple men after it tomorrow. In the meantime the
body will be safe from hunting animals." He looked over his

shoulder to ask Serena if she was ready to leave and found her kneeling in front of the fire, her hands held out to its meager warmth.

He noted her trembling shoulders and swore under his breath as a sudden thought brought raging fire to his eyes. He moved swiftly to hunker down beside Serena. Cupping her chin, he lifted it and gazed into her eyes.

His voice thick and unsteady, he asked, "Serena, Newcomb didn't . . . didn't . . ."

Serena shook her head as his sentence died unspoken. "No, Josh, he didn't. You came just in time, though."

Josh didn't respond, only pressed her face into his shoulder and gently stroked her head as great sobs shook her body.

Serena did not cry long; she knew it was a luxury she could not afford. When she wiped her eyes on her sleeve, Josh helped her to her feet and led her to the stallion. He had retrieved the lantern and started to boost her into the saddle, when he discovered the horse was limping.

"He must have stepped in a hole." Josh picked up the hoof and inspected the swollen joint beneath the fetlock.

Serena patted the proud arching neck and remarked softly, "I guess all three of us will walk, then."

Josh decided that the safest and closest route to take was to continue down the mountain and wait for the others at the bottom. Serena agreed, and they started the descent, Josh leading, the stallion trailing along behind Serena like a big dog.

The pair soon discovered the farther down the mountain, the thicker the fog and the larger the boulders. Soon Serena was faint from fatigue. And worse, the lantern began to flicker, then died out completely. As they moved on in total darkness, Serena could no longer contain a whimper of distress. Josh put a supporting arm around her waist.

"We'll be all right, honey. I'm going to let the stallion lead the way while I hold on to his tail. He'll take us down safely."

Serena staggered blindly on, too exhausted to respond.

Once Josh squeezed Serena's shoulder, signaling her to stand still. She knew from the tightness of his body he was listening to something. She attuned her own hearing and was rewarded with the sound of running feet and heavy breathing. A sigh of relief whistled through her lips as the footsteps faded away. She and Josh had barely avoided colliding with an Indian in the foggy darkness.

"Do you think he's one of Ira's group?" she whispered.

"I doubt it," Josh answered, a calmness in his voice that relieved her anxiety. "That rag-tailed bunch wouldn't split up."

The stallion was leading them into the foothills when a wolf's cry cut the night air. Serena's tired body stiffened and the big horse snorted uneasily. "It's all right," Josh soothed, hoping he had kept his own unease from his voice as they moved on, while he looked apprehensively over his shoulder every few yards.

The man, woman, and horse stumbled along in the darkness for some time before Josh's strained features relaxed somewhat. Bringing Serena to a halt and tugging the horse's tail, he cocked his head and listened to the muted sounds of the night. A smile broke over his face, and he nodded his head in satisfaction. He hadn't been mistaken. Off to his right sounded the soft lap of water.

"We've made it, Serena." He hugged her tightly, relief high in his voice. "We're almost off the mountain. There's a river nearby."

Serena opened her mouth to express her thankfulness, then snapped it shut. Louder, and much closer the wolf had cried again. Josh's breath sucked in when a little farther away another answered it. Had the animals picked up their scent? Were they sending messages to each other?

Very slowly and quietly, so not to frighten Serena more than she was already, he drew the rifle from its saddle sheath, praying that there wasn't a pack of the night hunters.

He felt Serena's fingers tighten on his arm, heard her low gasp, and spun around. Softly, in the still night, came the rustling of stealthy feet. How many are there? he thought tightly, trying to count the twin pairs of red spots that surrounded them and seemed to move ever closer and closer.

Josh felt the stallion's nervousness in the rippling muscles of his flank, sensed Serena go limp and wilt to the ground. "I hope she's fainted," he whispered hoarsely, raising the rifle to his shoulder. "She'll suffer less if I can't scare these bastards away."

His finger tightened on the trigger as he aimed between two

pinpoints of red light. The gun barrel spat fire, and the forest quiet was broken by a yelp of pain and yowls of startled fright.

Josh watched grimly as ghostly shapes skittered away into the eerie mist. Now if only they didn't regain their courage and return.

He was fumbling in the darkness, trying to reload the rifle, when glancing up he thought his eyes were deceiving him. He rubbed them and peered again, then suppressed a great shout. Dead ahead a flickering light broke the dense, foggy night.

In his relief Josh's fingers bit deeper into Serena's arm than he intended as he squatted down and shook her. She roused and muttered a protest as she stared up at him in confusion. "What's wrong?"

"Nothing's wrong," Josh answered, lifting her to her feet. "Maybe everything is gonna be right. Do you see a light shinin' straight ahead?" He turned her face to follow his pointing finger.

After straining her eyes through the swirling mist for a moment Serena gave an excited gasp. "Yes, I see it." She tilted her head to peer up at him. "Is it a campfire?" Josh felt a tremor pass through her. "Maybe Ira's Indians?"

"I don't know," Josh answered, keeping to himself his question of which would be worse, the renegade Indians ahead or a pack of hungry wolves behind. "We'll approach it real careful," he added, taking her arm and grabbing the stallion's reins.

The wavering light was farther away than Josh had thought as he and Serena stumbled along, the stallion almost stepping on his heels. He figured they'd covered about a half mile when the light disappeared.

"Damn," he muttered, coming to a halt and easing Serena to the ground. "You might as well rest while we wait for it to shine again."

Josh was about to sit down himself when suddenly a bright square of light flared up only yards away. "I see the outline of a cabin," Serena whispered wonderingly.

"Yes," Josh whispered back. "You stay here with the horse and keep him quiet while I check it out. There could be anyone in there." Serena shuddered slightly as her imagination furnished the collaboration of his statement: "Anyone from a friendly trapper to a cold-blooded murderer."

He approached the small building cautiously, coming up alongside the wall facing him. Flattening his body against the log exterior, he inched his way to the unadorned window and carefully peered inside. The first thing to catch his eye was an almost spent fire in a fireplace, giving its last burst of flame from a pile of live coals. That explained the inconsistency of the guiding beacon.

A quick scanning of the single room showed it void of human presence. Who lived in this lonely, isolated place? Josh wondered. A trapper, maybe. He could hear the flow of the river much more clearly now. It was probably full of beaver, he thought as he made his way back to Serena.

The cozy warmth of the room was the first thing to strike the shivering girl. She staggered toward the dying fire and, crouching down in front of it, held her cold hands to its heat. She smiled up at Josh when he filled his arms from a well-supplied woodbox and stacked the contents on the coals. When flames shot up the chimney he hunkered down beside Serena, warming his own hands. Then steam began to rise from their clothing, and Serena shivered. He stood up, bringing Serena with him.

"It's time you got out of those damp clothes and into bed." His gaze went to the bunk bed in one corner.

It did not occur to Josh to look away when Serena obediently disrobed, nor did it occur to her to be angry when he watched. She only knew how good the bed felt when he swept her up and placed her between warm blankets. She sank into the mattress of springy spruce boughs with a tired sigh and smiled drowsily as Josh tucked the covers around her shoulders.

"I'll join you as soon as I tend the stallion," he said softly.

She nodded sleepily, as though that too would be the natural thing for him to do.

Josh found a small shed in the rear of the cabin, and though it was barely large enough for the horse, it was warm and dry with a pile of hay staked beneath its slanted roof. He unsaddled the tired mount and tossed it a couple of forkfuls of the dried grass. Then, ready to drop from exhaustion, he plodded back to the cabin.

He closed the door behind him, his eager gaze going to the bed. Serena lay curled as he had left her. Quickly banking the fire, he climbed out of his clothes, his heart beating in anticipation as he slid in beside her.

But even as he drew her silky smoothness to him, a deep dreamless sleep closed over him.

CHAPTER
❧ 23 ❧

JOSH STIRRED, opened his eyes, and blinked against the bright rays of the sun shining on his face. For a fraction of a second he stared curiously at the small window, disoriented. Then he became aware simultaneously of a weight on the hollow of his shoulder and of satiny smooth legs lying close alongside his rough hairy ones.

He raised up on an elbow and gazed down at the perfect loveliness of Serena's face, flushed with sleep. He lifted a hand to finger the tousled curls spread across his chest, his eyes mirroring the love he felt for this woman. How many times he had dreamed of such a moment, Serena sleeping in his arms.

But had she ever dreamed such a dream about him? he wondered moodily, his hand lingering on her hair. In the light of day he was able to think more clearly. However, he wasn't so sure now that she had approached him last night to tell him of an undying love. She might have sought him out at Paw Landrie's insistence to apologize about the map.

He stared up at the raftered ceiling, lines of determination forming on his forehead. For once he was going to control his emotions and desire for this porcelain body. He was set on ignoring his need for Serena Bain. For an occasional taste of her body was no longer enough, nor was the closing of her heart and mind to him acceptable. He must have all three, or none at all. He had reached the end of his endurance.

He began to inch his arm from beneath the coppery head and had nearly succeeded in freeing it when she stirred, murmured fussily, then snuggled closer. And as his loins heated at the touch of her soft nakedness against him, the blanket slipped from her shoulders. "God!" he whispered, powerless at the sight of the creamy, full breasts pressed against his ribcage.

He was trying to gather his defenses against the need that raged through his body when a velvety smooth leg was raised and stretched sensuously across his hips. His large frame was still shuddering when Serena's green eyes opened slowly and gazed tenderly at him. A ragged breath caught in his throat when she offered him a small, shy smile.

"Did you have a nice sleep?" She murmured the question, her voice husky, painfully aware of every part of the hard body that touched hers.

Josh swallowed and nodded. "You?"

"Ummm, the best ever." Her red lips curved sweetly. "I haven't felt so safe in a long time."

God, I wish she'd cover herself up. Josh ached from her nearness. He was rapidly losing control, all firm intentions fading away. Another minute and the threat of death wouldn't prevent him from possessing the vibrant body that was melting closer and closer to him.

"Do you feel rested?" he asked, hardly knowing what he said, anxious to put his mind away from the temptation of lean legs and soft arms.

Serena's long lashes swept down to lie on her cheeks, hiding the frustration that had been building inside her since awakening. Why was Josh being so distant, so polite? Surely he was just as aroused as she was. She wished she had the nerve to slide a hand down that flat body and find out. She slid him a fast glance and felt better. His face was flushed, a sign that had given him away in the past. So why the curious reticence?

A thought came to Serena, so painful the anguish of it constricted her throat. What if, though his mind still rejected her, his body still desired her? Was he, right now, fighting a silent battle? And if so, which would win over the other, body or mind?

Please let his body win, she prayed silently, for if just once more we can make love together he'll return to me, and in time I'll regain his respect, and pray God, someday his love.

Her heart racing wildly, Serena raised her eyes and gazed into the hard face etched with experience. Will I succeed? she wondered as she compelled her eyes to tell Josh everything she felt.

For what seemed like a lifetime Josh gazed back at her, his strong expression causing hope to die in her breast. She could read the doubt and firm restraint in his eyes. In an unconscious and beseeching manner she raised a hand and stroked the implacable jaw, rough with whisker stubble.

At the first touch of her caressing fingers Josh lost all control. His arms reached for her as he moaned her name. A long, satisfied sigh whispered through Serena's lips as she waited for the long-awaited adoration of his hands and lips. She made a noise in her throat not unlike a purr when Josh began to trace her ruby lips with his tongue. And when his thumb pushed against her lower lip, opening her mouth for his invasion, her own tongue sparred with his eagerly before letting him capture it and draw suggestively.

Lost in the scent and feel of Josh, Serena's body, with its own will, writhed sinuously when the dark head moved from her lips and nibbled a trail down her throat.

And when the lean face finally rested in the valley of her breasts, Serena leaned up slightly to follow a pattern they had set the second time they made love. His name a caressing sound on her lips, she lifted a full breast and traced the passion-hardened nipple around his lips. She sounded a throaty moan when his eager mouth opened and almost enveloped the entire firm mound. She leaned back on her elbows, her eyes glazed over with desire as she watched his lips slowly releasing the rounded flesh until only the pink areola and darker nipple was left in the moist warmth of his mouth. As his tongue stroked and his lips sucked, she sobbed and moaned with pleasure.

Some minutes later, when the other breast had had its share of attention, quick kisses rained across a smooth, flat stomach, while the well of slim hips and soft inner thighs opened eagerly.

Finally Serena could no longer bear the exquisite pain of her need and whispered raggedly, "Please, darling, I hurt."

A triumphant glitter in his eyes, Josh moved up her parted thighs until their hips met, and then, with his hands braced on either side of her head, he lowered himself until just the tip of his arousal touched and teased her vibrant, waiting core.

"What do you need to ease your pain, Serena?" he whispered softly, his voice trembling from his own need. "What do you want?"

"I need you," she panted. Her hands moved down between their bodies and her fingers curled around the hard, throbbing muscle that teased and tormented her. "I want this . . . deep inside me."

"And that's where it wants to be," Josh rasped before bending his head and stripping a nipple through his teeth as he slid his hands beneath her hips and lifted them off the mattress. Then, still grasping her firmly, he curved his body over Serena's and slowly she guided him inside her.

A shudder rippled through him as he filled and stretched Serena, again amazed that she could take all of him. "Oh, God!" he gasped hoarsely.

For a long time Josh just let himself throb inside Serena, loving the loosening and tightening of her muscles that worked like tiny fingers on his manhood. Then, finding himself rapidly approaching a climax, he began to move on her, bucking in and out, trying to restrain the urge to increase his pace.

Minutes passed, and the lean body worked on, the bed creaking in time with the rustling mattress.

Heat simultaneously began to lick along their veins, and finally Josh quickened his rhythm and deepened his thrusts. In seconds the cabin rang with the cries of their release as together they reached the molten crest of desire.

Serena and Josh lay tightly in each other's arms, waiting for their ragged breaths to return to normal. Serena stretched lazily and Josh's lean fingers stroked down her slim waist and splayed across her silky treasure.

"I want you again," he whispered hoarsely. And reading a ready acquiescence in the slumberous eyes gazing lovingly at him, the bed protested as again he feverishly took the slender body that still glistened from their exertions of only minutes ago.

The fire died low, and Josh, as though he couldn't get enough of Serena, gathered her slight frame beneath him twice more. Her passion was equal to his, however, and she was content to rest only a short time between each bout of passionate lovemaking.

At last all virility was drained from their bodies and Josh turned over on his back, a drained man. Spent and relaxed, Serena snuggled against him, waiting for his declaration of love. He had said many things as they pleasured each other, instructing her, encouraging her, moaning how wonderful she made him feel, but not once had he uttered the word *love*.

As Josh remained strangely quiet, staring up at the ceiling, Serena's uncertainty increased. She, too, stared up at the ceiling, recalling his past coldness toward her. Then she remembered how virile he was, how amorous by nature, and a hard knot formed in her breast. She had been used. She had only been a handy body . . . a body that had asked for what it got. For she had done the seducing.

Serena sat up suddenly and scooted off the bed. If she continued to lie beside Josh he would see the despair on her face, and that must never happen. If she should ever see pity for her in Josh's eyes she'd shrivel up and die. Pulling a blanket off the bed and wrapping it around her Indian fashion, she padded across the bare floor and stared out the window.

In the daylight, she saw that the cabin sat in a miniature valley, isolated and lonely, dwarfed by the spruce-covered hills rising majestically to the skies. "Beautiful," she whispered when her gaze moved to the right and she looked on the silver sheen of flowing water. A fringe of cottonwood lined the banks that curved to run within yards of the small front porch.

Determined that Josh not know the agony she felt, she forced herself to remark lightly, "Oregon is a beautiful country, don't you think? I'm sure I'll like living here."

When Josh failed to respond, Serena glanced over her shoulder and found him watching her, a deep shadow in his eyes. She grew still inside. What was he thinking? Was he possibly going to say the words she so desperately wanted to hear?

But he only muttered, as his eyes slid away from her, "I think my northwoods has this country beat."

So, now I have my answer. Serena's head dropped dejectedly.

He's returning home once he delivers the settlers. Not trusting herself to speak, she turned back to the window. Somewhere inside me there sparks some of my old pride, she told herself, and I must find it, draw on it, otherwise I'll be flying across the room, begging him to love me, not to leave me.

While coaxing that inner strength to surface, Serena caught her reflection in a small mirror fastened to the side of the window. She frowned at the purple shadows under her eyes, remembering with aching bitterness why they were there.

Embarrassed by the telltale sign that her body had been well loved, she dropped her gaze to the narrow shelf affixed beneath the mirror. Her eyes ran over a razor, shaving mug, and comb and brush neatly arranged on the piece of rough plank. Evidently the man who lived here took pride in his appearance, she thought idly, picking up the razor and trailing a finger over the silver handle.

What did he look like? she wondered. Was he old, young? Was he fair, or was he dark, like that man over there, the one who refused to love her?

Her musing was halted when her fingers slid over some etching on the underside of the cold metal. She turned the smooth object over and after studying it closely shook her head in disbelief.

The engraved initials D.B. winked up at her.

Excitement thundered inside Serena. The blanket tangled around her feet, nearly tripping her as she tried to hurry back to the bed. Josh looked at her sparkling eyes quizzically as she tugged at the hindering blanket and knelt on the side of the bed.

"What is it?" he asked, leaning up on an elbow.

Serena opened her hand, revealing the folded razor. "You'll never believe this, Josh, but this is my brother's razor—this must be his cabin."

Josh shot her a surprised look then, taking the instrument from her, observed quietly as he examined it, "That's highly unlikely, Serena."

"It's Dorn's, I tell you." Serena jerked her shoulders impatiently, the blanket slipping down a bare arm. "I've seen it on his dresser too many times not to recognize it." She pointed to the blade. "It even had the same little nick up near the handle. One of the servants dropped it once while dusting."

"All right, calm down." Josh captured her fingers, quieting their agitated movement. "But there are other things to consider. Your brother could have lost the razor, it could have been stolen from him, he could have even lost it in a poker game."

"Maybe," Serena muttered, her tone betraying the fact that she wasn't convinced. She freed her fingers, and, gathering up the rough material to her knees, she walked about the room, looking for further identification.

The search was short. There were few items to be scanned in the sparsely furnished room. Besides the bed, there was a small table, a bench, and one chair placed beneath the single window, a rocking chair comfortably close to the fireplace. She deduced that a man lived here alone. A feminine touch was nowhere to be found.

Serena's jubilation began to wane. Although convinced that the razor was Dorn's, as Josh had pointed out, it was unlikely that in this vast wilderness they had stumbled onto his cabin.

She walked back to the window, disappointment displayed plainly on her face. She would have liked this small place to belong to Dorn. Oh, well, she thought, I'm sure he'll have a place equally pretty.

As Serena's thoughts moved to Josh, wondering when he planned to move on, he softly called her name adding, "Come back to bed, please. There's something I want to talk to you about . . . something I want to ask you."

Serena turned her head slowly to look over her shoulder at the roughly handsome man in the bed, afraid to get her hopes up again. She felt her bones melt before the soft light in his eyes. But what did the softness mean? That he was finally going to declare his love for her, ask her to marry him? Or did he only want her to return to bed for another bout of lovemaking?

And while she pondered—Should she go to him for whatever reason, or hang onto the tattered remnants of her pride?—she caught the familiar sound of wagon wheels. She turned back to the window and stared intently down the verdant valley.

There was no mistaking the proud carriage of the male figure handling the reins of the pair of horses pulling a bouncing wagon.

Forgetting everything but the fact that soon she would be re-united with a brother she hadn't seen in over four years, she cried triumphantly.

"I was right, Josh! This is my brother's place. I see him coming, right now!"

"Are you sure?" Josh asked skeptically as he sat up.

"Of course I'm sure." Serena laughed excitedly, taking a lit-tle skip, stepping on the blanket, causing it to slip and expose one breast. Then, as she blushingly pulled it back up it occurred to her that Josh was in the same naked state and that her brother would arrive within minutes.

She raced for her buckskins, calling out as she ran, "Josh, get up and get dressed. What will Dorn think, finding you in bed?" Her flying fingers paused at the lacings of her shirt and she added hurriedly, "Take one of the blankets and a pillow and lay them beside the fire, so it looks like you slept there. My big brother tends to be very protective of me."

He glanced at Serena, poised in the center of the room, breathless with excitement, and wondered how the Southerner would feel about marriage between a rough trapper and his baby sister. Eli had let it drop that it had taken some coaxing on Serena's part to persuade Dorn into agreeing to her engagement to his son. It had crossed Josh's mind at the time that the man had only been humoring his sister, that he had no intention of letting her marry the young man of no means.

The sound of a wagon creaking to a stop outside, the metallic jingle of harness fittings, brought Josh's musings to an end and Serena rushing to the window. She watched her brother stand up and wind the lines around the woodstock. A painful lump formed in her throat as she viewed the traces of the war's after-math in the deep lines of his face, and the gray in his hair. When he jumped to the ground she flew to the door and flung it open.

With one foot on the porch, Dorn Bain stopped and stared, open-mouthed. When he shook his head, as though to shake loose a mirage, he was nearly knocked over as a slender body hurled itself at him.

"Dorn, Dorn, it's me!" Serena laughed and cried at the same time.

Letting out a loud, hearty laugh, Bain grabbed his sister and hugged her. Then, holding her away, he scanned her face anxiously. "Are you all right, Serena? Eli Landrie told me that an Indian had grabbed you last night, and that the wagon master was out looking for you."

"Yes, Dorn, I was captured by an Indian, but worse, he took me to cousin Ira."

"Ira, that bastard!" Dorn roared, making Serena flinch as his fingers bit into her shoulders. His flashing eyes searched her face. "Did he harm you . . . in any way?"

Serena's face paled with remembrance. "If Josh hadn't come along when he did . . . I would have been harmed."

"That rotten little weasel," Dorn ground out through clenched teeth. "I'll kill him, if it's the last thing I ever do."

Serena picked up and patted the clenched fist. "Josh has beaten you to it," she said quietly. "Our cousin will never harm another woman. I'll tell you all about it later," she added, taking her brother's arm and leading him to Josh, who stood leaning against the fireplace. "Right now I want you to meet Josh Quade the wagon master."

"I can never repay you for what you've done, Josh Quade," Bain said, his hand outstretched, his voice husky with gratitude. "Serena is all I have in the world. She is very precious to me."

Josh wanted to say that Serena was precious to him also as he shook hands with the stern-looking Southerner, but he said instead, "I was mighty pleased to find her in time, and that's thanks enough." He wondered if it was his guilty conscience, or had he imagined that Bain's dark eyes flicked suspiciously from the bed to the blanket on the floor? He was thankful when Serena brought her brother's attention back to her.

"When and where did you see Paw Landrie, Dorn?"

Before answering his sister, Dorn quirked an eyebrow at her. "*Paw* Landrie?"

"Yes." Serena nodded solemnly. "Paw and I have become very close during these war years."

Dorn studied her grave young face a moment, then answered, "I saw Eli this morning, coming down the mountain. You see"— he shrugged out of his jacket and hung it on a peg—"I've been here at my line shack for the past week. I figured it was about time some wagons began rolling in. When last evening a friendly

Indian rode by and mentioned he'd seen a large group of wagons and people camped on top of the mountain I took a chance that you might be on the train and took off to meet you.''

He sat down and stretched his feet to the fire. "When Landrie told me what had happened I hurried back here to round up my men to go help search for you."

Serena started when her brother turned to her and teasingly switched the subject. "Have you learned how to cook yet, little sister?"

"Some," she answered, almost defensively, remembering some of the meals Paw had uncomplainingly choked down. "Paw taught me some. Do you want me to make you something to eat?"

"Sure. Then I think Josh should find Landrie and let him know you're all right. He's very upset and plans on forming his own searching party as soon as he leads the people down. Me and my men were to meet him at the foot of the mountain."

After Dorn had opened a cupboard and brought out a slab of bacon, a crock of eggs, and a chunk of butter to go with the sourdough bread, Serena busied herself between table and fire, listening to the men's comfortable conversation.

"What part are you from, Quade?" Dorn asked.

"The deep woods of Michigan. Just about as far north as you can go."

"I met a couple of men from the northwoods during my stint fighting Indians. Big men like yourself. Trappers."

Josh grinned. "That's about all a man can do in the frozen North. It's not much good for farmin'. The season is too short for most growin' things."

"I take it, then, you're a trapper too."

Josh hesitated. Would the friendly expression in the man's eyes change when he answered yes? Would his occupation bring rejection instead of acceptance when it was made known that he, a trapper, wanted to marry Serena?

Hell—his eyes narrowed fractionally—it's Serena I have to convince, not her brother. There was pride in his voice when he answered, "Yes. Since I was seventeen."

Bain slid a quick look at Josh's thick hair and grinned. "I'd say that was about seventeen years ago. Am I right?"

Josh laughed. "The gray at my temples gives me away, huh?"

"Just like these lines give away my age." Bain stroked his fingers down his cheeks. After a short silence he said, "The streams around here teem with beaver. There's a ready market for their fur in England. Beaver hats are the craze with the gentry. An ambitious man could make a fortune."

Serena paused while slicing bread, her breath held as she waited for Josh to respond. But when he spoke, it was to change the subject.

"Your sister tells me that you've started yourself a cattle ranch."

A wide smile lit up the handsome man's face. There was pride in his manner as he leaned back in his chair and clasped his fingers behind his head. "I sure have. This fall I'll have at least a thousand head to drive to market."

"That many?" Josh looked surprised. "Where will you take them?"

"Me and my men will drive them into Kansas. There's a railroad in Abilene."

"How did you ever get hold of that many cattle?" Josh tried to visualize a herd that size. "A thousand head seems an uncommon amount."

"That's only a splash in a bucket." Dorn's white teeth flashed. "There's hundreds of thousands of the wild beasts roaming around out there. Ever since the war started longhorns have been coming up from Texas in droves. All a man has to do is round them up and keep herd on them."

"It must take an awful lot of land to graze that many."

"That's a fact," Dorn acknowledged. "I own ten thousand acres and share the open land with a few other ranchers." He smiled at Serena. "I expect I'll be buying more land pretty soon, right, Sis?"

"If that's what you want, Dorn." Serena looked up from the skillet of bacon. "I've brought you the money for it."

"I've got the tract all picked out. Every acre borders the river, giving the cattle plenty of water. And there's a spot where I'll build our home, Serena.''

He grabbed his sister's hand as she passed him on the way to the table. "It will be a prettier place than the one you had to leave, honey. I promise that you'll be the lady of the manor again with all the same luxuries you had before.''

Serena glanced at Josh, a ready smile on her face, one that said she didn't want to be a lady, she wanted to be a trapper's wife.

The message died in her eyes when Josh didn't smile back, but only looked at her, his face refusing to betray his thoughts. Her voice was strained when she announced that the meal was on the table.

Josh avoided looking at Serena as he ate and talked only to Dorn. Her delicate features became pinched, aware that what he had planned to say to her earlier had been forgotten.

But why? She racked her brain, trying to figure out if anything she may have said or done could have changed his mind. When she had gone over her every word and action, and found nothing that could have brought on his cool aloofness, she was forced to conclude that he had simply changed his mind and that he wasn't ready to give up his freedom just yet.

When a short time later Josh stood up, remarking that he had better go look for Paw Landrie, Serena felt that a giant hand had grabbed her heart and squeezed. Although her pain was so acute she could barely keep from crying out, she stood up also and forced a smile to her lips as Josh shook hands with Dorn, then turned to her.

He gazed somberly into her eyes a moment then, murmuring huskily, "Take care of yourself," opened the door, stepped outside, and closed it quietly behind him.

Serena stood in tormented silence a moment, then, with an anguished sob that startled her brother, she ran to the window. Through tear-blurred eyes she watched Josh head down the valley at an easy lope that wouldn't hurt the mount.

When the clopping hooves died away, Dorn came to stand beside her. Putting a sympathetic arm around her shaking shoulders, he asked softly, "You like that big man, don't you?"

Serena nodded. "I love him."

She cried inwardly and wondered how Josh could act as though they were only mere acquaintances when just an hour ago they had shared the most intimate of relations. Dorn led her back to the table and sat down beside her.

"What about Jeremy Landrie?" Dorn tried to tease her. "I thought you loved him."

"I did love Jeremy." Serena sighed. "But that was the first love of a young girl, all sunshine and joy. I've learned a lot since then. True love can tear you apart." She stared into the black depths of her coffee. "Jeremy was killed in the war shortly before Paw and I headed west."

"Ah, that's too bad," Dorn exclaimed, regret in his voice. "That must have hit you awfully hard."

"For a while I didn't care what happened to me," Serena said. "I was tired of working like a field hand, hungry half the time. I was about ready to lie down and die when your letter came."

"It's all behind you, honey." Dorn took her hands and held them. "You're going to have a good, full life out here. You'll marry, have strong, healthy children, help this country to grow."

"No." Serena shook her head. "There will be no children for me. I shall never marry."

"Oh? What if that big man of yours says different?"

"He won't," Serena answered wearily. "As soon as the wagons reach their destination he'll head back north."

"Maybe," Dorn mused out loud. "Maybe." He glanced at the bunk bed in the corner. "For now," he said, standing up, "let's straighten things up here and head for the ranch."

Serena widened her eyes at him. "I thought this was your ranch."

"Naw, I told you it was my line shack, a place for the cowhands to stay when they're too far away from the ranch."

"Oh, I see," Serena murmured, not seeing at all.

CHAPTER
∽24∽

HIS FACE HAGGARD and miserable, Josh rode on, trying to leave the memory of Serena Bain behind him.

He had done the right thing, he knew in his heart, by parting with the southern girl forever. For as her brother had been quick to let him see, she wasn't meant to be a trapper's wife.

"She would hate me within a year," he muttered "livin' the kind of life I could provide for her."

Josh pulled the mount into a walk as he began to muse on what direction his future should take.

Should he return to his home country, or should he accept the old trapper's offer back at Fort Bridger?

"I'll decide that later." He lifted the reins, changing the gait back to the easy lope. "Right now I gotta catch up with the train. Eli is probably a wild man by now."

Half an hour later, when the stallion scrambled to the crest of a long rise, Josh pulled him in and leaned forward in the saddle. Below, his people had made their last camp of the long trip; they had arrived at their destination. Tomorrow would start the mad rush of claiming homesteads. "Good luck to you all," he said quietly.

Then, straining his eyes against the setting sun, he made out the Landrie wagon and the oxen grazing nearby. When a hand was raised and waved at him he knew that Eli had seen him. Smiling faintly, he sent the mount down the gentle slope.

"You didn't find her." Disappointment was thick in Eli's voice.

"I found her, and she's all right." Josh swung to the ground. "In fact, she's with her brother right now."

Although his heart beat joyfully at the good news, Landrie caught the tinge of bitterness in his young friend's tone. He sent him a curious look and opened his mouth to speak, but Josh jumped in, telling him of the confrontation with Ira Newcomb and how he and Serena accidentally stumbled onto her brother's line shack.

"What a relief," Eli said when Josh finally stopped talking. "Serena safe, and that mean little weasel gone for all time." He jerked his head toward the cheerfully burning fire at the end of his wagon. "Let's have a bite to eat while we talk over what happens now."

He patted a hip pocket. "I've got your money for bringin' us here. One of Hansen's men who stayed with us brought it to me."

Josh took the large roll of bills from Eli, stashed it in his saddlebag, then followed him to his fire.

"So, son, what are your plans?" Josh was handed a tin plate liberally filled with fresh trout.

"I'll be movin' on when I finish eatin'." Josh bit into crispy fried fish. "I haven't made up my mind yet whether to go home or to Fort Bridger. I'm kinda leanin' toward the fort. I liked that country. Good trappin' there."

For several seconds there was a tense, strained silence. Then, resentful fury in Eli's eyes, he rasped, "So, you're givin' up, are you . . . without even a fight. I ought to take a stick to you, Josh Quade, beat some sense into that empty head of yours."

Josh laughed lightly but avoided the brown eyes glaring at him. "I reckon you're fussed up about Serena, because I won't give up my freedom for her."

Disbelief shone in Eli's eyes for a moment, then the anger returned. "You listen here, you pumped up pup, my Serena is worth any man's freedom, and if it bothers you that much to give up yours, she's well rid of you. You don't deserve her."

And though everything inside Josh wanted to shout, "You're wrong, Eli, I'd give my soul, let alone my freedom, to marry her, to have her always,'' he concealed the pain that was like a dull knife jabbing him in the gut. Smilingly, he shrugged his shoulders indifferently.

"I agree with you, Eli. Serena is a fine woman, but . . ."

Josh watched his friend fighting to control his anger. He knew sadly that the man was genuinely fond of him and didn't want them parting with hard feelings.

"Eli," he said quietly, standing up, his smile gone and his eyes serious, "I'll be leavin' now. I'd like for you to think of me kindly once in a while. I'll remember you often, and remember you as my friend.''

"You're a plumb fool," Eli declared gruffly, rising also and offering his hand, "but I'll think of you a lot and regret that my best friend was a miserable coward when it comes to lovin' a woman.''

The two men shared a firm handshake, and Josh swung into the saddle. Eli watched him ride away, then suddenly called after him, "Josh, out here a man can be whatever he wants to be. He's just got to be man enough to take hold and wrestle it to a standstill.''

His only response was a wave of the hand as horse and rider disappeared down the valley.

The sun was sinking fast and the forest was still as Josh left the valley behind and again entered the sloping hills of forest. A sudden breeze sprang up, turning cool as the sun disappeared from sight. In the semi-gloom that comes before true night Josh pulled up his collar, unsaddled the stallion, then rolled up in his blanket beneath an outcropping of rock.

His last thought before sleep engulfed him: God, how I miss her.

Josh awoke at first light, hunger gnawing at his stomach. He rose, straightened out his buckskins, then caching his gear behind a rock he stalked into the forest in search of his breakfast.

Being a true woodsman, he walked swiftly, toe in, his fringed buckskins rustling softly. Within fifteen minutes a fat gray squirrel tumbled from a tree, its head neatly sliced off. Josh retrieved his knife and picked up the small animal.

The solemn silence of the forest was unbroken except for the scuffing of Josh's moccasins, until he was almost back to his gear and the stallion. Then he froze at the sound of a wolf's menacing growl.

"That bastard has someone at bay," he muttered, stirring into action, moving swiftly to his right.

Josh had taken no more than a dozen paces when he spotted a huge gray timber wolf, its jaws slavering, its small eyes flaming like fire. The animal's sides heaved with its rapid breaths, its fangs bared in a hideous grin. Josh looked in the direction the threatening snarls were directed and caught his breath.

Propped against a tree, old and obviously very ill, an Indian warrior stared back at the wolf. Acceptance of death was clear in his black eyes. Josh swung his gaze back to the gray, shaggy animal, saw the fur on its neck bristle, and prepared himself. When the beast snarled and leapt, he brought his knife to play. The blade struck home while the large body was in the air. He watched it collapse and come down limply, landing on its head and shoulders, its legs jerking spasmodically.

When he was sure that the wolf had received a fatal wound, he pulled his knife from the narrow chest, then walked over to the old man.

He stared into the peaked, wrinkled face. The high flush on the parchmentlike skin told him that the Indian was running a high fever and was quite ill. He squatted beside the lax figure and saw the eruptions of deep-seated pimples scattered over his face. He sat back on his heels. The old fellow had smallpox, a highly contagious disease.

Unconsciously he raised a hand to stroke a pox scar high on his left cheek. He had beaten the sickness at an early age.

"You're sick, old brave," he said gravely. "Why are you out here, all alone?"

The old Indian nodded gravely. "I am sick with the white man's disease." His words sounded low and crackly. "Since I no longer have any kin to tend me, I was brought out here to die."

"That's a hell of a note," Josh muttered, making no effort to hide the disgust in his voice.

"No." The red man lifted a weak hand in protest. "Do not

find fault with them. Why should I, an old brave ready to leave this land anyway, bring death to my people, especially the young?''

"Well, I've had the disease, so there's no danger of you passin' it on to me. I'm takin' you to my camp to feed you, and start gettin' that fever down. You stay quiet now while I go get my horse.''

A voice inside Josh nagged him all the way back to his campsite: "Now why do you want to burden yourself with a sick old Indian? He's only going to delay your getting away from here. It could be weeks before he gets on his feet . . . if ever.''

The inner voice was still picking at Josh even after he'd saddled the stallion and was on his way back to where he'd left the old man.

And that was the reason he didn't hear the galloping hooves until they were almost upon him. He swung around in the saddle, his eyes first widening in surprise, then in anger. The rancher, Dorn Bain, was bearing down on him. Bitterness grew in his heart. Was Serena's brother going to order him to leave the territory to make sure that he didn't get too close to his sister?

His face was hard and tight when Bain pulled up beside him, a genial smile on his face.

"So, Quade, you've decided to stay with us.'' His eyes searched Josh's face intently.

The trapper's lips thinned and the slashed grooves alongside his mouth tightened. "I haven't made up my mind yet,'' he answered surlily.

Dry amusement flickered in Bain's eyes. "Hell, don't be so thin-skinned, Quade. I only wanted to say that if you've decided to stay in these parts I'll sell you my line shack, along with the mountain area behind it. It's ideal for a trapper, overrun with 'most any animal you can name.''

"Why do you want to sell it?'' Josh eyed the rancher suspiciously.

"I have two reasons, actually,'' Bain said. "First, the line shack is too small. There's always at least two cowhands who have to share it, and that leaves one man to sleep on the floor, which always leads to an argument. I'll have to build another

one at least twice the size of the present one so that I can put in
more bunk beds.

"And second," he went on, "I can't graze cattle in the rough
mountain region, so it's of no use to me."

Josh remained silent for a long space after the rancher stopped
talking. With frown lines between his eyes he asked himself why
the man was offering him this property. Were his reasons sincere?

And what about Serena, the woman who made his pulses leap
with an eagerness that no other woman had ever roused in him.
Would he be able to stay away from her?

But Lord, he'd like nothing better than to own that tight little
cabin, the mountains rearing up behind it. He slid a glance at
the man who sat waiting for his answer. Taking a deep breath,
he asked, "How much do you want for the place?"

Something suspiciously like relief flashed in Bain's eyes.
"Whatever's the going rate per acre. I won't charge you for the
buildings."

Excitement began to build inside Josh. He was sure there was
enough money in his hip pocket to pay for the place, with enough
left over for traps and whatever staples he'd need. There would
be no problem in obtaining fresh meat.

"When could I move in?"

Bain shrugged. "Anytime. Today, if you want to."

"Good." Josh's eyes gleamed. "I'll go there now."

Dorn Bain had an infectious smile, and Josh couldn't resist
returning it when he said, "Fine, I'll drop you off some grub in
a couple hours." He lifted the reins and turned the big white
stallion around. As he urged it into an easy lope, he called over
his shoulder, "I'll tack its cost on to the price of the mountain."

Josh grinned, watching horse and rider disappear over a rise.
"I wonder if the two of us will ever tangle." He thought out
loud.

Memory of the sick old Indian waiting for him interrupted
Josh's musings. He jabbed the stallion lightly with a heel and in
five minutes he was again kneeling beside the slight figure.

"What is your name, old man?" He lay a hand on the hot
brow.

"I am called Red Feather." The answer was croaked from dry, cracked lips.

"Well, Red Feather, as soon as I collect some bark and roots to make a brew for your fever, I'm takin' you to my cabin."

Bird-bright eyes scanned Josh's face, as though looking for deceit or trickery. When he read only sincerity on the strong-planed features, he nodded gravely.

It was near sundown by the time Josh settled the old man in the bunk bed, made broth from the squirrel, simmered a tea from the ingredients he had gathered in the forest, and then bathed the feverish body with icy water that flowed from a spring in back of the cabin.

And now, as Red Feather slept, he moved about, stowing away the supplies Bain must have stacked on the porch while he was in the shed tending the stallion.

The last bag stacked on a shelf, Josh poured himself a cup of coffee and stepped outside to drink it. Leaning against a supporting post, his mind played with ideas for his future until twilight faded and darkness set in. Then, turning back inside, he checked on Red Feather, found him a little cooler, nodded his head in satisfaction, and rolled up in a blanket, close to the bed.

Soon the profound silence of his new mountain home lulled him to sleep.

CHAPTER
⇜25⇝

DORN BAIN'S ranch house was unusually large, considering the size of the dwellings put up by most settlers. Sturdily built of stone and log, durable enough to withstand blowing snowstorms and warring Indian attacks, it consisted of six rooms.

In the rear of the building, several yards beyond a flower border, sat a large barn, a long bunkhouse, and several other small buildings. About half a mile beyond these buildings were several small cabins where the help lived with their families.

The log structures were kept neat and clean, with vigorously growing gardens behind each one.

And Serena, standing in the kitchen door of the house that had been her home for the past four months, thought that the Bain ranch was almost like a small village. For, counting wives and children, there were close to a hundred people living on Bain Range.

She would have liked to become better acquainted with the women, she mused. Her lips curved ruefully. Serena didn't know when she'd find time to do so.

Every morning, seven days a week, she was up at dawn, turning her hand to whatever was most pressing, whether it be gardening, laundering, or even helping to cut out steers that still needed branding.

A soft, ragged sigh escaped her. She welcomed the arduous work, for when she fell into bed at night she was usually too tired to dream of Josh. She sighed again. But during the day there was nothing that interfered with thoughts of him.

A soft breeze, filled with the perfumed fragrance of wild roses blooming alongside the house, stirred the tops of the pines overshadowing the shake roof, bringing Serena back from thoughts of the handsome trapper who had ridden out of her life. She rested her glance on the valley of green grass rising to meet the darker green of tall spruce covering the rolling hills, and thought that this protected valley was perfect for her brother's new life.

A river flowed through its center, bordered by autumn wildflowers, providing clear fresh water year round. The hundreds of miles of ranch were lush with tall grass during the summer time, ensuring that the cattle would be strong and healthy, come time for the drive to Abilene.

Her eyes followed the course of the stream, where the grass always grew more luxurious, and where there were always several hundred head of cattle grazing.

She raised a hand to shade her eyes against the westerly sun, looking for Dorn. She spied him after a while, astride a light tan mustang among a sea of horns, some measuring six feet across.

It had been slow, back-breaking work, gathering the wild cattle, and only tough, excellent riders could round up the longhorns and keep them corraled. They were mean, nervous beasts, stampeding at every noise, sometimes taking days to be rounded up again.

Adding to the workload of Dorn and the cowhands were the marauding wolves. They traveled in packs, on the lookout for a young calf or a steer ready to die from old age. Besides those slain outright, many cattle were maimed by snapping fangs and limped off to die somewhere, while others were lost as the terrorized herd bolted and ran.

Altogether it was a rough life, she thought, but one that seemed to appeal to her hard-working, aristocratic brother. And the wild and lonely land was beginning to work its magic on her too. Already she had to rake her memory sometimes to recall her life on the plantation. She still missed Mammy Hessie, of course, and the absence of black faces had been strange at first, just as she had to get used to high-heeled boots on the cowboys, their spurs, chaps and tall Stetson hats. And she still couldn't half understand their special language.

Short bursts of wind worried at Serena's hair and tugged at her skirt, as though calling her outside. She stepped from the door and made her way to the flower bed Dorn had dug for her. She critically surveyed the jumble of bright-blooming flowers. Some of the settler women had shared their precious supply of seeds with her, and she gazed at larkspur, zinnias, hollyhocks, and many of which she didn't know the names.

She was about to bend over and pull a lone weed when crunching footsteps brought her swinging around, her hand dipping into a pocket where a little double-barreled derringer rested. Indians were still a threat, and Dorn insisted that she keep it on her at all times.

The wariness left her face and was replaced with a wide, welcoming smile. "Jessie!" she called, picking up her skirt and hurrying to meet her little friend.

As the pair embraced, Serena thought, as she had dozens of times, the trip west had certainly altered this young woman's life. The diminutive redhead was now the prosperous proprietor of her own fancy house. As soon as the building had been completed, she added two Indian and three Mexican girls to her original five. All were healthy and attractive, and every night "Jessie's Palace" swarmed with eager, randy men.

And though Jessie would never admit it, she was very pleased and happy that most of the settler women accepted her and now invited her into their homes. It appeared they had agreed among themselves that Jessie's girls were necessary in this piece of wilderness. There were too many single men, and too few single women.

"Men have to have their pleasurin'," they told each other, "and if they don't have an outlet, our daughters might be in danger to compromise."

Most of those daughters would like to be in such danger, Serena grinned to herself, taking Jessie's arm and walking her to the house. Inside the cool parlor she suggested, "What about a cold glass of milk and some ginger cookies while we have a good gossip?"

"Sounds good." Jessie smiled, taking off her elaborate red

bonnet and matching eyelet gloves. Her voluminous skirts rustled as she followed Serena into the kitchen where she was setting a pitcher of milk and two glasses on a tray. "Can't we stay in here?" she asked. "It's more friendly, don't you think?"

"Sure," Serena agreed, and chairs were pulled away from the well-scrubbed table.

Entertaining in the kitchen had taken Serena a while to accept and get used to. But when her lady callers continued to arrive at her back door, and wouldn't budge from the kitchen, she was forced to serve them there. She often wondered why those women even bothered to have sitting rooms. As far as she knew, very little sitting was ever done there.

She filled the two glasses with rich, creamy milk from her own milch cow, passed one to Jessie, then, pushing the platter of cookies within her reach, sat back and smiled widely.

"You're looking mighty handsome today."

The change in Jessie's appearance these days was startling, to say the least. The most obvious was her hair. It no longer frizzed all over her head like red yarn, but was pulled back from her small face and fastened in a smooth bun at the nape of her neck. The scanty silks and satins of the old days were gone, and the new hairstyle went perfectly with the dimities and sheer muslins she now wore.

Serena knew a small pang of nostalgia. Jessie's full skirt of black bombazine and white blouse with wide ruffles at throat and wrist were so like the ones she had worn at the plantation before the war.

She gave herself a mental shake, pulling her thoughts back from the past, and smiled at Jessie. "Come on, fill me in on the latest news and gossip. I haven't been to the village in two weeks."

Time flew by as the pair indulged themselves in the chatter they missed so keenly now that they lived apart.

Wiping milk and cookie crumbs from her lips, Jessie informed Serena that two more women they had crossed the country with were now expecting, and that Nancy Lewis had miscarried; she had worked too hard in the fields alongside her husband from dawn to dusk. "Then there's Becky James," she went on, "who is too lazy to lay her hand to anything. I'm told her cabin is a regular pigsty, and that poor old Tom is so skinny it's possible she doesn't cook much, either.''

Serena shook her head, in sympathy for the farmer, then asked jokingly, ''What about my old friend, Jane Scott? Is she enjoying her new status?''

Jessie's lips curved in amusement. ''I don't think the lady is all that hot about marriage. For one thing she's workin' herself ragged in her new husband's store. It would seem that he was lookin' for free labor as well as a bedmate.'' A glimmer of satisfaction shone in the green eyes. ''Rumor has it that her fat husband is a very randy fellow, demanding his rights night *and* day, even closing the store so he can take her into the back room. I'm thinkin' that snooty lady is findin' out what it means to be a whore.''

''But she's married, isn't she?'' Serena shot Jessie a puzzled look.

''So? There's no love in the union. Each wanted something from the other. If Jane chose to pay for that step up the social ladder with her body, that makes her as much a whore as any of my girls.''

''Well, yes, I suppose so,'' Serena was finally forced to agree after mulling over Jessie's line of reasoning. ''Put that way I think you're right.'' She looked across at Jessie, her grave eyes reflecting her new thinking. ''If it's true . . . the way you see it . . . there is many a whore hiding behind the vows of wedlock.''

''Exactly,'' Jessie answered crisply. ''You'd be surprised, Serena, at how many.''

''What about you, Jessie?'' Serena asked after a short silence. ''Would you marry without love?''

There was another short silence during which Jessie sat with her brow furrowed in thought. Then: ''I might be tempted to. I'd like to lead a respectable life again, have children . . .'' Her lips curved wistfully. ''But when it would come right down to it, I rather think that I wouldn't. If a man doesn't love his wife, nor she him, there isn't that tenderness between them. The consideration for each other's feelings is what makes a *good* marriage.''

Jessie watched Serena stare unseeing out the window and knew she was thinking about Josh. She touched the hand clenched on the table and asked gently, "What about you, Serena, would you marry without love?"

A large tear trickled down Serena's cheek as she shook her head mutely.

"Damn that Josh Quade!" Jessie slapped her palm down on the table. "I could break his stupid head."

Serena rubbed the heel of her hand across her wet cheek and laughed shakily. "He can't help it if he doesn't love me, Jessie."

"Hah!" Jessie snorted. "That big idiot is crazy about you."

Bewilderment clouded Serena's eyes at Jessie's outburst. "If he loves me so much why—"

"Why did he leave?" The small woman answered her unfinished question. "Who knows? Who knows anything about Josh Quade? I've been acquainted with him for six years, and I still don't know him.

"For one thing, he's never known a woman like you before. I think you scare the hell out of him. He has no idea how to handle a lady." She stood up and moved around the table to squeeze Serena's drooping shoulders. "Try to forget him, honey. Start looking more closely at those men who gaze at you like lovesick bulls. Most of them are real decent fellows. Get rid of that aloof austerity of yours, that frigidity that keeps them at bay. Like that young friend of your brother's. That Dr. Stevens. He's real good-lookin'."

When Serena only smiled wanly and patted the small hand lying on her shoulder, Jessie picked up her bonnet and carefully sat it on her head. "It's time I get back to the Palace and wake the girls," she said, tying the ribbons under her sharp little chin. "The men will be poundin' on the door as soon as it gets dark."

Serena walked with Jessie to the lightweight surrey parked in the shade of a spruce. "Think about what I said," Jessie ordered, climbing into the vehicle and picking up the reins. When Serena only smiled, she shook her head, clucked at the horse, and rolled away.

Serena watched her friend fade out of sight then, sighing raggedly, turned back toward the house. Her shadow reached far ahead of her. Glancing at the low-lying sun, she thought vaguely that she should start supper.

CHAPTER
∽ 26 ∽

THE FORMED BISCUITS laid carefully in a pan looked perfect to Serena as she popped them into a Dutch oven built inside the fireplace. Nell had taken pity on her—or on second thought was it her brother's stomach the good woman pitied? Serena grinned, for thanks to Nell's instructions she was becoming a fair cook. The mouth-watering aroma of a beef roast cooking slowly over a bed of red coals lent credit to that.

Nell and Paw, she thought lovingly. How happy the pair were together. Paw lived in a new world these days.

It hadn't been that way for him at first, Serena remembered, washing the dough off her hands. Lines of worry had been heavy on his face that morning when he had ridden to the ranch, determined to see for himself that she was all right. She had known right away that another worry was also pricking at him. The trip was over at last, and here he was, his entire wealth consisting of two thoroughbred horses and an old hound. And along the way he had taken on the responsibility of a woman and her four children.

Nell's confidence in him was lying heavy on his shoulders the next day when he returned to the ranch just to visit, he'd claimed. A smile hovered around her lips. She and Dorn had known that he was a man close to the end of his rope and didn't know what to do about it. There would be no place for him to find employment; no one could afford to hire him.

She had never loved her brother more than when he began delicately to lift up Paw's sore and ragged ego.

Refilling the visibly worried man's cup with steaming coffee Dorn remarked casually, "I guess you're concerned about getting your place built and getting in out of the weather."

"I surely am." The sigh that followed was heavy. "That's all I think about. That and makin' a livin', of course."

"Well, getting your place up is simple." Dorn pushed the sugar bowl toward him. "Get the men together, go stake out your claim, then with everyone working together, you start building your cabins. Before you know it, all of you have a roof over your heads."

Eli nodded. "That's right good thinkin', Bain, but what about food to put under that roof, not to mention clothin' for young-uns, shoes and coats for when the snow falls, all those things a growin' family needs?"

"That should be no problem for you." Dorn waved a dismissive hand. He paused to spoon sugar into his own coffee before adding encouragingly, "You're one of the lucky ones."

Serena and Eli stared at the rancher blankly, trying to understand his reasoning. Finally Eli said, "I don't get your meanin'."

"Yes, Dorn, what are you talking about?" Serena added.

Dorn grinned. "I'm talking about those two thoroughbreds of yours, Landrie. They're the finest pieces of horseflesh I've seen recently, maybe ever. You could build a fine herd with that pair."

While Serena suppressed a giggle, Eli looked at Dorn as if he wasn't overly bright. "It might have escaped your notice, Bain,"—he gave a short laugh—"but both them animals are stallions. I don't expect I'd get many colts from their matin'."

"I noticed," Dorn answered with dry amusement, "but have you noticed the hundreds of thousands of wild horses running around here? My foreman told me that there's some high-bred mares among them, ones that have wandered up here from Mexico. They're tough and durable, and mated with those beauties of yours, you'd soon have a horse ranch of exceptional mounts. And there's always a market for fancy riding stock."

As Dorn talked the doubt began to fade from the Southerner's eyes and by the time he had finished, hope and a new faith in himself were sparkling on Eli's face.

"Bain, you just may be right." He rose to his feet, his hand outstretched. "I'm sure gonna give it a whirl. Them two fellers have been raring to get at some mares, anyway."

"You'll find that I'm right." Dorn's calm assurance put a spring in Eli's step as he followed him to the door, adding that when he was ready Eli should let him know, and he'd lend him the help of his cowhands to round up some of the wild horses.

The next day the valley had begun to ring with the slap of steel on wood. Tall, slender trees were chopped down and trimmed, then with jubilant curses and cajoling, teams of mules and oxen dragged them down to the foothills. There several men waited, those who knew how to skillfully use an adz. These men would measure the trunks into equal lengths, chop them through, then notch each end.

Landrie's cabin had been the first to go up. No one knew or questioned why this should be. It might have been because it was he who had led them down the final mountain, but Serena felt that it was the man himself. He was generous and warm-hearted, never guilty of subterfuge, yet he could be hard when necessary and would take no nonsense from anyone. When men or women spoke of Eli Landrie there was always respect in their voices.

At any rate, within a week Paw had moved Nell and her children into a four-room cabin, plus a large loft where the boys would sleep. One by one, then, the other cabins went up. When the last one was finished, Paw and the widow were wed.

Serena smiled, remembering the Landrie-Simpson wedding. It had been the first social event, with everyone invited. Brother Dorn had been a big hit with the young women, with his whip-lean body, brooding eyes, and the silver at his temples adding dignity to his handsome good looks. He had disappeared around midnight, not showing up at the ranch until late the next morning.

She had been surprised at how pleased she had been to see all the women again. When she had voiced this to Dorn, he said, "That shouldn't surprise you. The lot of you practically lived together for nine months, and if you think on it, your lives will continue to be interwoven one way or the other for the rest of your lives."

And that is true, Serena thought now as she set the supper table. Their individual lives did spill into each other's. Everyone rejoiced at a new birth, shared their grief at a death, helped each other through sickness.

The same had been true in Paw's case when he started rounding up the wild horses. Most of the men, especially the young unmarried ones, had pitched in and worked hard at helping him. The wild dashing up and down hills on horses meant for plowing had appealed to the bachelors, and they decided that ranching would be their forte. Dorn had so many applying for work, he took to hiding every time a rider approached the ranch house.

But the hard work Paw and his new family had put into their ranch would soon pay off. Serena's eyes shone softly, proudly. From the hundred or so head gathered Paw had cut out some fine-looking fillies and they were now penned off by themselves, waiting to come into heat. Meanwhile the two sleek stallions, which were also kept by themselves, whistled impatiently.

Sadness darkened Serena's eyes. It would appear that only she was not to find fulfillment in the valley. For regardless of Jessie's coaxing, and sometimes downright bullying, the only man she would ever marry was two thousand miles away.

The clock in the next room struck six, and, yawning, she walked out onto the porch to watch for Dorn. As she stood there, another yawn was stilled midway. This is silly, she thought. I can't possibly be sleepy yet.

For the past two weeks she had been in bed by nine o'clock, and still found it difficult to pull herself out of bed by six o'clock the next morning. Maybe I've got sleeping sickness, she thought humorously, lowering herself to the top step and leaning back on the porch post.

Soon it will be "still time," she mused as the soft wind died down and the sun began to pass behind the timberline. The birds will roost and the small animals will hide in the night, leaving a silence behind them. And a lonely time for me, she sighed, for Josh will slide into my mind and refuse to leave.

Before she could get too deeply into depression, the thud of hooves interrupted her gloomy thoughts. Dorn was riding in and he would be upset if he imagined she was brooding over Josh.

Serena was smiling brightly as she watched her brother swing to the ground and motion a cowhand to come take the mount. His plain leather chaps showed marks of hard usage as he walked toward her, and the bright kerchief knotted loosely around his strong throat was limp with dust. Slapping the rest of the accumulated dust from his clothes he stepped up on the porch and, ruffling her hair, announced, "I'm dead beat and so hungry I could eat one of Eli's horses."

"What about one of your own steers?" Serena joked back and led the way to the kitchen.

Although breakfast was a hurried affair, the brother and sister enjoyed a leisurely supper. This period of easy conversation helped Serena somewhat to bear the lonely evening after Dorn had gone off on some pursuit of his own.

"My chickens are going to need warmer and sturdier quarters before winter sets in." Serena introduced the first topic for discussion when she thought the edge of Dorn's hunger had been dulled a bit. "That mesh wire won't keep the wolves and coyotes out when the snow comes and they can't readily find other game to eat."

With a fork of meat raised halfway to his mouth, Dorn teased, "You're more concerned over those hens and old rooster than you are for me. I don't hear you fretting about a hungry wolf getting me by the throat."

"Well." Serena's eyes twinkled. "My little pets are more valuable. They cost you ten healthy steers."

"I'll have a couple of the men build you a sturdy shed and put a blockade fence around it." Dorn poured himself a cup of coffee. "The old biddies' eggs go real good with the bacon in the mornings."

"Always thinking of your stomach, aren't you, brother dear." Serena gave his hair a tug as she passed behind him to pick up the pie cooling on the windowsill.

"Among other things," Dorn drawled. "I do occasionally . . ." He paused when from the kitchen door a soft southern voice spoke.

"I'd have a cup of coffee if was to be offered me."

Pleasure glowed on Serena's face. "Paw, come in." She peered over his shoulder. "Isn't Nell with you?"

"Not this time, honey. I left her and the younguns back in

the village. She and the girls were pawing over some yard goods the last time I seen them.''

Dorn nudged a chair away from the table with his foot. ''Have a seat, Eli.''

Eli sat down, removed his hat and placed it on the floor, then smiled at Serena as she set a cup of coffee before him. ''How about a piece of rhubarb pie?'' She returned his smile. ''It's still warm.''

''Well, I don't know.'' Eli feigned doubt. ''Has your baking improved any since the days on the trail?''

Serena slapped him lightly on the head as she took the chair beside him. ''You're going to have to taste it to find out.''

The three coffee cups were replenished twice, darkness descended in the room and Serena lit a lamp, and still the three talked on. They discussed cattle and horses, new happenings in the village.

Then Eli switched the subject. ''I'm pretty sure I saw Foster Jovan in the village a few days ago. Him and that Indian boy, Sato. I was wonderin' if he'd been out here to the ranch to see you.''

Serena shook her head. 'I haven't seen him since he left the train to go to his ranch.'' She paused a moment then, slightly put out, added, ''Do you know he didn't even tell me good-bye before leaving.''

''I suppose that broke your heart.'' Eli widened innocent eyes at her.

''Oh, yes,'' Serena agreed just as innocently. ''I'm not over it yet.''

''I'll tell him if I see him.'' Eli pushed his chair back, ready to leave.

Dorn would be leaving too, Serena knew, and suddenly the thought of another evening sitting home alone was unendurable to her.

''Paw.'' She laid a hand on his arm. ''If you'll wait a minute I'll ride in with you to see Nell and the youngsters, then go visit Jessie.''

''Glad to have your company, honey,'' Eli said, and she quickly cleared the table, stacking the dishes on the dry sink to be washed when she returned.

In her bedroom, Serena surveyed the dresses hanging on pegs and wrinkled her nose. The long, full skirts clung to her knees and ankles, hindering the free stride she had enjoyed in the buckskins. But she had known when her brother remarked that she could buy yard goods at a small trading post not far away that he didn't approve of her new apparel. So, taking his hint, she had bought several dress lengths of bright colors, and with Nell's help she now had some very pretty dresses.

However, she grinned, taking down her buckskins, regardless of Dorn's frowning displeasure, whenever she had cause to ride Beauty, the soft leather went on. Never again would she endure the discomfort and danger of riding sidesaddle.

She whipped the dress over her head then, sitting down on the edge of the bed, slid her long legs into the buckskins. She smiled in pleasure at their softness and stood up to lace them.

"What the devil?" she muttered as the two edges refused to meet over her stomach. "Have you shrunk?" She pulled at the thin leather laces, determined that they would pull the material together.

Finally one of the laces broke from her tugging, and she plopped back down on the bed, snorting impatiently. Have I gained weight? That's impossible; the way I work around here it's more likely I'd lose pounds. So what was the explanation? she pondered, smoothing her hands down over her breasts, frowning at the soreness in them.

Her palms followed the curve of her waist, then smoothed over the stomach. "I have developed a little paunch," she murmured, looking down at the slight protrusion and frowning again. Then suddenly her eyes widened. "My God!" she gasped, "I look just like the black women looked when they were 'bigged.' "

She stared at the floor for a long time, then a long sigh of despairing resignation fluttered through her lips. She was four months pregnant.

Serena had paid no attention when her menses hadn't arrived every month; she had always been irregular. But now she asked herself why she hadn't noticed the changes taking place in her body. She started when a sharp rap shook the door and Dorn called impatiently.

"Don't laze so in there. We'd like to get started before everyone in the village goes to bed. Get a hustle on, all right?"

Serena clapped a hand over her mouth, smothering a hysterical giggle. She was in no shape to go anywhere . . . unless it was to go hide herself.

Her movements trancelike, she moved across the floor to the door and called that she wouldn't be going to the village after all. "I've developed a splitting headache."

She only half heard her brother's disgusted snort, and Landrie's advice that she made sure she took something for it, as she stumbled back to the bed. Her burning, choking sobs didn't escape until the two men left the house.

"Oh, how I hate him for doing this to me." Her hands clenched into fists and the hot tears spilled down her cheeks. "How dare he be so careless, then ride off and leave me to face the consequences alone."

By the time, however, she had cried herself out, Serena admitted honestly that she couldn't put all the blame on Josh.

And that concession only made her lie in the darkness, remembering Josh's tender, almost savage love touch, every nerve in her body crying out for him even as she despised herself for loving such a man so much.

CHAPTER
∽27∽

As Josh Quade squatted before the small fire nothing was distinguishable beyond its light. However, by the time he emptied the canteen of water into a battered army pot and added coffee grounds from a leather pouch he carried with other items in a haversack, the stars had faded and a gleam of light showed on the eastern horizon.

The ex-wagon master had made camp the evening before after losing the trail of two wolves he had tracked all day. He glanced at the rumpled blanket laying in a heap close to the fire and stood up, stretching his entire body, his muscles stiff and sore from sleeping on the ground. He grimaced wryly, thinking that he was getting too old for that sort of thing. If he wasn't careful he'd end up like so many other trappers, full of rheumatism.

"I should have my head examined for letting Bain talk me into runnin' the varmints down in the first place," he grumbled. "Wolves are the most intelligent animals in the world, and it could be days before I spot them."

Josh directed a scornful grunt at himself. He knew why he had done it. When the rancher paid him a visit last week and complained that timber wolves were after his cattle, had killed and maimed several head, asking if Josh would go after them, he had looked into the eyes so like Serena's and agreed on the spot.

The aroma of brewed coffee mingling with the odor of burning wood and fresh morning air kept Josh lingering on thoughts of Serena. Disturbingly, she still remained in his mind all the time. Too many times he had almost given in to an ungovernable urge to see her. It had taken all his willpower not to ride down to the valley where the Bain ranch was located and snatch her away.

Thankfully common sense had always prevailed.

Josh sniffed deeply as he dug out a tin cup and filled it from the steaming pot. Squatting on the ball of one foot he sipped carefully, curling his lips away from the heat of the brown liquid. He sighed, almost contentedly. There was very little as satisfying as that first cup of coffee in the morning.

Josh finished his second cup of coffee as the rising sun reddened the crest of the hills. He stood up, adjusted the knife at his waist, then poured the remains of the coffee and grounds over the fire. He quickly and efficiently rolled up the army issue blanket and, along with the coffee pot and canteen, shoved it all into the bag. Pulling his collar up against the morning chill he picked up the rifle and struck out. He would pick up his gear on the way home, for whether he found the wolves today or not, he was finished looking for them. Bain could hunt the wily creatures down himself.

Luck was finally with Josh. Within five minutes he saw the doglike tracks leading upward, clearly visible in the dew-wet grass. As he began to follow their path, luck was with him again, for a light breeze had picked up, blowing against him, carrying his scent away from his prey.

The climb was longer and harder than he had thought at first, for the higher he climbed, the rougher the country. And once he narrowly avoided stepping on a coiled rattlesnake.

Finally he reached the top of the small mountain. He paused to catch his breath, wondering where the tracks would lead him next. And as he scanned the area, hoping to spot the animals, he saw the cave, barely visible in the jumble of rock and brush.

Excitement stirred his blood. He knew beyond a doubt that his hunt was about over. Caves were a favorite den for wolves.

He was checking the priming of his rifle when he heard the whimpering puppy sound. Damn! he thought. A bitch must have whelped recently.

Now what? Josh wondered, staring at the black hole from

which a strong fetid odor wafted. Though most men wouldn't hesitate to kill the mother and let the cubs die of starvation, he did not like to think of any animal having to die so painful a death. Nor could he see himself killing the helpless babies.

"But hell," he muttered hopefully, "the mother will probably stick close to her litter and not even show herself."

Slowly and cautiously Josh approached, thinking for the first time that he didn't actually know how many of the animals he'd have to face. There could be half a dozen, even a dozen inside the lair. The varmints hunted in packs.

When he was about three yards from the shelter he paused to check that the knife was handy to his reach and that the rifle was fully charged. Then, taking a deep breath, he picked up a good-sized stone and tossed it into the narrow opening.

Deep, threatening growls followed on the heels of a startled yip. Josh gripped the rifle with both hands as there came the rattling sound of disturbed stones, then the appearance of a gray shaggy shape moving stiffly into the pale morning light. Above the lips drawn back in a grinning snarl red eyes stared hotly at him.

Cold sweat bathing his body, Josh drew on his nerve and waited until the lean body settled into a low crouch. With an almost reluctant sigh, he swung the rifle to his shoulder.

The long barrel spat flames and the big male went slack in the middle of its gathering bunch to leap. There was no time for Josh to reload as a second wolf, old and grizzled, bounded from the cave and sprang directly for his throat.

With one smooth movement he dropped the useless weapon and whipped out the knife.

The weight of the hurtling body brought Josh to the ground, but the upraised knife had forced its way into the racing, battling heart.

For a long moment the fierce, burning eyes glared down at Josh almost as though they were human. Then, with a ragged sigh, the long body went limp, hung a moment, and crumpled on top of him.

Wasting no time, Josh jerked the blade from the old warrior's chest and pushed him aside. Scrambling to his feet and snatching up the rifle, he heard only warning growls from one throat. The bitch, he thought, rushing headlong down the hill—the most vicious fighter of all when it came to protecting her young. He didn't want to be around if she came out to challenge him.

Josh didn't stop until he came to the dead embers of his fire. Leaning against a tree, his broad chest moving with the rapid pump of his heart, his gaze swept the hillside. There was no sign of the mother.

"I'll not run down and kill another," he vowed, picking up his gear and heading homeward. Wolves were his favorite of all wild animals; they were brave, they killed clean. It had gone against his grain to coldly kill the strong-hearted fighters.

The cabin nestled into a frame of forest brought pride of ownership glinting in Josh's eyes as it came into view. The past four months had brought many changes to the log structure.

To keep himself busy, stave off thoughts of Serena, he had added to it.

The woodsmen of Michigan had taught him the use of the broadax and adz, and as the summer passed he added two flat-roofed rooms, one on either side of the original one.

It hit Josh now as he stood gazing at the cabin that subconsciously he had enlarged his home with Serena in mind. The wooden floors he had painstakingly laid had been done so that tender feet could walk about without risk of splinters, the windows fitted snugly to ward off drafts on delicate skin.

The oath that ripped from his throat was tormented and directed at himself. Was he to dream his impossible dream for the rest of his life? His broad shoulders hunched as he stepped up on the small porch.

Inside the cabin he found Red Feather bent over a pot, slowly drawing a long-handled spoon through whatever bubbled inside it.

The Indian had responded to the teas and broths that had been spooned into his mouth and had beaten the dreaded pox. He now stepped lightly around, much of his health regained. But he was still old, old all over, from his lean and dried body in its breech cloth to his deeply wrinkled face and stringy white hair that hung to his shoulders.

A warm bond had grown between them, and as Josh dropped

his gear and hung up his rifle, he drawled teasingly, "Have you got somebody's dog cookin' in there?"

"No." Red Feather didn't look up. "It's the squirrel the dog was chasing."

"Well, whatever it is, I'm starved." Josh threw himself into a chair. "I haven't eaten since dawn this morning."

"It is good to be hungry sometimes, to thirst, to fight the elements. How else does a man become strong?"

The tender stew was quickly consumed and the two moved to sit in front of the fire. The elder puffed on a long-stemmed clay pipe and the other stared into the fire, his expression one of mute misery as he conjured up a lovely face in the flames.

The cry of a distant wolf broke the silence between the pair. Red Feather took the pipe from his mouth and looked closely at Josh.

"Have you ever been married, Quade? Have any children? You are of the age."

The dark shadows hid the pain that filmed Josh's eyes, but the old Indian discerned the flinch of the broad shoulders. He held his silence until Josh answered quietly, "No, I've never been married; have no children."

It was silent for several more minutes before Red Feather spoke again. "You are a young man, Quade. Not healthy for you not to have a woman.

"I know of a white squaw who could draw away your unrest at night, ease away the tiredness from you in the winter after you have run your traps all day. This a man needs."

"Thank you friend." Josh grimaced. "But I have no desire to sleep with a whore."

"Oh, but this one is no whore. She is young and good to look at." He paused to add frowningly, "She has one flaw. She has a very sharp tongue."

Josh eyed his friend suspiciously. "How do you happen to know a white woman? Is she a captive of your people?"

A hint of anger darkened the black eyes. "If this woman I speak of lived with my tribe she would belong to one of the chiefs, and he would kill you if you tried to take her away from him, such is her beauty and spirit."

"All right." Josh held up a silencing hand. "I spoke too hastily. Where does this woman with the sharp tongue live?"

The old man's pride was still ruffled, and several seconds ticked by before he said stiffly, "She lives about a half day's ride from here, with her brother."

Josh sat up with a jerk, all amusement gone from his face. The old Indian could only be talking about one girl. "How in the world do you happen to know Serena Bain?" The question snapped from his mouth.

An almost gloating look slid over the bronze face. He had managed to stop his friend's sporting with him.

"The first time I saw the woman with the golden hair she was about to plant some vegetable seeds. I explained to her that it was too early. I could see in her flashing eyes that she resented my advice as she questioned me why."

The thin lips twitched slightly at the corners, and there was a little boasting in his tone as he continued. "When I explained that we would have more killing frosts, she nodded and put away her hoe. 'I will wait,' she said and went into the house."

"Have you seen her since?"

"Yes." This time there was a full smile. "Several times I have watched her from a distance. Like I said before, she is good to look at. As she moves about outside, tending her garden, feeding her chickens, milking the cow, she sways like the graceful willow when a gentle wind stirs it."

Josh closed his eyes against the remembrance of how Serena Bain moved.

His head thrown back against the chair, he asked, "Are there ever men about this woman you take such interest in?"

Mischief flickered in Red Feather's eyes. "She is seldom alone. Men ride in from the village, and the cowhands find excuses all the time to be near her." He knocked out his pipe on the wide hearth. "That is why you shouldn't let too many moons rise before you also make a trip to the Bain ranch."

Josh sent the old man a bitter look. "I won't be goin', friend. The young lady is not for a rough character like me. One day a man of her own kind will come along and she will marry him."

Red Feather gave a scornful grunt. "She could marry no finer man than you, Quade. You are a fool not to try for her hand."

Josh's only response for the moment was a short, mirthless laugh. The old man didn't know about the brother and the plans he had for his sister.

Red Feather stood up and reached for the blanket he folded each morning and placed at the corner of the hearth. Spreading it on the floor, he grunted, "Good-night, Quade."

Josh was a long time falling asleep. Serena's face swam before him, hauntingly beautiful. Of those many men who came to court her, had any of them caught her interest, touched her heart?

CHAPTER
∽ 28 ∽

SERENA TOSSED a handful of beans into the basket at her knees, then rose tiredly to her feet, thinking, that's the last of these for the year. She bent over and dusted off the lower part of her dress where it had dragged as she crawled along the rows laid out in the garden. She would miss the fresh vegetables it had provided all summer. She straightened up.

However, the long ropes of beans she had strung on thread and hung in the loft to dry wouldn't taste half bad this winter. Soaked in salt water overnight they would regain most of the lost moisture and become almost plump. And the kernels of corn dried slowly in the sun would respond equally well to a good soaking, swelling to their normal size. As I will swell to great size when winter sets in, she thought ruefully, leaning on the hoe and drawing an arm across her perspiring brow. God, she was tired, mentally and physically. She had forced herself to work full steam today, hoping to keep her mind from wandering to the calamity that had befallen her. And she had lain awake for hours last night, her mind too active, her nerves too stretched to sleep. Repeatedly she had asked herself, What in the world am I going to do?

And always she came up with the same answer. There was nothing she could do but have the baby, a poor innocent little bastard. Its father was over two thousand miles away, but even if he lived next door she would never go to him and say, "I'm expecting your baby, you must marry me."

Oh, he would marry her, she knew, for Josh Quade was an honorable man. He would want a child of his to carry his name legitimately.

Serena shook her head to break her train of thought. What nonsense, wasting time speculating on events and words that would never come to pass. She would never see Josh again, so she would never know how he'd react to approaching fatherhood.

No, she sighed, her second biggest problem, and one she should give a lot of thought to, would be her brother's reaction to her plight. What would he think, or say? He was so strong himself, would he understand ordinary human weakness? Like being held helpless against the warmth of Josh's sweet lips, his seeking hands on her body.

She didn't know. Perhaps it was well that Josh was no longer around.

And Paw, he would be so disappointed in her . . . and in Josh. He thought so highly of the Northerner.

Then there were the people in the village. Would they whisper and snicker when she could no longer conceal the swelling of her stomach?

Enough of this. Serena firmed her lips and gauged the sun's position over the tree line. Soon it would be time to return to the house and mix up the corn bread, and she had the chickens and cows to tend to yet.

The sun was losing most of its heat as it broke through the shiny window, bathing Serena in a soft golden glow as she bustled around the kitchen. It turned the color of her hair red as she popped a pan of corn bread into the clay oven, then added carrots and potatoes to the pot of meat simmering over the fire.

She stood a moment in thought, then with a remembering snap of her fingers, walked out the kitchen door and moved the short distance to where Dorn had stretched two clotheslines between towering pine trees.

She sniffed deeply of the fresh-smelling laundry as she removed dry articles and folded them into a large reed-woven basket. A short time later, balancing the wicker on a hip, she returned to the kitchen and placed it in a corner out of the way. Tomorrow she would heat the irons in the fireplace and spend half the day pressing the clothing that had taken all morning to scrub clean.

Spicy, pungent steam rattled the heavy lid of the cooking pot as it sought to escape, and Serena hurried toward it, a long-handled spoon in her hand. Swinging the smoke-blackened crane away from the fire she uncovered the pot. It was done cooking and she lifted the crane away from the fire and walked through the front room and out onto the porch. Dorn should be coming in soon. He and most of his men had been gone for three days and nights, combing the brakes for cattle.

She leaned against a roof support, shading her eyes, looking in the westward direction Dorn and the others should arrive from. Had everything gone all right? she suddenly worried. Wild cattle were so dangerous, more so than the fiercest buffalo.

Finally Serena's searching gaze was rewarded and she heaved a great sigh of relief. Away in the distance she could discern a faint trace of dust drifting into the air. She gave a glad cry and stepped into the yard when she made out the chuck wagon leading the way in.

Gradually, through the rolling dust, Serena began to make out the figures of horses and riders moving alongside the sea of horns. When a tall, lean figure waved his hat at her and pulled away from the herd, Serena flew across the yard, her skirts flying as she raced toward the weary horse and rider.

The tired lines in the handsome man's face lessened as he caught his sister in a bear hug. "Have you been all right, *cascososi*?" He put Serena away from him, searching her face, frowning at the purple shadows beneath her heavy-fringed eyes.

"Of course I have." Serena smiled up at him. "And stop calling me *child*. I missed you, though," she added, as with arms around each other's waist they moved toward the house, the drooping mount clomping along behind them. "It was lonesome in the evenings."

"When I leave for the cattle drive next week you're going to sleep at Jessie's," Dorn said firmly. "I won't have you staying alone for that length of time."

Serena couldn't suppress a giggle. "Can you imagine the expression on Mammy's face if she knew her missy was going to sleep in a house of prostitution for several weeks?''

''Shhh.'' Dorn chuckled. ''She may be getting vibrations this very minute and put a spell on me, make me break a leg so I'll have to stay here with you.''

And what would Mammy think if she knew I was expecting a baby without benefit of a husband, Serena thought, the laughter going out of her eyes.

''Hurry and get supper on the table,'' Dorn called over his shoulder as he walked to the porch to wash away the grime and dust of the day.

Soon it will be too cold to use the basin on the outdoor bench, Serena mused as she brought the stew and corn bread to the table. For already the nights and early mornings were quite chilly.

When Dorn sat down at the table he was too hungry to do more than just bring the food to his mouth, dispatching two plates of pot roast in quick order. Finally Dorn's appetite was sated, and with a repleted sigh he sat back with a cup of coffee. Would he be going into the village, Serena wondered, or was he too tired? She needed to see Jessie to seek her counsel. No, not her counsel, for how could her little friend give her any advice after the deed had been done? It was the comfort Jessie would give that she sought.

Dorn answered her silent question by standing up and announcing, ''I'm going to get some clean clothes and take a dip in the river.'' His white teeth flashed devilishly. ''After I shave I'll see what I can scare up in the female department.''

''I'm going with you.'' Serena stood up also. ''I need Jessie's witty chatter for a change. I'm tired of ranch talk all the time.''

''Well, hurry it up,'' Dorn grumbled. ''I guess that means I'll have to hitch up the buggy. I'll not have you wearing those buckskins you're so fond of wearing when you ride in the saddle.''

Serena stared after his disappearing back, thinking wryly, If only you knew, big brother, that the buckskins no longer fit me.

By the time Dorn had bathed, dressed, and hitched the bay to the buggy, Serena stood on the porch, waiting. The kitchen was in order, a fresh blue gown pulled on, and her hair brushed until it shone like pure gold in the moonlight. Dorn swung her inside the light carriage, grunting that she had gained weight. Serena let the remark pass unanswered.

The night was frosty, cold and clear as the wheels whirred along, sending up dust in their wake. Off in the distance, in the luminous light, night riders walked a slow circle around a bedded herd. When up in the mountains a lone wolf sounded his plaintive yowl at the full moon, Dorn muttered, "Stay up there, you bastard, and leave my cattle alone."

There came poignant memories to Serena, of burning leaves and autumn before the war turned her world upside down.

She wondered if the war was over. Newspapers never reached the frontier, but every man passing through had something to tell. Still, there had been no mention of an agreement between the states.

A score or more lights flickering through the trees several yards ahead drew Serena back. On the ragged edge of the wilderness the settlers had carved out their piece of civilization. The village had started out small: a blacksmith, a store, and Jessie's Pleasure Palace. Then, within the month, another train of emigrants had rolled into the valley, and a tavern had gone up, and a Dr. Saunders had hung up his shingle. By the time summer was in full swing the little settlement bore no resemblance to its humble beginning.

There were business properties now, a bank, a saloon, a combination dress and millinery shop run by two old maid sisters. Finally, a restaurant and hotel had gone up.

Serena lifted her gaze to the hills where the private homes were situated, neat and cheerful-looking with soft lights shining through clean windows. In the daytime one could see the gay curtains at the windows and bright flowers growing in the yards. Also in this area were the church and schoolhouse.

Jessie's establishment was set some distance from the homes and places of business. Most of her customers were raw frontiersmen, rough and sometimes mean-tempered when they had been drinking. Fights broke out regularly, and the little madam wanted to save the growing town the annoyance of rowdy noise and vulgar language.

The pleasure house's only companion building was the sawmill. Every day there was a steady hum from its large blades slicing through the logs that were cut down in the mountains, then dragged to the mill by teams of mules and oxen. Off to one side were tall stacks of lumber, waiting for more emigrants to arrive and start building.

Dorn pulled the bay up in front of Jessie's two-story structure. It had an outside stairway leading to its upper floor, as well as the one rising up from inside. Jessie had confided to Serena that the outside one was used by the men who didn't want it known that they visited the second floor, which was subdivided into small bedrooms. She had added with an amused sneer, "Such men as husbands and so-called respectable businessmen."

Jessie's living quarters were located in the back of the first floor, and Serena was surprised to see it lit up so as Dorn helped her from the buggy. Usually only one light burned.

Dorn lifted a fist to knock on the door, then hurriedly stepped back as the door flew open, revealing a pale-faced, wild-eyed Jessie.

"Jessie! What is it?" Serena stepped forward.

"Serena, thank God." The little woman grabbed hold of her arm. "I was just about to send for you. Josh is here." Her fingers tightened on Serena. "He's badly wounded, honey."

CHAPTER
∞29∞

FOR THREE DAYS Josh and Red Feather had rode up and down the mountain, finding and marking likely places for Josh to lay his traps once the season arrived, not too far distant. Any morning now a man could rise and find frost on the ground, followed closely by a tight freeze.

"There is a place I want you to see." Red Feather rode up alongside Josh. "A place we've never been."

Josh nodded, and the old brave, riding with only a saddlecloth made of buffalo hide, took the lead, urging his shaggy pony up the incline of the foothills. His companion followed him readily, for these were the old man's haunts and he obviously knew every inch of them.

It was nearing sunset, the forest still and lonely, when the Indian drew in his pony. He pointed off through the trees. "There is a river a short distance away. There is no other stream in this region that has more beaver in it."

The stallion snorted, a tired and thirsty mount. Red Feather lifted the pony's reins, saying, "We go to the river now, water the horses."

It was cool beside the clear-running stream, and after all four had drunk their fill, Josh and the old man sat down on a rock, reluctant to leave the shady spot.

But neither man wanted to be caught in the mountains that

were overrun with wolves after dark, so after a short time they rose and swung onto their mounts' backs.

With Josh leading this time, the stallion wound his way around a large, low sweeping pine and was then reined in sharply.

A few yards ahead were two riders, a white man and a young Indian lad. Josh's body jerked in angry surprise as he recognized the beautiful white horse the man rode.

"Jovan!" He swore under his breath. "What's that bastard doin' in this neck of the woods?"

His heel jabbed the stallion into a lunging gallop, leaving the old Indian staring after him and the pair ahead swerving around in their saddles. Surprise, apprehension, and defiance chased each other across the rancher's face as Josh pulled up even with him, his hostility unmistakable.

"Well, Quade," he drawled silkily, "I see you're still here in Oregon country. I figured you'd be back in your northwoods by now. Are you still hankerin' for Serena Bain?"

"I was wonderin' the same thing about you." A feral smile twisted Josh's lips. "What other reason could you have for being so far from home? There are no cattle in this high country."

Jovan had difficulty meeting Josh's cold, level gaze. Staring off into the forest, he said stiffly, "If it's any of your business, I'm on my way to Jessie's Place. I've been a while without a white woman."

Josh gave a contemptuous snort, eyeing the man with withering scorn. "Don't try to match wits with me, Jovan." He slid the Indian a knowing look. "We both know you have no use for whores." He jerked a thumb over his shoulder. "Jovan, turn around and head back where you come from," he ordered. "You'll be a sorry man if you don't."

Jovan's hands clenched on the reins and his jaw corded. "Are you threatening me with blackmail?"

"That's a possibility, Jovan, but what I'm really sayin' is if you go around Serena Bain I'll put a bullet in your belly and blow you so far into hell the devil himself won't be able to find you."

His face working with futile rage, Jovan tried to stare Josh down. When he failed, he affected unconcern by shrugging his shoulders indifferently and turned his mount around. "If you feel that strongly about it, I can always go back to squaws until more white women come along.''

"I'm sure," Josh said sarcastically as the rancher set off at a brisk canter.

"You heard?" Josh asked as Red Feather quietly came to stand beside him.

"Yes. There is evil in that man. You have not seen the last of him, friend. Make sure you watch the trail behind you. Such a man is a back shooter.''

Josh made no response as he gazed in the direction in which both riders had now disappeared.

Red Feather waited until the rigid body eased and the lines around the firm mouth relaxed. Then: "What you do now?''

In the dead calm of the forest there was no sound or movement, but there was still a prickling of Josh's skin, as though eyes were upon him, a shadow awaiting. "We'll continue on home," he finally answered the old Indian, "but I want you to hang back, keep an eye peeled. I don't think Jovan will try anything, but he might. It will depend on how badly he wants the girl from the South. If he's really got his mind set on havin' her, who knows what he might try.''

Reins were lifted and the pair started off, Red Feather trailing several yards behind Josh, his eyes constantly roaming the surrounding forest. He nodded when Josh spotted wild turkey tracks in the dust and motioned that he would follow them.

Josh heard the nervous gabble before he came upon the large, long-necked birds in a burned-out clearing. Unfortunately the dozen or so saw him at the same time and took off, thudding over the ground. Their running start spread their wings and they launched into a whirring flight. Excitement stirring his blood, Josh rested the smooth stock of the gun against his shoulder, started to squeeze the trigger, then froze.

A bullet had struck the ground a foot in front of him, throwing a dusting of earth and pine needles into the stallion's face. The animal whinnied in alarm and Josh was hard put to wheel the animal and spur him into the shadow of a large boulder. Sliding to the ground, he shoved the gun into the saddle sheath and drew his knife. Josh doubted that Jovan would hang around, but if he did come looking, he would find his prey waiting.

At first Josh saw nothing that didn't belong among the trees as he peered carefully around the huge formation of granite. Then he glimpsed the nearly naked Sato skulking from tree to tree.

A grim frown gathered between his eyes. The Indian's intent was clear. He meant to circle his master's enemy, get behind him. "Well, bucko, I'll put a stop to that notion," Josh muttered.

Using the Indian's tactic Josh moved from tree to tree, determined to get behind the Indian. Suddenly there came the twang of a bowstring, and white lightning exploded in Josh's head. He felt his knees buckling, felt the ground seemingly rise up and hit him. Blood flowed down his forehead and into his eyes as he clung to consciousness with clenched teeth.

He lost the battle as the forest spun around him and the setting sun disappeared.

The sun was almost gone when Josh opened his eyes and gazed into the wrinkled, worried face of Red Feather. Through the painful throbbing in his head he heard the concern in the aged, cracked voice.

"You are hurt bad, friend. I use all my skill and knowledge on your wound. It is not enough. Is there someone I can take you to?"

"Take me . . . to Jessie's . . . place," Josh answered in a faltering croak. "Do you . . . know . . . where?"

"Me know," Red Feather grunted. "The whorehouse."

The stallion snorted uneasily, not liking the smell of blood. But he stood quietly when Josh spoke to him, allowing him to grab hold of the stirrup and slowly pull himself up. It took several agonizing moments and the old Indian's help to crawl onto the broad back.

Josh was only vaguely aware that Red Feather climbed up behind him to support his body as they began the long trek to the village and Jessie.

CHAPTER
~30~

SHIVERING VIOLENTLY from the dread that gripped her, Serena followed Jessie into the frilly, feminine bedroom, her fear growing as the usually unflappable woman explained almost incoherently that all her efforts to stop the flow of blood from the deep head wound had been ineffective.

"I have sent for the doctor," she said, and after that Serena heard nothing else Jessie said. Her undivided attention was on the man who had almost destroyed her.

She stared down at him a moment, then bent over him and gently stroked the fine weather lines radiating out from his thick-lashed lids, then down to tenderly trace the grooves, intensified by his pain, carved near the corners of his firm lips.

He looks so helpless, she thought, lying so quiet, his skin so pale compared to his usual sun-baked look. Her hand moved to the blood-soaked bandage wrapped around his head.

"Oh, Jessie," she whispered unsteadily, "tell me that he's going to live."

"Of course he is." Dorn spoke behind her, at the same time pushing a chair against the back of her knees and pressing her onto it. "Men like Josh Quade don't give up easily. You can bet he's fighting like hell right now."

"He's lost an awful lot of blood, Dorn," Jessie worried out loud and received a warning look from him. She hurriedly added,

"But the doctor will be here shortly and he'll do what's necessary to keep this hellion alive."

Serena knew this last comment was meant to reassure her, and she gave Jessie a wan smile just as the bedroom door opened.

All eyes jumped to the tall, angular man who stood there, his brown hair mussed, a small black bag in his hand. "Good evening, Bain, Jessie." He nodded although his eyes were admiringly on Serena.

"Dr. Saunders, I don't believe you've met my sister," Dorn said. "Serena, meet doctor Robert Saunders."

Serena acknowledged the introduction with a brief nod of her head, anxious for the man to get on with attending to Josh. She rose, relinquishing her chair to him.

When the doctor's skillful fingers began to unwind the bandage Jessie had wrapped around Josh's head, Serena could not watch and moved across the floor to the small fireplace. For the first time she became aware of the old Indian as she blindly, because of tear-blurred eyes, almost tripped over him.

"I beg your pardon," she murmured and sat down in a cushioned rocker a few feet away.

What is this old man to Josh? she wondered, secretly studying Red Feather as he remained squatting before the fire, one bony hand stretched out to the blaze. Her eyes dropped to his other hand, which tightly gripped what she recognized as a sacred medicine idol. Todd Simpson had found one up in the mountains shortly after arriving in the valley. He had excitedly informed her that its Indian name was *taime*.

Serena shivered at the fierce expression carved into the wood. The elderly Indian, thinking that she was cold, dropped a log onto the fire. As sparks shot up and smoke curled upwards to be lost in the chimney, she said, "Thank you."

When she received a nod, she asked, "Are you the one who brought Josh here? Are you his friend?"

"Yes, I bring Quade here. I am his friend."

Serena leaned forward in her chair. "Have you known him long?"

A nod, then a stoic, "I know Quade for several moons."

Serena sat back, a quizzical frown marring her smooth forehead. Does that mean several months? she wondered. And did Josh now live in some Indian camp, sleep with a young squaw?

The thought brought on such a surge of jealousy, Serena suddenly felt ill. Her hands gripped the chair arms until reason returned. She didn't know for a fact whether Josh now lived with Indians or slept with squaws, she was only afraid that he did. A few discreet questions was the reasonable course to take, not all this conjecturing.

She glanced at the expressionless, wrinkled face and phrased her question carefully. "Where has the trapper built his cabin? Is it far from here?"

Serena saw the flicker of amusement that touched the corners of the thin lips and realized she hadn't fooled the old man at all. She wasn't surprised when she received another baffling answer.

"Quade's cabin is only a few echoes away from your valley."

Drat the wily old devil, she thought, but had to grin at his cunning. He had, however, let the information drop that Josh had his own place . . . wherever that might be. A few echoes away, indeed.

"I haven't seen you around the ranch lately." She changed the subject. "I wondered what had happened to you."

"I been helping Quade."

"Oh?" Serena looked at him questioningly.

"Yes."

She blinked at the single-word answer. I'll say no more to the rude old man, she decided and stared into the fire, still afraid to see what was going on with the man in Jessie's fancy bed.

Several minutes passed before Serena became aware of the old Indian's brilliant, curious gaze upon her. She gasped at the directness of the question he suddenly shot at her. "I see that you are with child, does it belong to Quade?"

She continued to stare open-mouthed. How did this old brave know she was expecting when no one else had discovered it?

He's only guessing, she thought, casting a fast glance over her shoulder to see if those who were gathered around Josh's bed had heard the impertinent question.

No one appeared to be paying any attention to them; the doctor bent over Josh, Jessie and Dorn watching him intently.

"I don't know what gives you the idea that I'm with child,"

she hissed, low-toned, glaring at the Indian, running a palm over her nearly flat stomach.

"I do not see it there." Black eyes followed the action of her hand. "I read it in your eyes. There is a new softness in them."

Serena opened her mouth to deny his charge, then closed it. He knew. It would be futile to call him a liar. She lifted her eyes to the stony face and said quietly, "Yes, I am with child."

"Does Quade know?" A widening of his pupils was the only sign that the old brave was pleased by her admittance.

"Why do you insist that the father of my child is Josh Quade?" She turned a stormy gaze on him.

"There are two reasons. You are not a woman who carelessly give body to any man. You must have strong feelings for man you take to your blankets. The trapper Quade is that man. I see pain on your face when you look on him."

Serena didn't bother to answer. Any argument would be but empty words and both of them knew it. Besides, there was another matter to be discussed. One of great importance to her.

"Red Feather," she began slowly, "there are circumstances that make it impossible for me to tell Josh about the coming child. I have good, strong reasons not to, one being that he wouldn't be happy to hear it. So I'm begging you not to tell him."

A dark frown deepened the wrinkles between Red Feather's eyebrows, and Serena was sure he was going to refuse her request. But finally he nodded and grunted, "As you wish." He penned her with black, reproachful eyes. "You do Quade injustice. Every man has a right to know when he is a father. You did not come to your present state alone."

Evidently he did not expect Serena to respond, for he stretched himself out on the floor, and in seconds was snoring softly.

Why is it taking so long? Serena fretted a few minutes later as the harsh odor of astringent added to the water the doctor used invaded the room. She glanced up at the clock. Twenty minutes had passed since Saunders had started ministering to Josh. Hadn't he stopped the blood flow yet? The long, lean body couldn't afford to lose much more.

She jumped and gave a startled cry when a hand came down

on her shoulder. Her eyes flew to Dorn's face, a desperate searching in them.

"He's all right, honey," the hastily spoken words assured her. "He has to have some stitches taken in the wound, though, and you have to help me and Jessie hold him down."

"Oh, I couldn't, Dorn," Serena objected in a tortured whisper. "I couldn't stand to see the doctor—"

"Serena," Dorn cut across her faltering sentence, hunching down beside her chair. "I've never seen you go to pieces like this before. When I remember how coolly you used to take care of our blacks, tending cuts, bruises, boils—why the faint heart now?

"Unless"—Dorn took her chin and tilted her head to look into her eyes—"you still love him that much. Is that it, Serena?"

Serena could only nod as the tears rolled down her cheeks.

Dorn rose and, taking Serena by the arms, pulled her up to stand beside him. "That's all the more reason you should help us. If it hurts too much to watch, then don't. All you have to do is sit on one of his legs. You can keep your eyes closed."

Serena swallowed, nodded her head, and willed her feet to walk across the floor to the bed. Jessie gave her an encouraging smile, and after one long look at Josh's pale face, she climbed on the bed and settled her weight on a muscular calf, her hands settling on the long, firm thigh above it.

She ran a fast glance over the body that was usually so vibrant with health, then closed her eyes, unable to look any longer at the form lying as quietly as death.

But at the first sharp sting of the needle entering his flesh, Josh's body came alive. Groaning and muttering oaths, he struggled against Dorn's powerful grip on his shoulders and strained against the weight that stubbornly bore down on his legs. Then the doctor sighed with relief when the thrashing body went limp in a dead faint.

Saunders's work went quickly now, and the tall man was soon straightening up and replacing his shiny instruments in the black bag and rolling down the sleeves of his white shirt. As he shrugged into his coat, he said, "He's going to be all right. He has the strength and resilience of a tough whipping sapling."

He grinned ruefully. "However, he's going to have one hell of a headache for a while, and possibly run a high fever."

Speaking to no one in particular, he added, "I'm leaving some laudanum. When you feel it's necessary give him forty drops in a glass of water."

He picked up his bag, and Dorn and Jessie walked him to the door, leaving Serena alone with the unconscious man. "A very beautiful girl, your sister, Bain." Serena heard the doctor's statement floating back to her.

She sat down on the edge of the bed and tenderly stroked Josh's forehead. "As if I'd be interested in him, eh, darling?" she murmured. "Or any other man, for that matter."

She ran her palm down the side of Josh's neck and out over a smooth shoulder. *Maybe Red Feather is right.* Her eyes were thoughtful. *Perhaps I should tell him about the baby. I know he has a feeling for me, even though it's mainly for my body. We are wonderful together in bed. And maybe, given time, that fact could lead to that which I desire more than anything else. His declaration of love.*

Serena was still perched on the edge of the bed, holding Josh's hand, when Jessie returned, a gown and robe draped over one arm and a tray propped against a narrow hip.

"I've brought you some coffee," she said, depositing it, along with a pitcher of water, a glass, and a spoon, on the table beside the bed. Then from a pocket she brought out the bottle of laudanum and placed it on the tray.

"This gown and robe came from Kate," Jessie half whispered.

"Thank her for me, will you." Serena smiled crookedly as she took the two articles from Jessie and held them up for inspection. Both were bright red, and very sheer.

Jessie giggled. "If Josh doesn't have a fever when he comes to, he'll soon get one when he sees you in those." She took Serena's arm and urged her to her feet. "Change now, then have a cup of coffee. It's gonna be a long night for you." Her green eyes sparkled. "I'd offer to spell you, but I know it would be a waste of breath and words."

"You're right." Serena smiled, then asked, "Where has my brother got off to?"

"Oh, he, well, I, I . . ."

"That's all right, Jessie." Serena came to the aid of Jessie's stammering tongue. "I have a pretty good idea where he is. If you should happen to see him again tonight, tell him I'll see him tomorrow."

The little woman was gone then and Serena had Josh to herself. "Except for you, you old red devil." She glanced at Red Feather's sleeping form in front of the fireplace. Humor twitched her lips. "And a stick of dynamite wouldn't get you out of here, right?"

The slithering feel of the gown brushing her naked flesh reminded Serena of Josh's caressing hands as she crossed to the fireplace and added a log to the fire. How she longed to crawl in bed with him, to know his lovemaking again.

Her eyes dropped to the curled figure at her feet. Are his old bones warm enough? she wondered, then grinned as she plucked a colorful throw off the sofa. Jessie will probably have a fit, she thought in amusement as she carefully placed the knitted cover over the old Indian.

She walked back to the bed, sat down on the chair Jessie had pulled up for her, and began her lonely vigil.

The clock had just struck two when Josh began a toneless, rambling mumble. When he started to toss about restlessly, then attempted to lift his head, Serena rose and gently pressed him back to the pillow.

"You must lie quietly," she soothed, "otherwise you will start your wound to bleeding again."

She knew by the visible start Josh gave that he had recognized her voice even as he floated in the dark shadows of the netherworld. She watched his eyes slit open, watched him struggle to focus in on her. She gave a soft little cry and clasped his hand when he could not.

"It's all right, darling," she whispered, sitting down on the bed and gently stroking his flushed cheek. "You'll be able to see me tomorrow."

"Tomorrow?" The confused question feathered through his lips.

Serena's answer was interrupted by a groan of pain. When

Josh's slim fingers lifted to the white bandage around his head, she jumped to her feet and hurriedly filled a glass with water from the china pitcher Jessie had placed there.

Her fingers shook a bit as she measured forty drops of pain-relieving liquid. After whipping the spoon around the glass a few times, she sat back down beside the lean body. Leaning forward, she carefully raised his dark head.

"Drink this, Josh," she coaxed, "then the pain will go away."

Serena was unprepared when the glass was dashed from her hand and her wrists were caught in fingers of steel. Her startled gaze dropped to Josh's face, and she caught her breath at the raw desire flaring in the fever-clouded eyes. Before she could insist gently that he shouldn't exert himself, she was jerked so hard against his chest the breath was knocked out of her.

Oh, dear, her mind panicked, he doesn't know what he's doing. He's going to hurt himself.

She pressed gently but firmly on Josh's broad shoulders, at the same time cajoling softly, "Let me go, Josh, you're hurting me. You'll hurt yourself."

It was as if she hadn't spoken. For the man lying partially beneath her had slipped an arm across her back, bringing her yet closer to him. She knew a leaping of her heart as, just before his lips seared the valley between her breasts, Josh murmured brokenly, "Ah, Serena, you tear at my very soul."

Long moments passed as Serena lay passive, her smooth throat beginning to sting from the scratchiness of a full day's whiskers moving against it. But she knew it was imperative that she do nothing that would inflame the desire that was already making the big body writhe with need. So she lay quietly, her head nestled on Josh's shoulder. If this man ever wanted to punish me, he has done so this night, she thought.

It was a relief to Serena when Josh's pain finally overrode his desire. With a deep moan his head slid off her shoulder and he pushed impatiently at her weight leaning against him. She sat up, then rose to mix the prescribed dose of laudanum in water again. She stood a moment chewing thoughtfully on her lower lip, then moved across the floor to where Red Feather slept.

The old man came awake at the touch of her hand on his shoulder. His bright, birdlike eyes looked at her inquiringly. "I need your help to get Josh's medicine into him. He knocks it out of my hands. Do you think you could hold his arms?''

There was a faint creak of old joints as Red Feather rose slowly to his feet and preceded Serena to the bed. When she would have raised the ill man's head, the Indian shook his head and took the glass from her.

''Your touch will excite him,'' he muttered knowingly.

Serena blushed furiously, wondering if the old scamp had really been asleep, had instead watched what had gone on in the bed a few minutes ago. She watched in surprise as Josh meekly swallowed the mixture held to his mouth by a red, wrinkled hand.

The tincture worked swiftly, Josh's body relaxing as the pain diminished. It caused dreams, however, to float through his mind, and his voice revealed what they were about.

Serena figured in them, for her name was mumbled often, as was Silas Hansen's, Paw's, and Jessie's. Then he spoke Foster Jovan's name, in a tone heavy with anger and threat.

''That man Jovan put Quade here,'' Red Feather said stonily.

Serena gaped at Red Feather. ''Foster Jovan shot an arrow?'' she exclaimed. ''I can hardly believe that.''

''No, his hand does not do it. The young Indian with him use bow and arrow after Jovan missed Quade with rifle.''

''What was the rancher doing in these parts? He lives a long way from here.''

''Quade accused him coming to see you. Told him stay away from you.''

Serena was mulling over the Indian's astonishing statement when Josh asked, quite clearly, ''Serena, how could you keep the map from me?''

He's still reliving the journey. Serena's eyes held sympathy for the man who now rolled his head back and forth. Hurt had been with him that night, as well as anger when he found her poring over the map.

''Josh,'' she said gently, reaching for the fingers that plucked at the blanket covering his naked torso, ''I explained that to you, don't you remember?''

Shock drained the blood from her face when Josh jerked his hands free and cried out savagely, ''Stay out of my life, Serena

Bain! I don't need you, or want you." And while she stared at him mutely, he swung a hard arm across her chest, sweeping her from the bed, landing her heavily on the floor.

Red Feather was quickly beside Serena, helping her to stand. "He does not know what he says." The timbre of the old voice was softer than Serena had heard it yet. "It is fever talking."

Serena wiped the free-running tears from the corners of her mouth with a wrist, then shook her head with numb acceptance. "No, old man." Her voice was low and shaken. "It is the truth speaking. Josh does not need or want me. All the need and wanting is on my side. I came awfully close to making a fool of myself tonight. Thank God I was saved from that at least."

Sighing raggedly, she took her folded clothes off the chair where she had placed them a few hours ago. "Will you sit with him, Red Feather?" she asked as she changed clothes behind a folding screen. "I find that I am dreadfully tired and would like to go home and to bed."

The old brave nodded solemnly, then asked quietly, hopefully, it seemed, "You return tomorrow? Quade will be his old self then."

Her hand on the doorknob, Serena smiled wanly at the anxious-faced Indian and shook her head. "No, Red Feather, I'll not be coming back."

CHAPTER
∾31∾

IN THE OPAQUE LAND in which Josh drifted, he tossed and moaned, his hand going often to the wide bandage that was no longer tinted with red. Each time his hand was tenderly grasped and firmly put back beneath the blanket that was pulled up to his chin.

Although his fevered sleep was troubled, he was aware that, though the hand that sought to comfort him was soft and smooth, it was not the same touch that had successfully soothed him before.

The sun was just peeping over the mountain when, with Serena's name a breath on his lips, he struggled from the dead sleep that had taken over when his fever broke a few hours before. When his eyes slitted open, he gazed into Jessie's sparkling ones.

Licking his dry lips, he croaked, "Hi, Jess."

"Hi yourself, you rangy wolf." Jessie laid the back of a hand on his forehead. "You feel cool. How is your head?"

Josh smiled ruefully. "I think it's parted company with my body."

"I'm not surprised. Thanks to that little weasel, Sato, you have a deep gash in that hard head of yours." When Josh lifted a questioning eyebrow at her, she explained, "That arrogant old Indian friend of yours finally told me what happened. After about an hour of questioning," she tacked on.

"Yeah, he's like that," Josh said noncommittally.

323

Jessie's lips thinned into a stubborn line. "He said that bastard Jovan tried for you first."

Josh's only response to the heated statement was a flash of violence in his narrowing eyes. He would decide Foster Jovan's fate when his head stopped pounding.

Jessie had known the big man too long to press him further. Whatever he decided to do about the rancher he would do quietly, and in his own time. It was not Josh Quade's way to rant, rave, and loudly swear vengeance.

She dropped the subject and, smiling brightly, said, "I'll bet you're starvin'. The old Indian brought in a couple of squirrels and my cook has made some broth from them, at his orders, I might add. Would you like a cup of it?"

Josh grinned crookedly. "I'd like a quart of it."

"Good!" Jessie grinned and stood up. "Hunger is a sure sign that you're on the road to recovery."

Josh's question stopped her just as she was ready to step through the door, on her way to the kitchen. Propped painfully on an elbow, he asked, "Was Serena here last night, Jess?"

"What makes you ask that?" Jessie returned evasively after a moment.

He hunched a shoulder. "It seems like I remember her talkin' to me, touchin' me."

"Maybe you were dreamin'. You were delirious most of the night."

Josh lay back down with a soft sign of resignation. Serena had only been a figment of his fevered mind.

From her stance in the doorway Jessie saw the defeat that darkened his eyes, the hope that faded from them. I should tell him, she thought, then remembered another despair-filled face and hardened her heart. It won't hurt him to suffer a little longer. After he's eaten I'll tell him.

"That sure smells mouth-waterin', Jess." Josh sniffed at the steam rising from the bowl Jessie carried into the room.

"Yes, it does." Jessie looked down at him thoughtfully. "Now, how are we gonna get it inside you? Can you manage the spoon, or should I—"

"I don't need no woman spoon-feedin' me." Josh cut short

Jessie's question. "If you can just prop my head up a bit, I'll drink it from the bowl."

"You and your all-fired pride," Jessie snapped, plumping up the extra pillow and carefully inserting it under the dark head. "It's gonna be badly shattered one of these days, my friend. It's been comin' for a long time."

"You think so, huh?" Josh took the bowl from her. "What if I should tell you it's already been badly bruised a few times?"

"I hope it's true, but I somehow doubt it." Jessie sat down and watched him drink deeply and hungrily. "I just can't see you takin' that chance."

"So, those cat-eyes of yours miss somethin' once in a while." Josh raised an eyebrow at her.

Jessie shrugged. "Maybe . . . occasionally. No more talkin' now. Drink your broth."

Josh had just drained the bowl and handed it to Jessie when both of them were startled when the door was flung open.

"So, Josh, you *are* back!" A concerned Eli bore down on the bed, his southern drawl deeply pronounced in the expression of aroused emotions. "And wounded. How are you feelin', boy?"

Jessie suppressed a giggle as the two men shook hands. A thirty-six-year-old man a boy?

"Besides hurtin' like hell," Josh answered, "I feel pretty dumb, lettin' a scrawny teenage Indian almost do me in."

Eli's eyes turned frosty. "I understand he had some help from a certain rancher."

Josh turned a questioning gaze on the older man. "You sound pretty well informed, Eli. Who gave you all this information? Red Feather?"

"I don't know any Red Feather. Serena told me."

Josh's lean body stiffened beneath the blanket, and his increased breathing was discernible under the cover. His accusing gaze swept to Jessie's bent head. "You've got a streak of meanness in you, Jess, do you know that?"

The small woman lifted eyes that sparkled with mischief and apology at the same time. "I was gonna tell you that she was here last night, Josh. I just wanted you to eat first."

"Yeah, I bet," Josh grunted, then waited for her to explain, to say some balming word that he could cling to in the winter months ahead.

When the silence dragged on he asked hoarsely, "Did she sit with me last night?"

Jessie threw up her hands in resignation. "Yes, she did. The better part of it, accordin' to that old Indian. She was gone when I got up to relieve her."

Josh's eyes searched the green ones as he asked quietly, "Is she comin' back, Jess?"

"I honestly don't know, Josh," Jessie answered softly. "Like I said, I was asleep when she left. Red Feather might know. I don't know where he is now. He laid the squirrels on the table this mornin', then stalked out."

"He's gone to check on the place," Josh said half to himself, then turned his questioning gaze on Eli. "Did she happen to mention to you whether or not she's comin' back?"

Eli looked down at the drawn face and shook his head. Then, reproach in his voice, he said gruffly, "She'd been cryin'. Did you give her the sharp edge of your tongue as usual?"

"Of course I didn't." Josh half sat up, then fell back with a groan, his hand going to his head. "I wasn't even sure she'd been here. I thought maybe I'd dreamed it."

Concerned when a gray cast of pain washed over her patient's face, Jessie filled a glass with water and measured in the laudanum. "Drink this, Josh. You've had enough excitement for a while."

"That's right, son." Eli was instantly contrite. "You sleep now." He awkwardly patted Josh's shoulder. "I'll be back tomorrow and we'll catch up then."

When Eli closed the door behind him Jessie straightened the pillows under Josh's head and smoothed the blanket. "Josh," she said quietly, "what difference would it make if Serena didn't come back?"

She waited long moments for his answer, the expression on his face giving nothing away. "What difference, Josh?" she persisted.

When he finally said, "None, I guess," she barely restrained herself from slapping him in the head.

"That's what I thought," Jessie snapped. "I'm ridin' out to

the Bain ranch now, and while I'm there I'll tell Serena that she'll be wastin' her time to come see you again."

She slammed the door on Josh's angry, "Damn you, Jess, keep your nose out of something that doesn't concern you!"

In the pale light of early morning, Serena stared out over the valley. In her exhaustion, her hand trembled as she raised a cup of coffee to her lips and took a slow, appreciative sip.

She hadn't slept last night, most of it spent crying out her grief, the rest of the time staring at the dawn stealing through the window.

She lay a hand on her stomach, covering the baby that lay beneath her heart, the consequence of her folly. What would it think of its mother when it had grown up and was called bastard? Would her son or daughter hate her?

The sound of trotting hoofbeats broke Serena's melancholy reflections. She smiled at the feminine figure riding up the trail. When Jessie brought her mount to a halt beside her she affected a brightness in her voice as she asked, "What brings you out so early, Jessie?"

"I'm lookin' for a horse thief." Jessie smiled, giving Serena a swift, intent look at the same time. "I was told that a long-legged blond was seen riding it. Would you know anything about that?"

"Oh, Jessie, I'm sorry I took your mare without asking. But truly, I was going to send one of the hands in with her this afternoon."

"I don't mind you takin' the mare, Serena, you know that." Jessie slid to the ground and dropped the reins over the head of the mount she had rented from the livery in the village. "I'm out here to find out why you felt it necessary to return to the ranch at two o'clock in the morning. That was a rash thing for you to do. These mountains are overrun with wolves, not to mention the two-legged kind."

Serena pretended a careless shrug. "Josh was sleeping, and I thought that I might as well go home."

"You're lyin', you know." Jessie took her arm and turned her toward the house. "I'll have a cup of that coffee while you tell me the truth."

"Now." Inside the kitchen Jessie folded her hands on top of the table after Serena had poured two cups of dark, steaming liquid. "I want no quibblin', no pretendin'. Tell me exactly what Josh said or did to you that would send you tearin' off in the middle of the night."

"Really, Jessie, I don't know what makes you think that Josh had anything to do with my leaving. It's like I said, I just wanted—"

"Wanted nothin'." Jessie slammed a small fist on the table. "What you want is Josh Quade. Now what happened last night? I warn you, I'll stay here until I get the truth."

Serena opened her mouth to tell the impatient woman that she was wrong, then, surprising herself as well as Jessie, she broke into tears. Her hands over her eyes, she sobbed out everything that had happened, ending with the heart-stabbing words Josh had used to lash her at the end.

"Oh, honey." Jessie rose and came around the table to put her arms around the shaking shoulders. "Don't take that to heart. It was only the fever talkin'."

"No, Jessie," Serena cried impatiently, "it was the truth speaking. Fevered people and drunks always speak the truth. And the truth is, although Josh Quade lusts after my body, there is no love in him for me. With him it has always been, 'I want you, I need you.' "

Serena stared bleakly into her coffee, then blurted out, "Jessie, I'm carrying Josh's baby."

It was a long time before the stunned Jessie could speak. She finally managed to croak, "How far along are you?"

"Around four months, I think."

Jessie jumped to her feet and began to pace. "You should have told me the first time you had morning sickness. It's too late for me to give you anything now."

"Jessie, sit down," Serena said sharply. "I would never take anything to hurt Josh's baby."

Jessie sighed softly and leaned her head back against the chair. "No, of course you wouldn't." She turned her head and met the steady gaze of the pale-faced girl beside her. "Naturally you'll tell Josh. For all his faults, he's an honorable man. He won't hesitate to marry you."

Serena looked away. "I would never want him . . . not that way. When he's well he can return to wherever he's been all this time and be happy in his ignorance." She brought her gaze back to Jessie. "Where does he live, anyway?"

Jessie laughed shortly. "This is gonna floor you, but accordin' to that old redskin, he and Josh have been livin' at the other end of the valley, in the wild country." She leaned forward and said quietly, "It seems that your brother sold Josh his line shack and the thousand acres surrounding it, including the mountain."

She waited for Serena's angry outburst, but it never came. Instead Serena said in a small, wavering voice, "How could Dorn have kept this from me, knowing what a miserable time I've had of it?"

"I don't know, honey," Jessie said, looking out the window, "but why don't you ask him? He's comin' up the valley now."

"Oh, I'll ask him all right." Serena jumped to her feet. "And he'd better have some good answers."

"Well, I'm gettin' out of here before you do." Jessie rose also. "I'll be back next week to see how everything is goin' with you."

Serena barely acknowledged Jessie's words as the woman left, her attention intent on her brother sliding off his mount.

"What's eating you?" He stepped up on the porch, frowning at her stormy face.

"Why did you sell Josh Quade your line shack?" Serena came right to the point.

Guilt washed over Dorn's face. "So you've found out," he said, entering the house and walking through to the kitchen.

"Yes, I've found out." Serena followed him, her heels clicking angrily on the floor, her skirt swishing. "I want to know why you did it."

"Look, Serena." Dorn tossed his hat on a chair and plopped down at the table. "I knew that you had strong feelings for the man and I wanted to keep him around. That if it was meant to be that you two would get together, then it would happen."

"But I remember distinctly that you tried to discourage him

that morning when you found us at the cabin. You as good as told him he wasn't good enough for me.''

"No, you're wrong. I only wanted to see if he loved you enough to fight for you." He looked up at Serena, a rueful smile on his lips and regret in his eyes. "I'm sorry, Sis. I should have kept my damn mouth shut."

"Don't blame yourself, Dorn." Serena relented. "Josh Quade never had marriage on his mind."

CHAPTER
∽32∽

JOSH SAT on Jessie's second-floor balcony, his chair tilted back, his feet propped on the railing. The comfortable warmth of the early autumn day settled over him, drowsily and lullingly.

It was the first time in two weeks he'd been allowed outside, and he felt like a man who had been released from prison. He had begun to hate Jessie's bedroom as his head wound slowly mended. The mattress was too soft, he grouched to himself every night, its fluffy down as different from his own of fragrant pine boughs as the winter winds were to their summer counterpart. And sometimes the perfumed scents Jessie and her girls wore swirled around his head, almost stifling him. It was at such times he yearned with all that was in him to be back in his cabin, breathing deeply of the fir-scented mountains.

He hadn't complained, though. How could he be so inconsiderate when Jessie and her girls did everything they could think of to make him comfortable? Josh smiled wryly. Even offering to sleep with him.

His smile turned cynical. The one female he wanted in his bed, the one who made him look hopefully at the door every time it opened, never came to make the offer.

Now, he spent long hours every night, tossing and turning, asking himself unanswerable questions. Why hadn't Serena returned? She had been here that first night; that fact had become clearer as his fever left him. He knew she had tended to him

with a tenderness and care he hadn't known since he was a very
young child and his mother had lovingly soothed a bruised knee
or a bloody nose.

So, he would think as he stared into the darkness, why had
she now apparently forgotten all about him? And why wasn't her
name ever brought up? The few times Paw Landrie had stopped
by to visit he hadn't mentioned her name. And that damned
Jessie never breathed a word about her, and damn her, she knew
very well that he wanted to talk about Serena, that he had a
hundred questions to ask.

The nagging voice of his conscience nudged him and
sneered, "You could bring up her name yourself if you weren't
so damned proud. That doctor Saunders doesn't hesitate to say
what is on his mind. And anyway, aren't you forgetting something? Didn't you decide four months back that she wasn't the
one for you?"

Josh ignored the last question, his mind occupied with Saunders. He was remembering the second time the handsome man
had come to check his stitches. All the time his fingers worked
expertly changing the dressings he had talked to Jessie about
Serena. "That Miss Bain is one of the most beautiful women
I've ever seen," Saunders had begun.

And Jessie had shot him a fast glance before answering the
man's statement with amused eyes. "Yes, Serena is quite an
eyeful."

"I suppose someone like her is already spoken for," Saunders had gone on, hinting for information.

And despite the warning sparks shot at her, the little madam
answered blithely, "As a matter of fact, to my knowledge, she
isn't." Then she had had the nerve to turn wide, innocent eyes
on him and say in a tone of melting sweetness, "Josh, do you
know of anyone who might have claims on Serena?"

And while he had glared at her, she had rambled on, driving
home her barbs. "Our Serena is kinda stand-offish. She's very
choosy. It will be a rare man who will capture her interest."
She had tossed him another wide-eyed look and asked, "Don't
you agree, Josh? I mean, she wouldn't give her heart lightly.
Right, Josh?"

His answer had been a glaring stare at Jessie, but a pleased smile had curved the doctor's rather thin lips. "I'm rather picky myself when it comes to the opposite sex." His fingers deftly tied the new bandage in place on the healing stitches. "Maybe Miss Bain and I can find in each other that rare quality we're both searching for."

As he closed the black bag he had placed at the foot of the bed he added smoothly, "Generally she and I come from the same kind of world. I'm sure we'd have many interests in common."

On his way the neatly dressed man paused at the door. "Miss Bain lives with her brother, is that right?" He directed his question at Jessie.

"Why do you ask?" Jessie counter-questioned, the corners of her lips twitching, her eyes gleaming devilishly. "Are you plannin' on ridin' out to the ranch?" she teased.

"I thought I might." Saunders raised a questioning eyebrow. "Don't you think it's a good idea?"

Josh had sensed rather that seen the flash of mischief directed his way before Jessie answered brightly, "I think it's a fine idea, don't you, Josh? I'm sure you'll agree that it's time Serena settles down and starts raising a family."

Fire sparked in Josh's eyes now. He had ignored Jessie's hardest jab, but if he could have reached the little redhead, he'd have squeezed the breath out of her scrawny neck.

Clouds of dust now rose from the dirt-packed street below as a team of mules hauling logs to the sawmill rattled by. As the dry silt settled on everything and everybody, Josh forced his mind to think of other things.

He meditated first on the trapping season that was fast approaching, deciding that he would set most of his traps along streams to catch the beaver. Its soft and beautiful fur was in demand for coats, muffs, and particularly hats. They were very fashionable with the wealthy gentlemen in both America and Europe.

A few minutes later he was thinking of Red Feather. The old brave hadn't been around for a few days, and he missed him— missed his presence, that was, for the elderly Indian never talked much. He had seen him sit for hours, staring out over the valley, never uttering a sound. He had often wondered what went on in the snow-white head but had never asked. Chances were that he wouldn't have been answered anyhow.

Without being conscious of when it happened, Jovan Foster had stepped into Josh's musings. He impatiently brushed the image of the rancher away. In his days of idleness he had thought of many things but had made only one decision. He would not go after the man. Since the bastard had failed to kill him, he felt sure that he wouldn't show himself in these parts again. Besides, after all the killing he had done in the war he no longer believed in the claim of an eye for an eye. In time, Foster Jovan would spin out his rope and receive his dues.

The clip-clop of hooves brought Josh's attention back to the street. His lazy squint became a wide, interested stare. When he saw Serena driving a buggy and coming his way, he let the chair down and his burning gaze engulfed her entire body, his eyes gleaming with the memory of it. His eyes fastened on the jutting firmness of her breasts, and his loins knotted as he remembered how they filled the cupping of his hands. When she passed Jessie's house without a glance, he wondered with a sharpness in his chest if the doctor had visited her yet.

The soft buzz of the young whore's chatter floated through an open window and Josh stiffened and listened intently when he heard Serena's name spoken.

"Serena just rode by, girls. Come and look at the men starin' at her. She does fill out her dress."

"I saw her last Sunday," a new voice said. "She was talkin' to doc outside the church."

"I saw them havin' supper together Saturday night," someone else put in. "They looked real cozy, their heads together, talkin' and laughin' soft like."

"It looks like everything is over between her and Josh," remarked another, a tinge of disappointment in her tone. "I always thought she and Josh would make a match of it. The two looked so good together. She so delicate lookin' and he so—"

"So dumb lookin'." The scathing tone belonged to Jessie, who had evidently just joined her girls. "Don't you ladies have anything else to do besides chatter about Serena's love life? It's Saturday and a busy night comin' up. Why don't you all take a nap?"

It grew quiet as the girls left the room and Josh stared straight ahead, his eyes dull and bleak. His question had just been answered.

The sun had disappeared and the gray of dusk was settling in when he leaned his elbows on the narrow ledge of the railing and stared down at the now empty street. A hard-fought resolution lay in his eyes.

As he had paced for the better part of an hour he had accepted the obvious. It was no use trying to stay in the same vicinity with Serena. He had thought he could cure himself of the hold this slip of a girl had on him, but he had been mistaken. It would be impossible for him to live with the knowledge that not too far away another man took her to bed every night, and there made love to her.

He would get through the winter somehow, probably going back to his old ways, drinking and whoring. Then, come spring, he would start the long trek back to his northwoods and eventually find peace. He hoped.

There was a sag to his broad shoulders as Josh straightened up and descended the stairs to Jessie's quarters. He would tell his longtime friend that he was leaving her place tomorrow morning.

Jessie slowly cut her steak into bite-size pieces, shooting Josh studied looks at the same time. He was unusually quiet tonight, and she suspected the reason why. She had spotted him through the window when her girls had been rattling on about Serena and the doctor, and he was hurting now, she knew. It showed in the lines of bitterness around his mouth.

She was unprepared however, when he said bluntly, "I'll be goin' back to my place in the mornin', Jess."

"But Josh . . ." She flicked a glance to the shaved spot above his ear. "Shouldn't you wait a few more days? You've not fully regained your strength yet. And you'll only have that old Red Feather to look after you. God knows what kind of roots and barks he'll feed you."

Her hand covered Josh's lying on the table. Squeezing it persuasively, she coaxed, "Stay a little longer. Your color isn't all that good. I don't think you fully realize just how much blood you lost. You were more dead than alive when the old man came poundin' on my door. I thought every ounce of your blood had drained out of your body.

"So please stay a while longer. You need good food and a blood tonic from Saunders."

"Those roots and barks you speak so lightly of," Josh said, stirring his coffee, "will build up my blood faster than anything that sawbones would give me."

A knowing look came into Jessie's eyes at his sarcastic tone. "You don't like Dr. Saunders, do you?" she asked gently.

Josh shot her a fleeting look, his eyes refusing to meet hers. He shrugged and answered stiffly, "I don't have any feelin' about him one way or the other."

"He's a competent doctor."

"Probably."

Jessie grew impatient. "Josh," she said, ending a dragged-out silence, "admit it. You're jealous of the man. It's gnawin' your insides that he's courtin' Serena."

She flinched and leaned back in the chair when Josh erupted savagely, "Yes! I could cheerfully put my knife in his heart."

"Well, dammit!" Jessie shot back. "Why don't you fight for her?"

Expelling a sigh, Josh lifted angry, resentful eyes. "What do I fight with, Jess? My wealth?" he added with self-scorn. "The big house I could give her, the sort Saunders could provide. And let's not forget how pleased brother Dorn would be to have a lowly trapper for a brother-in-law."

"You misjudge both the Bains," Jessie retorted sharply. "Neither of them are impressed by money. If Saunders wins Serena's heart and hand it will be because he's worth lovin' in his own right."

Josh shook his head and set the empty coffee cup back in its saucer. "Look, Jess, if you want to fool yourself, thinkin' that, go right ahead, but I know better. I fought the southern gentry. I know all about their pride and arrogance."

Jessie gazed at the big man hopelessly. She knew him too well. It would be a waste of breath to argue further. "I'll miss you." She smiled. "Take care of yourself and come visit as often as you can."

* * *

Serena stepped outside and blinked as the early-morning sunlight blinded her. Another beautiful fall day, she thought, stepping off the porch and heading for the chicken pen, a pail swinging from her hand.

She was unlatching the gate to the wooden enclosure when her name was called brightly. "Jessie," she cried happily, recognizing the voice and turning around. "I didn't hear you coming. What brings you out so early?"

Jessie swung to the ground and flipped the reins over a bush. "Just some chit-chat," she grinned. "I get tired of the girls' singular concerns."

Serena hurriedly tossed the feed to the clucking hens, then led the way into the kitchen and motioned Jessie to sit down at the table. When she had poured two cups of coffee and took a seat across from her friend, she smiled at her quizzically.

"So, what *did* bring you out here so early?"

Jessie looked up from stirring honey into her coffee and frowned slightly at the shadows in Serena's eyes, the lines around her mouth that spoke of deep unhappiness. Damn Josh Quade, she thought, then forced a teasing grin to her lips.

"Plain old nosiness brought me out. What's this I hear about you and Saunders?"

"Me and the doctor?" Confusion looked out of Serena's eyes. "What have you heard?"

"Well, I heard the two of you went to church together last Sunday, and that the night before you had dinner with him."

Serena's tickled laughter rang out. "That sounds like your gossipy girls talking, Jessie. The doctor and I did not go to church together. He was there but we didn't even sit close to each other. He was in the back of the room and I was up front. When the services were over we talked outside for a minute.

"As for having dinner with him, he happened to come into the hotel just as I was finishing eating and sat down and had a cup of coffee with me."

Jessie shook her head with a small laugh. "Those girls. I'm gonna cut their tongues off one of these days."

She looked at Serena soberly. "You do realize, don't you, the man is pursuing you; showing up everywhere you go. Maybe you should encourage him. It would solve your problem if you and he wed."

"Jessie!" Serena's eyes brightened with shock. "I couldn't foist another man's child on any man."

"Well, tell him about the baby. The man is besotted with you. I bet anything he'd marry you anyway."

"Jessie," Serena scolded with a shake of her head, "I know that people marry for all sorts of reasons, but only love would work for me. I seriously doubt if I could go to bed with any other man than Josh."

Jessie patted her clenched first. "So, he's still strong in your heart?"

Serena nodded, blinking back angry tears. "Yes, dammit, his memory grows stronger with each passing day."

A silence grew, the only sound the ticking of the clock and the snapping of the fire. Serena stared into her cup, then brought her head up swiftly when Jessie said, "For God's sake, Serena, if that's how it is why don't you go to Josh, tell him that you love him, and that you're goin' to bear his child in five months."

"Are you crazy, Jessie?" Serena gasped. "I would never do that."

"Well, if you ever want to get him in front of a preacher you'd better had. He's goin' back to the north country come spring."

Jessie rose and came to sit beside Serena. "Look, honey, I've known Josh Quade for a long time, and in all those years I've never seen him affected by a woman. But you—he's worse than useless when you're around him. The man is wild about you, but he's prouder than Lucifer. He's got it in his head that he's not good enough for you, couldn't give you the things he thinks you deserve."

Serena stood up and walked to the window. Was it true what Jessie said? Did Josh truly love her? She was afraid to hope. She had been disappointed so many times.

"Well, Serena?" Jessie prodded.

"I don't know, Jessie." Serena sighed. "I'll have to think about it."

Jessie made an impatient sound. "You can't think too long, Serena. Once Josh gets snowed in you'll never see him again. He'll head for the north from there."

Jessie couldn't have chosen more convincing words. Her "You'll never see him again" was a statement that must never come to pass. Serena would do anything to make it so.

She wheeled around, alarm in her eyes. "All right, Jessie, I'll do it. And pray God it works. Otherwise . . ." She left the sentence unfinished.

CHAPTER
∽33∼

It was the last day of October. Since peeking over the eastern timberline the sun had been unable to penetrate the dark clouds that had rolled ominously in from the north. An hour before noon large white, lacy flakes had began to float in the air. Two hours later, having drawn strength from the steadily falling temperature, snow covered the valley in a thin white blanket.

Josh's whip-lean body turned from the window that looked down on the trail leading to the settlement and moved across the floor to squat beside the wide hearth of the fireplace. With a jerky movement that betrayed the unrest inside him, his long fingers took the handle of a battered coffee pot and lifted it off the hot glowing coals. Filling a pewter mug with the steaming fragrant brew, he rose, crossed to the door, and stepped outside. Leaning against a rough-hewn supporting post of the small porch, the snow catching in his long lashes, he sipped carefully from the cup, staring through the rising steam at the dark green of spruce and pine, the only color in the stark white world.

Gloom had been his constant companion for a week now. Was Serena still seeing the doctor? Maybe married him. Much could happen in five weeks.

He turned back inside, set the empty coffee cup on the table, and flung himself into a chair. When he moved around restively, crossing and uncrossing his legs, Red Feather, sitting cross-legged in front of the fire, sent him a quick glance of understanding. He took the pipe from between his withered lips and spat into the fire.

"The snow has stopped," he said. "Only a forewarning of the big one that will come next."

The grunt Josh uttered could be taken either as agreement or denial.

Red Feather studied him gravely, then spoke. "Better you ride to the Bain ranch before the Big White blows in. February is only four months away. No time to waste."

Josh gave the old man an impatient look. "I have two questions of the riddle you talk in. Why should I ride to the Bain ranch, and what does February have to do with anything?"

Red Feather looked up at him without expression. "Serena Bain lives at the Bain ranch. She will have your child in February. You must go to her, make her aware of this deep feeling you have for her."

Josh looked at the Indian incredulously. Then, giving a scornful grunt, he asked, "How could you know that? Have you been listenin' to the wind song in the trees? If so, it's told you some ridiculous things."

Red Feather ignored the barb and answered quietly, "She say it was true. I ask her about it."

Stunned, it took Josh a while to think coherently. He turned a dark, accusatory glower on Red Feather. "Why didn't you tell me this earlier?"

"Serena make me promise I would not. She say she don't want you unless you feel love for her, and that she know you don't."

"How can she know that?" Josh jumped to his feet and paced agitatedly.

"From things you say to her the first night you wounded."

"What did I say, for God's sake?" Josh wheeled on the old man.

"You say you don't need her, you say for her to get out of your life."

Josh threw himself back in the chair. Words said in delirium had cheated him of months, nights, and days that could have been spent with the woman who lived always in his dreams.

He turned his head to look at the Indian, who watched him intently. "Would you say, old man, that she returns my feelin's?"

"She does." The thin lips cracked. "And it was not the wind song who told me."

Josh jumped to his feet again and reached for his jacket. "I'll be back when I can convince Miss Serena Bain to come with me."

Red Feather nodded, a glimmer in his eyes suspiciously like humor. "I look for you tonight."

Serena stood outside the kitchen door, gazing down the valley. Thankfully it had stopped snowing, leaving only a skimming of white on the ground. She had gathered the courage to go to Josh, and when the first soft flakes had began to fall the memory of Jessie's words had swept in on her.

"Once he gets snowed in you'll never see him again."

She gazed up at the mountaintop still touched by the setting sun, praying that it wouldn't snow tonight. For tomorrow she would swallow her pride and go to Josh. If he was honorable as Jessie claimed, at least her baby would have a name even if he didn't marry her out of love.

Serena went back into the kitchen and lit a lamp. Picking up a plate she carried it to the fire where a black kettle sat simmering over the coals. She ladled her plate full of stew then carried it to the table. She sat down with a long sigh. She would be eating alone tonight. Dorn and the men were out on the range and he wouldn't be home until sometime the next day.

She picked up her fork, mentally forming the words she would say to Josh tomorrow and dreading his reaction when she told him about the baby.

A sudden knock on the door startled her, making her drop the fork to the table. She sat frozen a moment, uneasy that she was alone in the house. The knock sounded again and she rose, stood a moment, then moved to the door. Her voice a little wavering, she asked, "Who is it?"

She went weak all over when a familiar voice answered, "It's Josh, Serena."

"Josh!" she whispered and swung open the door.

There was a moment of silence as Josh and Serena stared at

each other, she praying that he couldn't see the excited rise and fall of her breasts, he hoped that her thick-lashed eyes wouldn't notice the trembling of his body.

"Aren't you goin' to ask me in?" Josh finally spoke, his voice husky, his eyes wistful.

"Yes, of course." Serena held the door open a little wider. "I was just going to eat supper. Beef stew. Would you like some?"

"Sounds good." Josh smiled at her, leaning his rifle against the wall and shrugging out of his jacket.

Serena ran hungry eyes over the broad shoulders, the strong throat, then blushed a deep red when she found him watching her. She grabbed up a plate and hurried to the fireplace.

"Your cookin' has sure improved," Josh said teasingly a moment later after he had swallowed his first mouthful.

Serena lowered her lids against the pleasure his words of praise had brought her. "Nell has been giving me lessons," she said quietly.

"She and Eli seem to be gettin' along just fine." Josh forked more stew into his mouth.

"Yes, they're very happy. Nell and her family have been good for Paw. They've helped ease the pain in losing his son."

There was a thickness in Josh's voice when he asked, "Were you deeply in love with Eli's son, Serena?"

Serena gave him a startled look, unaware that he knew about Jeremy. She looked back down at her plate. "I thought that I was at the time. Later I realized that it was only a deep friendship that I had mistaken for love."

Josh's heart hammered in his chest, and his words were thick as he asked, "What led you to that discovery?"

Their gazes locked, each seeking an answer. Then Serena looked away and said quietly, "It was a person."

Hope mingled with uncertainty as Josh laid a hand on Serena's and asked, "Do I dare think that someone is me?"

The logs in the fireplace hissed as Serena looked back at Josh and asked in a voice that trembled slightly, "If I said yes, Josh, what would it mean to you?"

"It would mean everything to me." Josh's eyes bored into hers. "Is it yes?"

When Serena didn't answer right away, but continued to look searchingly into his eyes, Josh cried hoarsely, "I love you, Serena. Put me out of my misery and say yes."

A wide smile grew on Serena's lips and a happy tear slid down her cheek. "Oh, Josh, do you mean it? I've waited so long to hear those words."

They were both on their feet then, rushing into each other's arms. His breathing ragged and uneven, Josh groaned, "It's been so long," as he curved her body into his and captured her mouth with hungry lips.

Her heart hammering, her pulses leaping, Serena leaned into him, deepening the kiss.

Minutes later, her head tucked under his chin, feeling the heavy thud of his heart, she asked, "Why have you waited so long to tell me that you love me? I have been living in such hell."

Josh tightened his hold on her and, giving a small derisive laugh, answered, "I was half afraid of you. The first time I saw you, sitting in the wagon, your nose in the air, your eyes spittin' hate at me, you had my heart." He rubbed his chin on her head. "And though you scared me witless, I decided right then and there that this haughty lady was goin' to have my baby someday.

"And you know what else?" He tilted her chin and looked into her eyes. "Every chance I got I tried god-awful hard to get you with child."

"Josh! What a rotten thing to do!" Serena tried to look reproachful, but amusement twinkled in her eyes. "Why didn't you come right out and ask me to marry you?"

"I don't know." Josh sighed. "Every time I got up the nerve we always ended up havin' an argument. Then, when I met your brother, I knew his plans for you didn't include a man who trapped for a living."

"But you were mistaken about Dorn. He was only testing you, to see if you truly loved me. His only interest in who I marry is that the man make me happy."

"I hope so, for I intend to marry you as soon as possible, and whether he likes it or not, he's gonna be stuck with me as a brother-in-law."

"Now"—his eyes twinkled seductively—"are you about ready to put me out of my misery?"

Serena felt a growing arousal pressing against her stomach and caught her breath. "Oh, yes," she sighed as Josh swept her into his arms.

Serena roused and snuggled closer to the heat of the muscular body curved at her back. The movement brought a tightening of the strong arm wrapped around her waist. A contented smile touched her lips. At long last she knew that Josh Quade truly loved her.

But as she savored the comfort of his warm, loving arms, she wondered how to tell him about the baby. What if he thought she was only marrying him because of the child? She gave a strangled sob. It would kill her to lose him now.

Before the sound of her cry died away Josh was sitting up and fumbling to light the lamp. In its light he looked at her anxiously. "Serena! I didn't hurt you, did I? Hurt the baby?"

Serena's body went still. "How do you know about the baby?" she finally managed.

Josh gently smoothed the tousled hair and answered softly, "Red Feather told me."

"Red Feather? But he promised me that—"

"He wouldn't tell me," Josh finished the sentence. "But he saw my sufferin', and unlike a certain young lady, felt it was my right to know that I was to become a father."

Serena flushed guiltily. "I thought so, too, Josh, but I was afraid you'd be angry, think that I was trying to trap you."

"Oh, Serena." Josh lay back down and gathered her in his arms. "So many misunderstandings. It's got to stop, you know. We can't have our little son growing up with battling parents."

"Nor our little daughter either." Serena patted her stomach.

Josh chuckled. He could see plenty of arguments ahead with this fiery one. He smiled. He'd love and cherish every one.

ATTENTION
ROMANCE
CUSTOMERS!

SPECIAL
TOLL-FREE NUMBER
1-800-481-9191

Call Monday through Friday
10 a.m. to 9 p.m.
Eastern Time
Get a free catalogue,
join the Romance Book Club,
and order books using your
Visa, MasterCard,
or Discover®

Leisure
Books

GO ONLINE WITH US AT DORCHESTERPUB.COM